THE CHRONICLES OF E

BOUNTY on a DRAGON

J. R. KNOLL

ARTWORK BY SANDI JOHNSON

ISBN: 145281306X

ISBN-13: 9781452813066

CHAPTER 1

Early Summer, 989 Seasons

A squire's life is not meant to be an easy life. He must learn strength, battle, wisdom and humility before entering the realm of knighthood, that and a hundred other things. But these things are often far from the mind of a boy of only sixteen seasons. Never having experienced much of what life offers can prove to be a constant distraction as the call of adventure and the allure of every maiden within his field of vision constantly tantalizes the fancy of a young man who craves to be more than what he is.

The early summer days grew hot this season, yet could not drive away the rains that kept the Abtont Forest green and the grain fields flourishing. Humans and other lower animals always seemed to prosper during the warm times and food was never in short supply. Only the humans could not seem to realize this as they prowled the forest, killing everything they thought they could eat, only to leave much of their kill to the scavengers. Whether this can be said to be wasteful or generous depends on one's point of view, but their gluttony would eventually thin out the northern forest herds to dangerously low numbers and drive the forest predators to the herds the humans raised for themselves, even the dragons.

Humans and dragons have never coexisted easily. When humans hunt in the hunting grounds of the dragons, trouble cannot be far behind. While human meat is not at all appetizing to most of us, there are those who do not mind the putrid taste, and others who will hunt and eat humans out of spite. This would eventually give rise to a different kind of hunter, those of the human clans who hunt dragons for bounty, and those who yearn to follow them. Glory or gold drives them. It is difficult to say which is the stronger attraction. The last Great War between our people took huge tolls on each side, and as we ended the war, I was certain that wisdom and experience had enlightened both our peoples.

How wrong I was!

Humans and dragons learned from the war, but not what I and the other elders hoped they would. They learned to kill one another. For dragons, killing humans has always been almost embarrassingly easy. For the humans, killing dragons has worked its way to being a science. Magic and metal, potions and courage have been melted together to form lethal weapons which the humans turn against us. Not many of them have the power or the knowledge, but those few who do have paid a heavy price in gold and blood and the cost to the dragons is even higher.

This is where our squire comes in.

Ambition never seems to be in short supply where humans are concerned and young Garrin would prove to be no exception.

Not especially large nor small, heavy or thin, he was the kind of lad who could easily be lost in a crowd of others. In the crowd of the banquet hall at Caipiervell Castle, a human stronghold that lies on the south bank of the Spagnah River and only eighteen leagues east of the Hard Lands, he was not the only squire present as many knights attended. All of the squires were dressed the same, wearing the castle colors, blue tunics with silver trim and black belts. Each of them carried a sword and wore black riding trousers and a white swordsman's shirt beneath his tunic. On the left breast of the tunic was the crest of the knight who sponsored the squire. Unlike the simple soldiers of the time, a knight in training, a squire, would have to learn more than just the brutal waging of war against his fellow humans. There would be things that Garrin had never even considered when he entered this world of chivalry, battle and gentlemen.

On one summer evening, as he and the other squires stood ready in the cavernous banquet hall, ready to spring into action should their knight need anything, his thoughts wandered to other things, mostly the young maidens who milled about in their best evening wear. These maidens were largely of highborn blood and were forbidden to a mere commoner or squire and would not even acknowledge his existence as they casually glanced his way. Still, his lack of birthright and status could not bridle his fantasies or his imagination as he watched them mingle with the highborns. He had vowed two seasons ago that he would someday catch the eye of a beautiful young maiden and take her for his mate, or bride as the humans often say. He knew this would probably be after his knighting, but he was certain that a few acts of chivalry or some glorious act in battle would have them clamoring for his attention.

His brown eyes darted around the room, hopeful of any chance to impress one of the many maidens present, or perhaps a knight or some highborn. He combed his light brown hair back with his fingers as he often did when he felt anxious about something as he searched for an opportunity to be noticed by the nobles. Honor and chivalry had been ground into him when he was a young boy. As the son of a soldier who aspired to be more, this was passed to him aggressively and he absorbed it like the food he ate. It was in fact through his father that Garrin came to be in the service of Sir Kessler at age ten, the very knight his father served on the battlefield. A season later on a nameless battlefield fighting a forgotten enemy over some meaningless matter of land or someone's opinion of insult, Garrin's father would fall in battle. Still too young to accompany his knight on the battlefield, the squire would not be told of his father's death until the next day. To honor his father, the boy would not grieve; he would not weep for the loss of his father. Perhaps he mourned within, no one would know. They only saw a strong, willing lad who carried on, one who seemed eager to please those around him, and yet there was an impatience about him that could not be fully silenced.

Another squire, a taller boy with red hair made his way to Garrin and pointed across the room to the opening, ornately decorated double doors.

Garrin was not impressed at first as a few servants and two palace guards entered, but when one of the guards stopped and announced, "Her Royal Highness, Princess Bellith," Garrin's eyes widened as he saw a blond young woman in a long silver satin evening gown walk into the hall. He watched her with his absolute attention as she strode gracefully into the banquet hall a few steps. He did not notice that, as she scanned the room, her chin was raised as if to bring her above everyone present. He also failed to notice how stiffly she moved, as if she was trying hard to appear more graceful than she was to impress everyone in her presence. No. She was well made and attractive to an adolescent young male no matter how unsuccessfully she tried to hide her lack of physical prowess.

Princess Bellith was not the heiress to the throne of Castle Caipiervell, but she wore her jewel studded silver tiara as if she was, and had the manner of a spoiled princess who expected to be. She seemed to know that her blue eyes were captivating to any man or boy whose eyes she snared with her gaze. Her shape, very well developed for a girl of sixteen, would catch their attention should her eyes not. Still, she had missed no meals and she appeared to have worked physically not a day in her life. Her skin was pale from a lack of sunlight but very smooth to the eye, free of blemishes or scars.

Her father, a tall, lean man who was already milling about in the ballroom, strode toward her. He clearly expected the other people present to move out of his way as he walked, and they did. He did not wear the colors of Castle Caipiervell; rather he wore a purple tunic and red arming pants, a white swordsman's shirt beneath his tunic and a satin black cape with a crimson lining. His boots, which reached nearly to his knees, were shined black with a hint of blue as the light hit them. He wore no ornament or armor over his black, shoulder length hair and his beard and mustache were short and well groomed. He was Prince Tahmrof, the brother of the late King of Caipiervell and high royalty, but was also not heir to the throne, nor was he free of parasites. Most would never know this, though he was clearly not as well as most others, always lean no matter how much he ate and always pale no matter how hot the sun.

He strode to his daughter with the same conceited look and his chin held up, a silver goblet of wine in his hand, which he swirled constantly and unconsciously as he walked.

Garrin took only brief notice of him as his eyes were almost entranced by the Princess.

The red haired young man nudged him again and said in a low voice, "Tell me you would not kill to have her in your bed, even once."

Garrin rolled his eyes to him and replied, "There is more to having a woman to that."

"But not much," the red haired boy insisted.

Shaking his head, Garrin looked back to the Princess as she took her father's arm and walked with him toward the center of the room. After a second, he asked, "And when you tire of her?"

"Who could ever tire of *her?*" the red haired boy countered.

"There is much more to her than what you see," Garrin informed. "She *is* beautiful, though…" He finished with a long breath and shook his head. Clearly, through the haze of adolescence and inexperience, he sensed something about her was amiss.

The red haired boy huffed a laugh. "You act so chivalrous, but I know you would not hesitate should she approach you."

Garrin finally smiled. "That depends on what she approaches me for, my friend."

"Garrin," a gruff voice summoned from one side.

Both squires spun toward the gruff voice and Garrin snapped to attention. A knight approached, *his* knight.

Sir Kessler was a sizeable man with a full beard and short cut blond hair. He wore the colors of Castle Caipiervell, his brown riding boots and blue and silver cape. His family crest, a silver shield with a gold eagle flanked by two black stars, was worn to the left of the kingdom's crest, a gold crown with two silver swords crossed behind it. Worn to the left and not below the crest of

Caipiervell showed that he was a landowner of stature. His family crest was the very crest worn by Garrin.

Holding a goblet of wine, the knight strode to the boys, looking down at Garrin as he ordered, "I would speak with you." His eyes then shifted to the red haired boy, who took the hint, bowed his head to the knight and left their presence.

Sir Kessler watched after the red haired squire for long seconds, clearly not impressed by him and making no secret of it, though he would say nothing openly out of respect for the boy's knight. When his eyes moved back to Garrin, they betrayed a certain annoyance that was confirmed in his voice as he said, "I have been trying to get your attention for some time, lad. I should never have to find you when I need you."

Garrin felt as if his heart was in his throat and he looked to the floor, his eyes training on his knight's perfectly polished boots as he explained, "I am sorry, my Lord. I was distracted."

The knight huffed a laugh and asked, "Maidens again?" Without waiting for a response, he advised, "You should keep your distance from them for a while, lad. A maiden's pretty face and soft curves have brought down many a man and kingdom."

Garrin smiled and looked back up at his knight, asking, "I should find an ugly one, then?"

Kessler laughed again and shook his head. "No lad. That is not what I am saying. Just don't let your lust overpower your wisdom."

Clearly, Garrin wanted to do as his knight said, but as his eyes locked on a maiden who strode past and followed her into the crowd, he informed, "That is much easier in words than in deed, my Lord."

"Something I know all too well, lad," the knight confessed. "Just do your best to avoid them and keep them from your thoughts as much as you can, and let what happens happen."

Garrin looked up at his knight and asked, "What should I do if some beautiful girl approaches *me?*"

Sir Kessler took a gulp from his wine and answered, "Just let what happens happen, and don't make an ass of yourself."

Nodding, Garrin smiled and agreed, "Yes, my Lord."

"Good lad," the knight commended, then he glanced around the ballroom and said, "Somewhere, wandering about out there is a visitor to the castle, a Duke Malchor. I spoke to him earlier and offered your services to him should he need a squire during his stay." He turned his eyes back to his squire and asked, "Up to it?"

"Of course, my Lord," Garrin confirmed, trying hard to sound enthusiastic. Most humans prefer certain safety zones, like tending to the needs of a knight they already know. Acting as squire to a man he had never met was, at best, an uncomfortable thought for Garrin as it had taken him half a season to grow accustomed to Sir Kessler. No matter. This would be a way to be noticed, to stand out in a room full of average young men who all aspired to be more than they were.

Kessler seemed to take little notice of his squire's uneasiness of the matter. Why should he? He stood to gain more than the squire did, or so he thought.

"May I ask who this Duke Malchor is?" Garrin asked, trying to sound interested.

"He is a man of importance," was the answer from his knight, "a dragonslayer."

Garrin's eyes lit up. The thought of meeting a dragonslayer--an actual dragonslayer!--was as exciting a thought as he had ever had. With a sudden surge of enthusiasm, he threw his chest out and barked, "I shall not disappoint you, my Lord. I shall endeavor to be the best squire who has ever served him."

"That's what I want to hear," the knight said with a nod. "Go on and wander about the ballroom and see if you can happen upon him, and stay by his side after you do."

"I will, my Lord," Garrin assured. "I shall not disappoint you."

The response he got was simply another nod, then he watched his knight turn and slowly stalk back into the crowd. Fear and enthusiasm are a strange mix, one that seems to be unique to humans. While he did not look forward to his first meeting with this knight, this Duke, the thought of finding himself in the service of a dragonslayer had his heart racing as never before. Careful not to be offensive, he found himself at a quick pace to find this dragonslayer before some other detached squire could.

Not especially tall, he could not see over any of the men in the crowd, nor could he see over most of the women. Still, a smart lad knows how to overcome and he would find one of the marble staircases that would lead to the circular balcony that overlooked the ballroom from almost three men's heights high. Racing up it, he hoped to be able to find this Duke Malchor quickly, as he would no doubt be accompanied by quite an entourage who would be clamoring for his attention.

Once at the top, he found a slower pace as he intently scanned the ballroom for just such a collection of people, his hand sliding along the dark marble rail that would offer protection against a nasty fall for some unfortunate soul. Even from his higher vantage point, he found his search just as difficult and he quickened his pace slightly as he scanned the mass of people even harder. So involved was he with his search that he did not know there was a young lady standing in his path until he collided with her, almost knocking her to the marble floor. When he finally looked and realized what he had done and who he had done it to, his mouth fell open and he found himself frozen where he stood, his wide eyes locked on the young woman who turned a fierce glare on him.

When she pulled herself back up fully by the rail, her eyes still stabbing at him, she revealed that she was a slight young woman, not quite as tall as the squire who was about to find himself on the receiving end of her wrath. Other than a very angry appearance about her, her face was very pleasing to the eye. This was a very attractive girl, well made yet very lean. Her gown was silver and light blue and fit her very tightly and her long black hair was restrained behind a gold tiara that was laden with jewels. This was the heir to the throne of Caipiervell, Princess Faelon herself.

When she faced him and folded her arms, her brow low over her eyes, he finally managed, "Are—Are you okay? Uh, Highness?"

"I was," she snarled back, "until some little buffoon tried to push me over the rail to my death. What do you think you are doing, anyway?"

"Um," he stammered, "I'm, uh… I'm looking for Duke Malchor."

She rolled her eyes. "Ah. The supposed dragonslayer, you mean. Why would you want to find him? Do you want to be a dragonslayer yourself?"

He glanced around and found himself unable to meet her eyes. This was actually his first meeting with the princess of his own castle, and things were already not going well. "I was, uh, directed by my knight to find him."

"But instead," she pointed out, "you tried to push me to the hard stone below."

"I wasn't really trying to do that," he argued. "I was just trying to find Duke Malchor and didn't see you."

She turned away from him, toward the huge doorway that led to a balcony overlooking a courtyard outside of the castle. "Perhaps you should keep your eyes where you are going before you run over someone else."

Perhaps her cruelty was not her fault. Perhaps the loss of her parents a season earlier was responsible. Garrin just could not accept that she was a cruel, spoiled child of royalty. She was just too pretty in his eyes.

Without fully realizing what he was doing, he followed her outside into the sultry summer night and offered, "Highness, I'm sorry for the loss of your parents."

She stopped.

He stopped right behind her. "I lost my father in battle five seasons ago."

Half turning her head, she didn't quite look at him as she replied, "So he was lost in battle. Defending his kingdom, was he?"

"He was, my Lady. He fell defending Caipiervell."

Princess Faelon nodded. "So he wasn't murdered in his bed with your mother by some coward in the night. He died in battle. At least you have that." She strode stiffly out to the balcony outside and leaned on the marbled railing there, looking out into the sky as the sun began to touch the treetops to the West.

Once again, Garrin followed. "Highness, I didn't mean to upset you. I just wanted—"

"It was a season ago," she interrupted. "The sting of losing my parents has since passed and I don't need to be reminded of it."

"I'm sorry," he offered softly, turning his eyes to the floor.

"Why don't you go on and find your dragonslayer," she suggested. "Perhaps he wishes to hear your mindless banter."

He loosed a deep breath, knowing his first meeting with the heir to the throne of the castle he intended to one day defend had not gone well. It had, in fact, gone very poorly. Still, he had done his best to be polite and a pang of anger sounded loudly within him and released before he realized. "I'm happy to see my father's death was not in vain, and protected the worthy and gracious royal blood of this kingdom."

Princess Faelon's hands clenched into tight fists and she slowly turned, her narrow eyes finding the squire's. She glared at him, then half turned her head and hissed, "What did you say, squire?"

"I'm sure you heard me, your Highness," was his answer. He bowed to her and informed, "I have duties requiring my attention, so I should take my leave of you." He turned stiffly and walked back toward the banquet hall. He glanced back as the Princess wheeled around and turned her eyes up to the sky as she gingerly laid her hands upon the cold marble of the railing.

With a deep sigh, he turned back, gasping and flinching away as he almost ran into someone else.

Princess Bellith also flinched and took a step back, but quite unexpectedly she smiled, then giggled a little as she said, "I didn't know the young soldiers of the castle frightened so easily."

"I don't usually, Highness," he informed. "I, uh… I find myself distracted. I've been instructed by Sir Kessler to find Duke Malchor and offer him my service."

"Ah," the Princess drawled, "our guest of honor. I wonder if you'll get to see him slay any vengeful dragons in the coming days."

Garrin shrugged. "I don't know, your Highness."

Looking past him to the balcony overlooking the courtyard, Princess Bellith shook her head as she saw her cousin leaning on the rail. "It's so sad, really. Ever since the deaths of her parents she's been in such a dreadful melancholy. I don't know how she intends to run the kingdom when she feels so."

The squire looked back at the lonely princess, sighing almost wistfully. "I wish I knew what I could do or say."

"You seem a sweet boy," Bellith observed, speaking as if she was not a few months younger than he was. "Perhaps we should try and cheer her up."

Turning his eyes down, Garrin shook his head and admitted, "I've said enough to her. She doesn't want my company."

"Nonsense," the Princess insisted, taking his arm. "I think we can find her smile." She pulled him along, prodding, "Come on."

He reluctantly allowed her to pull him toward the balcony, unable to look at either of them and feeling a certain sense of foreboding as he drew closer.

"Cousin!" Princess Bellith greeted. "You are missing the banquet."

"What do you want, Bellith?" Faelon snarled, a certain venom in her words.

"I've brought someone to meet you." Bellith looked to the squire and asked, "What is your name again?"

"Um," he stammered. "I'm… My name is Garrin, squire to Sir Kessler."

Princess Faelon finally turned, slowly. "We've met. This is the boy who tried to ensure that you would be queen one day by pushing me to the ballroom below."

Raising her brow, the blond Princess turned her eyes to Garrin.

"It was an accident," he defended, still not looking at either of them. "I apologize again for my clumsiness."

"As you should," Faelon growled, her eyes narrow. "Should Sir Kessler hear about this clumsiness? I'm sure he could find a way to cure you of it."

Unable to find an answer for her, Garrin clenched his teeth and looked beyond her, out into the courtyard below.

"Oh, come now, cousin," Bellith pressed, almost laughing. "He's a nice boy and very easy to look at. Perhaps we should forgive his indiscretion and enjoy the banquet with him."

Faelon folded her arms, her eyes narrowing as she hissed, "Draining my treasury to entertain someone who claims to have killed a dragon is no reason to have a banquet."

"You really should learn to enjoy yourself," Bellith insisted. "Let go of the past and realize that you are the ruler of this kingdom now."

"Not if your father has anything to say about it," Faelon grumbled.

"Oh, don't start that again. He's simply attending the affairs of the kingdom until you are ready to."

"And taking more and more power from me."

This dispute was actually common knowledge around the kingdom and Garrin found himself not wanting to hear the story yet again, even from the two beautiful princesses at the center. He loosed a deep breath, wanting to be almost anywhere else, wanting to resume his search for this Duke Malchor. He would even rather be tending to Sir Kessler's horse than listening to this mindless debate. Still, the company of two lovely girls such as these had its place in his mind as well so he would not excuse himself too quickly.

Movement outside caught his attention. Something was rising over the treetops of the surrounding forest. Garrin squinted, focusing on the huge form that drew closer.

"Having a dragonslayer about can be very advantageous," Princess Bellith insisted.

"Only if we manage to anger a local dragon," Princess Faelon countered. "What are the odds that a dragon lives even close to here?"

Long wings swept downward, lifting the huge form higher over the trees. It was half a league away and drawing closer with frightening speed. In only a few seconds it halved its distance and was charging right toward them.

"I need more wine," Bellith informed. "Faelon, you should come and join us. At least talk to the man and get to know him. Do you know what that could do for your status among the nobility?"

Rolling her eyes, Faelon snarled, "I don't care what they think."

As the dragon's wings swept forward and it extended its talons, Garrin sprang into action without even thinking. He grabbed both girls by the arm and almost threw them back into the castle then followed himself, pushing them along.

"What do you think you're doing?" Princess Faelon barked.

With a glance back as the dragon slammed into the balcony, the squire grabbed handfuls of dresses and threw the girls to the marble floor to the side of the doorway, then dove on top of them.

"How dare you!" Faelon screamed.

Fire exploded through the door, just a brief burst, and suddenly two girls of privilege were grateful to have some boy of no birthright lying on top of them. The fire scorched his back and legs as it exploded through the doorway and managed to burn the exposed parts of their dresses.

When it thinned and died, Garrin pushed himself off of them and turned toward the doorway, pulling his sword from its sheath as he could hear the beast outside clawing at the doorway to widen the hole. As half its snout entered the castle and red scaly lips curled back from forearm length teeth, the squire turned and first took Princess Faelon's arm, pulling her to her feet, then he took Princess Bellith's and pulled her up, ordering as he did, "Get back downstairs to safety!" She spun back as the dragon ripped part of the wall away and began to squeeze into the castle, turning its orange glowing eyes on the squire as a growl erupted from its throat.

Clinging to each other, the Princesses slowly backed away.

Garrin looked back at them and shouted, "Go!" then he turned and charged the dragon. He slammed his sword hard into the dragon's nose, then again, and again.

Flinching away, the dragon grunted and blinked each time it was struck. Ripping more of the wall away, it managed to reach in and swipe at the impudent human who dared to stand against it.

The squire dodged the clumsy blow, backpedaling and swung his sword hard at the dragon's arm. Though steel met scales again, he was doing no damage.

With an angry roar, the dragon crashed further into the castle, turning fully on the young man who stood against him. Now with enough room to be more mobile, the dragon was able to raise its head and crash a shoulder into the castle, swiping again.

This time Garrin met the strike with his sword and was nearly knocked over.

The dragon's orange eyes went fully to red as they locked on its puny foe. Garrin met those eyes, his own narrowing as he poised his sword to continue the fight, and for a moment the world around ceased to be. Time itself seemed to stop as the two hesitated to stare each other down. The crowd below was in a panic and screams and shouts of terror reached the squire, but he could barely hear them. For the first time in his life he was fully engaged and this beast before him had his full attention unlike anything or anyone ever had. The rush of battle mingled with his combat training and he did not even have the time to be frightened, nor did he have the time to consider his safety or his station. Quite the contrary. For the first time in his life everything was coming together in his mind with absolute focus.

He backed away from another clumsy strike and the dragon entered further. When he raised his sword and charged yet again, he realized too soon that the dragon had entered far enough to strike at him with his full speed and accuracy, and the fingers of a clawed hand slammed into his chest with a solid blow, sending him backward toward the protective railing. Only his ankles caught the rail and he flipped over it, hurling back-first to the floor of the banquet room below....

"He's coming around."

Ever so slowly, Garrin's eyes opened and as they did many different pains revealed themselves to him. As the blur left his vision, he saw many people standing around him, looking down on him with a mix of expressions. He finally realized that he was lying on what remained of a wooden table, one that had been laden with food for the banquet. The many different smells of the dishes he was lying among converged in a sickening buffet in his nose.

Sir Kessler finally appeared with a large nobleman behind him. The knight knelt down beside him, looking him over for a moment before asking, "How do you feel, boy?"

Garrin tried to move and finally reported, "I think I broke everything, my Lord."

His knight smiled and patted the boy's chest, correcting, "Not everything, just dinner." He stood and offered his squire a hand and pulled him to his feet. "That was quite a battle you fought. Everyone at the banquet saw you up there fighting off the dragon single handed, or trying to."

Lowering his eyes, the squire admitted, "I didn't stop him, Sir, but I did my best."

The nobleman finally stepped forward and confirmed, "As your sword shows, boy. I don't think I've ever seen a blade beaten up so badly. It would have faired better against the anvil it was forged on."

This was a man who was well decorated, one who was clearly a man of importance. His knight's tunic was white, decorated with dark green and gold braid along its edges. In the center was his crest, the image of a green dragon with crossed swords through its body. This was in a circle of gold, the whole thing consuming most of his chest. Like most of the knights and nobility present, he wore no helmet or head ornament and his stringy black hair hung as it would down his head and nearly to his shoulders. Black swordsman's trousers and high, well polished black boots showed him to be ready for battle nonetheless as a very ornate sword hung on the thick, black and gold belt on his left, a matching dagger on his right. Piercing blue eyes scrutinized the boy and he nodded, finishing, "That was truly an act of courage. Your minstrels should be writing songs about it as we speak."

Garrin's whole body was sore and he seemed to hurt all the way through. Still he managed to hold his head up, then bow to the nobleman. "Thank you, my Lord."

Patting the lad's shoulder, the nobleman smiled at Sir Kessler and observed, "This is the boy you spoke of, eh? I'd say you left out the best of him. I'll be taking that offer of yours, Sir Kessler. I think such a lad could serve me better than any other."

Garrin's eyes widened as he finally realized that this nobleman was the Duke Malchor that his knight had spoken of, the dragonslayer. Managing a smile, the squire looked to his knight, then to the Duke and assured, "I will, my Lord. I'll be at your side day and night should you need anything."

The men laughed softly and exchanged glances and the dragonslayer patted the boy's shoulder again. "You just rest up tonight, boy. We've a dragon to find in the morning and I'll need you well rested and with your wits about you. Ever hunted a dragon?"

"No sir, I haven't."

Sir Kessler roughed his squire's hair and assured, "Tomorrow you do just that."

Prince Tahmrof finally found them and demanded, "Is this the boy?"

Turning to greet him, the dragonslayer informed, "This is him, probably the bravest lad in the castle."

The Prince regarded Garrin coldly as he growled, "But clearly not one who is competent enough with a sword to keep that beast from making off with my daughter and niece!"

Once again Garrin's eyes widened as he realized that the Princesses had not gotten to safety. Surely dire consequences awaited him.

"Your highness," Sir Kessler finally said, "this boy stood in battle with the beast to buy them time to get away. I can't say—"

"And where were you?" Prince Tahmrof shouted. "All of these knights and warriors in the castle and still this thing made off with my daughter!" He looked to the dragonslayer and growled, "Even with you here he still attacked and took my two most precious gems, and you did nothing to stop him!"

"It made its escape quickly," the Duke casually defended. "I thought our young squire would delay it long enough and he nearly did. This boy tried to kill the beast single handedly and no doubt gave it pause about staying longer."

"It still took my daughter," the Prince pointed out.

"And tomorrow we go to get her back," the dragonslayer assured. "Dragons tend to keep maidens in their company for many days before they eat them, so we have time to attack him and recover the girls. Believe me, I've been up against such a beast before."

Nodding, Prince Tahmrof said, "I will, of course, reward you handsomely for her safe return, but I will be horribly irked if she is harmed."

"Not to worry, your Highness. I'll have her back before dinner tomorrow."

"How can you be so sure," the Prince demanded.

"I know of this dragon," Duke Malchor explained. "It is the scarlet beast that has a lair only five leagues from here and is said to have an appetite for human girls."

Garrin puzzled and spoke before he realized. "It won't eat men?"

The Duke laughed softly, almost expecting everyone around him to do the same. "Come now, lad. What dragon would want a tough and gamy man for a meal? The tender and pure flesh of a virgin girl is what dragons like the best."

Nodding, the squire tried to make sense of that. How would a dragon know if a girl was a virgin? Why would any dragon turn down an easy meal even if it was a man?

"It's been that way for centuries," the dragonslayer continued. "In fact, in some parts of the land there are those who still sacrifice young virgins to vengeful dragons to placate them." He took the boy under his arm and led him toward a couple of chairs. "Two seasons ago I killed such a beast. It had eaten hundreds of the local girls over the decades, so many that their lottery had thinned any chance a man might have of finding a virgin wife. It was becoming quite the problem."

Garrin sat down when directed and watched as the dragonslayer did the same. "So they called you to attend to the beast?"

Nodding, Duke Malchor confirmed, "That they did. I was passing through the area and heard of their plight from a farmer who had lost two daughters to the beast. I couldn't very well let that continue so I demanded an audience with the king of that land and told him I would smite this beast down to save his kingdom."

With his eyes wide and lighting up a little more each second, Garrin listened intently, forgetting about his sore and aching body for a moment as he leaned forward and gave the dragonslayer his full attention.

"Oh, he was reluctant, of course," the dragonslayer went on. "His fear was that the dragon's ire would be so severe that the kingdom would be lost should I not prevail. I finally convinced him and took my forces out to meet the beast."

"You went to its lair?" the squire asked, sounding a little astounded.

"It's not a good idea to fight a dragon on its own terms. I had to lure the beast to a battlefield of my choosing, which was easy enough."

"How did you do that?"

"Very simple. Dragons tend to be creatures of habit. The lottery went on as usual and a maiden was chosen to give her life to keep her kingdom safe." His eyes narrowed. "But this time I was waiting for him." Looking to one side, the Duke casually took a goblet of wine a servant offered him and looked down into it. For a moment he did not speak and appeared to be collecting his thoughts. Finally turning his eyes back to the boy, he continued, "I almost lost my life that day. This beast was larger and stronger than I had anticipated and I definitely had my hands full with him."

"How did you slay him? My sword did not even mark the dragon that attacked here tonight."

Smiling, Duke Malchor reached over and roughed the boy's hair. "Your sword was not made to kill dragons. You see, to kill such a beast takes more than steel and courage. I have two mages in my company, one a warlock who concocts the potions that my blades are forged with and one a wizard who can control the elements and keep the beast on the ground. I also have with me a few soldiers who assist with the kill, but only one can actually approach and do battle."

"That would be you," the squire guessed.

Malchor nodded. "That would be me. The soldiers are largely for show and they will use their weapons against a beast that might be particularly large, but I do most of the fighting myself."

"All this time I thought is was just you against the dragon."

The Duke laughed and shook his head. "No, only a fool would do that."

Garrin nodded and turned his eyes down. "A fool like me."

"That wasn't the fool in you, boy. That was a warrior protecting his kingdom and his princess. I think had you the weapons that beast would be lying dead now, and I would have some fierce competition." He winked.

Suddenly feeling better, the squire dared to ask, "May I go with you to find this beast tomorrow?"

"Of course you can," the Duke assured. "I wouldn't even think about going without you at my side. Dragons fear the courage of men, and with you facing this beast with me I'm sure he'll have no chance. I'm hoping your presence will even take some of the fight out of him."

Garrin smiled. "I'll do my best, sir."

Prince Tahmrof approached, holding another goblet of wine as he scolded, "While you sit there telling this boy your fanciful stories my daughter is out there in the talons of this horrid beast!"

His eyes shifting to the Prince, the dragonslayer assured, "She won't be by high sun tomorrow, Highness, and you'll have a trophy in the form of a dragon's head to show off to the other royalty. Believe me, most of them do not have such trophies."

Tahmrof nodded and took a drink of his wine. "Just so long as my daughter is returned safely."

His failing to mention the safe return of Princess Faelon, the true heir to the throne, did not escape Garrin's notice, but he wisely said nothing regarding that, saying instead, "How will we approach this dragon?"

"We will bring him to us," was the Duke's answer. He turned his eyes to Prince Tahmrof and asked, "Tell me, Highness.

Are there any maidens of your kingdom who will volunteer to help us lure this beast into the open?"

The Prince nodded and assured, "We will find one, I'm sure. I'll have the guards round up some volunteers tonight. Is there anything else special you might need?"

"Just make sure she's a virgin of marrying age and dressed in white. Flowers in her hair would be good. And make sure my mages and I are not disturbed. We have much to prepare for tonight and little time."

"I will have guards posted so that you aren't disturbed," Tahmrof assured, "and I will see to it you have everything you might need."

"Thank you, Highness," the dragonslayer offered. "I'll try not to be too much of a burden."

"Not at all," the Prince assured, "so long as I get my daughter back."

As Prince Tahmrof turned and walked away, Garrin enthusiastically asked, "May I help in your preparations, my Lord?"

Duke Malchor smiled at him and replied, "You can help me best by resting yourself for the hunt tomorrow. You'll need all of your strength for the battle this beast will put up when we finally engage him."

"I will, my Lord." Garrin looked to Sir Kessler, who watched from a couple of paces away. He seemed to need reassurance from his own knight, which he got with a smile and a nod. Without realizing, the squire asked, "Lord Malchor, will Sir Kessler join in the hunt tomorrow?"

Malchor could sense the boy's loyalty to his knight and he responded just as the lad had hoped. Looking to Kessler, the Duke nodded and assured, "A knight of Sir Kessler's courage and stature is always welcome at my side, should he choose to honor us with his company."

"I believe I will," the knight said, "and thank you for the invitation." He looked to Garrin and ordered, "Well, come on, boy. We've little time to tend your injuries and rest before the hunt tomorrow."

Responding to his knight's order, Garrin stood and faced Duke Malchor, bowing his head to the dragonslayer before following his knight from the ballroom.

Sleep would be elusive as excitement and anticipation coursed through him like a surging river.

CHAPTER 2

Evening in the forest usually meant the time was at hand to wind down, to find some place safe in the grass to lie down and relax before drifting off to sleep. With the sun below the treetops the time was right to do just that, and most of the day dwelling forest animals already were.

One pony-sized white unicorn was not.

Her big brown eyes were locked intently on the large form that was lying in the grass before her.

Near the tree line, the black spotted tan and white forest cat waited patiently for nightfall, watching the field of grass that would eventually bring about a potential meal as the sun went down. Most of the deer and other plant eating animals of the forest knew of his presence already and avoided the area. Those with burrows stayed in them. No matter. Forest cats were always known for their patience. Some hapless creature would make the mistake of wandering into the open just a little too close to get away, as forest cats are difficult to spot in tall grass, and after a brief chase would end up as just another meal.

This was far from the mind of our unicorn. Her ivory horn with its ribbons of gold shimmered in the dim light and her gold cloven hooves stepped noiselessly onto the soft soil and pine needles of the forest. Holding her head low, she crept closer, six paces, five, four…

Still oblivious to her presence, the forest cat was nothing more than relaxed, watching patiently as they do.

Three paces, two... The unicorn hesitated as the forest cat's ear flicked her way. When his full attention returned to the field, she closed the gap more, her eyes narrowing.

Half a pace away she stopped, reaching her head toward the big cat, and when she was almost close enough to touch him between the ears, she whinnied as loudly as she could before springing away.

Screaming in surprise, the cat sprang up and tried to swing around to face whatever had just startled him into soiling himself. Standing, he was as tall at the back as an average horse and built with enough muscle to take down almost anything he wanted to eat–including unicorns!

Before he could get his wits about him, the little white unicorn leaped over him and galloped toward the center of the field.

When he finally realized what had happened and who it was that caused it, the big cat cried out in anger and launched himself in pursuit. Much faster than he appeared, the forest cat was able to rapidly close the gap between himself and the fleeing unicorn.

Looking behind her, the unicorn slowed her pace a little more to allow him to catch up, bringing him to within about four paces before she lengthened her stride again.

When the cat kicked his own stride longer to catch her, she planted a front hoof and turned sharply, galloping the other way before he had time to react. When he tried to match her turn his big paws were unable to stay under his bulk and he found himself rolling across the field.

The dust had not quite settled when he finally rose from the grass and shook his head. Then his eyes fixed on something and he growled.

Watching from only nine paces away, the little unicorn snorted back.

Stalking toward her, the forest cat held his head low and his ears flat against his head, his eyes locked on the defiant unicorn who just stood there. Half way to her and preparing to spring, he suddenly raised his head and looked behind her, his ears swiveling to the front. With another growl, he turned and stalked back toward his resting spot downwind of the field, not even looking back at the little white unicorn who just stood there and curiously watched his slow retreat.

Whinnying to the cat, the unicorn seemed a little irked when he did not respond. She snorted at him, then turned and flinched as she saw a big bay unicorn standing right behind her.

He held his lips tight, his eyes locked on the little white unicorn's. He was a big unicorn, as big as a horse and well muscled. Ribbons of copper glistened within his spiral and his long black mane, tail and beard shined even in the dimming light of the forest evening. As the white unicorn turned fully toward him, he loosed a deep breath and asked, "Shahly, what are you doing?"

She raised her head, her ears perking up as she countered, "What do you mean?"

"We normally avoid predators, remember?"

Glancing at the forest cat, she agreed, "Oh, yes. I was, uh… I was… He was lying there and—and I—"

"Provoked him again," the big bay unicorn finished for her.

Turning her eyes down, the little unicorn kicked at the earth and admitted, "Yes. I was only having fun with him."

"I'm sure he did not share your joy," the bay pointed out. "Shahly, you simply *have* to stop pestering the forest predators so."

"I know," she conceded. "I just get bored and I want to have fun."

Whickering a sigh, the big unicorn turned and paced back toward the forest. "I can see I'm going to have to keep my eyes on you every moment."

She cantered to his side, looking affectionately up at him as she pointed out, "That can't be so bad, having you watch over me so."

He glanced at her. "Not for you. What are you going to do when one of those predators actually catches you?"

Stopping, her eyes widened and she grimly admitted, "I hadn't thought of that."

"I know," he growled, walking on toward the forest.

She caught up to him again and tried to lighten his spirits with, "That won't happen as long as you're about. You're the strongest unicorn in the forest."

Another glance was all the response she got. He was not pleased with her and made no secret of it.

She finally loosed a loud breath and offered, "I'm sorry, Vinton."

The bay could see that she was near tears and his already soft heart trembled for her. When she looked away from him, he butted her with his nose and pointed out, "You've got every predator in the forest so nervous they keep watch behind them most of the time expecting ambush any moment."

She glanced at him.

He continued, "You're fast becoming the most feared creature in the land."

Not wanting to look at him, she could not help whickering a laugh.

"Of course," he went on, "before you know it you'll—" A deep roar overhead cut him off and they both turned and looked skyward.

Flying rather low over the forest, the winged form stroked its wings for speed, roaring yet another warning before him.

Shahly squinted slightly. "Is that Ralligor?"

"I don't think so," the bay answered, "and it looks too big to be Falloah. What is that he's carrying?"

Pacing forward a few steps as if pursuing, the white unicorn looked hard, then her ears stood straight up and she declared, "He's carrying women! Vinton, he's got human mares!"

The big bay paced to her side and mumbled, "I didn't think dragons actually did that."

As the dragon flew out of sight over the trees, Shahly looked to her stallion and asked, "What is he doing?"

"I've heard stories of dragons carrying away human mares, taking them to their caves. I'm not sure why or how the stories began, but it appears to be true."

"That doesn't make sense," the white unicorn complained. "Why would they? Ralligor says dragons don't like the taste of humans."

"That one appears to," the bay observed.

"Should we follow him?" Shahly asked.

Finally turning his eyes to his smaller mate, the bay countered, "How do you propose we do that? Unless you've figured out how to fly we'll never keep up with him."

"Well, if we travel in the same direction long enough we should find him."

"Unless he turns, or we turn in the forest without realizing."

"Vinton, we have to do something."

His eyes widened. "We do? Why is that, exactly?"

"We can't just let him eat them."

"Why not?"

Shahly snorted. "Vinton, what if it was me up there."

"It isn't you up there, Shahly. Just let the humans attend to him."

Shahly looked at where the dragon had disappeared. "It just doesn't seem right. I still think we should go and find him."

"And then what?" When the little white unicorn turned a very hurt look on him, the bay finally conceded, "Fine. But only until sundown. Traveling after dark is just too dangerous."

"Do you think we should find Ralligor and–"

"No, I don't," the bay interrupted.

"But he's another dragon and he could–"

"We don't even know if we're going to find that other dragon, Shahly. I tell you what. If we find this other dragon and we aren't able to help the human mares then I will personally go and find your friend Ralligor to attend to him, okay?"

Turning her eyes down, Shahly nodded and agreed, "Okay. I just hope he hasn't eaten them before we find him." She looked back up at the bay and asked, "How do you know that other dragon is a male, anyway? It looks an awful lot like Falloah."

"The pitch of his roar," Vinton answered. "It was too deep for a female. A male dragon will often announce his approach to warn off other males who might want to challenge him. He might also have been telling them that he was just passing through and did not intend to fight."

"Oh," Shahly said. "You sure know a lot about dragons."

He looked back at her and softly whickered a laugh. "You've had more experience with them lately than I have. I'm thinking you're twice the expert that I am."

She butted him with her nose. "Now you're just teasing me again. Vinton, do dragons ever live in human strongholds?"

Glancing at her, he replied, "Uh, it's not unheard of. Why do you ask?"

"There is an old castle the way he is flying. He might be taking the human mares there."

"First of all, how do you know about the old castle?"

"I've been there before. I went in and wandered around for a while. It sort of reminds me of Red Stone Castle, but it is older and really—"

"Second," the bay interrupted, "Why do you think he would take the human mares there?"

Shahly glanced at him. "Vinton, where else would he take them? They're humans."

He drew a deep, calming breath and explained, "He could take them to a cave or a lair like that. He's not necessarily interested in their comfort."

The white unicorn considered. "So, why would he have them?"

"I suppose we could ask when we find him?"

Her ears perked and she looked to him. "Really?"

"No, Shahly."

She snorted. "Well, I think that's where we'll find him. We need to try to get there before dark."

"Why do you think we'll find him there?"

"There aren't any caves that way, so where else would he take them?"

"Okay, Shahly, but if we don't find him there—"

"I know, I know. I still think we should find Ralligor."

"We will, as soon as we know more."

She glanced at him again. "You don't like him, do you?"

Vinton glanced back. "Ralligor?" He huffed a sigh. "He's a dragon, Shahly. I don't have trust for dragons."

"But he helped us. He's the reason we get to still be together."

"And you are the reason he was reunited with Falloah," the stallion pointed out. "You know, sometimes I wish my heart was as open as yours."

Slowly, she turned her young brown eyes to him and a smile. "I think it is."

Many hours passed as they made their way through the forest toward this ancient castle. As always, each reveled in the company of the other, and before nightfall they stood at the edge of the tree line about a hundred paces from the old castle. The clearing around the castle was overgrown with young trees and bushes, tall grass and vines. Of the four towers, only two still stood, as did only half of its defensive wall. The palace itself suffered from many decades of disrepair and was half reclaimed by the vines and green things of the forest.

Sitting atop the tower closest to them was the dragon they had seen. While its color was difficult to make out in the dimming light, its size and build were the same. It warily scanned the forest, mostly the treetops, and would occasionally turn its eyes skyward.

Torchlight illuminated two of the windows of this tower and four more on that side of the palace.

Vinton's eyes narrowed and he observed, "Odd."

Shahly glanced at him. "What do you mean? I told you we would find him here."

"Not that. The place appears to be inhabited. A form just moved in one of those windows that is lit."

"Why would that be odd?"

"Why would humans be there if that dragon is right on top of them?"

Considering, Shahly finally answered, "Well, it would be safer than being outside with him, especially if he likes to eat humans."

He glanced at her. "Shahly, did you see any humans the last time you visited here?"

She looked away, then shook her head. "No."

"But there are now."

"Maybe he's bringing them here for a reason."

The stallion's eyes narrowed again. "Or maybe they were expecting him to be there."

Turning her eyes down, Shahly considered his words again, then she looked to him and said, "That doesn't make sense."

"Have you ever known humans to actually make sense, Shahly?"

She looked back to the castle. "No, not really. I was human myself for three days and I still don't understand them. Should we go and talk to that dragon?"

Vinton quickly raised his head and bayed, "No, we're not going to talk to the dragon!"

"We have many questions," she insisted, "and he can answer them all."

"He can also kill us!" the stallion pointed out. "Shahly, not all dragons are like Falloah and your Ralligor. Many *will* kill us if they see us."

She loosed an impatient breath and looked away from him.

His lips tightening, he assured, "We can go talk to Falloah in the morning. Her cave isn't far from here."

Shahly turned her eyes to him and asked, "Promise?"

He nodded and confirmed, "Promise. Now let's put some distance between us and this place before night consumes the forest fully."

Awakening early for such errands was not something unicorns did, and yet two unicorns trekked south on just such an errand. They only knew of one red dragon in that part of the forest and perhaps their answers were there. Having visited this part of the forest many times, the big bay knew right where he was going. The little white unicorn remained at his side, not trusting nor mistrusting his sense of direction, just happy to be with him. Yet, something stirred within her, something that craved excitement, something that frustrated her stallion so.

After many hours of morning travel, stopping occasionally to nibble grass or berries, the land abruptly ended. The lush grass grew right to the edge and they stopped and looked down into the deep water of the river four human's heights below. The current moved slowly here and the water turned deep blue, but was clearly shallower down river and ran more rapidly. Also down river the bluff they stood on sloped downward toward the river where an easy crossing only fifty paces away was evident. Looking across the river, they saw another hill that climbed from the river flood plain, one that was overgrown with green things. Some of the short trees and bushes and vines partly concealed the cave that opened near the base of the hill.

The bay unicorn motioned across the river with his head, informing, "That's her lair. We just need to hope she's in there and not out hunting or something of the like." He looked to the white unicorn, finding her gone. Turning his attention behind, he summoned, "Shahly?"

Hoof beats drew close at a gallop and Vinton saw her as she ran past him and hurled herself off of the cliff with a loud whinny. He watched her careen toward the deep water, his mind scrambling to understand what she was doing. As she slammed into the water's surface with a great splash, he guessed that she did not want to walk all the way around and was just looking for a faster way across, in her own special way.

Breaking the surface seconds later, she snorted and shook her head, then swam hard toward the shallows downstream. As she strode from the deep water, she turned toward the bank she had leaped from and scrambled up the shallow slope from the water and ran back toward her stallion.

Now her actions were a complete mystery.

Veering behind him again, Shahly ran about twenty paces behind Vinton and turned toward him, then she galloped toward the cliff, whinnying as she passed the stallion and launched herself off of the cliff again.

Vinton was a little stunned, and yet he had gotten used to her increasingly eccentric behavior. Watching her splash into the river again, he loosed a deep sigh and shook his head. The reality was all too clear. The unicorn he loved was a maniac.

He watched as she swam to the shallows and scrambled up the bank, turning his head to keep his eyes on her as she ran behind him. Looking the other way, he watched her run toward the cliff a third time.

Whinnying as before, Shahly threw her head down as she launched herself from the cliff, somersaulting hooves over head toward the water. A turn and a half later she hit the water flat on her back. The once pristine water's surface was now so turbulent one might think that a waterfall was nearby. Her waves lapping both banks, the little white unicorn struggled to the surface and toward the bank, exiting the water closer to the cliff side and scrambling up the half-height climb toward the slope.

As he sensed another presence approaching, Vinton looked behind him to see an old human with long white hair and a long white beard approaching. He wore a green wizard's robe of light material that was just enough to keep the sun off of him. A black headband with a green jewel in it was all he wore on his head. As he approached the unicorn, he smiled and raised his hand in greeting.

Vinton did not like the company of humans, but today his instinct to flee from this human's sight was silent. He knew this one, this gentle man of the forest. Shahly had met him in the spring and now even the stallion felt trust for him. Like only one other, he felt this human had a strange link to the forest, to the land itself.

As the wizard reached him, Vinton turned the other way and watched the little white unicorn hurl herself off of the cliff side yet again, shaking his head as she whinnied all the way to the water.

The human also watched, and as she splashed head-first into the river, he asked, "So, how long has *this* been going on?"

"Four times now," the bay unicorn answered dryly.

They both looked on as Shahly swam to the shallows and scrambled up the cliff side at an even higher point. She was clearly growing impatient with the traveling and wanted to be at the top quickly.

Vinton looked to the wizard as Shahly ran behind them again and he asked, "What brings you this way? I rarely see you venture far from the scrub country."

"I was seeing someone at Enulam," the wizard explained. "While I was meditating in the forest I saw a red dragon in the distance, one carrying two maidens."

"We saw him last night," Vinton confirmed. "We followed his path of flight to an old castle not very far from here. There seemed to be some humans living there, but only recently arrived."

The wizard nodded. "Strange. I know that castle you speak of. It's been abandoned for almost a century. You are sure there were people there?"

Shahly galloped by again, greeting, "Hi," as she passed the stallion and human.

They glanced at her, then Vinton answered, "I'm sure."

As the white unicorn splashed into the river below, the wizard nodded, his eyes narrow. "I was hoping it wasn't Falloah I saw. I can't really see her approaching a castle and carrying off a couple of maidens."

"I didn't think dragons really did that," the bay unicorn said. "I'd always considered that a myth since it really doesn't make sense for them to behave so."

"I'm certain it *is* a myth, my friend. I've known Ralligor for over forty seasons and he's never even mentioned an appetite for women."

"He doesn't think highly of your kind. I think you are the only human he spends any time with."

"He doesn't trust my kind, and with good reason. Too many of my kind are consumed with greed and gain, too much so to realize what it is they've lost."

Vinton nodded. "Their connection to the land, you mean?"

"Yes," the wizard confirmed softly.

As Shahly ran by them again, movement in the cave across the river drew the stallion's attention and he looked to see a red form emerging.

A scarlet dragon slowly crept from her cave on all fours, watching the top of the cliff across the river. Her eyes followed the white unicorn all the way to the water and she drew her head back as she watched the unicorn swim to the shallows and climb back up. Turning her eyes to the cliff top again, she stood and opened her wings, gracefully lifting herself into the air. Her ocher belly and wing webbing was like fire in the late morning sunlight and her scales glistened as she soared effortlessly to the cliff where the human and unicorn were standing. Settling on the grass nearby, she stood to her full three human's heights and folded her wings to her. Her curvy, lean muscles were not tense and ready for battle in the presence of two natural enemies, rather she was at ease as her amber eyes looked the visitors over. Not once did her dorsal scale ridges even stand up, which would show an enemy she was ready for a fight.

Sitting catlike before the wizard and unicorns, the scarlet dragon wrapped her tail around herself on the ground as she said, "I didn't expect visitors today."

"We aren't disturbing you, are we?" the unicorn asked.

Shahly sprinted by, half out of breath as she greeted, "Hi, Falloah."

The dragoness watched the white unicorn launch herself from the cliff. "Uh, what is she doing?"

Laughing, the wizard replied, "She's trying to find her wings."

Falloah looked to the bay unicorn.

"Since we got here," Vinton growled.

Raising her brow, the dragoness nodded, then she looked over the cliff and asked, "You've come about that dragon I saw last night?"

Wizard and unicorn exchanged glances.

"He flew right over my cave," Falloah went on, "and then he turned back to the North. I think he was carrying a couple of humans. I wasn't sure what he was doing, flying so close to my lair like that, especially with Agarxus' lair only about twenty five leagues from here."

Vinton's eyes narrowed. "You don't know this dragon?"

The dragoness shook her head, watching Shahly scramble back up the cliff. "The only drakes in this part of the forest are Ralligor and Agarxus."

"So you're sure this was a drake?" the wizard asked.

Her eyes panned to him and she lifted a brow.

He nodded. "Of course you are. We came her hoping to find answers, like why he would abduct two girls."

Falloah shrugged and watched Shahly run toward the cliff side again. "I'd thought about finding you to ask the same."

The white unicorn whinnied all the way to the water.

The bay reported, "Shahly and I followed him to an old castle not far from here. He was glancing about pretty nervously from the look of him."

"He should be nervous," Falloah confirmed, looking toward the North.

"I wonder if Ralligor could help us shed some light on this?" the wizard guessed.

"He needs to be told regardless," the dragoness answered, her eyes on the white unicorn as she swam toward the bank again. "If another drake is trying to claim territory here then he will have to be dealt with."

"Especially if he intends to start attacking castles in the area," the wizard added. "The last thing we need is another war between men and dragons."

"Who would you side with?" Falloah asked with a steely tone as she watched the white unicorn swim toward the cliff.

Smiling, the wizard answered, "Why, the dragons, of course."

She turned her eyes back to him and the hint of a smile curled her mouth.

"But," the wizard continued, "let us try to avoid such a war, just so that I am not forced to betray my people."

Vinton considered. "Would this new dragon have an appetite for human mares?"

Her lip curling up, Falloah snarled, "I don't know why. I'd almost rather eat carrion, myself."

"So, you've tasted humans before?" the unicorn asked.

"I've smelled them," she answered, then looked to the wizard and offered, "No offense, of course."

He smiled and assured, "None taken, Falloah. I know we have an odor about us."

They all looked toward the slope as Shahly scrambled up. Running too close to the cliff edge, part of the land beneath her hooves gave way and she stumbled to keep her balance, but more of the cliff behind her collapsed and, with wide eyes, she whinnied as she tumbled off.

All the onlookers could see was a plume of dust where she had gone over, and a splash in shallow water let them know she had found the riverbed.

Many long seconds of silence followed.

Vinton turned fully and whickered, "Shahly?"

"Ow," was her pitiful response

He cantered forward. "Shahly!"

"I'm okay," she strained to whinny.

He stopped, staring at the edge of the cliff.

The wizard and dragoness approached.

Falloah raised her brow and finally said, "Well, I think I should let you two take care of this. I'm going to fly north and see if I can find that other dragon."

Turning his eyes up to her, the wizard asked, "Shouldn't you find Ralligor first?"

"I can handle it," she assured. "We're closer to Agarxus' lair, so if he wants to fight I'll just have him chase me there." She took a couple of steps back and opened her wings. "I'll be back shortly. Let me know if she needs to be carried somewhere."

Vinton and the wizard watched the dragoness lift herself into the sky, then they turned their attention back to the cliff edge.

"Vinton," Shahly pitifully whinnied, "I think I hurt myself."

The stallion closed his eyes and lowered his head, whickering out a little exasperation.

Patting his neck, the wizard assured, "Well, my friend, you'll never be bored with her."

CHAPTER 3

The reality of slaying dragons was far different than Garrin had imagined. Sitting atop their horses and looking out into the meadow from their hiding places in the trees of the forest a league or so from the castle, he and the dragonslayer, Sir Kessler, the Duke's thin, gray and black haired wizard and thirty soldiers watched and waited for their quarry to happen upon the bait. Earlier that morning, a tall timber post had been planted in the ground in the center of the meadow. A reluctant blond haired girl of around Garrin's age had been forcibly bound to the post. Per the dragonslayer's instructions, she was dressed in white and had flowers in her long hair.

Garrin felt for her. The hour they had spent awaiting the arrival of the dragon had been spent watching the girl cry. Occasionally she would turn to the men who waited in the trees to beg for her life. Only the squire seemed to feel for her. To the other men present she was simply bait.

This would be the first time Garrin wore his armor in actual battle. He had helped Sir Kessler into his armor before leaving the castle and made sure it was polished and oiled along with the knight's sword. His own armor was not full suit; rather it covered his torso, his upper arms and upper legs. High, polished black leather boots would be the only protection his lower legs would have, and heavy leather gauntlets protected his forearms.

A new sword hung at his side, one that had been given him by the dragonslayer that morning.

All of the soldiers present wore light armor similar to Garrin's, armor that was meant for quick maneuvering. Unlike the squire, they already had their helmets on, anticipating a fight that could come at any moment.

Duke Malchor himself sat on an armored horse closest to the meadow. Though his armor was well polished and oiled, it was clearly scarred from many battles, probably with dragons. Metal covered almost every part of him as plate armor was layered over chain mail. He appeared to be ready for very close combat with this dragon. A long sword hung on his left, a barbed lance to his right. His eyes shifted constantly from the girl to the sky, the sky to the girl.

Garrin's horse shifted nervously and he patted the animal's neck to reassure him.

The dragonslayer looked to the horse, then to the squire, ordering in a low voice, "He senses the approach of the dragon. Get that helmet on. It's almost time."

Swallowing hard, Garrin took his helmet from the saddle horn and slipped over his head. Having no face shield, his helmet did not offer the protection the other soldiers present would have. No matter. Excitement lanced through him as he pulled his chinstrap tight and turned his eyes to the Duke.

Smiling at him, Duke Malchor winked and assured, "This promises to be an eventful day, boy. Are you ready?"

Garrin nodded.

The wizard pointed up, hissing, "There."

Everyone's eyes turned skyward.

A red, winged form soared into view from the East and trumpeted a challenge, then flew on toward the West, descending sharply. Against the morning sun it was difficult to make out, but for its shape and color.

Long moments passed. Everyone was on edge, scanning the heavens with sharp eyes.

Garrin's heart thundered as watched for the beast to return. Wings cutting the air overhead and behind had him turn in his saddle, his wide eyes trying to pierce any gap in the canopy for a glimpse of the beast. A shadow above soared past over the trees.

"He's circling," the Duke whispered. "Make no noise and be ready. He'll be landing to get the girl in a moment."

The dragon flew lower over the clearing, his full attention on the girl who was bound to the stake. Her screams as she saw him drew Garrin's attention to her. She struggled against the rope that held her until her wrists bled, though she could not seem to feel the pain through the terror that had its grip on her.

As the dragon flew out of sight again, the squire leaned to Duke Malchor and whispered, "Will we be able to get to the dragon before he gets to the girl?"

The dragonslayer shrugged as he continued to watch for the dragon. "Perhaps so."

Garrin turned his eyes back to the terrified girl as she looked back at them again.

"Please!" she screamed. "Help me! Don't let him get me! He's going to kill me!"

His lips tightening, Garrin's had found his sword, his eyes on the girl's. He glanced at the Duke again and insisted, "We can cut the girl loose and have her back before he lands."

"If we do that he won't land," was the dragonslayer's answer, "and if he suspects we're here he will likely fire us from the air. We really don't want that. If we are going to kill the beast and get your princess back then we have to get him on the ground."

"What if he gets to the girl first?" the squire pressed.

Malchor drew a breath, not looking at the squire as he replied, "She may have to be sacrificed so that many others might live."

Feeling a chill, Garrin tried to understand, but everything he had been taught cried out in one voice. His sword was to uphold justice, to protect the weak and the innocent, to be wielded against evil. In his heart he knew that sacrificing the girl was wrong, and yet if this saved the lives of others, perhaps hundreds...

A dragon's deep trumpet from the South alerted the soldiers and everyone's hand found a weapon.

Long seconds passed.

The dragon sounded again, the same call but higher pitched this time.

Nerves were pulled taught. Even the bait girl fell silent.

All Garrin could make out at first was the flash of ocher soaring over the trees on the other end of the field. As the dragon drew closer and swept its wings forward, the squire noticed quickly the red scales on its flanks and head. He also noticed that the dragon suddenly looked smaller.

Stroking its wings forward in wind grapping sweeps, the dragon lowered its talons and gently settled onto the ground about fifty paces south of the bait girl. Garrin fully expected the dragon to go right for her, but it just stood there, scanning the sky all around. As its amber eyes panned back and forth, the girl screamed hysterically, drawing its attention.

The Duke leaned to Garrin and whispered, "The moment is at hand, boy. Be ready to charge."

Nodding, the squire slowly pulled his sword and held it firmly, ready to engage the beast again. As before, excitement mingled with his battle training and he found himself barely holding back.

Staring down at the girl, the dragon approached, leaning its head as it neared. It stopped less than ten paces away, suddenly raising its eyes to the sky again. Its eyes were a little wider and Garrin could swear he saw fear in them. Its jaws opened slightly and the tips of its teeth gleamed in the morning sunlight.

"It's looking for something," Garrin whispered.

"He smells us," the Duke whispered back. Looking to the wizard, the dragonslayer nodded once.

The wizard raised his hands, his eyes locked on the dragon.

"Please help me!" the bait girl screamed.

Taking a step back, the dragon looked down at her, its jaws opening further.

"Now!" the dragonslayer shouted.

Hot white light lanced from the wizard's hands and slammed into the dragon's chest, sending it backward to the ground. As it went down, the Duke kicked his horse forward, shouting a battle cry as he swung his sword. A ball of fire that ignited at the hilt grew larger as it sped down the blade and was slung from the tip of the sword, striking the dragon as it tried to right itself. The explosion sent the beast back down.

Garrin kicked his horse forward, holding his weapon ready as he closed the distance between him and his quarry. All of the men were riding toward the dragon in a staggered line, weapons ready.

Rising to all fours, the dragon looked to them, quickly scanning their ranks, then it turned toward them and backed away, roaring back at them. When it opened its wings, the wizard struck again, this time hitting the side of its neck near the shoulder and it shrieked and staggered, backing away more. As the soldiers neared, it gaped its jaws and loosed a blast of fire, sweeping it along their line.

This stopped them and the men turned their horses and raised their shields against the flames. From here, only Duke Malchor continued to charge, holding his shield ready and raising his sword.

The dragon blasted him with fire, but he raised his shield against it and urged his horse on faster. Swinging his sword as before, he sent another fireball at the dragon which it tried to dodge but was hit on the wing anyway. Screeching again, it retreated further, angling away from the dragonslayer.

Malchor's blade erupted into flames and when he was close enough he swung it hard, the burning sword slashing through the armor of the dragon's upper arm.

Grasping its wounded arm, the dragon retreated further, shrieking in pain. As the dragonslayer charged again, the dragon unexpectedly wheeled around, its tail catching the horse's legs and upending the animal.

The dragonslayer rolled from his toppled horse and was quick to find his feet. Holding his sword ready, he faced the retreating dragon and motioned for his men to move in.

As they advanced, the dragon stood and blasted them with its fire, then turned to the dragonslayer and blasted him.

He took the fire on his shield, then swung his sword and struck back, this time hitting the dragon square in the chest.

Stumbling backward, the dragon did not go all the way down this time. It turned and ran toward the charging men, giving them a short blast of fire as it opened its wings and swept into the sky.

The wizard got in one more shot, striking the dragon along the back as it struggled to remain airborne.

Watching its retreat, Garrin feared for the safety of the princesses this beast had stolen and charged after it, his sword still in his hand as he raced toward a forest trail. Keeping up with a flying creature was a problem, but occasional glimpses of orange through the canopy of trees and the calls the dragon made in flight made it easier to track. He did not know how long he pursued the beast. He only knew that two girls were counting on him.

As he rode into a clearing he saw the dragon in the sky before him, barely remaining above the treetops. Ahead was a large, grass covered meadow, almost half a league wide and long.

Clumsily stroking its wings, the dragon finally descended and lowered its talons, landing awkwardly and finally collapsing onto the grass.

"I have you now!" the squire shouted as he charged to finish his quarry.

Lying sprawled before him, the dragon heaved and it struggled to catch its breath. Many wounds were evident as Garrin drew closer and its arm still bled badly. As he dismounted and strode toward the dragon, he hesitated as the beast crooned pitifully.

The dragon half turned its head and tried to pull its limbs under it to stand, but clearly lacked the strength. All it could do was watch Garrin approach and await his death blow.

Now, as he stared into the dragon's amber eyes, Garrin felt pity for it. He stopped his advance and lowered his sword, just staring back at those eyes for a time.

It crooned again, clearly in pain.

Studying the beast before him, Garrin suddenly realized something very important. This dragon was smaller than the one that had attacked the castle. Much smaller. Its eyes were not even the right color, amber and not orange. The dragon that had attacked the castle had four large teeth protruding from its lower jaw. The teeth on this one were completely covered by its scaly lips. Slowly, he backed away a step.

This was the wrong dragon.

The dragon's eyes shifted to his sword.

Garrin also looked to his sword. This blade was meant to protect the weak and innocent. It was meant as a tool of justice. His father flashed into his mind and he hoped he had not disgraced his family's honor. He could not know of the guilt and shame in his eyes as he looked back to the dragon, meeting its eyes. When Duke Malchor and his men arrived this dragon would surely be killed.

His lips tightened and he approached, stabbing the point of his sword into the ground and kneeling down beside the scarlet form.

It cooed again.

"You didn't attack the castle yesterday, did you?" he asked.

It just stared at him and a tear rolled from its eye.

Hoof beats in the forest drew his attention and he looked over his shoulder. In a moment the Duke and his forces would come charging out of the trees to finish this dragon. To him, it would be just another trophy. Garrin knew he could go back to the castle a hero, unless he did what honor demanded.

Slowly he stood and turned toward the approaching riders, holding his sword ready. When he heard the dragon move, he looked over his shoulder, then turned fully and backed away as his eyes were filled with the huge black form that swept in right at him.

Landing with its back talons first, the black dragon slammed hard onto the ground, dropping to all fours and bringing his head right over the scarlet dragon's. This one was easily twice the red dragon's overall size, a mammoth beast with heavy armor, menacing black horns and glowing red eyes beneath a thick, angry brow. Muscles of unimaginable strength bulged beneath his scales and the dorsal scales that ran from between his horns all the way to the end of his tail grew erect as his scaly lips curled back from sword sized white teeth. Just his snout was as long as Garrin was tall. One did not need but to guess that this was the mate of the red dragon. One thing was perfectly clear: This dragon was angry.

With the dragon's nose and teeth only a pace away, Garrin stood there dumbly, staring into the eyes of sure death. He was unaware how wide his own eyes were, that his mouth was hanging open, and that he had dropped his sword.

The dragon sniffed, then blew out through is nostrils with enough force to cause the puny human before him to step back. Those horrible teeth parted slightly as a deep growl rolled from the dragon's throat.

A hiss from the forest was the only warning of the power of Duke Malchor's sword being unleashed and it struck the black dragon's head with a true aim, exploding with enough force to send Garrin stumbling backward.

The dragon's head swung over slightly—only slightly. Growling and with narrow eyes, he turned toward the treacherous human who dared strike at him.

Garrin also looked, seeing Duke Malchor and his men and wizard charge from the trees. Looking back to the dragon as the great beast stood, bringing his head five heights from the ground, he realized that the same power that had badly stunned the scarlet dragon and caused her grave injury had merely angered this brute.

The black dragon turned fully, lowering his body and lifting his long tail so that he was parallel to the ground and still nearly two heights from it. Holding his arms at the ready, he gaped his jaws and roared loud enough to shake the very ground he stood on. Even the red dragon cringed and Garrin covered his ears and sank to his knees.

Duke Malchor and his men stopped as their horses were thrown into a panic, many of them rearing up in fear.

Raising his head slightly, the black dragon waited for the dragonslayer and his men to organize themselves. While this happened, he looked to the squire and growled again. He reached toward the boy, and as Garrin scrambled away, the dragon plucked the sword from the ground with two fingers.

As his weapon was taken away, Garrin raised his eyes as the dragon looked it over, then he cringed as the beast easily snapped it in half and dropped it. When the dragon turned those menacing eyes on him again, the squire felt he was next.

The dragon simply raised a brow, then turned his attention back to the dragonslayer and his men as they regrouped.

This was the kind of thing Garrin had read about, an epic battle between man and dragon, a dragonslayer's skill, steel and courage against the most powerful creature in the world. In the stories, the dragonslayer always won, but as men and dragon closed for battle Garrin could only shake his head, knowing that they had little chance of victory. Ambushing the smaller dragon had seemed almost easy. This one was huge, seemed invulnerable to the Duke's powerful sword, and he knew they were coming.

With long strides, the dragon roared as he closed the sixty pace gap between him and his enemy. The men raised their weapons, yelling their battle cries as they charged him head-on. The dragonslayer's sword sent its deadly fireball at the dragon again, but this time the beast batted it away, smashing it in mid-air. The wizard struck with his deadly white light and the dragon raised a hand and caught the attack in his palm. Arrows and spears flew, all of them enchanted with dragon killing potions and all of them bouncing off of the dragon's scales.

As they drew closer, the dragonslayer slung one more fireball with his sword, then he sheathed it and reached for his lance. The tip of the lance began to glow an ominous blue and seemed to burn as if it was aflame. Holding his shield ready to ward off fire, the dragonslayer charged right at the beast.

The wizard struck again, this time hitting the dragon's side.

Lurching slightly from the blow, the dragon struck back with a blast of fire.

Only powerful magic could shield one from such an onslaught of flame, and powerful magic was called upon to do just that, which it did barely.

Dragonslayer and dragon closed quickly and the lance struck the dragon's chest, bouncing off in a brilliant flash of blue light. One swipe from the dragon's hand dismounted the Duke and he slammed onto the battlefield and rolled to a stop.

Far more nimble than he appeared, the dragon turned toward the fallen dragonslayer, his jaws agape and his teeth gleaming in the sunlight as another roar erupted from him.

His men closed on the dragon quickly. Spears and arrows flew and all bounced off of various parts of the dragon's head and body, but it was enough to distract him and give the Duke time to get to his feet and find his weapon. Reacting quickly as the lance charged again, the dragonslayer rammed the weapon into the dragon's belly with all of his might and a powerful explosion sent him stumbling backward. By the time he regained his senses only half of his smoldering weapon remained and the dragon's scales were barely marked.

With deceptive swiftness, the dragon's hand slammed into the Duke and knocked him through the air easily ten paces where he hit the ground and rolled to a dusty stop.

The soldiers moved in to protect their Duke, swarming on the dragon almost like ants.

Distracted by the battle, the dragon did not notice the departure of the wizard, who rode fast and hard toward Garrin. When he reached the boy, he waved his hand along the red dragon, and as he did a cloak of darkness fell over her, appearing as enchanted silk linen. It draped over her body and consumed her, then settled to the ground and faded from sight, and the dragoness was gone. Riding up to the boy, the wizard offered him his hand and urged, "Hurry up, boy. They'll not keep him but a moment."

Garrin took his hand and was pulled up onto the horse right behind the wizard, and as they galloped away, he held on tightly to the wizard's waist.

As they rode wide around the battle, Garrin asked frantically, "Where is the dragon?"

"I have her," was the answer. "Don't fret. She'll pose no more danger." As he passed the battle about fifty paces away, he raised his hand and struck the dragon's back with a powerful burst, but only succeeded in drawing his attention.

Batting another man from his horse, the dragon wheeled around to respond and immediately turned to where the scarlet dragon had been. Less concerned with his human enemies now, the dragon strode to where she had been.

Men scrambled to find their mounts and ride hard back toward the forest.

Garrin and the wizard met the Duke and five of his men on the main road back to Caipiervell Castle and all pushed their horses as fast as they would go.

"We haven't much time," the wizard shouted over the hoof beats. "The men will only be able to draw him off for so long before he discovers us."

"We'll be safest back at the castle," Duke Malchor shouted back. "We can regroup there and hope he doesn't discover where we've gone."

"Were we able to find where the dragon took the Princesses?" Garrin asked in a loud voice.

The dragonslayer answered, "I believe they're in an abandoned castle not far from here. When we get back I'll lead a party to go fetch them."

"Be sure to be on your guard," Garrin advised. "The red dragon we fought today was not the dragon that attacked the castle."

The Duke and wizard exchanged looks and the Duke assured, "I'll pass that on."

CHAPTER 4

Walking at a human's pace down the wide forest path was slow, but they knew where they were going and had time. Infinitely patient, Vinton kept his pace slow and stayed abreast of the wizard as they trekked north. Shahly on the other hand kept up with some difficulty as she paced along with a bad limp, favoring an injured shoulder and leg. Staying at her stallion's side, she discovered her frequent, pitiful glances went unnoticed and the bay unicorn simply engaged in conversation with the wizard.

Almost two leagues later, she finally looked to her mate and bade, "Vinton…."

"No," was his immediate response.

"But it hurts," she complained.

"I know it does."

"Please heal it," she begged.

"No," he responded.

"Please?"

"No."

"But, Vinton."

"No."

"I can hardly walk."

"That means you can't *run* off of any more cliffs."

"I didn't hurt myself jumping into the water I hurt myself climbing back up. Besides, it wasn't my fault."

The stallion turned his eyes to her.

"The side of the hill gave way," she argued.

He just stared at her.

"I was only having fun," Shahly continued. "Please heal my leg. I've learned my lesson. Please?"

Listening to the exchange, the wizard just smiled and kept on his way.

"I won't run off of any more cliffs without your permission. I promise!"

The wizard stopped and stared blankly ahead.

Vinton stopped a few paces later and turned to him, raising his head.

Shahly also stopped and looked back to them.

His eyes widening, the wizard mumbled, "Falloah."

Turning his ears to the wizard, Vinton's eyes widened as he almost demanded, "What about Falloah?"

Slowly shaking his head, the wizard just stared blankly a moment longer, then finally blinked and looked to the stallion, informing, "Ralligor's coming. Something's wrong."

Shahly limped to him and asked, "Something is wrong with Falloah? Did that other dragon hurt her?"

"I'm not sure," the wizard answered. "We need to get to the clearing ahead. Ralligor will land there." Without waiting for the unicorns, the wizard, old as he was, ran through the forest trail toward the clearing.

Vinton turned and followed.

Shahly watched them for a few seconds, then assured, "I'll catch up. Never mind my injured leg, I'll just limp along as fast as I can." She snorted as she limped after them, grumbling, "I just wanted to have some fun, I got hurt, now he's all irked. You're *so* welcome I rescued you from the humans at Red Stone Castle, *Vinton.*"

Arriving in the clearing well out of breath, the wizard stopped just outside of the tree line and turned his eyes up.

Vinton stopped at his side and waited with him. "You still don't know what's wrong with Falloah?"

Answering only with a shaking head, the wizard continued to watch for the black dragon.

"I'm fine, thanks," Shahly whinnied from somewhere behind.

Ralligor's approach was fast and low. He swept his wings forward and descended rapidly, landing hard in the middle of the clearing. His eyes found the wizard immediately and he strode forward to meet him.

"What happened?" the wizard demanded.

"She was attacked by humans," was the black dragon's answer, his voice filled with rage. "One of them was clearly a dragon hunter. He had thirty soldiers and a wizard in his company and used enchanted weapons. I intervened before he could strike his death blow and the wizard..." he looked away. "He made her disappear. He used magic to take her somewhere. I just don't know where."

"Did you recognize armor or crests?" the wizard questioned.

Shaking his head, the black dragon admitted, "I didn't study what they wore. I wanted to defend Falloah." He closed his eyes, baring his teeth as he roared, "I failed! They've taken her!"

"Take me to where she last was," the wizard ordered. "We'll find her, mighty friend, and we'll get her back."

"I'd better find her alive," Ralligor growled.

"They would not have abducted her just to kill her," the wizard informed. "Take me there."

Vinton stepped toward the dragon, looking up at him with desperate eyes of his own and said, "Tell me where you're going. I'll meet you there."

The dragon glanced at him. "I'm to believe you would help your enemy?"

"My enemy helped me once, didn't he?"

Ralligor did not consider long before he looked back to the stallion and nodded. "We'll be not quite a league north of here. Just follow the trail there." He crouched down and lowered his head and the wizard climbed aboard him, right behind his horns.

As the dragon stood again, the wizard looked down to the stallion and said, "Your help is appreciated, Vinton. Catch up as soon as you can."

Shahly limped from the trees just in time to see Ralligor take off and she snorted as she watched him sweep over the trees on the other side of the clearing, clearly annoyed that her big friend did not stay to at least say hello.

Vinton looked back at her. "There you are. Come on. We've a short journey to take and little time to get there."

Her eyes narrowed as she turned them on him. "I guess we should run there to save time, shouldn't we?

"We should," he confirmed.

They just stared at each other for a moment.

"I'm faster with all four legs healthy," she pointed out.

Vinton whickered a laugh and lowered his horn to her injured shoulder.

When they arrived at the scene of the prior day's battle and Falloah's abduction, the unicorns found the wizard standing near the center of the field with his arms out and his palms held down. Slowly he turned, taking a few steps before turning again. Ralligor stood a few paces away, watching him.

Shahly ran right to the dragon, looking tenderly up at him as she assured, "We'll find her, Ralligor. I promise we'll find her."

Only a glance was his response. He was distraught, and clearly still very angry.

The wizard stopped and turned to the dragon, looking up at him with commanding eyes. "Ralligor, I want you to sit down and calm yourself."

The big dragon looked away and growled.

"Your emotions are clouding your judgment," the wizard went on, "and inhibiting your *facultas*. To defeat this dragonslayer and reclaim Falloah you need a clear mind and focused thoughts, and your emotions held in check."

Venting a deep breath, Ralligor sat on his haunches and settled his hands to the ground, wrapping his tail around him, his tense eyes on the wizard.

Nodding, the wizard continued, "We're faced with two kinds of magic. There's a warlock to contend with along with the wizard you saw."

The dragon growled, baring his teeth slightly.

"I know, mighty friend. There are few warlocks of this skill in Abtont and we both know who we're dealing with. The next time you meet this dragonslayer he will be ready for you. You must be ready for him." The wizard drew a breath and tightened his lips. "I want you to consider involving Agarxus."

Snarling, the dragon stood and turned away. "I don't need Agarxus! I will take care of this dragonslayer myself." He strode away a few long paces before he stopped and for long seconds he just stared into the forest.

"I don't doubt your skill or your strength, mighty friend, but he and his wizard and men will be ready for you. Don't allow your pride to eclipse your judgment."

Ralligor spun around and roared, "I will kill this puny human and his wizard on my own! I don't want the Landmaster here!"

His eyes narrowing, the wizard shouted back, "Why do you already seek vengeance? Is your judgment already so impaired by your rage?"

"Perhaps it is!" the dragon shouted back.

Shahly cringed and backed away.

"Then you will condemn yourself to death–*and* Falloah!" The wizard's gaze was unwavering even as the black dragon strode toward him again.

Ralligor's breaths came deep and vented out in growls. His lips tightened as he stared back down at the white haired human.

"Your pride or her life," the wizard said flatly. "Choose now so that I'll know if I should help you further in this matter or just walk away."

His eyes widening slightly, the dragon took a step back, then finally sat back down. He looked away again, finally and softly offering, "Forgive me, *Wizaridi Magister.*" He huffed a loud breath and growled, "I don't want Agarxus involved. He'll only come here and kill the dragonslayer himself."

Nodding, the wizard observed, "And again your pride overwhelms you."

"I'm her *unisponsus*," the dragon pointed out. "I failed to protect her. I should be the only one at risk to save her."

The wizard laughed under his breath. "What makes you think Agarxus would be at risk? He's had more experience with dragonslayers than any dragon alive."

"I had to call on him this spring," Ralligor pointed out. "I don't want him involved now."

Vinton finally stepped forward and said, "And when the drakenien attacked our herd this spring I didn't want *you* involved. Shahly involved you anyway and it turned out to be the right choice."

"You were ill equipped to handle the drakenien," Ralligor pointed out.

"And you don't know exactly what you are walking into this time," Vinton countered. "You always seem to have an advantage and this time you don't."

"Why do you care?" the dragon growled.

"If it was just you I wouldn't," the unicorn admitted, "but it isn't. There's Falloah to consider, and that other dragon we saw."

Ralligor's eyes snapped to the bay and he asked, "Other dragon?"

"We thought you knew," the wizard informed. "The four of us saw another red dragon last night carrying off two maidens. We came to ask Falloah about it...." His eyes widened slightly. "She went north to investigate."

The black dragon's eyes narrowed. "Falloah is the only scarlet anywhere in Abtont."

Vinton added, "This other dragon is male, we all agree on that."

"A scarlet *drake?*" Ralligor asked as if to himself. He raised his head, his eyes widening as he looked back to the wizard. "That other dragon wasn't red at all!"

"Of course he was," Shahly corrected. "We all saw him."

"That's not his natural color," the dragon informed.

"What if it comes to fighting them all at once?" the wizard questioned. "Falloah was clearly made to seem like she took the maidens."

Ralligor considered, then he looked to the wizard. "You know where she is, don't you?"

"I do, mighty friend, and I'll tell you when you are ready."

Shahly danced excitedly and declared, "We should go and save her, then!"

Looking down at her, Ralligor simply asked, "We?"

"I have a debt to repay," she reminded. "You helped me rescue Vinton from Red Stone Castle and got us all out of there."

"I sent you in there for Falloah," he reminded.

Vinton added, "And you stayed behind to fight the ogre while we made our escape. You didn't have to do that."

Ralligor looked away and admitted, "No, I suppose I didn't."

"Then we're going to do whatever we can to help you free Falloah," the stallion insisted.

Nodding, the black dragon finally conceded, "Very well."

"Might I offer a suggestion, mighty friend?" the wizard asked.

Loosing a breath in frustration, the dragon replied, "You still want me to go for Agarxus, don't you?"

"As his *subordinare*, it's your duty to inform him when another dragon invades his territory, isn't it?"

"Or run the other dragon off," Ralligor grumbled through bared teeth.

"How will you do that when you are locked in battle with the dragonslayer?" the wizard asked straightly. "If you are already involved with that matter then the task of finding the other dragon will fall to your Landmaster, won't it?"

Raising an eyebrow, Ralligor admitted, "I suppose."

"Go on, mighty friend," the wizard ordered. "I will make preparations here."

Looking to the unicorns, the dragon locked his eyes on Vinton and said, "Keep her out of trouble."

"I'm trying," the bay grumbled.

Ralligor opened his wings and ran into the wind, lifting himself into the air with seemingly little effort, then he turned south.

Scanning the forest, the wizard pointed north and informed, "What we seek is that way, toward Caipiervell." As he started walking, the unicorns glanced at each other and followed.

"Who is Agarxus?" Shahly asked.

Vinton glanced at her. "Would you believe that there are dragons even bigger than Ralligor?"

She raised her head, her ears perking as her eyes widened. "Bigger than Ralligor?"

"Agarxus is said to be the biggest and most powerful in the world," the bay went on.

"Wow," Shahly declared. "Will we get to meet him?"

"Let's hope not," Vinton mumbled. "He has no great love for unicorns."

Her eyes narrowing, Shahly snapped, "And what do you mean you're trying to keep me out of trouble?"

A glance was the only response she got.

CHAPTER 5

The ride back to Caipiervell Castle was a swift one, and yet it seemed to take an eternity. They arrived to the expected accolades, and yet the Duke did not appear to want to celebrate, nor did he want to even talk to anyone. He and his wizard and men dismounted immediately and made their way into the palace. As Garrin tried to follow, one of the soldiers stopped him at the door that led to the catacombs beneath the palace and simply shook his head as he backed inside and closed the door, locking it from within.

Garrin turned and glanced around, realizing that Sir Kessler had not yet returned.

In a chamber on the second level was a table with soft chairs. This was a hall for knights and only knights. Squires were forbidden unless they were with their knights, and then it was only to serve their needs.

Garrin went in anyway, stopping just inside the door as he scanned the score or so of knights who ate, drank, tended armor and weapons and conversed in small groups. They all seemed to ignore him, clearly expecting Sir Kessler any moment.

The squire approached one, a man of rank called Sir Bidainne and snapped to attention, asking, "May I be heard, sir?"

The man had a wine goblet in his hand and was comfortably dressed. His full beard was dark brown as was his long, well groomed hair. He regarded the boy with only half interest, took a gulp from his tankard and demanded, "Out with it, boy."

"Has anyone seen Sir Kessler?" was the squire's question.

Most of the room drew silent and looks were exchanged.

The bearded man looked to Garrin with narrow eyes and answered, "The last we saw he was armoring up to go take on that dragon. I thought you were with him."

"I was," Garrin assured, "but we got separated in the battle. Another dragon attacked, a huge, black beast with unimaginable strength. Everything Duke Malchor and his men wielded against him simply bounced off."

"And the red dragon?" another knight demanded as he approached.

"Taken by the Duke's wizard," Garrin replied. "Did Sir Kessler not come back?"

"He would be here if he did," Sir Bidainne assured. He scanned the room and shouted, "Hear me! One of our own lies on a battlefield and is in need of us. We ride within the hour to retrieve him."

"And if the dragon is still out there?" another shouted back.

Sir Bidainne raised his chin and insisted, "If we find it there we will face it like men. Those who haven't the courage to go may stay here with the women." He turned and strode across the room where his squire was working on his armor and ordered, "Worry over dents and rust later, boy, and help me get that armor on."

Most of the knights did, and eventually they all did.

A half hour later they all had their mounts and were ready for battle, twenty four knights and their squires. With Garrin they numbered forty-nine, yet he knew they were still not enough.

Garrin rode his horse to the bearded knight and asked, "Sir, will we have infantry along?"

The knight shook his head. "No, boy, they'll only slow us. We have little time if we're to come to our comrade's aid. Lead the way and get us there fast."

Turning his horse, Garrin shouted, "Yes sir!" and kicked his horse into a run.

Again, despite the fast pace, time seemed to move slowly, but they finally arrived at the battlefield. All were hopeful until they actually left the trees.

Including Sir Kessler, Duke Malchor had attacked the dragon with thirty-two men. Seventeen still lay on the battlefield along with twelve dead horses.

Knights dismounted and had their weapons in their hands as they strode into the churned up grass to find survivors. All were dead.

"Boy," a knight called to Garrin.

He ran to the knight as best as his armor would allow and his eyes found the remains of Sir Kessler. His knight lay awkwardly with an arm twisted beneath him and his head lying at an awkward angle. His chest and side armor had been opened in three gashes that penetrated deep into his body, spilling his blood and some of his entrails. His eyes were still open, locked in a glare of battle.

For the first time since his father's death, Garrin's heart sank and he dropped to his knees, his eyes fixed on the powerful man who lay broken before him. This time nothing held his tears in his eyes and he found himself weeping shamefully.

Sir Bidainne took his shoulder and assured, "He fell in battle, lad. That is the best way for a knight, a warrior, to die. He mentioned you fondly many times, kept saying what a great knight and gentleman you would be someday. He was proud of you, boy. Be proud of him."

Garrin nodded, sobbing, "My father also fell in battle."

Patting the boy's shoulder, the knight comforted, "He fell protecting his kingdom. I can only pray that I can be such a great man as your father and Sir Kessler. I should also try to live up to the man and knight you will become. Keep them in your heart, boy. Keep their spirits alive inside."

Nodding again, the squire wiped his eyes and assured, "I will, sir."

Another knight with a battle axe approached and asked, "Squire to Sir Kessler, this dragon was a black beast, you said?"

Garrin stood and faced him, nodding.

"How tall when he stood?" the knight questioned.

"Five heights, perhaps six."

Turning his eyes to Sir Bidainne, the knight with the axe cried, "Do you know what that imbecile Malchor has done? He's brought upon us the wrath of the Desert Lord!"

Everyone within earshot turned in stunned silence.

"Are you sure?" another knight asked.

"Of course I am," the knight with the axe assured. "How many black dragons that size live in this part of the world? It has to be him! And this Malchor fellow has drawn his ire taut for sure."

A low roar of mumbling and questions began among the knights. Concern thickened the air. The dragon they spoke of was one of the most powerful in the land and Garrin realized he had been less than a pace away from him.

Bidainne raised his hands and shouted, "Gentleman and protectors of Caipiervell. We have a mission before us. Let us attend to our fallen comrades before we worry over this dragon."

Another knight approached on horseback, heavy red leather visible between the joints of his polished steel plate armor. "My squire is attending to the girl he used for bait. She's a bit bruised and chapped raw from her bindings but I think she'll be okay otherwise once she sheds the hysteria she's drowning in."

The ranking knight turned and growled, "I don't care what Prince Tahmrof says or feels for this dragonslayer. I don't see him bringing us anything but ruin, and I'll be damned if I'll just sit by and watch our walls fall to his recklessness."

The knight with the axe pointed out, "We dare not speak out against him while he is in the Prince's favor. There's no telling what his Highness will do."

"This is turning into a very delicate matter," another knight observed. "Acting against the Prince is treason, and acting against this dragonslayer is acting against the Prince."

Turning to Garrin, Sir Bidainne asked, "Do they know where this dragon took our Princess? I mean our rightful Princess, not that other brat."

Garrin nodded. "They think he is holding them in an abandoned castle about a league from here."

A red bearded knight grumbled, "No doubt held there by this Duke's men."

Clearly, the entire Knight's Legion distrusted both the dragonslayer and Prince Tahmrof. Garrin could not even remember a time when Sir Kessler spoke fondly of the Prince.

Perhaps Princess Faelon had been right all along and Tahmrof was after her throne. It seemed to make sense.

A brown bearded knight picked up Sir Kessler's sword from the ground near the fallen knight's body and held it with both hands to the squire, asking, "Would you be up to checking it out for us?"

Raising his chin as he took the sword, the squire assured, "I shall be swift, sir. And if I find our Princess I shall rescue her."

Smiling, Sir Bidainne roughed the squire's hair and ordered, "Just don't get yourself killed. If you find her and you are able to rescue her, bring her secretly to the Knight's Hall. Even if you aren't able to rescue her, come to the hall and report your findings. I'll be waiting there for you."

"I'll bring her back, sir," Garrin assured. "Honor's word." He ran to his horse and mounted quickly, riding hard to where he knew the old fortress to be.

Early evening found him tying his horse's reins to a tree limb in a glade near the old castle. Knowing that his armor would offer little protection anyway, it came off. He would go into the castle only with his dagger and Sir Kessler's sword.

He crouched low in the tall grass as he slowly made his way across the hundred pace open expanse that separated the old castle from the forest, taking his time and making as little noise as he could. This took almost an hour. When he finally reached the first of the broken down castle walls, he noticed lights burning in a couple of windows. Someone was living there.

His stealthy approach had him inside the walls unseen and he went about the task of searching for his princesses, praying he would find them both alive. With the sun not yet down, shadows were his allies and he exploited them as best he could, staying near walls and behind whatever availed itself to him.

Stories of maidens being held in a castle's towers came into his mind as he entered the dilapidated structure and he crept toward the stone spiral stairs that would take him there. Along the way, he looked toward what had been a banquet hall. Torch or lamplight poured from the room, but it appeared that at least one wall was down. As he turned from the stairs and drew closer, he could hear something from within, something that sounded like armor and weapons were being worked with, and voices! Men were in there!

He crept closer, staying near the wall as he neared to have a look inside. Wind from within revealed that a wall was indeed down and the smell of sweat and leather reached him with the smells of something cooking, wild boar probably. Not quite close enough to see inside, he heard hoof beats approaching and turned to the opening in the wall he had entered. Now his heart raced as never before and he glanced around him, finding a doorway half closed by a rotted out door. Slipping around the door, he was careful not to touch it, fearing it would creak and alert those within to his presence.

Looking out one of the holes in the door, he listened as the riders dismounted and watched armored soldiers file into the ruined palace.

Outside, he heard Duke Malchor order, "Keep those horses quiet and out of sight. Feed and water them and be sure they are ready to ride within the hour."

Garrin's eyes widened as the Duke entered with two more men and his wizard behind him. With purposeful strides, Malchor went right for the banquet hall, clearly annoyed about something and making no secret about it to the men around him.

Once they were all inside, Garrin slipped from his hiding place and approached the door again, crouching in a shadow right outside of the room.

"Lord Malchor," one of the men within greeted.

"Hold your tongue!" the Duke snapped. "I need someone to tell me how this is anything but a festering boil of incompetence and disaster!"

The wizard answered, "There is a way to turn this to our advantage."

"I don't see how," the dragonslayer grumbled. "None of the weapons worked!"

"They worked nicely on the red dragon," one of the men pointed out.

"But not the black one," Malchor growled back.

"Black dragon?" a man who sounded quite ancient questioned. "You saw a black dragon?"

"I could have killed him had your potions worked," the Duke scolded.

"The potions were of such power to battle the scarlet," the old man pointed out. "If this black dragon is the one I think it is then you did well to survive against him."

A winged form swept overhead in the night sky outside, out of sight of those within. Through a hole in the ceiling that looked to the sky Garrin got a look at a wing and fear surged within him as he guessed the black dragon had found them and would seek revenge.

Inside the room, the squire heard something hit the ground beyond the broken wall and the men within grew silent as something approached with heavy footsteps.

Daring to peer inside, Garrin first made out a long wooden table or bench in the center of the room, torches on the walls, lamps on the table, and at least twelve soldiers and other men within. The hole in the wall was just as he had expected. Half of the stone wall was gone. The rest was in disrepair and striped with vines. Many crates and shelves were in the room along with a four wheeled wagon that appeared to be half unloaded. From what he could see, the far wall, the half that was left, was twenty or twenty-five paces away and the room looked nearly as wide.

Outside in the darkness, a huge white form moved into the firelight. What entered was the head of a dragon, not unlike the head of the black dragon, but its features were different other than its fair color. Its snout was a little shorter, its eyes a pale yellow. The horns were not like those of a bull like the other dragon, rather they curled outward more like a goat's would. From what Garrin could see as the men backed away from it, his head was almost an arm length shorter than the black dragon's, but still almost a man's height long.

Its eyes darted around from man to man, finally landing on the Duke, and as its lips curled away from white and ivory teeth Garrin feared a fight, dragon against dragonslayer in yet another battle.

Instead, the dragon roared in a deep voice, "You idiot! I told you this would happen!"

Raising his hands to the dragon, the Duke ordered, "Calm yourself, Ckammilon."

"Calm myself?" the dragon shouted in a roar. "You have involved the Desert Lord himself and attacked a dragoness that is his mate and I should be calm about it? Did you go spit in the eye of the Landmaster as well?"

"I was calm through *your* little disastrous mistake yesterday," Malchor pointed out, "you can be calm tonight."

"How was I supposed to tell them apart?" the dragon snarled. "You should have kept them separated so that I would know which one to take!"

"We'll work it to our advantage anyway," the Duke assured, "just as we will this new matter."

The dragon looked away and snarled, "I don't see how."

Finally speaking up, the wizard informed, "We have taken the scarlet dragon alive."

Slowly, Ckammilon's eyes turned to the wizard and he raised an inquisitive brow. "Have you, now? How did you accomplish that?"

"The secrets of a wizard," was the wizard's response. "Point is she is an advantage."

"I'm sure you think so," the dragon growled. "You do realize that he's going to come for her. If you used a wizard's tricks to whisk her away somewhere he'll know how to find out where. It's only a matter of time before you have to deal with him and you've simply not the weapons or power to do that."

"Combined," the dragonslayer insisted, "we can bring him down."

Ckammilon looked to him.

"And," the Duke continued, "your lair can be filled with *his* hoard."

The dragon considered, then shook his head. "I can't see this as anything other than another hair brained scheme of yours with no chance of success. You can't underestimate him."

"And we won't," the wizard assured. "I've never underestimated any dragon before, have I? With the scarlet in our grasp we hold an advantage over him, and with the tools we need to take him specifically—"

"He'll grind you all into little human stains where you fall," the dragon interrupted.

"We have another advantage," the Duke pointed out.

"And what would that be?" Ckammilon snarled.

"You," Malchor answered straightly.

A silence gripped the room.

"This is madness," the dragon growled.

"Think about it," the dragonslayer urged.

"I have," Ckammilon snapped. "I've tangled with Ralligor before. Even before this wizard started training him he was too strong and too skilled. Fifty seasons later he's even stronger *and* he has that wizard's power to call upon."

The wizard informed, "He's never fought a wizard, a dragonslayer *and* a dragon all at once. He'll be overwhelmed."

Ckammilon looked away and growled. "We'll only have the one chance."

"We'll formulate a strategy tonight," the wizard said straightly. "We have the warlock concocting some potions that will be more effective against this dragon's armor."

"You'll be lucky if he concocts a potion that will scratch his armor," the dragon growled. He huffed a breath, then nodded and looked to the wizard. "Fine. I'll have to strike him from behind while you have his attention. But if the fight starts to go badly I won't stay to be killed by him." He backed from the room, warning, "And you'd better pray that the Landmaster doesn't catch wind of any of this or we're all dead."

As he left, many men within the room sighed away the tension and seemed to relax somewhat.

Duke Malchor shook his head, grumbling, "This will either be very profitable or very disastrous. We will need to get this right the first time."

"What about the girls?" one of the men asked.

"I'll take Princess Bellith back tonight," the Duke informed. "As far as anyone knows she's been kept by the dragon to be eaten later."

"And the other one?" the same man asked.

"Take her to the field where we fought the second dragon in the morning and kill her. Make sure it looks like the work of a dragon."

The wizard suggested, "We could probably enlist Ckammilon's help for that."

"He's grown timid of late," the dragonslayer grumbled. "I'm sure he'll not want to be caught in the open."

"I'm sure he won't mind," the wizard corrected. "I will have him attend to her in the morning. In the meantime, we should collect Princess Bellith and be on our way. We don't want to arrive too long after dark."

"Continue preparations here," Duke Malchor ordered. "We'll be back sometime tomorrow morning for the other girl. If Ckammilon should come out of his hole before we return then tell him of our plan and make everything ready."

Garrin crouched into the shadows as the men filed out and went upstairs. His eyes narrowing, he reasoned that he would find Princess Faelon up there as well.

Waiting for them to come back down taxed his patience, but in short order he heard boots on the stone steps and the unmistakable voice of Princess Bellith as she complained.

"And the food I was served was quite horrible," she went on. "I suppose with all the money you have you couldn't afford a cook?"

"We did the best we could," the Duke assured.

"You can be sure my father is going to hear about this."

"You'll be back in your own bed this evening, Princess," Duke Malchor told her patiently. "We'll even have a banquet in your honor."

"I don't like the way some of your men were looking at me," she continued.

"I'll see to them, Princess. Let's just get you home."

Garrin shook his head as they left the palace. Never had he heard such a roll of complaints from any one person. Waiting for the hoof beats outside, he slowly stood from the shadows, making sure no one in the ruined banquet hall could see him, and slipped upstairs.

There were two chambers at the top. One was dark and its door stood wide open. The other had light coming from under the door and was sealed. This area seemed to be a little better kept, as if someone had spent quite a bit of time cleaning it up for a long stay. Glancing around, he saw a hook jetting out from the wall between the doors right beneath the single torch that illuminated the short hallway. A key dangled from this hook, one that looked as if it should fit the lock on the doors.

Slowly and noiselessly, he took the key from the hook, glancing down the staircase to be sure no one was coming, then he turned to the door. His hands shook a little and getting the key into the lock quietly was a bit of a problem, but in it went. Ever so slowly he turned the key and as the mechanism within the lock opened it announced this with a horribly loud series of clacks, and he cringed, gritting his teeth.

He gently pulled on the door, grinding his teeth more as the antiquated hinges creaked. Only opening it halfway, he slipped in, first seeing Princess Faelon standing in front of a crude bed. Little else was in the room, only the bed, a stand with a bucket of water and a single lamp by the door to light it.

Her eyes were wide and she was wringing her hands together nervously. Her gown was torn and tattered and she appeared to have a bad scrape on her arm.

When her lips parted, Garrin quickly raised a finger to his mouth to silence her, then he beckoned and extended his hand to her.

Hesitantly, she reached to him, finally grasping his hand and allowing him to gently pull her from the room. Ever so slowly he closed the door, cringing again as the hinges creaked, then he turned the key and locked it.

As he replaced the key, she whispered, "Why did—"

"Shh," he ordered. Her reaction was one of shock, but no matter. He took her hand and they slowly crept down the stairs, his wary eyes piercing the darkness for any movement.

The journey to the glade where his horse waited was a nerve-racking one. The Princess did not know how to stay down *or* walk quietly through the grass and brush. Garrin patiently kept the pace a slow one and said nothing to her, simply gesturing from time to time for her to be as quiet as possible. The more he gestured, the more annoyed she seemed to get.

At the horse finally!

She stood and watched as he untied the reins. In the dim light this was a difficult task. Still, the Princess was impatient and eager to get home.

As the night grew darker, Garrin knew riding back to the castle would be a problem, even on well ridden roads, so time would be of the essence.

When the reins were finally free, he turned and offered his hand to the Princess, urging, "Up you go, Highness."

She stubbornly folded her arms. "You'll not ride with me. You will lead the horse back to the castle."

He loosed a sigh and, as patiently as he could muster, informed, "Highness, we haven't time for this."

Princess Faelon raised her chin. "I'll not be caught riding with some lowborn commoner and be groped the whole way home."

"Then you can ride behind me," he conceded. "Now please mount the horse."

Her lips tightened. "Mere squire, I am ordering you—" She took a step back as he advanced on her.

Garrin's patience had clearly run out as he ordered through clenched teeth, "Get your behind on the horse now!"

Faelon finally realized he was just a little taller than she was and as she stared up into his eyes for that long few seconds that followed she felt humbled by a commoner for the first time in her life. Salvaging her dignity, she lowered her eyes and stepped around him. Grabbing the saddle horn, she looked sharp for the stirrup in the dimming light and finally got her foot into it, then hopped a couple of times before climbing to the saddle.

The squire pushed her the rest of the way up with a hand on her buttock and when she was safely nestled into the saddle, she turned narrow eyes on him and spat, "I hope you enjoyed touching me so."

"Move your foot," he growled back.

She jerked her foot from the stirrup.

When he was mounted behind her, he reached around both sides of her to take the reins and slowly guided the horse to the road that would lead back to the battlefield. This was the first time he had ever held a girl this close, but he was too annoyed with her and his nerves too taut for him to enjoy it.

Not quite half an hour into their journey, she complained, "You need a bath."

Speaking without realizing, he replied, "So do you."

She turned her head, hissing, "How dare you? You speak down to me, you touch me inappropriately—"

"And I rescued you and saved your life," he finished for her. "You're welcome."

"I'm sure one of the knights of the castle would have come for me," she informed with a snide tone. "I was more expecting to see Sir Kessler than his mere squire."

"Sir Kessler is dead," Garrin informed straightly. "He fell in battle against a dragon with a dozen others who wanted nothing more than your safe return."

She turned her eyes ahead again.

"I'm sure you appreciate their sacrifice," he continued, "just as I'm sure you appreciate me saving your life tonight."

Faelon was silent for a moment, then she drew a breath and said straightly, "I don't think you saved me at all. I think someone would have come for me first thing in the morning and—"

"Killed you," he finished for her again. "I overheard their plan. Your uncle saw this as an opportunity to get you out of the way, just as you've suspected."

Her spine went rigid and a chill ran through her. Still, she argued, "Then... Then why would Bellith have been taken as well? Have you an answer for that?"

"The dragon couldn't tell you apart," the squire informed, "so he took you both to make certain he got the right one. Duke Malchor is already on his way back to Castle Caipiervell to deliver your cousin to Prince Tahmrof."

"You seem to know a little too much about their plan," she said coldly.

"More than I want to," he grumbled.

She vented a deep breath, then ordered, "Get me back to the castle. If this is true then Uncle and I are to have words."

Garrin turned his eyes to the sky and shook his head. "Princess, are you sure that's a wise idea?"

"How dare you question my judgment?"

"I'm in Hell," he mumbled. "Princess, he's already conspired to kill you to get you out of his way once."

"And he has a good scolding awaiting him when I return," she countered.

"There's something else you should consider, Princess."

She sighed. "What, then?"

"As soon as you step into the castle he will most likely arrange to have you killed."

"In my own palace? You're speaking madness. He would be arrested and tried for treason."

"Highness, how many of your soldiers can you still trust?"

"I should be able to trust all of them."

"But, how many have been swayed to support Prince Tahmrof?"

Faelon considered for a moment, and after this frightening thought sank in she finally spoke. "You... You mean my own soldiers could conspire against me?"

"Many have already, I think," he informed grimly. "I feel you may still be able to trust the Legion of Knights, as they appear to support you, but I'm not certain how deeply he's divided the kingdom. I do know that you are currently in great danger."

The Princess fearfully asked, "May I ask where your loyalties are?"

Garrin answered carefully, yet deliberately. "My loyalties lie with Caipiervell, and with her rightful heir."

Faelon leaned back into him, just a little. "Thank you, squire."

"You're welcome, your Highness."

"What should we do?" she asked fearfully, finally trusting him.

"I've been ordered to take you to the Hall of the Legion of Knights. That is where the heart of the loyalty to you seems to be strongest. Getting you back to the castle at all shall prove to be an undertaking in itself."

She half turned her head, asking, "What do you mean?"

"When they discover you missing then their first task will be to silence you before you can reach the castle. I don't believe they want you in a position where you may be able to regain control of your throne or tell anyone about your experience with your capture."

"And the knights will help me?"

"I believe they will, Highness." He looked around. "I can barely see the road. We're going to have to stop for the evening."

"And sleep in the wilderness?" she asked a little fearfully.

Garrin held her a little tighter and assured, "I'll keep you safe, my Princess. You have my word on that in the name of my father and Sir Kessler, I will keep you safe from harm."

Still afraid, she lowered her eyes and whispered, "Thank you."

CHAPTER 6

Procrastination was not something considered common to dragons, and yet the night would see the Desert Lord doing just that. He spent many hours sitting outside of the scarlet dragon's cave, just staring inside. Twice, and in the language of the dragons, he called to her, knowing she would not emerge and yet hoping she would.

A short flight took him to the hot springs, but he did not enter the water. He sat on the edge, staring into it. The quarter moon offered little light, but dragons' eyesight has no equal in night or day. For Ralligor, this was unfortunate this night. All he saw in the water was his own emptiness. Hours later a slight glow started to the East. Morning was coming and time was running short.

Reluctantly, the Desert Lord opened his wings and took to the sky again, flying south past his dragoness' lair, past a human settlement cut into the south part of the Abtont forest. Ahead was a mountain rising from the trees. Circling around the mountain, he looked to an area nearly half a league in diameter that was devoid of brush or trees. Only patches of grass grew here. Many trails led through the forest to the clearing, mostly from the human settlement. Right around the mountain and halfway up it everything was scorched down to stone. This scorched land extended halfway to the forest in all directions. In the center was a huge opening in the mountain itself, perhaps ten heights high and nearly as wide that looked like a seemingly depthless pit. Here was the dreaded place Ralligor had to go.

Circling four or five times, he descended slowly, finally settling to the burnt ground a hundred paces from the cave opening. He stared into the blackness for a time, then finally drew a deep breath, gaped his jaws and roared loudly.

Not half a moment passed and his call was answered by a deep growl from within the cave. Heavy footsteps drew closer and, as the glow from the East grew brighter, a gargantuan, ominous form emerged.

Ralligor sat catlike before the cave, raising his head as he watched his Landmaster emerge.

His massive head was nine heights above the ground when he stood fully. His scales were a very dark, metallic green, almost black in the pre-dawn light. The scales on his belly were even darker. The dorsal scales that ran from between his thick, bull-like black horns were obsidian black. When he spread his wings, the webbing was a dark blue. His features were not pleasant, even by dragon standards. Very dark green eyes glistened beneath a thick, scaly brow. Tusks protruded from his heavy lower jaw, half way up his upper jaw. As he bared his teeth, some of them the length of a broadsword, powerful muscles tensed beneath the armor that was his scales.

Striding forward, the massive dragon curled his black claws, taking heavy steps. His brow was low over eyes that were locked on the black dragon in a deadly stare. As he reached the smaller dragon, he swiped once and hit the Desert Lord at the base of the neck with one mighty blow, slamming him hard onto the ground.

Slowly, Ralligor pulled his arms under him and looked up at the huge dragon.

With a curious growl, the massive dragon drew his head back and demanded in a deep and thundering yet somewhat gravelly voice, "What's wrong with you? You made that too easy." He reached down and took the back of the black dragon's neck, hoisting him easily to his feet.

Ralligor sat back down, his eyes on the ground before him.

Leaning his head, the dark green dragon stared down at him for long seconds, then sat in front of him and growled, "Out with it. Why are you here?"

Venting a deep breath, the Desert Lord was slow to answer. Too slow.

"I hadn't intended to awaken so early," the huge dragon informed, "and you never come here unless I summon you." He raised a brow. "You obviously aren't here to challenge me, either."

Shaking his head, the black dragon confirmed, "I'm not here to challenge you."

"I was almost hoping you were," the massive dragon admitted. "Trostan won't send me the next crop of dragonslayers for nine more days."

Ralligor nodded, still staring at the ground.

The dark green dragon raised a hand and punched the black dragon in the chest, making him lurch backward. "Out with it."

"Falloah," was all the Desert Lord could say.

His eyes narrowing, the Landmaster growled, "What about her?" He bared his teeth and added, "Did Terrathgrawr come to reclaim her after all this time?"

"No," the black dragon answered. "She's been...." He growled and looked aside, into the forest. "She was attacked by a dragonslayer yesterday. I intervened, but he had a wizard with him. While I attended to the dragonslayer and his soldiers, the wizard took Falloah. I don't know where she is."

"Is she alive?" the Landmaster asked.

"Yes," Ralligor answered. "I can still feel her. She is very weak."

Nodding, the huge dragon guessed, "It sounds like he's using her as bait. You have many enemies."

"This dragonslayer did not even know I was coming," the Desert Lord informed. "He was there specifically for Falloah. He seemed to be hunting dragons for glory and status and his weapons were enchanted for battle with a smaller dragon."

"And had no affect on you," the Landmaster finished. "You come here with a certain sense of guilt, Ralligor. Did you fail to kill the dragonslayer that attacked Falloah?"

Ralligor closed his eyes. "Agarxus, I failed to protect her. With all of this wizard training one would think that I—"

"Stop your whining," the Landmaster growled. "Do you want me to take down this dragonslayer and his wizard for you?"

"I should do it myself," Ralligor replied. "Falloah and that part of the land are my responsibility. I've only come to tell you about the other dragon."

His eyes narrowing again, Agarxus bared his teeth and asked, "What other dragon?"

"Others saw him and insist he was red. Falloah is the only scarlet in Abtont."

"That we know of."

Looking up at his Landmaster, Ralligor corrected, "I don't think this other dragon is truly a scarlet."

Agarxus raised his nose slightly. "A color shifter?"

The black dragon nodded. "I feel he may be in league with this dragonslayer."

"Why do you think that?"

"It answers all of the questions." Ralligor looked beyond the massive dragon, continuing, "He goes to red, he steals maidens from a castle and this dragonslayer hunts down the only red dragon in the forest."

"And unwittingly involved you," Agarxus finished.

The Desert Lord nodded.

"I've only had dealings with two color shifters," the massive dragon informed. "One is dead. We both know the other."

"I thought he knew not to return here," Ralligor growled. "Apparently he feels stronger with this dragonslayer riding on his tail, and far too confident."

Nodding, the massive dragon agreed, "It would seem so. Perhaps he needs to be taught that he isn't so strong after all."

The black dragon replied, "If I reach him first that's exactly what he'll be taught."

"So why did you come to me?" the Landmaster asked.

"My *wizaridi magister* insisted. I told him I would report the other dragon's presence to you. I think he wants you to intervene."

"And intervene I will," Agarxus assured. When the black dragon lowered his eyes again, the Landmaster continued, "Ralligor, what is it you want exactly?"

"I want Falloah back."

"Then go and get her."

Slowly, the black dragon raised his eyes to the Landmaster.

"Do you think you can defeat them all?"

Answering honestly, Ralligor replied, "I'm not sure. I just want Falloah back alive."

"And what good is this wizard training going to do you? You've got to fight a wizard too, don't you?"

"Yes."

"I never approved of this training, Ralligor."

"I know you didn't," the black dragon replied softly.

"But," Agarxus continued, "if you're going to fight a wizard, it sounds like it will come in handy. There's a reason I gave you the desert and the western Abtont Forest, and it had nothing to do with keeping you out of my way. I trusted you to watch over that part of my territory. I trusted that you would one day be strong enough to face down Territhgrawr on your own should he come this way again. Today, I trust you to overcome this dilemma of yours and free Falloah."

The black dragon's chest bulged out just a little. "So you won't be fighting this fight yourself?"

"This human who teaches you seems to want to look out for you," the Landmaster observed, "but I think he underestimates you. Perhaps it's time the humans in the Abtont Forest learned about the wrath of the Desert Lord. Wouldn't you agree?"

"I would," Ralligor confirmed with bared teeth.

Agarxus raised a brow. "By the way, did you destroy that human colony in the Dark Mountains this spring like I told you to?"

Turning his eyes away, Ralligor countered, "Define *destroy.*"

"You didn't destroy the colony," the Landmaster growled.

"I have another agenda for it," the Desert Lord defended, then he looked up at the massive dragon and informed, "There's plenty of gold in those mountains and the humans I had occupy the settlement are mining it for me."

The Landmaster's eyes narrowed.

His brow arching slightly, Ralligor added, "The next load of gold will be coming here, of course."

"Of course," the massive dragon snarled. "You and your schemes. For now, concentrate on the matter at hand. I want Falloah freed from this dragonslayer by nightfall."

"No more than I do," the Desert Lord assured.

Agarxus stood and turned back toward his cave, informing, "I'll fly north at about high sun, but I don't intend to intervene. You'll attend to this on your own."

As he watched the Landmaster enter the cave, Ralligor found himself surging with new determination. He stood and wheeled around, opened his wings and swept himself into the sky. The words of his Landmaster had ignited a fire within him, one that this dragonslayer would be hard pressed to extinguish.

CHAPTER 7

Sleep was elusive as the forest was full of sounds so late, but a squire and a princess who were curled up beneath a horse blanket would finally find it somewhere near midnight.

With the sun peering through the canopy of leaves and pine needles in the treetops, Princess Faelon slowly opened her eyes, blinking herself awake. Garrin had chosen a boulder for them to bed down beside, making their bed on the south side of it where it would be the warmest. As she awoke fully, she realized he was still asleep and had his body pressed to her back and his arm laid over her. This was the first time she had ever awakened with anyone, and the loneliness of her station suddenly blurred away as she felt him lying next to her. Knowing she should awaken him, she felt herself reluctant. This was such a nice feeling, lying beneath a blanket with a warm, sweet boy beside her. She had always imagined herself sharing a bed with some noble in an arranged marriage, one meant to benefit the kingdom, but now thoughts of that seemed less and less appealing. She was marrying age, but knew that it could be put off for a time. This squire was not especially strong or rich, nor was he even of highborn blood, but as the sun rose, he just felt perfect. Besides, he was cute. At least Bellith had been right about that.

Her eyes found Sir Kessler's sword, just within reach where the squire had laid it before they settled in to sleep. He had told her that he would keep her safe and, good to his word, had done so, staying ready through the night to defend her. Looking to the nearby glade, the unsaddled horse, tethered loosely to a tree stump, grazed peacefully in the sunshine.

The morning seemed perfect. If only she was lying with this squire in a bed surrounded by roses and candles… She simply did not want the moment to end.

As she saw the white haired man in the green robes sitting on a small boulder only two paces away, the moment ended in a loud scream as she sprang up and retreated, wrapping herself in the horse blanket.

Garrin's sword was in his hand and poised for battle before he realized he was standing and facing the white haired man who sat calmly two paces away, staring back at him with a slight smile. Awakening fully, the squire stepped between the stranger and his Princess, holding his sword ready as he glared back at the man.

"You hold that blade well," the old man complimented. "I never learned to use one, myself, never had the need for one. And, as you can see, I don't have one now."

"What is it you want?" the squire demanded, trying unsuccessfully to make his boyish voice sound as threatening as he could.

"I have a great many wants," was the old man's answer. "But, I'll not bore you with them. I've been waiting for some time for you to awaken. Looks like you two had a rough night." He turned his eyes to the Princess and greeted, "Good morning, Faelon."

Her eyes widened, her lips parting slightly as she breathed, "You know me?"

"Of course," the white haired man replied with a friendly tone. "I've known you all of your life. I was there the day you were born. In fact, King Elner and I were quite good friends for many seasons. He was a good man and I'm sorry to hear of his passing. I almost wish I had stayed on as his court wizard."

Garrin was slow to lower his sword. "What are your intentions now?"

"I am simply a man who guides others," the white haired man explained. "Perhaps one of you can tell me what exactly happened with this whole red dragon business." He looked to the Princess. "I feel your insights would be most helpful."

She glanced at Garrin, holding the blanket closer to her. "What is it you want from me? I can tell you nothing beyond the night of my abduction."

"Then tell me about that night," the wizard prodded.

Glancing about, she recalled, "There was a banquet for Duke Malchor. I was on a balcony overlooking the courtyard and it came and forced its way into the castle." She blinked, trying to remember more, then she looked to the squire. "You tried to fight it off. While everyone else watched dumbly you went at it with your sword. It struck and you went over the baluster to what I thought was certainly your death."

The wizard nodded. "This Duke Malchor wouldn't be a dragonslayer, would he?"

Faelon nodded. "Yes. My uncle arranged a banquet in his honor."

"I see," the wizard sighed. "And, conveniently, while he is at the castle a dragon attacks and carries you off."

"He got Bellith and me both," the Princess corrected. "I fainted shortly after he took us from the palace and awoke some time later in an uncomfortable bed in a small room where this squire found me."

"And I suppose there were men to take care of you," the wizard guessed.

"Yes," she recalled. "An unkempt man brought me food and water. He also warned me to remain quiet." She looked away. "When he went in to visit Bellith she did nothing but complain. I thought for sure he would strike her or at least scold her, but he did not."

"How convenient," the wizard observed. He looked to Garrin and asked, "And you? Anything you can tell me?"

"I overheard their plans," the squire told them. "They didn't know the other dragon was coming and the Duke was rather irked when his weapons did not work against it. They took Princess Bellith back to the castle and meant to kill Princess Faelon this morning. I would wager they are looking for her now."

"I would wager they are," the wizard confirmed. "Tell me about their plan."

"They have the red dragon," Garrin reported. "They mean to use her as an advantage over the black one somehow. They are going to get new potions for their weapons that will be more effective against him and they will wait for him to strike." He considered for a moment, looking into the forest, then his eyes snapped back to the wizard. "The other dragon!"

His spine going rigid, the wizard's eyes widened and he raised his chin.

"They said the other dragon would be yet another advantage. He was there last night, talking to the Duke. He didn't seem happy about it, either. Something had gone wrong and they were trying to figure out how to take advantage of it or something."

"What does this other dragon intend to do?" the wizard asked, his eyes narrow.

Garrin's lips tightened and he answered as best he could. "He said something about striking from behind. They said they would only have the one chance. I think they're afraid of the black dragon, this Desert Lord that they will have to face soon."

The wizard nodded. "With good reason they're afraid. You've done well, boy. I've something to attend to. Can you get Princess Faelon to somewhere safe without being discovered?"

The squire nodded, assuring, "I will, sir."

"Good to hear," the wizard complimented as he stood. Waving his hand, a thick mist began to pour from two trees and completely obscured everything beyond, forming a thick wall of fog between them. "I'll find you in a while. Stay on your guard and get Princess Faelon safely home, and find any who are loyal to her. Most importantly, find the scarlet dragon they have abducted. That is important above all. I'll catch up with you when I can." He turned to the wall of mist and walked into it. His footfalls faded in a couple of seconds and the mist cleared. The wizard was gone.

Garrin did not allow himself to be stunned in amazement for long. He picked up the saddle and looked to the Princess, ordering, "We need to get the horse ready to ride. There's much to do."

She nodded.

He raised his brow. "That blanket will have to go on before the saddle."

Faelon pulled it from her and looked down at it, then turned her eyes to the squire as she held it to him and asked, "Will you show me?"

⁂

Showing her meant saddling the horse as she watched.

Some time passed as the rode slowly toward Caipiervell Castle. As before, Faelon rode in the saddle in front of him, holding onto the saddle horn with one hand more out of reflex to steady herself. Conversation was trivial as Garrin had too much on his mind. Inexperience conspired against him as he tried to formulate some kind of plan to restore his princess to her rightful place and bring down those who were attempting to kill her. For the first time in his life he had an attractive girl sitting right in front of him, actually leaning back against him, yet this escaped him as he was so distracted with other matters.

Half turning her head, she observed, "You've been so quiet today."

"Sorry, Highness," he offered. "I'm a bit preoccupied."

"Like you were the first time we met," she reminded. "Don't get too preoccupied or you might push me off of the horse."

"I wouldn't do that!" he barked, sounding offended.

Faelon giggled. "I'm only jesting."

"Oh," he responded.

"You were very harsh with me last night," she observed.

"I know, Highness," he confirmed. "Believe me when I say I had your best interests in my mind when I was."

"Spoken just like my uncle," she grumbled.

"I'm not your uncle," he snarled back, "nor am I anything like him."

"Do you at least know where we're going?" the Princess asked, trying to change the subject.

He did not answer right away, but finally admitted, "I'm not sure."

She rolled her eyes. "I suddenly don't feel quite as safe as I did a moment ago." An impatient sigh from him told her she had offended him again, and for the first time in her life this actually bothered her. "That isn't what I meant. Well, I meant it, but... How safe *should* I feel? You're a squire. If I had a legion of soldiers surrounding me I might feel safer..." Finally looking back at him, she asked, "I'm not making you feel better, am I?"

He raised his brow and slowly shook his head.

Turning her eyes forward again, she mumbled, "Fine." She fumbled for something to say, finally asking, "Have you figured out where we are going yet?"

"Not in the last moment or two," he confessed.

She looked around her. "I think I know where we are now. There is a road that will come into this one on the left, one that is not well traveled. Take that road."

"I have orders to take you back to the castle," he reminded.

"Orders from a knight," she informed. "I believe my commands supercede his."

"Once again, your Highness, I have to consider your safety above all."

"Tell me, squire. Is it more important to you to serve your ego or to serve the crown of Caipiervell?"

His jaw tightening, Garrin replied, "I don't serve my ego, Highness."

"Then do as I said."

"You're going to get us lost."

"I know where I'm going!"

"You're not even certain where we are."

Faelon's lips pursed. "Are you questioning my judgment?"

"That has nothing to do with it, Highness. If you don't know where we are then you can't very well determine where we're going."

"That does it! Stop the horse!"

"What?"

"I said stop the horse!"

Shaking his head, Garrin stammered, "What... What are you talking about?"

"I'm getting off. Now stop the horse."

"I'm not stopping the horse."

She half turned her head. "Should I jump off while we're moving?"

"You'll end up hurting yourself."

"I want off of this horse right now!"

"Princess, I'm not going to just leave you here."

"You'll do as I say!"

He finally reined in and stopped the horse. "Fine. Get yourself killed. Do exactly what they want so that your uncle can have your throne. I guess I'll be in his service after all once you're dead."

Princess Faelon did not actually expect him to stop and just sat there dumbly for a moment, staring down the road. No one had ever acted so defiantly toward her. Ever! Tears welled up in her eyes and her mouth quivered. She was unsure what to do. She dare not stay on the horse, nor could she very well strike out on her own. Frustration and pride battled within her.

When her sobbing caused her entire body to quake, Garrin's anger collapsed, and when she wept openly, his pride went with it. He vented a deep breath and conceded, "Highness, I'm sorry. I—"

"No you're not," she cried. "You just want to get me back to the castle so that my uncle can finish his dastardly crime against me." She raised a hand to her eyes.

His lips tightening, Garrin finally found the right words. "Princess, if you have no other ally in the world or any loyal soldier to protect you, I shall be at your side." That was actually something he had read in a story once, but she did not have to know that.

She sniffed and lowered her hand, half turning her head toward him as she asked, "Do you really mean that?"

"I do, Highness."

She nodded, then looked forward again and offered, "Thank you, squire. Now let's find that road I told you to take."

"Princess…"

She leaned back into him, laying her head against his shoulder. "And hold me a little tighter. I feel safe when you hold me so."

Garrin found he had no choice but to comply. He held the reins with one hand, wrapping his other tightly around her as he reluctantly kicked the horse forward.

"You'll see I know where I'm going," she assured.

He just sighed, shaking his head. "Where exactly are we going, Highness?"

"There is a summer cottage my parents used to take me to. Not many people know about it. When the castle was under siege four or five seasons ago my mother and I were sent there to be kept safe during the battle. Although I enjoyed the outing, I was still a little frightened and very relieved when news came that our soldiers had handily prevailed."

"My father died in that battle," Garrin said softly.

Faelon turned her eyes his way, her lips parting as the words sank in. This was a commoner, and his commoner father was a soldier in Caipiervell's army. He was not of noble blood at all. One soldier giving his life was not supposed to matter. This was the way of things. And yet, at this moment, it mattered.

Fumbling for the right words, she finally managed, "I think I heard of this soldier. I heard of a soldier whose courage put pause into the hearts of our enemies and he felled a hundred of them before he was struck down himself."

Garrin knew she was just trying to make him feel better and actually smiled slightly. "That's what I've always believed too, Highness."

"Well," she stated straightly. "It seems they stayed away because they knew his son would enact a horrible revenge should they return."

"That I would, Highness."

"Your courage far surpasses your age, squire. I think you should be in the Legion of Knights now."

He smiled just a little more. "I suppose when I'm ready, Highness."

"I shall knight you myself upon our return," she informed.

He held her just a little tighter. "Okay, Highness. I'm going to trust your judgment."

"As well you should," she pointed out. "I'm an educated woman, after all."

"Yes, Highness."

Idle conversation resumed. They found the road and traveled down it for about two leagues before finding a humble cottage just above the flood plain of a fast running creek. The cottage itself was difficult to see from a distance as a few trees grew between it and the road and vines had completely consumed three of its stone walls.

They rode around to the side that faced the creek where the only door was. It was not large at all, only about ten paces by eight. Small, shuttered windows flanked the door and grass grew tall all around it. With a grass roof, it was truly difficult to make out as a man made structure.

Garrin dismounted first, then reached up with both hands to help his princess down. As she settled on the ground before him, their eyes met for a long, tense moment. He no longer seemed like the clumsy boy at the castle, one who stumbled over his own words. She finally realized she was still grasping his shoulders, and he finally realized he was still grasping her waist. They stepped away from each other, Faelon looking toward the cottage and Garrin turning toward the horse.

"I, uh, should attend to the horse," he stammered.

She nodded, not looking at him.

He led the horse to the creek, looking back over his shoulder as she opened the door to the cottage. He met her eyes again as she looked over her shoulder at him. She seemed confused, and he shared this inner turmoil as her lips parted. Quickly, she turned away and entered the cottage.

With some effort, Garrin managed to catch his breath and lead the horse to the creek for a drink. Somewhat reluctantly, he turned back to the cottage, very nervous about going inside. He could not understand why.

Once inside, he found the cottage to be as simple on the inside as it was outside and lit only by the windows and open door. Within, it seemed deceptively large. On one side were three beds, in the center was a wooden table surrounded by four chairs and an oil lamp sitting on the center. The wall on the other side was consumed with shelves that were laden with supplies. The far wall was bare but for the fireplace that protruded nearly a full pace into the room. It was very quaint.

Faelon stood near the table, her eyes on the lamp. Hearing his approach, she turned and hopefully asked, "Do you know how to make a fire?"

He looked beyond her to the fireplace and saw the flints and shavings neatly placed to one side. With a nod, he assured, "I'll have you a fire before you know it."

As promised, both the fireplace and the lamp were burning the windows and door were open for ventilation against the summer heat and the crude stone floor was swept. A pot above the fireplace was filled with water and dried meat, a few vegetables he found outside in a discreet and neglected garden and spices from the shelf. Garrin himself ate a few wild pears as he prepared her meal. Meanwhile, she did what she could to help, but she did not know how to do much.

Once he knew she was settled he only had to take a short stroll to the creek to fetch the horse, but she was not quite settled.

Faelon strode gently to him, her brow high over her wide eyes as she asked, "You can't stay here with me?"

This would be the perfect moment, the perfect time to forget he was a squire, forget she was a princess, forget about his duties to a kingdom that barely knew he was alive and just stay here with this beautiful girl forever. She clearly wanted him to. She did not want to be alone. All he had to do was forget about the rest of the world.

Alas, reality prevailed. She was a princess. He was merely a squire.

He gently took her hands and assured, "I'll be back for you, my Princess. Before the sun sets, I'll be back for you."

Hesitantly, she nodded, fighting back tears. "I'm afraid, but I trust you, my brave squire." She took the last half step toward him, raised her chin and ever so gently touched her lips to his.

Not even the battle with the dragon excited Garrin as much as that single, first kiss. As she backed away just enough to look into his eyes, bewilderment turned to quite a hefty grin. She could not help but smile back.

"You know I'll be back for more of that," he informed straightly.

The Princess' smile broadened and she blushed. "You may just have more waiting, but only *if* you come back for me."

He nodded. "I should hurry, then." When he turned toward the door, she only released one of his hands, holding onto the other as she followed him out.

Garrin felt that for the first time in his life things were going his way—until he got outside and found his horse missing. He growled a sigh, looking right, then left. His entire body went rigid, his eyes looking as if they were going to burst from his head.

Princess Faelon screamed and grabbed onto the squire from behind.

The black dragon lay on his belly in the grass just outside of the cottage, staring down at them. His head was a height and a half from the ground, his thick arms crossed before him. One finger rhythmically tapped the ground and his claw had already left a deep hole where it had repeatedly struck there. His brow was low and the blue of his eyes surrounded a red glow.

Garrin instinctively reached for his sword. He did not glare at this dragon as he had the one that had attacked the castle. This beast was different. He had seen what it could do and how easily it could kill a man.

Faelon breathed in shrieks as she clung to her squire, knowing that the cottage would be no safe haven from this monster.

Backing away a step, the squire murmured to the Princess, "This is the beast that killed Sir Kessler."

The dragon's eyes narrowed and he stopped tapping the ground.

Garrin's grip tightened on his sword.

Unexpectedly, the dragon thundered, "Perhaps you are wondering why you are still alive, human."

"It talks!" Faelon whimpered.

His eyes darted to the Princess, locking on her in a predator's stare as he confirmed, "I speak thirteen languages."

Now it was Garrin's eyes that narrowed and he prepared to pull his blade. "This is between you and me, dragon. Leave her out of it."

"She is very much involved," the dragon snarled. "You both are." His eyes found the squire again, his brow low above them. "Where is the scarlet dragon?"

The squire raised his chin slightly. "The one we fought yesterday or the one that attacked the castle?"

"Which one do you think I would be asking about?" the dragon growled impatiently.

"Then they aren't the same," Garrin countered.

"Now is not a good time to test my patience," the dragon snarled. "If you expect to live through the day then you will tell me where she is."

The squire swallowed hard. "What if I don't know?"

"Then you should not expect to grow any older," was the dragon's answer.

"I know the man who took her," Garrin explained. "He is at Caipiervell Castle. I don't know if the dragon is there as well."

"And this dragonslayer?" the dragon thundered.

Garrin found himself shaking but knew he dare not back down or show weakness before this massive predator. "He's with the wizard. They were plotting to kill Princess Faelon and I believe them to be conspiring with her uncle to that end. I was about to return to the castle to tell the League of Knights that I have found her."

"I'm not concerned with any plots against your princess," the dragon growled. "I am ready to lay waste to every human settlement and kill every human I see until the scarlet dragon is returned to me. Perhaps you should tell your League of Knights about that."

"You are the Desert Lord, aren't you?" the squire asked before he realized.

Raising a brow slightly, the dragon countered, "And if I am?"

"Duke Malchor plans to attack you next," Garrin informed. "There is a man he calls the warlock who is concocting stronger weapons to turn against you. There is also another dragon. He is part of their plan as well and they said they are going to use the red dragon as an advantage against you."

Drawing his head back slightly, Ralligor's eyes narrowed again as he observed, "You seem to know an awful lot about their plans."

"I overheard them when I went to rescue Princess Faelon," the squire said straightly. "They talked of a battle with you and planned to kill Princess Faelon this morning and make it look like the work of a dragon."

Looking toward the creek, the Desert Lord growled, clearly considering this news.

Garrin offered, "I can try to find out more when I reach the castle."

His eyes sliding to the puny humans before him, the dragon snarled, "What reason do I have to believe you? You were standing over her with a weapon in your hand when I arrived to help her."

Taking his hand from his sword, the squire admitted, "I was part of Duke Malchor's hunting party and felt we were doing the right thing. Then I saw your red dragon lying helpless on the battlefield and I realized she was not the dragon that attacked the castle. I think the white dragon that spoke to Duke Malchor last night was."

Raising his head, the dragon demanded, "This Duke was speaking to a dragon last night? A white dragon?"

Garrin nodded.

"As I suspected," Ralligor growled. "How long will it take you to get to the castle and back here?"

The squire shrugged. "I can be back well before dark, halfway from high sun, I think."

Standing to his full five heights tall, the dragon's hands balled into tight fists and he informed, "I will be back then and you will tell me what you find out. Fail to come back and your Duke Malchor will meet his end along with your entire kingdom and all who live there." His eyes shifted to Faelon and he added, "Starting with her."

As the dragon opened his wings and strode away, his footsteps shaking the ground as he walked, Faelon raised a hand to her head and stumbled back into the cottage. Garrin turned and caught her before she could fall completely. She was very pale and looked like she could faint at any moment.

"Princess," he called to her.

Though her head wobbled slightly, she managed to turn her eyes to him, her brow arching as she whimpered, "Why does everyone want to kill me?"

"Not everyone does, Highness," he assured. He pulled her from the doorway and practically held her up as he led her inside, helping her to sit on the closest bed. "I need to get to the castle and back quickly. I'll bring help and we'll get you safely home. My word on that."

Staring up into his eyes, she nodded back.

He could hesitate no longer. Though reluctant to leave her, he turned and bolted from the cottage. He found his horse in the garden beside the cottage, mounted and was on his way in a moment. Twice now he had survived an encounter with the most powerful dragon in the land. He had even spoken to the great beast. They no longer seemed like creatures of lore, monsters that swooped down from the heavens to burn kingdoms and sweep away maidens. No. What he had seen was a powerful, intelligent creature, far removed from the legends he had been told his entire life. During his long ride back to the castle, he would have plenty of time to consider this new perspective.

At a fast pace he arrived at the castle sooner than he expected to. After turning his horse in to the stable master, he wasted little time hurrying into the castle, stopping by the kitchen where a kind, older lady who had known him most of his life made sure he had something to eat.

He left before he finished his last gravy soaked biscuit and was on his way to the Hall of the League of Knights when something out a window caught his eye. He paused at the window, looking out for many moments as he wondered why such a crowd had gathered at that corner of the west courtyard near the battlement wall. A part of the palace jetting out obscured his vision and he could not see what caused such commotion down there. Perhaps the knights could wait a few moments more while he found out what was going on.

Once outside, he discovered that the crowd was more angry mob than curious onlookers. He had seen such anger directed at notorious criminals, but this gathering was of a much greater magnitude, as was their hostility.

With much effort and over quite a stretch of time he was able to make his way through the crowd, which seemed to number over two thousand, and toward the front. The first thing he saw was the hundred or more heavily armed soldiers who held the surging mob back with some difficulty. Many people fell to the back or were carried, sporting wounds from sword or halberd. Still, angry words and shouts were not directed to the guards, rather what was just beyond them.

Finally managing to maneuver himself to the front of the mob, Garrin froze as his wide eyes found the chained and wounded scarlet dragon.

She was surrounded on all sides by timber posts that were sunk into the ground and covered with some kind of heavy netting. Heavy chains bound her to eight stakes that were sunk deep into the ground, shackling her four limbs, her neck, binding her wings down, and one even restraining her tail. Lying barely conscious amid the roar of obscenities and cries of anger, she seemed lost in a sea of despair. Her eyes were only half open and trained on the ground for the most part. She suffered from her many wounds and her pain was evident only to those who might be sympathetic to her. In this mob, only one was.

His lips tightened as he stared at her. If that black dragon saw her like this he would surely carry out his threat to flatten the kingdom and kill all within. Never had he felt such hatred, and for the first time he felt ashamed of his own kind.

In only half a moment he was pushed aside as others worked their way to the caged dragon and he stumbled toward the rear of the crowd. When he finally made his way clear of them he ran back into the palace and the entire way to the Hall of Knights.

Bursting into the hall, he ran in about five paces before he stopped to scan the ranks within, finally finding the knight he sought striding toward him.

"Sir Bidainne," the squire called to him.

No longer dressed in his field armor, the knight only wore his arming shirt and riding trousers and polished black boots.

He turned and raised a finger to his lips, glancing aside as he approached, and he took the boy's shoulder as he reached him. Guiding him back toward the door, the knight did not speak until they were outside and the doors were closed, softly asking, "You found her, lad?"

Garrin nodded and confirmed, "I did, sir. She is safely at a cottage only two leagues from here."

"Does anyone else know where she is?" the knight questioned.

"No sir," the squire confirmed. "I've told no one."

"Good lad," Sir Bidainne complimented. "The fewer people who know the better. There aren't many left who can be trusted. Let's get to our mounts and fetch her home."

Once again the ride seemed to take forever, even at a quick pace. A half hour of travel and they arrived at the hidden cottage. Its location and its very existence seemed to surprise the knight as they approached and his eyes never left the cottage even as he followed the squire to the other side.

Garrin noticed first that the window shutters were closed. Stopping his horse, he dismounted quickly his hand on his sword as he approached the half open door.

Sir Bidainne dismounted and followed, staying right behind him.

They were only about ten paces away when the door opened and the Princess emerged, smiling as her eyes found Garrin.

Smiling back at her, the squire assured, "I told you I'd come back."

Seeing the Princess, Bidainne grabbed the boy's shoulder and rammed his dagger into his back.

Garrin's face contorted into pain and surprise, his wide eyes still on the Princess as he staggered and fell.

She froze, her mouth falling open as she watched him fall. Slowly, she looked to Sir Bidainne.

With blood still dripping from his dagger, the knight turned malicious eyes on Princess Faelon.

Shaking her head, she retreated into the cottage as Bidainne stepped over the fallen squire and advanced on her.

"Your escape was admirable," the knight complimented, "but as you can see it was very futile."

Stopped by the table, Faelon cringed away from him, grasping the table behind her as she stared back at him with disbelieving eyes.

Sir Bidainne reached for her, saying, "Come along, Princess. Let's make this easier on us both." He threw his head back as his shirt bulged right beneath his ribs, and as the bulge retreated, he staggered back a step. He grimaced and lurched, then staggered back again, this time turning around fully and reaching a hand behind him. He bled badly from two deep wounds, one in his lower back and one right under his shoulder blade.

The Princess retreated around the table, seeing the knight squaring off with Garrin.

Anger filled the squire's pale face and his brow was low over his eyes as he bared his teeth and poised his blood stained sword for another strike. "Feel the price for your treachery, Sir Bidainne," he hissed, retreating from his larger enemy, "and know you will have your place waiting in Hell."

The knight coughed, blood spewing from his mouth. He dropped his dagger and reached for his sword, drawing it too slowly and unable to avoid Garrin's next thrust which plunged right into his belly, just below the ribs.

Garrin staggered backward a few steps as he wrenched his weapon from the knight again.

Coughing up more blood, Bidainne finally got his sword out and poised it unsteadily for battle.

The squire swung his weapon hard and steel rang as the two swords met. Spinning completely around with the blow, Garrin angled his weapon high, the blade finding the side of the knight's head and felling him at last. Stumbling into his vanquished foe, Garrin fell over Sir Bidainne's body and hit the ground hard, but did not lose his grip on his weapon.

Faelon rushed to him, dropping to her knees beside him as he rolled to his back.

His eyes were closed tightly at first, but slowly opened and quickly found his Princess. He coughed, cringing against the pain that caused, then he looked to her again and rasped, "I guess he could not be trusted after all."

She shook her head, tears filling her eyes.

"I'm not sure who can be," he continued. "I thought we could trust him, but clearly not. You should find that wizard, or hope he finds you."

She raised her brow, shaking her head as she argued, "What do you mean? You have to come with me!"

He managed a smile and reached up to stroke her cheek. "I didn't want anything to separate me from you. You were the first kiss I ever had."

"Just lay still," she urged as tears began to roll down her cheeks. "You will be fine."

Garrin shook his head. "I'm sorry, my Princess. He has struck his death blow."

Faelon raised a hand to her mouth and shook her head again, tears freely flowing from her eyes.

"I did my best for you, Highness," he assured.

"I know you did," she sobbed. "You are the bravest knight to ever serve Caipiervell."

"I'm not a knight," he reminded, "only a squire, and your humble servant."

She stared into his eyes for long seconds, then she wiped hers and tried to regain her composure. She reached to his sword hand and took the weapon from him, then stood and placed the tip of the blade on his shoulder. "By the crown of the kingdom of Caipiervell and for your unbridled bravery in defending your kingdom and Princess, I knight thee, Sir Garrin."

He was a knight at last. Garrin offered her a smile and slowly closed his eyes.

CHAPTER 8

No one would know exactly how long Faelon lay on her bed crying. The first sparks of a first love only hours old had already been snuffed out when he had given his life to defend her. Outside still laid the man who would have her dead and the boy who fought to the death to defend her.

Curled up in the middle of the center bed and hugging a pillow, the Princess wept with no chance of stopping. Already exhausted from the day, she had given up hope and simply did not know what to do next. She had nowhere she could go, no one she could trust, so she just cried.

At first she did not notice the shadow fall over the doorway, but the shuffle of an old boot drew her attention and she slowly lifted her head from the pillow, tears still streaming from her eyes as she looked to see the man who had just entered. She could not quite focus, but she knew who he was by the green robes and long white beard.

The wizard's bushy eyebrows were high over his eyes as he stared back at her.

Laying her head back down, she kept her eyes on him, her body still quaking from the sobs that continued to escape her.

Slowly, the wizard approached, never taking his gaze from her. He sat down on the bed beside her, his lips tightening as he asked, "Faelon, what happened here?"

She sniffed and wiped her eyes, then looked down to the pillow and shook her head, a sad frown curling her mouth downward. "Garrin thought we could trust him. He said he would take me home and bring my uncle to justice."

"The knight outside?" the wizard asked.

Faelon nodded, her eyes staring blankly ahead. "He just stabbed Garrin right in the back. He just stabbed him. Garrin trusted him so and he just stabbed him."

"What happened to the knight?"

She finally turned her eyes to the wizard. "He underestimated Garrin's courage and his valor. Garrin fought with his last breath to protect me." New tears streamed forth. "He was the only one I could trust. He was all I had left. I—I kissed him before he went for help. He promised he would come back and he did, and I felt so strongly for him. I was so cruel to him before, but..." She turned her eyes away. "I wish he had never saved me now."

Nodding, the wizard observed, "Your first pangs of love have ended so bitterly. Don't let this darken your spirit or harden your heart. Such things are best learned from."

The Princess looked to him, silent for long seconds before she asked, "What do I do now? I can't go home. There is no one I can trust."

The wizard smiled. "You can trust me, Faelon. At last I can repay a great kindness lent to me by your father many seasons ago."

"Is there anyone who doesn't want to kill me?" she whimpered.

"You have many still loyal to you at Caipiervell," the wizard countered. He stood and offered her his hand. "Let's set in motion your restoration to the throne."

Hesitantly, she took his hand and, with his help, finally got to her feet. She wiped tears from her cheeks and turned her eyes up to his. "If you mean to kill me, just do it and please just be swift."

He patted her cheek. "Faelon, no one is going to kill you while I'm around."

"Garrin died to defend me," she pointed out. "I cannot bear anyone else doing the same. Please don't put yourself at risk for me."

The wizard took both her hands and assured, "Child, you just proved you are well worth putting myself at risk for. You are the rightful ruler of Caipiervell, and you are a young lady of conscience. I can think of no one better to sit on that throne."

She shook her head. "We can't beat my uncle."

"Oh, we will," he informed straightly. "It's time you learned to start wielding your power for the greater good. Will you finish Garrin's work and protect the innocent?"

Some sense of importance finally entered the Princess. She raised her chin, asking "What can I do?"

He pulled her toward the door. "Someone is in great need of your compassion."

As they got outside, she gasped loudly and backed away a step as she saw the black dragon sitting where he had been before.

His eyes on the fallen squire, the dragon slowly shook his head. "*Magister,* he stood against me twice, and I see he's fought to the death with one of his own. That kind of courage is rare in your kind."

Faelon did not expect to hear compassion in the dragon's voice. She even heard a hint of admiration. When he turned his eyes to her, she no longer felt so afraid. She took the wizard's side and his hand and returned the dragon's gaze, raising her chin as she said, "That dragonslayer has taken someone important from you. My uncle's treachery has taken someone important from me. They are allied, and so are we."

Glancing at the wizard, the dragon growled, "We have a common enemy."

The Princess nodded. "Tell me what I can do to help you and I am yours."

Ralligor simply stared back for long seconds, then he looked down to the fallen squire again, asking, "What happened here?"

She answered straightly. "Sir Bidainne assured Gar—Sir Garrin that he could be trusted, but he was just as treacherous a snake as my uncle. Sir Garrin fought him to the death to protect me."

The black dragon nodded. "I see. He didn't happen to tell you if he found the scarlet dragon, did he?"

Faelon tensed up and simply shook her head.

"He was good to his word, nonetheless," Ralligor observed. He reached down and picked up Bidainne's body, then stood and turned, hurling the dead knight across the creek and into the forest beyond. "At least he will be a good meal for the flies and scavengers." He looked back down to Garrin and informed, "When this is over, he will need to be properly attended to."

"He has a place of honor awaiting him," Faelon assured. She looked to the wizard and asked, "Were their horses still here?"

"Hiding in the woods," the Wizard replied as he walked to a pear tree. "Ralligor has that affect on most creatures."

She glanced down at Garrin once more, then walked right up to the dragon. "Tell me what you would have me do."

Riding side by side, Princess Faelon and the wizard did not appear to be in a great hurry. The dragon had flown toward the South for parts unknown, clearly to plan his own strategy.

An hour of travel seemed to get them nowhere. They did not seem to be traveling toward the castle. The wizard did not really even speak, but to answer the Princess' simple questions, and even then many of his answers were cryptic at best. A long period passed with no conversation between them.

She glanced at him yet again, seeing that his eyes were still forward as he just seemed to stare into the distance. Finally, she asked, "Can you at least tell me where we are going?"

He nodded.

Waiting many long strides, she prodded, "Well?"

The wizard finally looked to her and smiled. "We're going southeast."

Faelon just stared at him for many long seconds, then, "Southeast toward what?"

"We have a rendezvous with someone," was his answer.

"Can you be a little more specific?"

He laughed softly. "You simply wouldn't believe me, Faelon. You'll just have to see."

"Well so far I've spoken to a dragon, so at this point I would believe almost anything."

The wizard nodded.

She loosed an impatient sigh, her lips tightening as she said, "I demand you tell me where we are going!"

"Ahead to a grassy clearing in the forest," he replied.

Turning her eyes ahead, she loosed another breath and shook her head.

Their destination was not much further. With the sun already halfway toward the horizon, time already seemed horribly short, and yet the wizard did not seem concerned or in any great hurry.

Turning her eyes to him yet again, the Princess asked, "Can you tell me about the dragon?"

"What would you like to know?" was his response.

Her mind scrambled for specifics, and finally she confessed, "I don't know, anything. Everything. Why is he so determined to save the red dragon? How do you know him? Why does he call you *magister*? Tell me everything."

Smiling, the wizard finally turned his eyes to her. "I haven't the seasons left in me to tell you so much. Perhaps I should just tell you what you are most likely to understand."

"I understand more than you think," she informed, raising her chin.

"You understand more now than you did yesterday," the wizard countered. "As Garrin gave his life to protect you so Ralligor feels about Falloah, but theirs is a union seeded forty seasons past."

"They've known each other since childhood?" she asked innocently.

Shaking his head, the wizard informed, "That black dragon is more than twice my age, some one hundred forty seasons and still very young for his kind."

Faelon's brow shot up. "How long do they live?"

"No man knows for sure. It is said that his Landmaster is over six hundred seasons old himself, and has seen most of the recorded history of the land."

"His Landmaster?"

"A dragon king, as it were. He was not born to that position as men are; he won it in battle long before even Ralligor was born."

"I didn't know dragons had kings."

"Oh, he is a king of sorts. As dragons go, he is established by his own strength and cunning, his skill and fortitude. He controls a territory far larger than any mere man will ever control, and he controls all of the dragons within."

"There is a bigger dragon than the black beast?"

The wizard nodded. "In stature, he's probably the largest in the known world. Ralligor actually looks small standing beside him."

"So, Ralligor is like one of his knights."

"In a manner of speaking. He is one of a few loyal drakes in the Landmaster's large territory and controls a smaller territory within. He is charged with keeping other dragons out, keeping other large predators under control and he will alert his Landmaster if another Landmaster invades."

"He *is* like a knight." Faelon shook her head. "In all of the stories of knights and dragons I've ever read, knights and dragons are enemies, and yet they are so similar."

"In many ways we are similar to them, and yet we are so different."

Turning her eyes away, the Princess guessed, "The red dragon is his wife, isn't it?"

The wizard glanced at her. "You learn quickly."

"And it was another dragon that took Bellith and me from the castle."

"One that seems to be in league with your dragonslayer."

"Who is in league with my uncle," she added. "What about the red dragon? How did it manage to become involved in this?"

"By accident or design, it's difficult to say. They seem to have needed a smaller dragon that they could deal with easily, and apparently they thought Falloah would fill that need."

"Falloah?"

"The scarlet dragon."

"Do dragons feel such things like love and devotion the way we do?"

"They feel such things much more so than we do. I don't remember a time when I've seen Ralligor so distraught. Even during that fiasco at Red Stone Castle a season ago he had better wits about him."

"What happened?"

"Oh, nothing I should burden you with. Suffice to say it was the first time his inexperience as a wizard really caught up to him. I'm proud that he managed to solve the problem and I'm hoping he can find a solution this time that will not get them both killed."

Faelon nodded. Questions whirled in a cyclone in her mind. "How did the black dragon and the red dragon meet?"

The wizard first responded with a glance and a smile, then, "Oh, it was some forty seasons ago. Falloah was barely of age when she fled the Territhan Valley. She was never specific about why, but she was determined to leave, and her Landmaster was not far behind."

The Princess' eyes widened. "He was chasing her?"

He confirmed this with a nod. "It was clear that he did not know right away that she had left. You see, a dragoness, especially one so young and just coming of age, is considered more prized by a Landmaster than most anything, and he will do his utmost to keep as many as he can."

"But she didn't want to be there."

"No, she didn't. He was only a few hours behind her. A long flight over the hard lands saw her drained and thirsty. She landed at a small but deep lake that is fed by the Spagnah River for a drink, and that is where she first encountered the Desert Lord himself."

"The Desert Lord?"

"Ralligor. It's how most people in these parts know him. He had seen her in flight and followed her at a distance until she landed. From what I understand she was not quite so impressed with him at first. He was just another cocky young drake clamoring for her attention."

Faelon smiled.

"But," the wizard continued, "as the fates would have it that is when her Landmaster, finally found her. Terrathgrawr is a dragon of horrible wrath, short temper and seemingly boundless strength."

Biting her lip, the Princess hesitantly asked, "He didn't hurt her, did he?"

"Oh, I'm certain he would have, but for the young drake who intervened. I actually witnessed that fight."

A slight smile curled her mouth as she declared, "And he battled and won her from the horrible Terrathgrawr from across the desert."

"Oh, no," the wizard corrected. "Ralligor was quick and agile, but did well just to survive. He was either too proud or too foolish to back down when he should have. Terrathgrawr was easily twice his size at the time."

Feeling herself becoming anxious, Faelon arched her brow and insisted, "But he must have won somehow."

"Not exactly. Fortune was with him that day and his own Landmaster, the massive Agarxus the Tyrant was close enough to hear the commotion. Once he joined the fray the battle took a decisive turn against Terrathgrawr."

"You said before that Agarxus is a bigger dragon. He taught the other dragon a lesson, huh?"

"That he did. What was to Ralligor a fight to the death to impress a young dragoness turned quickly into a territorial battle between Landmasters. Agarxus and Terrathgrawr have tangled many times, and that would prove to be the last. Unlike Ralligor, Terrathgrawr knew when to withdraw. That is actually the day Ralligor and I first met. I felt he had a strangely active gift within him, one that I could cultivate."

"What kind of gift?"

"The *wizaridi*. As I learned from my own *magister* I was able to go beyond my teachings and draw my gift directly from the land itself. This would prove to be a source of almost limitless power that I knew would take me decades to teach someone, and I could not trust just anyone with such power as this."

"So you chose a dragon? Why wouldn't you choose a younger man?"

He raised his brow. "Dragons already have such a connection with the land, so teaching him that much would not be necessary. I only have to teach him the disciplines of the *wizaridi*, which he was already very strong with when we met, and hope he will one day pass the knowledge on to someone worthy."

"If he is a wizard *and* a dragon, then shouldn't he be able to easily defeat Duke Malchor and his wizard?"

"One would think, child, but he has yet to bring himself as a dragon and his teachings as a wizard together. He is potentially the most powerful wizard in the world, yet the disciplines still elude him. I'm not sure why."

"All he has to do is learn how to be a dragon *and* a wizard at the same time?"

Nodding, the wizard master confirmed, "Yes. It sounds easy, and yet he's been unable to accomplish this for nearly forty seasons. He easily controls the *wizaridi* and can cast spells, control certain elements and even project his *facultas* with amazing strength and skill, but all on a human level. He seems to have no idea the fathomless power he could wield as a dragon. I just wish I knew what is stopping him."

Her lips tightening, the Princess dared ask, "Do you think he can beat Duke Malchor?"

Venting a deep breath before he answered, the wizard finally replied, "For his sake and Falloah's, I'm praying he can, but I fear he will have to call upon potential he does not yet know he possesses to do so."

"Time is short for him to learn how to do that," Faelon observed.

"I know it is," the wizard confirmed.

They rode in silence again for some time before the Princess finally organized her curiosity again. "You said you knew my father."

He finally smiled. "Many, many seasons ago. He was having some problems with a troublesome sorcerer, one who was allied to an enemy of Caipiervell. I happened along simply looking for shelter against the spring storms, and the next thing I knew the guards were escorting me to his court for an audience. I don't normally involve myself in such nonsense as kingdoms warring with each other, but he truly wanted his kingdom spared the ravages of that war." The wizard looked to her. "He didn't start the war and he would not surrender his lands and holdings to a tyrant and have his people subjugated. Sadly, he did not have the mind of a warrior, so he relied upon generals who did not know how to deal with this sorcerer who had cost them battle after battle."

"So my father had you fight this sorcerer," she guessed.

Turning his eyes back down the road, the wizard corrected, "Not exactly. I countered his spells and simply took away the advantages the sorcerer gave the other side. King Elner's forces were still rather overmatched, so I may have done some things that evened the odds a bit."

Faelon leaned her head. "Like what?"

The wizard smiled. "Oh, I would arrange for catapults to not work, horses to become stubborn right before they rode into battle, wagon wheels to fall off, weapons to become brittle and snap in half right before the battle, bowstrings to break... Just a few annoying little things that made the fighting impossible. Of course, Red Stone's sorcerer did what he could to counter *my* spells, but as the fates would have it he was young and relatively inexperienced. He demanded a meeting and he and I settled things amongst ourselves and agreed to abandon the war."

"How long ago was that?"

"Oh, I think you were four seasons old at the time."

"But Red Stone attacked us again only three seasons ago."

Nodding, the wizard confirmed, "Yes, I know. It seems the young sorcerer grew stronger and a little too bold and seemed to forget about our agreement. He helped the Queen of Red Stone rebuild her army and the machines of war. You see, she was bitter about the first war fought against your kingdom. Her king and husband never returned from the last battle and she was left to raise her young prince on her own."

"My father never went into battle with the army," Faelon informed.

"He was more diplomat and gentleman than warrior," the wizard told her. "He was wise to stay at Caipiervell and encourage his people. When the renewed battles started to go poorly, your father recalled me, much to the ire of my apprentice."

She raised her brow. "The dragon, you mean?"

"The dragon," the wizard confirmed. "When I told Ralligor that I had to go and stop the war he was furious, and a dragon's anger is not something to be trifled with. I thought I had convinced him it was for the best, but he clearly did not want his studies to wait or my attention to be shared with someone else again. Even as I helped Caipiervell repel the first of Red Stone's invasions, his rage swelled and he finally put a stop to the war himself."

"What did he do?" the Princess asked a little fearfully.

With another glance at her, the wizard answered, "Queen Hethan's troops regrouped and reinforced at Red Stone Castle. They doubled their numbers, leaving only a third of their forces to protect the castle. As they were marching from the castle with their catapults and siege engines on route to meet us on the battlefield again and attack Castle Caipiervell itself, Ralligor descended upon them. Most of them were in the open and fell quickly. They retreated behind the walls and their sorcerer stood against him but that only infuriated him more and he destroyed much of the wall and palace to get to them. By the time he left, their siege weapons were burning and destroyed, much of the castle was burning and almost half of their army lay dead."

"What happened to the sorcerer?"

"He paid the dearest price for standing against an angry dragon."

Faelon covered her mouth.

"It put a stop to the war," the wizard admitted, "but Ralligor still had a good scolding awaiting him when he returned. He's stubborn though, and each time Red Stone tried to rebuild their army he returned to decimate them anew."

"To be honest I'm glad he did," the Princess said straightly. "They spent most of my life trying to bring down my kingdom. I'm glad he kept them at bay for so long."

"Many innocent people died when he attacked," the wizard pointed out. "Those who did not know he was there to keep their army in check took shelter within the castle."

"How many of my people would have died if the war had continued?" she countered.

"Perhaps only soldiers," the wizard offered.

"Soldiers like Garrin's father," she replied. "Why did they go to war with us, anyway?"

The wizard shrugged. "Land, someone felt insulted, a trading dispute… I fear the only people who truly know are long dead."

"But not dead enough to stop them from killing my parents."

He glanced at her again. "I don't believe Red Stone was responsible for that."

She raised her brow. "Why don't you? We fought for over a decade with them."

"As I said. He was not a warrior king. Your uncle is more of a military threat to them than King Elner ever was." His eyes slid to her. "Unless they find an ally in him."

Something cold swept through her and her eyes widened. Looking forward again, she allowed that knowledge to sink in for a moment.

"Did they ever find your parent's killer?" the wizard asked.

Faelon shook her head.

"Is anyone looking?" he continued.

"My uncle assured me that he would not rest until…." She trailed off, not wanting to believe what was right in front of her, what she had truly known for over a day already. Finally, she conceded, "He isn't even looking. He never was."

The wizard shrugged again. "Not for me to say."

"My parents were just the first of his obstacles," she went on. "He took power until I was old enough or married someone who could help me rule Caipiervell, but he never intended…." She slowly shook her head, staring blankly forward. "He planned this all along. He was never going to step down once I was ready." Her breathing seemed labored as tears filled her eyes once again. "He's all the family I have left and he planned to kill me from the start. He killed my parents!"

The wizard glanced at her again. "Did Duke Malchor wander to Caipiervell on his own or by invitation?"

"I don't know," the Princess admitted softly, her gaze still somewhere in the distance. "I thought the day that dragon kidnapped me was the worst of my life, but each day since has just been getting worse."

"Had you ever seen a dragon before?" the wizard asked.

She was long seconds in answering, but finally nodded. "I saw it many times high and in the distance. I thought two days ago it was the same dragon."

"What did you think about her three days ago?"

Faelon turned her eyes down, again taking time to answer before she finally admitted, "I thought it—she was beautiful, so magnificent and free, yet I was so afraid of her. I was always afraid of her swooping down to get me, but many times I saw her I could not look away from her. She was just so… So beautiful."

"How many times did you see her?"

"It seemed every few days we would see her in the distance. It was almost a routine, and then last season sometime she disappeared from the sky for a long time. I didn't see her again until late this spring."

Smiling, the wizard assured, "I'll tell you why someday."

The Princess nodded. "If we all live through this I shall look forward to hearing the story."

"Have faith, Faelon."

"I have no more. I can't go home, I have no kingdom or family and now the red dragon I admired and feared most of my life is imperiled by people who also want *me* dead. My life may as well be over."

Laughing softly, the wizard corrected, "Oh, I think your day is about to get better." He raised his chin as they rode into a clearing and stopped.

Following his gaze, Faelon looked into the middle of the clearing and gasped as her eyes found the little white unicorn who grazed peacefully in the tall grass. She did not dismount right away. She could not move. The unicorn she saw consumed her.

The wizard smiled as he looked to Faelon and swung down from his horse, then he took a couple of pears from the saddlebag, turned and strode toward the unicorn.

Tearing her eyes from the unicorn, the Princess looked to the wizard and scolded in as quiet a voice as she could manage, "What are you doing? You're going to frighten her away!"

He looked back at her and smiled, informing, "You or I would be hard pressed to frighten *that* unicorn."

As he strode on, Faelon just watched in amazement. The unicorn looked directly at him and the Princess was certain she would turn and run, but to her shock she turned and approached him. She was not afraid! Faelon simply watched, barely believing what she saw as the unicorn and wizard met and she smiled a little as the wizard offered the little unicorn a pear and she took it. Slowly, she got down from her horse, hesitantly approaching a creature of myth and legend, a creature she had dreamed about seeing her entire life. Fear crept into her, fear that her approach would frighten the unicorn and she would flee, but as she drew closer and heard the unicorn and the wizard actually speaking to one another, that fear slowly faded from her mind.

As she reached the wizard, she stopped behind him, her eyes wide and locked on the unicorn. The Princess simply could not look away.

Staring up at the wizard as she listened to him tell her about finding the Princess and about the fate of the young squire, the unicorn slowly chewed on the last of the first pear, eyes showing a little pity.

"I wish we had arrived an hour sooner," the wizard continued. "We were fortunate that Garrin was such a brave lad as to stand and fight his larger opponent to protect her even after he was mortally wounded. The only good news I have is that Ralligor seems to be reining in his anger enough to think clearly."

"That's good," the unicorn whickered.

Faelon gasped again.

"I've never seen him like that," the unicorn continued. "He's frightening when he's so angry. I don't like being so afraid of him."

"You *are* natural enemies," the wizard reminded.

Snorting, the unicorn rolled her eyes and scoffed, "I think people are enemies when they don't understand each other."

With a smile, the wizard agreed, "Shahly you have wisdom well beyond your age." He looked to the Princess and introduced, "This is Faelon of Caipiervell, one of the maidens you saw that other dragon carrying away."

Shahly looked to her and greeted, "Hi. Did you bring pears, too?"

Faelon covered her mouth and was unable to answer.

The unicorn slid her eyes to the wizard. "Is she okay?"

Laughing, the wizard finally managed, "She is simply awed at the sight of a unicorn."

"Oh," Shahly said dryly. "I don't even think about it anymore."

"I can understand you," Faelon breathed.

Whickering in a little relief, the unicorn almost sighed, "*That's good to hear. The last humans I met couldn't.*" She looked to the wizard's other hand and asked, "*Are you going to eat that?*"

The wizard laughed again and offered her the other pear. "You seem hungry."

"*I'm famished!*" she declared, eating half the pear in one bite. "*Vinton and I have been running all over the place all day with almost no time to stop and eat anything.*"

"Where is Vinton?" the wizard asked.

Chewing the last of the pear, Shahly answered, "*He said he is going Caipiervell to see if he can find Falloah and see if there is a way to free her if she is there.*"

The Princess' eyes widened, her mouth falling open as she demanded, "He went there alone? Doesn't he know what can happen if he gets caught?"

"*He won't get caught,*" Shahly assured. "*Most of your kind are very easy to trick into not seeing us and Vinton is very experienced at that.*"

Her mouth falling open, Faelon breathed, "He is another unicorn?"

"*Of course he is,*" Shahly confirmed. "*What else would he be?*"

Tearing her eyes from the unicorn, the Princess asked the wizard, "How many unicorns do you know?"

"Just the two," he answered.

"And you are sure they won't see him?" Faelon persisted.

"They have ways of not being seen," the wizard assured.

Arching her brow, the Princess informed, "A unicorn in the middle of Caipiervell will be just a little conspicuous."

"*Only if they know he's there,*" Shahly countered, then she looked beyond them and beamed with excitement as she declared,

"There he is!" She bolted around them and ran to the approaching unicorn.

Faelon and the wizard turned and the Princess raised her hands to her heart as she saw the other unicorn, the stallion.

"I don't believe it," she breathed.

With a sidelong glance and a certain smile, the wizard said, "I told you your day would get better."

Watching the two unicorns approach, Faelon nodded.

Vinton seemed to ignore the Princess as he paced steadily toward them, his eyes on the wizard. Shahly paced at his side and looked as proud as a unicorn could, holding her head high as she walked very close to him. This did not escape the Princess as she knew right away that just being in the presence of the big bay unicorn brought the white unicorn unimaginable joy. The bay did not seem quite so happy. Most people cannot read the mood of a unicorn at a glance but to both Faelon and the wizard at her side something was clearly on the bay's mind.

As he reached them, Vinton's eyes never turned from the wizard and even showed some anger as he reported, "They have her at the castle. It looks like most of the humans who don't already have something to do are swarming around her. I've never felt such anger from so many creatures all at once."

"How is she?" the wizard asked in a solemn tone.

"She's weak," the stallion reported. "Somehow I don't think they mean to leave her there until she dies. She is under heavy guard and they've even offered her food." He huffed a breath and looked away. "She's badly injured. I don't think she will survive more than another day or two there."

"Then we have to get her out," Shahly declared, looking at Faelon. "You're from Caipiervell. Perhaps you can help."

The Princess found herself at a loss for words, and when she met the stallion's narrow eyes she felt overwhelming shame for her people.

"What's the matter?" Shahly asked, clearly sensing something was amiss.

Vinton glared at the Princess for long seconds more, then he looked to the wizard and advised, "We need to find some answers.

With that dragonslayer waiting for Ralligor I don't see how we can safely get her out of there."

Nodding, the wizard agreed, "They would kill her as soon as he attacked. That's why I don't want him going there yet. She's clearly alive for some reason, no doubt to draw him in on their terms."

Vinton snorted. "Then they hold all of the advantages. Even if we knew their plans for her, how could we possibly stop them from carrying them out?"

"We should first figure out what they intend to do," the wizard insisted.

"How do we do that?" the stallion questioned. "We don't know for certain where this dragonslayer and his men are, and even if we did they would be under heavy guard."

"The old castle," Faelon said before realizing. All eyes turned to her and she suddenly felt very uneasy.

"I just came from the castle," the bay pointed out dryly.

"Not Caipiervell," she corrected, "the old ruin they took me to when I was captured. Garrin found them in the banquet hall there and overheard part of their plan. Perhaps we can learn something more there."

Vinton and the wizard exchanged looks and the wizard added, "And it is not far from here."

The stallion nodded. "After nightfall, I think. They should be making their move soon and if we can discover what it is then perhaps we can counter it somehow."

"I can go!" Shahly announced.

"You aren't going," the bay corrected.

"But—"

"No."

"You have a more important mission, Shahly," the wizard informed, "one that will require your particular gifts of speed and your special way of communicating." He got a look from the stallion and continued, "Do you remember the people you helped this spring?"

She considered, turning her eyes down, then she looked back to the wizard and her ears perked. "I remember. There was the tall woman and the really big man who I watched over. It was such an ordeal keeping them safe that I was sure they would not survive their journey. They could not even understand me. The woman did after some coaching from Traman. He had to tell her—"

"You will need to find them," the wizard interrupted. "They should be near Castle Zondae. If you can get word to them and give them a message we can, perhaps, end this whole ordeal safely and restore what should be." He looked down and reached into a pouch on his belt.

As Shahly watched him, Faelon finally noticed the gold chain that the white unicorn wore around her neck. Animals, even enchanted beasts like unicorns, did not commonly wear jewelry and she felt compelled to ask, "Where did you get the necklace?"

Shahly glanced at her, then turned her head trying to see the chain. "Ralligor gave it to me. It is an amulet that made me human when I said the right words."

"It's very pretty," the Princess complimented, then her eyes widened. "Wait. Made you human?"

Nodding, the white unicorn confirmed, "I had to get into Red Stone Castle and rescue Vinton. Ralligor gave me the amulet to make me human so that I wouldn't be noticed."

Snorting again, the stallion looked away again and growled, "Sure worked out nicely."

"It did," Shahly innocently confirmed. "Nobody there knew I was a unicorn."

"We thankfully will not need you to endure that again," the wizard assured.

"Dark will be settling soon," Vinton observed. "I'd better get to that old castle and see what I can learn."

"I'll go with you," Faelon offered. When all she got was a dry, distrusting look from the stallion she continued, "I know where to go and how to get there once we're inside. I'll also know what to listen for. Please let me help."

Turning unsure eyes to the wizard, Vinton whickered for any sign of yah or nay.

"I feel she could be helpful," the wizard assured. "But, she must be kept safe. She is the rightful heir to the throne of Caipiervell.

Why she is not there is something I will gladly explain when time favors us."

"Or I can tell you on the way," the Princess said, trying to win his trust.

Clearly still uncomfortable with the idea, Vinton reluctantly conceded, "I suppose it will be wise to have someone along who knows what to listen for. You'll have to leave your horse here. He will be too easy to spot and I don't think I could mask you both."

"I'll keep up with you as best I can," she assured.

With a sharp look, Shahly whickered something to him, or at him.

The wizard raised his brow.

Looking away, Vinton grunted and said, "No, you can just ride on my back. We will get there quicker that way."

"I don't want to burden you," Faelon said softly. "You are already kind enough to let me stay in your company."

He turned his eyes to her and assured, "You won't burden me unless I have to keep waiting for you. Just ride on my back, and on the way there you can tell me how you managed to get yourself mixed up in all of this."

The wizard patted the white unicorn's neck and ordered, "Shahly, come along with me. We have much to do and little time. I will explain everything as we go."

Hesitating, the white unicorn looked to her Vinton once more and softly assured, "I will be back at your side quickly, my stallion."

He whickered back to her, then his eyes narrowed and he ordered, "Don't take any unnecessary chances."

"I won't," she conceded in a sigh, then she turned and took the wizard's side as they walked across the clearing.

"Okay," Vinton announced as he approached the Princess, "on my back. Let's get this journey on the road."

As gingerly as she could, and on her third attempt, Faelon settled herself on his back, and as they started down the road toward the ancient castle she offered, "Thank you. I am in your debt."

He glanced back at her. "I hold no such debts over anyone. So, tell me what happened that caused you to be out here like this and not on your throne at Caipiervell."

A long, horrible story was ahead, one which she would have to relive yet again.

CHAPTER 9

Traveling such great distances was easy with the help of a wizard. Walking through a dense fog was a simple thing, even though seeing what was on the other side was impossible. For a short time there was extreme cold, then warmth, then the air felt normal again.

Shahly emerged from the mist on a human built road a day's travel from the clearing near Caipiervell castle, way up the Spagnah River where she had been that spring. Months of wandering were suddenly both ahead of her and behind her.

Stopping in the center of the road, she took a moment to look around her to get her bearings, aware of the important scrolled up note that was tied with bark twine to her gold chain. Only now did she wonder how she was going to get back to where she was and find Vinton again. Yet, something more important was at hand. As before, she found that many people were counting on her, this time a mix of species. Humans and dragons both depended upon what she did next.

Now to find which direction to go. The sun would tell her. The wizard said to keep it to her left. She looked up and found it, then paced down the road with the sun on her left side. Each time the road turned she found herself growing anxious about her direction, but kept going despite this.

Not far down the road she heard horses approaching. She also heard the casual conversations of humans with them, all female. Shahly raised her head and looked for them somewhere beyond a turn in the road ahead. Instinct tried to speak and speak loudly, but her experience argued it down once again. She felt some excitement about seeing some new humans and the fear she knew should have been there would not arise.

They were five in number, each riding a saddled horse that was sleek and powerful. These were tall, muscular women, each dressed in light steel and leather armor and under-padding, riding boots and not really much else. Heavy coverings were more a hindrance on a hot summer day. Bows and swords were at the ready hanging from their saddles, but dispositions were very relaxed. Four of them had dark hair. One, clearly the leader and the largest and most muscular of them had blond hair, and only hers was restrained behind her. She rode at the front, but her attention was uncharacteristically behind her as she listened to a darker haired warrior behind and to her left.

So involved in some conversation or debate were they that Shahly went unnoticed until she was about thirty paces away. No surprise to her that it was the youngest of the group, a black haired girl not quite sixteen seasons old and riding in the middle of the staggered procession, who saw her first.

"Captain Pa'lesh!" the girl cried.

"Do not call rank out here!" the blond warrior shouted. When the girl pointed ahead, she turned and instinctively reached for her sword, then froze as she saw what approached her.

The entire procession stopped and all of them stared at her with wide eyes.

Shahly stopped right in front of them. Most of them were in their mid twenties or older, but for the black haired girl who had seen her first. Remembering her encounter with a Zondaen before, she dryly whickered, "I don't suppose any of you can understand me, can you?" Once again, she was not entirely surprised when only the black haired girl nodded.

"A unicorn," the woman second in line breathed.

All of the riders behind steered their horses abreast of the field captain.

Raising her hand, the blond warrior ordered, "Don't frighten her."

Shahly drew a deep breath and loosed it hard and quickly, then she turned her eyes to the black haired girl and asked, "Will you tell them I'm not afraid?"

"She's not afraid," the black haired girl complied, her eyes locked on the unicorn.

Turning her eyes to the girl, the field captain demanded, "How do you know?"

Clearly hesitant to answer, the black haired girl's eyes shifted to her and she stammered, "Uh, she... She told me to tell you that." It was obvious that no one believed her and she glanced around at the others, insisting, "She did! Didn't anyone else hear her?"

"This *has* to be some kind of trick," the captain snarled.

"It isn't," the girl assured. Looking around at the other warriors, her frustration mounted and she looked to the unicorn, declaring, "I'm not mad!"

Shahly could not help a subtle little smile and no longer felt alone in the communication line. "It's okay," she assured, taking a few steps forward. "The last one of your people I encountered couldn't talk to me either without a lot of coaching."

"Why can I hear you?" the girl asked.

"I don't know," the unicorn admitted. "I think sometimes your kind forgets how to hear us. A friend of mine had to teach the last one of your people how to hear us."

"Last one of my people? You mean from Zondae?"

"Yes," Shahly replied.

The captain's eyes narrowed. "What about Zondae?"

The girl glanced at her, answering, "She knows someone from Zondae." Looking back to the unicorn, she asked, "Who is it you spoke to?"

Shahly looked away, into the woods as she tried to remember. "What was she called? Ell something... Something Ell...."

The girl's eyes widened. "Le'ell?"

"That sounds right," the unicorn confirmed. "Vinton and I helped her and her stallion this spring. They had much to do and I'm a little surprised they survived it all."

"Wait a minute," Pa'lesh ordered. "What about Le'ell? How does she know Le'ell? What am I saying? This is insane! Animals can't talk."

Shahly snorted at her.

"Le'ell talked about speaking to a unicorn when she got back to Zondae," a brown haired woman to the girl's left recalled. "This must be the unicorn she spoke to!"

A murmuring of agreement stirred among the warriors.

Glancing at them in turn, Shahly informed, "I'm kind of in a hurry."

The girl swung down from her horse, her eyes on the unicorn.

"Traw'sann!" One of the women scolded. "What are you doing?"

With only a glance, the girl assured, "It's okay, Traw'linn." With her attention fully on the unicorn again, the girl asked, "What is it you need us for?"

"Well," Shahly started, "the wizard told me everything as we walked, but we both knew I wouldn't remember it all so he scribbled on this cloth or whatever this is and tied it to my amulet chain." She turned her head to reveal it.

Pa'lesh also dismounted and was cautious to approach, looking to the note that was tied to the unicorn's chain.

Hesitantly, the girl asked, "May I take that off of you?"

"You're almost going to have to," Shahly informed. "Don't be afraid. I don't bite."

"You're still talking to her?" the captain asked.

Traw'sann was still a little afraid to touch the unicorn, but nodded and confirmed, "Yes." Her hands shook a little as she untied the twine and removed it from the chain. She unrolled the paper and read for a moment, then she looked to the blond warrior and offered it to her. "Captain Pa'lesh, you should see this."

With a glance at the unicorn, the captain took the note and started reading, shaking her head as she made out the first words. "This handwriting is terrible. Must have been a man that wrote it." Her eyes panned back and forth over the words, then she looked to the unicorn with wide eyes and demanded, "Where did you get this?"

"From the wizard," Shahly answered.

Gasping loudly, Pa'lesh grasped her chest and stumbled backward a few steps, her wide eyes still on the unicorn. She clearly did not actually expect a response.

The girl smiled. "I think she can hear you now."

Shaking her head, the blond warrior declared, "But animals can't talk!"

Shahly rolled her eyes, countering, "*You* can talk and you're an animal."

The girl covered her mouth and giggled.

Pa'lesh rubbed her eyes and looked the note over again, then she conceded, "Okay, for the moment I'm going to assume we haven't all gone mad and this is for real. If that's the case we have to get this to the Queen right away."

"He was hoping you would," the unicorn said.

"Who was?" the Field Captain asked.

"The wizard who wrote that," Shahly answered in a matter of fact tone. "I should get back. If you see Le'ell tell her hi for me and that I look forward to seeing her again."

As the unicorn turned to leave, Traw'sann raised a hand toward her and bade, "Wait!"

Shahly stopped and looked back at her. The girl was still hesitant to approach and it was clear that she wanted to touch a unicorn, so Shahly turned fully and took the last steps, laying her head on the girl's shoulder and closing her eyes.

Traw'sann slowly raised her arms to embrace the unicorn's neck, and as she hugged her tighter and brushed her cheek against her soft hair, she wept and offered in a whisper, "Thank you."

Shahly looked to the other humans who stared back with looks of disbelief and envy, and she softly whickered, "Oh, okay. Come on, everybody."

She did not expect to spend so much time with the Zondaen warriors, but unicorns have little perception of time. An unknown time later would find her trotting down a forest trail, not really thinking beyond the fun she had experienced with the women. With her mind wandering about, she was not as alert as she should have been and did not notice the wizard leaning against a tree on one side of the trail until she was only a few paces away from him.

He was munching on a bright red apple when she stopped and she was startled a little at his apparent sudden appearance.

Still chewing, the wizard observed, "You took longer than I thought you would."

"How long did you think I would take?" she countered.

"It isn't important," he said, reaching into a pouch to remove another apple. "We should get back to Caipiervell. I need to find Ralligor."

Shahly's ears perked. "Are we going to walk through the mist again?"

He smiled as he held the apple to her. "Yes, I think it would be faster than walking."

She took the apple from him and ate it in short order. "You seem tired after you do that."

"It's a little draining," he admitted. "I'm not as young as I once was."

"Well, don't get too tired," she advised. "We will have our hooves full getting Falloah away from that castle." Looking up, she observed, "It's going to get dark soon, too."

Waving his hands repeatedly between two trees, the wizard informed, "The sun will be a trite higher near Caipiervell."

Shahly raised her head, looking on him with some confusion. "It will?"

Mist began to pour from the two trees and swirl together between them. As the unicorn started toward it, the wizard commanded, "Wait," and she stopped. The mist grew heavier, denser, and a soft blue glow illuminated it from within. "Okay," he finally said, "it's ready."

She was not quite so hesitant to enter this time since she knew what to expect and paced into the mist fearlessly, emerging into the clearing where she had entered before, this time almost forty leagues away. She walked some distance away from the mist before she stopped and looked back for the wizard, who emerged a second later. As soon as he walked from the mist, it thinned into nothingness.

The wizard stopped and just stood there for long seconds, rubbing his eyes.

Shahly turned and approached him. "Are you all right?"

He offered her a reassuring if strained smile. "Fine. A bit fatigued." He looked into the forest behind her, his eyes narrowing as he announced, "We need to find Ralligor."

Turning to scan the forest with her essence, she found the dragon in the distance and her ears perked up. "He's that way." She trotted around the wizard and came along to his side, bumping her shoulder into him as she ordered, "Quickly! On my back. We'll get there faster that way."

With great effort, the wizard fought back a hearty laugh as he looked at this little, pony-sized unicorn with more of a deer's build than a horse. "Shahly, I think I should—"

"We don't have time to discuss it!" she insisted. "We need to find Ralligor."

"Um…" he stammered. "I appreciate the offer, but I should probably just take one of the horses."

She raised her head and looked back at him, then across the clearing where the horses still grazed peacefully. "Oh. Yes. I forgot about them."

Tenderly patting her neck, the wizard shook his head as he walked to the waiting mounts. "Shahly, you are a refreshing change from the people I spend way too much time with."

She followed, responding with, "Thank you."

And still the journey to find the black dragon would be delayed as Shahly insisted that they not leave Faelon's horse there alone, so as the Wizard rode in front down the forest trail, Shahly followed with the second horse right behind her. They did not seem to travel far or for very long, yet half a league was behind them before they realized. Ahead was the flood plain of a small river, one that fed into the Spagnah River, and this would be a good landing area for a large dragon.

The wizard stopped, sensing something was amiss.

Shahly stopped at his side, looking up at him as she asked, "What is it?"

Just staring blankly ahead, the wizard suggested, "Perhaps you should remain here."

"Why?" she asked.

"There is something ahead you should not see," was his answer.

She snorted. "Oh, I'm mature enough. It won't bother me."

Slowly, he turned his eyes down to her. "Shahly, you should stay here. Please."

The white unicorn just blinked, then she laid her ears back and angrily looked away, whickering, "Fine."

"Promise you won't follow," he insisted.

"I don't want to be left out again," she grumbled, stomping her hoof on the ground. "Everyone always treats me like I'm a filly, but I'm a grown mare with a stallion and mate and I've already saved my stallion and Falloah and helped those people from Enulam and Zondae find their way and—"

"Shahly," the wizard interrupted. When he had her attention, he continued, "I'm not questioning your maturity or the great tasks you've performed, but some things are better left in your unknown."

She snorted again and looked away from him. In her eyes was an annoyance rare to her, one that only seemed to surface when she felt left out.

Unable to avoid succumbing to her, the wizard shook his head and urged, "It really isn't a good idea for you to go. Some things are best left unseen."

She turned her eyes down and lowered her head, still refusing to look at him.

Pouting was not a trait most would associate with unicorns, yet this unicorn proved they could as she had well mastered it, and the wizard's will yielded. With rolling eyes and a sigh, he finally said, "Where we need to be is another two hundred paces or so. The horses will have to remain here."

Her ears perked up and turned toward him.

He dismounted and led his horse to the second one. "If you could convince them to stay here that would be most helpful."

Slowly, she looked to him.

"Just remember," he added, "I'm not responsible for what happens when we get there."

Something about her seemed to smile and she assured, "I'm a big mare. I can take care of myself."

The wizard's brow arched and he turned and continued down the path.

Shahly followed for a time, just watching him. She finally trotted to his side and asked, "What is so horrible that I shouldn't see?"

He glanced at her.

Something ahead roared a deep roar, something very big!

Shahly stopped, her wide eyes trained ahead of her.

"Having second thoughts?" the wizard asked.

"No," she assured, catching up to him again. "I'm not afraid."

He raised his brow and turned his eyes to her again.

She just glanced at him. "Well, I'm not afraid enough to not go and see."

The wizard snickered and shook his head.

Another roar ahead made Shahly cringe, but she kept pace with the wizard.

Running water was ahead in the distance. The thumping of some gigantic beast's feet slamming into the ground as it walked actually drowned that noise out intermittently. Shahly could sense the black dragon's presence, but also another, a presence that was very powerful and unfamiliar to her. It was another dragon, one which she did not know. Despite a little fear of the unknown, she felt a little eagerness and held her head up as they neared.

They seemed to enter the flood plain of the small, fast river quickly. The grass was laid flat as recent rains had caused the river to swell from its banks. A little debris consisting of branches and clumps of gray plant matter littered the area and shoots of fresh grass sprouted up to about ankle high.

Shahly stopped and sniffed the ground, smelling the new grass as well as the stench of decay and river bottom left by the flood, then something very large moved near the river and she lifted her head to look. She first saw Ralligor's back. He was sitting there facing the other way. Then her eyes widened as a mountainous dark green form moved in front of him, something that she had not seen right away. It was clearly the other presence. This dragon was on the other side of the Desert Lord, who was an enormous dragon in his own right, and yet he was dwarfed by the mammoth beast that paced angrily before him. Swallowing hard as the huge dragon stopped and seemed to look her way, Shahly instinctively folded her essence around herself and backed into the trees. She lowered herself almost all the way to the ground and retreated under a clump of course, leafy brush, her eyes on the enormous dragon before her.

The wizard watched her retreat and felt her deception. But for his knowledge that she was there and for his knowing her for some time, she would have disappeared completely from his sight.

She finally laid completely to her belly and scooted herself a little further into the brush, her wide eyes never leaving the gargantuan beast near the river.

Raising his brow, the wizard advised, "Why don't you just wait here."

Shahly nodded, her wide eyes fixed on the huge dragon.

Shaking his head, the wizard turned and approached the dragons. Most humans would know to avoid even one, but these two he knew and he neared them without fear.

The biggest of the two dragons bared his teeth as he paced back and forth and growled, "Nightfall. That means before sundown. You haven't even attacked the castle where you think she is yet."

The wizard stopped beside Ralligor and informed, "A direct attack is not what is called for now. We must be patient and await their first move and mistake."

With another thunderous growl, the massive dragon stopped pacing and slowly turned toward this puny human who dared speak to him.

"If we strike now," the wizard went on, "they will surely kill her." When the huge dragon only glared at him, he continued. "They will choose the battlefield and do something to lure Ralligor to it. That would be the ideal time to move against them."

"How does that free her by nightfall?" the huge dragon snarled.

"It doesn't," the wizard informed straightly.

His brow low over his eyes, the massive dragon growled, "It is your kind that has her, human."

"Yes, it is," the wizard informed. "That means I have unique insight into their actions. Attack now and they are poised to kill her while most of their forces are doing battle with Ralligor. If we wait for them to use her as they intend or leave her unguarded, even for a moment, we can get her back alive. Her safe return to you is what you want, Agarxus. It's what we all want."

The Landmaster raised his head slightly. "Why should I trust you?"

Ralligor finally spoke up. "I trust him."

The massive dragon's eyes shifted to the Desert Lord.

"I would ask you to trust me," the black dragon continued. "I will do whatever is necessary to reclaim Falloah. If that means trusting my human *magister* and waiting until morning to attack then that is what I will do."

"Against my command to you?" the Landmaster growled.

"If that wins Falloah her freedom and her life, then yes."

Agarxus' eyes narrowed. "That sounds like a challenge."

His eyes also narrowing beneath a low brow, Ralligor countered, "And while you assume that, Falloah is still a captive of the humans. I would rather have her back alive tomorrow than enact my revenge on the humans now to placate you and get her killed."

Stomping toward the smaller dragon, the Landmaster lowered his head until his nose was only a pace away from the Desert Lord's.

Ralligor did not flinch.

The two glared at each other for a moment.

Finally, Agarxus observed, "She is more important to you than your own life." He raised his head, staring down at his *subordinare* as he continued, "At least I know you listen to me from time to time."

Ralligor raised his brow. "Of course I do. You are the second most important dragon in my life."

One would have thought that Agarxus actually smiled slightly.

Nodding, the Landmaster growled back, "You are defiant and callous. That tells me you're getting your wits back about you." He looked to the wizard, his eyes narrowing. "What is your role in this, human?"

"Simply to prevent them from starting a war between your kind and mine," was the wizard's answer. "That and I don't want anything to happen to Falloah. She means a great deal to Ralligor—and me."

"And yet she was not your first thought," the massive dragon observed.

The wizard simply smiled at him. "She was not my first answer. I no more want to see anything happen to her than I want to see humans and dragons at war. With you as our enemy, I fear my kind would be extinct in Abtont in short order."

The Landmaster's eyes slid to the black dragon. "Such defiance as this is not the way to stay in my favor, Ralligor. I said I want her free before sundown tonight."

"Even if it means they kill her?" the black dragon countered.

"Do I have to attend to this myself?" the huge dragon roared.

"If you want her death on your head," Ralligor snarled back.

Dropping to all fours, the Landmaster roared again and slammed his horns into the Desert Lord's chest.

Crashing back-first to the ground, the black dragon quickly rolled to all fours and faced the larger dragon, glaring back.

The wizard backed away, his eyes shifting from one dragon to the other.

A standoff followed, each dragon growling and raising his head, baring his teeth. Ralligor was clearly outmatched, but there was a point to be made. Growls were exchanged and dorsal scales stood erect as tails thrashed furiously.

This was not at all what it appeared. To those who do not know dragons and our hierarchies it would appear that Agarxus and Ralligor meant to fight for power. In reality, the Landmaster had to know how strongly was his *subordinate's* will to do what he needed to do. He had to test the Desert Lord's resolve, and Ralligor would have to demonstrate this and not waver. It is the dragon way.

To an ignorant human or naïve unicorn, this would be a mystery. The wizard had seen this test many times between these two. Ralligor was always a strong willed drake, but with his Landmaster he always knew the limits of his patience. Today, that limit would have to be tested, as would the Desert Lord's own strength. The wizard knew this. The unicorn did not, and once again good judgment would abandon her.

With her fear temporarily and foolishly displaced, she exploded from her hiding place and galloped to her big friend's defense. With a loud and sharp whinny, she galloped to the dragons, veering around the black dragon and stopping right between them. Her eyes glowed emerald and the same glow enveloped her horn until nothing of it could be seen but a bright emerald light. Her hooves were spaced wide and her tail swished violently from side to side as she looked up at the Landmaster and snorted, kicking at the ground as she lowered her head to bring the tip of her spiral to bear on the huge dragon's chest.

Ever so slowly, Agarxus' scaly lips slid over his bared teeth, leaving the tips of eight of them and his tusks exposed as he lowered his nose to see the new threat that challenged him.

Shahly bayed at him and half charged, stopping abruptly to kick up some dust. With another challenging whinny, she reared up and lunged at him, stopping only a pace forward as her hooves slammed back onto the ground. Projecting her essence and thoughts at him, she showed a horrible threat, the most horrible images and emotions she could muster from her short life.

The Landmaster's eyes turned to the black dragon and he boomed in a thunderous voice, "Ralligor, what the hell is that?"

His lips tightening, the Desert Lord snarled slightly as he answered, "It's a unicorn."

"What is it doing?" Agarxus murmured, his jaws barely moving.

"She appears to be trying to intimidate you," the black dragon answered.

Shahly snorted yet again as the huge dragon turned his eyes back down to her, but when he bared his teeth and growled, her courage failed completely, her essence faded from her eyes and horn and she backed away, right between the black dragon's arms.

Loosing a deep breath, Ralligor reluctantly informed, "She's here with me."

Once again the Landmaster's eyes found the black dragon and he raised his brow, his heavy dorsal scales folding down to his back as he asked in clear disbelief, "What?"

"It's a long story," the Desert Lord growled.

Daring to step toward the massive dragon again, Shahly scolded in a shaky voice, "You shouldn't be fighting with Ralligor! Falloah needs our help so you need to listen to him or they could kill her!"

This time a slight snarl curled Agarxus' lip and he arched his brow. "You have a pet unicorn and I'm trusting you with most of my western border *and* with the task of freeing Falloah. Does this have something to do with that wizard training?"

"I am not a pet!" Shahly bayed, but when the Landmaster's eyes found her again she cringed and backed up behind Ralligor's hand and arm.

"It doesn't, Agarxus," the Desert Lord assured, turning his eyes down.

The wizard finally approached again, looking up at the Landmaster as he informed, "At your bidding I shall tell you the whole story, but currently I would humbly ask that we be given until morning to free Falloah from this dragonslayer." When the huge dragon's eyes found him, he continued, "My goal and purpose is to ensure that Ralligor and Falloah are reunited, and to get her back alive. I know you want her freed today. We all do. But I fear for her life should we move too quickly."

Cocking a brow up, Agarxus asked, "Just how are you and the unicorn so involved in this?"

"Ralligor is my apprentice," the wizard replied, "and he is my dearest friend. I would gladly lay down my life for him as I would for Falloah. On that you have my word."

Hesitantly nodding, the Landmaster looked back to Ralligor and stood fully, half opening his wings.

Ralligor did the same.

Suddenly in the open again, Shahly sprinted to the wizard and behind him, peering around him up at the Landmaster.

Agarxus shook his head. "So you've involved yourself with humans *and* a unicorn. I'm not entirely sure how I should feel about all of this." He looked away, growling, then continued, "You're reckless and arrogant. You get yourself involved in things that no other dragon would bother with." He turned his eyes down to Ralligor. "You've always been a huge pain in my side.

Why I continue to tolerate your antics escapes me, and yet I do."
He looked to the wizard, to the unicorn who tried desperately to
hide behind him. "I've not seen any of those in South Abtont for
many seasons now."

"Some of the humans here have taken to hunting them for
their horns," Ralligor informed. "They built a talisman to kill
dragons with them."

The Landmaster nodded. "And you dealt with them?"

"I did," the Desert Lord assured.

"And that's where this unicorn came to be in your company,"
Agarxus guessed.

Ralligor nodded, straightly answering, "Yes."

The Landmaster growled. "All for the greater good, I suppose."
He looked to the black dragon, his eyes narrowing. "I'll be
watching, Ralligor, and I'll give you until tomorrow to free her. If
you fail I will take the matter up myself." He looked to the wizard
and snarled, "And your kind will pay a heavy toll for this deed."

Raising his chin, the wizard countered, "Then we shall not fail
you, Agarxus."

With another sharp look at Ralligor, the Landmaster turned
and strode toward the river, opened his wings and swept his bulk
into the sky.

As he flew away, Shahly finally crept around the wizard, her
eyes on the departing dragon as she asked, "Is that why you did not
want me to come with you?"

Nodding, the wizard confirmed, "That's why."

She looked to him, raising her head as she informed, "Well,
it's a good thing I did. He was not so willing to fight Ralligor once
I came up and scared him. Did you see how I scared him? He
didn't want to fight after that."

The wizard met the Desert Lord's eyes and assured, "I'll explain it
to her later. In the meantime, we have some preparations to make."

As they turned and walked toward the forest and the waiting
horses, Shahly rambled on, "Did you see how he just flew away?
He wasn't ready to deal with Ralligor *and* me. I think he knows his
place now."

"I'm sure he does," the wizard confirmed.

"He won't try anything like that again," the unicorn continued.

Ralligor vented a deep breath and looked toward the departing Landmaster. Preparations indeed. This was a fight to the death, one way or another.

CHAPTER 10

Darkness was less than an hour away and an annoyed unicorn carried a human princess back toward Caipiervell, a place he did not want to be.

"I said I was sorry," she offered yet again. "How was I to know they would abandon the ruins and take everything to the castle?"

He loosed a hard breath and glanced back at her. "I'm not upset with you, just the whole situation. Ever since this last spring Shahly and I can't seem to turn around in the forest without getting ourselves involved with some kind of trouble involving your kind."

Faelon could not help but feel bad about this. Slowly shaking her head she suggested, "You can let me off just before we're in sight of the castle. I can go inside and try to find something out."

"And I suppose no one will recognize you," Vinton countered. "I believe the idea is to ensure that you are not seen by those who want to see you dead."

She nodded. "I know. I just don't want to endanger you."

He whickered a laugh. "Oh, don't worry over me. Your kind is very easy to trick into not seeing what I don't want them to see."

"How do you do that?"

"The same as I would do a predator in the forest. I can use my essence to make them think they see a horse when they look at me, or a big forest cat, or nothing at all. After many seasons of practice it's almost easy."

"But they will still see me," she pointed out.

"They will see you," he assured, "but they will not recognize you. Within my essence they would see just another rider, no one that they would know or be interested in. I would take common traits and apply them over you. If I wanted to I could make you look like someone of your kind that is very old, tattered and poor and not worth a second glance. I could also make them think you are very ordinary and make you disappear into the crowds of those they've dismissed in their minds."

"That sounds almost like magic," she observed.

He nodded. "It probably does to humans, but it's something we unicorns have grown accustomed to, much as you've grown accustomed to many things that you take for granted."

"Like what?"

"Well, like walking on two legs. You really don't seem to be well made for it and I'm still not sure how you do that without falling."

The Princess shrugged. "I've never really thought about it."

"And yet you do it. I suppose it's similar." He glanced back at her again. "So do you know where to go to find out what it is we need to know?"

"I was raised there," she pointed out. "I'll find them and discover their plan one way or another."

"You don't seem afraid. That's encouraging, I suppose."

Faelon was silent for some time, clearly immersed in whirling thoughts. When she did speak again, it had nothing to do with the purpose of their journey. "I've wanted to see a unicorn since I was a little girl. I have unicorn toys, unicorn tapestries, I've even dreamed of you almost every night of my life. The best I'd ever hoped for was to just be touched by one of you, and now, here I am riding a big, beautiful unicorn to my castle, one who speaks to me and has vowed to help me."

"We need to get Falloah away from your people first," he said flatly. "If we can find someone still loyal to you, do you think you could command them to release her?"

She turned her eyes down. "No one listens to me. I feel like someone in the way more than the princess who will one day rule Caipiervell."

"Perhaps that is at the heart of your problem," he guessed. "Perhaps they need to see your strength. Most will follow someone who is strong."

The Princess shrugged. "I don't know. I never really expected to find myself as the heir and ruler. I thought I would marry and... I suppose I always expected my father to rule the kingdom. His death and my mother's were the furthest thing from me."

Vinton paced on in silence for a time, then he glanced back at her again. "So, what did you expect this first unicorn to look like?"

Torn from the memory of losing her parents, Faelon smiled and straightly answered, "Just like Shahly."

Whickering a laugh, the bay confirmed, "That's what I thought."

"What do you mean?"

He answered her very directly. "White unicorns are very rare. They are also very easily seen in the shadows of the forest. That is why your kind sees so much more of them than the rest of us, which is all the more reason for me to worry over her so."

Faelon puzzled for a moment. "Really? I thought most unicorns were white."

He laughed, "Only an unlucky few."

"Unlucky? Just because they are white and can be seen easily?"

"Our survival often depends on others not seeing us. Shahly and other white unicorns can use their essence to hide and disguise themselves, but only against threats they know about. If some predator or human sees a white unicorn in the forest they will know her right away if she doesn't see them first."

"But," the Princess continued for him, "if someone sees one colored like you they may not know what they are looking at. They may not even notice you in the shadows."

He looked back at her. "Exactly. You learn very quickly for a human."

She smiled and rolled her eyes. "Thank you, I guess." She settled herself on his back to try to get more comfortable, then she looked ahead, raising her chin as she informed, "Someone is coming toward us."

"I see them," he assured casually.

Something happened in that moment and Faelon felt something she had never experienced before. Something warm wrapped around her, something so soft and pure that she closed her eyes for long seconds as it enveloped her. It made her feel like she was somewhere between asleep and awake, a safe place long forgotten to her kind. Looking forward again, she saw many soldiers approaching and fear crept back to her.

"Don't be afraid," the stallion said to her in a calm voice. "They won't know who you are. They will look at you, but they will not know you. Just make yourself feel ordinary."

She mustered her courage and felt safe within his strange, comforting power. As the soldiers drew closer, her confidence in the unicorn grew until it was absolute and when they were only ten paces away she dared to smile and wave at them.

Of the five in the patrol, they all looked right at her, and three casually waved back.

One of the younger among them asked, "Come to see that dragon?"

Faelon's heart raced but she swallowed back her fear and answered, "Aye, and I hear it's a copious big beast."

"That it is," another soldier answered.

"It'll be answering for what it's done to Princess Faelon," still another assured as they passed. "You'd best have you a look before they kill it."

Vinton waited until they had some distance from the soldiers, in fact waiting until they were out of sight before he looked back to the Princess again. "Feeling a bit overconfident, aren't you?"

"You said not to be afraid," she reminded.

"That doesn't mean get cocky," he snarled back.

She smiled.

They encountered many more riders as they neared the castle and the same deception worked over and over.

Long ago the tree line had been cut some five hundred paces away from the castle on all sides and they exited forest and found themselves on a plain of rich grass and grain, cut down from ankle to knee high all the way around by grazing animals. Many animals grazed here from cattle to sheep to horses. Many humans tended them, mostly very young and all clearly peasants by the simple, drab garb they wore.

The road they traveled on did not approach from the front of the castle, rather it was a side road that led straight to the main road and met it halfway between the tree line and the castle. There appeared to be only one way in from this angle as this side of the castle wall lacked any gate inside.

Looking up to the battlements, Faelon observed, "I've never seen that many guards up there unless we were under attack."

"Or expecting one, perhaps," the stallion countered.

"Do they really think they can fight off that dragon?"

"That's more for you to say than me," he replied, veering off of the road and into some deep grain. "Excuse me."

As he plunged his nose into the grass and grain, Faelon hesitantly asked, "What are you doing?"

He lifted his head and looked back at her with long shoots of grass hanging out of his mouth, answering, "I'm hungry."

As he went about grazing again, she slid from his back and just watched him for a moment, then turned around and leaned back against him, staring at her castle, her home. "I've never felt as distant from Caipiervell as I do right now."

"It's right over there," the munching stallion pointed out.

"And yet so far away," she said softly. "I used to come out here with my father when I was a little girl, just to pet some of the sheep and watch the animals graze. Sometimes he would put me on a horse's back and lead me around like I was really riding." A smile touched her lips. "Sometimes I would imagine unicorns grazing out here, just like you are now. I could swear sometimes I actually saw some."

He raised his head and looked to her, meeting her eyes.

Slowly, her lips parted, her eyes widening. He whickered, and she knew he was laughing at her. Faelon shook her head. "You mean...."

"Since long before you were born," he confirmed. "You can't have such lush grazing and not expect us to find it sooner or later." He snickered again and went back about munching on the rich grains and grasses.

"So I really saw unicorns here?" she breathed

Vinton glanced at her. "You were looking for us, weren't you?"

"But I thought… I thought I couldn't see you if you were using your unicorn powers to keep me from seeing you."

"From keeping threats from seeing us," he corrected, still grazing. "Young humans like you have never been considered a threat."

"So, I might even have seen you."

"Probably," he confirmed. "I've grazed here a great many times."

Smiling, she looked back to the castle. Memories fluttered around her, memories from her earliest childhood. Such happy memories so long absent from her began to rage like a fire within her and a tear rolled from her eyes as she was once again that little girl looking for unicorns in a field of tall green grass so long ago.

Vinton looked back at her again, still chewing on a mouthful of grain as he asked, "What's wrong?"

She shook her head, softly answering, "Nothing. Everything seems perfect."

Hesitantly, he nodded, then he turned back to the lush grass.

Faelon did not know how long she daydreamed or how long Vinton grazed. What was clear was she did not notice the two palace guards, each dressed in light armor and arming shirts and thin blue tunics with the kingdom's crest in silver embroidery right in the center of the chest. She barely noticed the clanking of swords and daggers and the heavy footsteps until they were only a few paces away. Palace guards had never made her nervous before, but today she tensed up as she saw them, pushing off of the unicorn she had been leaning against. Almost in a panic as they approached, she patted Vinton's back many times to get his attention, but to no avail. He just calmly grazed away.

The guards strode right up to her, one stopping less than a pace away and folding his arms as he turned narrow eyes down to her. And older and slightly overweight fellow with graying black hair and beard and a big belly, he was tall and intimidating, just as a palace guard should be. He just eyed her for long seconds, then asked in a gruff and harsh voice, "Who gave you permission to graze this animal here?"

"Um…" she stammered, struggling to find an answer.

"Nice steed," the other guard observed. This was a younger fellow with light brown hair and mustache, but something about him seemed cruel and unsympathetic. "It would make a fine addition to the mounted guard."

"And he will," the first guard confirmed, "unless this young lady can tell us who gave her permission to graze on Caipiervell's grains."

Faelon's mind scrambled. The best way out of this was to reveal who she was. They would not feel so smug then. They could also be loyal to her uncle and kill her where she stood. Instead, Garrin entered her mind as if to return from the dead to rescue her yet again. Raising her chin slightly, she finally answered, "I am Shahly, Sir Kessler's niece. Word got to my village that he was killed in battle. Is it true?"

The two guards exchanged looks and the older one looked back down to her, his voice softer and more sympathetic as he confirmed, "It is true. Sir Kessler was felled in battle against a dragon that attacked the castle a few days ago."

Faelon covered her mouth and turned her eyes down, shaking her head as she forced tears to emerge from her eyes. "I'd hoped it wasn't true. I'd hoped it was all just a lie."

His lips tightening, the guard just stared down at her for a moment, then he assured, "He died a hero's death, maiden, and fell in battle a brave man. People around the castle and throughout the land are still telling stories of his bravery."

Covering her face with both hands, she bowed her head and nodded.

The other guard asked, "Would you like an escort into the castle?"

Vinton whickered and swished his tail. The guards could not know that he was speaking to the maiden in front of them.

Faelon shook her head. "Thank you, no. I would just like to be alone for a while."

"Very well, maiden," the older guard said softly. "I'll see to it you aren't disturbed again. I will also send word to the Knight's Hall to expect you."

"Thank you," she offered as they walked away.

When they were far enough away, Vinton raised his head and looked at them, then to the Princess. "You are Shahly now?"

"I couldn't think of another name," she grumbled back, "and I couldn't very well use my own. Besides, I got us out of that, didn't I?"

"I suppose so," the unicorn confirmed.

"It didn't help that you stopped to eat when you did, right out in front of everyone."

"I was hungry," he countered. "Besides, it's not like I've never grazed here before."

Faelon smiled and stroked his mane. "When I am restored to the throne you will always be welcome here. You have my promise."

He seemed to smile. "You'd better get back on. I think we still have a lot to do." He jerked his head up, looking toward the sky over the forest right across from the castle's main gate.

Alerted to his sudden tension, Faelon also looked, her eyes widening.

Animals and humans alike fled in all directions as a shadow fell over the grassy field.

Sweeping his great wings forward, the black dragon slammed onto the ground only fifty paces away from the castle's gate, roaring in nightmarish volume through bared teeth. He stood fully, looking over the battlements of the castle's defensive wall and growling at the fleeing guards. His eyes shifted back and forth and he finally turned his attention down to the closing timber gates. Fully opening his jaws, he belched a hellish blast of fire right at the gates and they exploded in flames and fleeing, smoldering debris. His throat and chest swelled again and he turned his attention to the top of the wall, fire lancing from his jaws as he swept his head and burned the battlements, the battlement defenses and all of those who did not flee in time.

Vinton's mouth hung open as he watched the attack and he slowly shook his head, asking aloud, "What the hell is he doing?"

Many animals and their human tenders ran by, fleeing toward the safety of the forest.

The dragon took a few steps back, sending two bursts of fire toward the palace itself and blowing holes into the stone walls in violent explosions. He glanced around at the fleeing people and animals. They were easy targets, yet he did not attack them. He raised his head slightly as his eyes found Vinton, and it was clear that he saw through the unicorn's deception. His attention did not stay on the unicorn long. Baring his teeth further, he stepped further away from the castle's gate and waited.

Faelon shook her head, barely believing what it was she was watching. "He must know that Duke Malchor and his men will come out to meet him."

Vinton confirmed, "I think that is exactly what he wants."

Moments passed and the dragon watched the smoldering, wrecked gate entrance to the castle. He leaned his head slightly, then his jaws gaped and he roared again.

Another dragon within responded, though it sounded weak and almost pitiful.

More moments passed, and finally Duke Malchor and his wizard, followed by at least fifty men cautiously emerged from the castle, holding their shields and weapons ready. More men appeared on the still smoking battlements, aiming bows and crossbows at the dragon. Some readied spears. Against this dragon, all that they could muster seemed to be in vain. Many of the men coming out to meet the dragon did not even have all of their armor on and were clearly not ready to do battle.

Blue fire engulfed the Duke's sword and he poised it to strike. The wizard, now dressed in white robes, raised his hands and seemed to suspend a glowing blue ball of light that randomly spat little discharges of lightning in all directions.

His eyes narrowing, the dragon snarled at them, but more than anything he studied them. He loosed one mighty blast of fire, deflected barely in time by the wizard, then he stood and slowly turned away, walking toward the forest as he opened his wings. Surprisingly, he casually took to the wing and lifted himself over the trees, then higher and higher until he flew out of sight.

Faelon puzzled, shaking her head slightly as she asked, "Why did he just leave? Why didn't he stay and fight?"

"He didn't come to fight," Vinton informed. "He was here to send a message. He'll be back, and when he returns blood will be shed. Let's just hope Falloah's won't be the first." He shook his head, finishing, "Reckless bastard."

"Can we tell him not to damage my castle too badly?" she asked hopefully.

The stallion glanced at her. "We can try, I suppose. I don't know how receptive he'll be, but we can try. Come on. While they're confused we can enter easily and find out what we need to know."

She got onto his back with only one try this time and they made their way cautiously toward the castle. As Vinton suspected, no one took notice of them through all of the confusion, people with buckets of water running to and fro to control the many fires that still burned, and they actually got there before the Duke and his men even returned into the castle. Pausing to graze again, Vinton and Faelon were able to overhear what was said, and what they heard did not sound encouraging.

"We can't just kill the scarlet," the wizard insisted. "Do that and there is no telling what kind of wrath he will bring down on us."

"Keeping her alive didn't do us much good today," Malchor insisted.

"She's the only reason he withdrew," the wizard informed. "As long as we have her he won't dare attack us with all his power."

"*All* his power? What do you call that?"

"*That* was simply a challenge. He is coming back for her and means to take her when he returns. We will need to be ready when he does so."

"I'm not so sure," the Duke argued. "If the castle is damaged much more or more soldiers killed we will have to deal with Tahmrof as well, and I'd rather have him in our debt than be in his. We'll have to get the red dragon away from the castle and to a battlefield of our choosing."

The wizard nodded. "He will surely go to where she is. We can ambush him as we did the red, and hope our weapons are strong enough to contend with him this time since we won't have the aid of the castle's defenses."

"They will be," Duke Malchor assured. "For the price I'm paying, they will be or that warlock will have plenty to answer for."

"Still," the wizard continued, "We'll need her far enough away so that Ckammilon can do his part without being seen. We'll also have to keep the local soldiers away from the battle until the black dragon is down."

The Duke nodded. "I'm not that worried about Ckammilon being seen. I can explain his presence away easily." He looked around, his eyes finding Faelon.

Knowing she had been seen, she prayed the stallion's deception still worked as she folded her hands before her and asked, "My Lord, can you kill the beast and make us all safe again?" She arched her brow and appeared as vulnerable and frightened as she could.

He raised his chin, eying her as if for the first time, then he nodded and assured, "We will kill it surely, and bring its head back to Caipiervell as a trophy." He turned his horse and rode back into the castle, his men following.

When they were a safe distance away, Faelon breathed a breath of relief and observed, "Well, he didn't seem to know me."

"And at least we know what they're doing," Vinton added. "While we're here, let's go in and see what else we can find out and see where they are holding Falloah."

With confusion still rampant, entering the castle was easy, but for the half panicked people who came and went, some looking for safety and others fleeing the castle. Vinton searched with his essence, finally finding the scarlet dragon and pacing toward her with a calm stride. Most people retreated from her, apparently no longer interested in being so close to the black dragon's object of revenge. As they drew closer, only a few guards and the very curious remained, and not even they could see through Vinton's deception.

Much of the inner perimeter was already lit by torch or lamplight as the sun was quickly abandoning its place in the sky and its light seemed to fade a little by the moment.

As they got closer and finally saw her lying bound to the cold earth beneath her, Vinton laid his ears flat, his lips tightening as his heart suddenly felt very heavy. Faelon slowly shook her head, not believing what she saw before her. This dragon was the same color as the one that had abducted her, but was clearly smaller. This one also did not look well. Badly injured, the dragon suffered from her wounds and the Princess could not help but feel pity for her.

The unicorn glanced around subtly, then whickered to her, "She won't last much longer here. She is very weak."

"What can we do?" Faelon whispered, sliding down from his back.

Nine guards remained around the dragon, five of them nervously watching the sky. The other four seemed to want to be almost anywhere else. Only the closest two seemed to notice Faelon's approach. She joined only a very few curious people who remained after the black dragon's visit. Two of them were determined to get drawings of the dragon. Two others engaged in some low discussion. One simply stared.

One of the guards approached, raising a hand before him as he ordered, "That horse will have to be kept away from here. It might cause the dragon to get excited."

Tearing her eyes from the dragon, Faelon looked up at him and nodded, then turned to the unicorn, her eyes begging for instructions.

He met her eyes only briefly, then he looked to Falloah and whinnied.

Turning her head as best she could, she looked pitifully at him and crooned, then a growl escaped her.

Vinton whickered back.

"Run along, now," the guard ordered. "Get that horse away from here. The beast is getting agitated. Don't need it breaking loose, now."

"I'm sorry," Faelon offered. She turned to Vinton to lead him away. Since he was wearing no tack, she simply patted his neck and hoped he would follow her toward the palace, which he did. Her lips were tight as she wandered toward the north side of the palace. This is where water collection was done. This is also where clothing and linens were washed. They air dried on long lines of twine stretched between high poles about fifteen paces from the palace. Walking through the maze of hanging linens, she found a line of commoner's dresses, those used by castle servants, and pulled a carefully selected one off of the line. It was a simple dress, light blue with a low neck line and long skirt that looked like it would be comfortable and easy to work in. From another line she took one of many white ribbons, then she turned toward the palace.

Two stone walls met and were joined by a timber wall to form an open storage area that was already half full of crates and baskets, mostly food, as well as a couple of wagon wheels, leather pieces and some tack for horses. It was illuminated by two oil lamps that appeared to have been recently filled and lit for the night, as were many of the lamps that flanked the doors into the palace. About three paces wide and about as deep, it was plenty large enough to serve the Princess' needs, but not quite large enough for the stallion.

His eyes panning back and forth as she pushed some baskets of vegetables out of the way, he asked in a low whicker, "What are you doing?"

"I'm going to change," she answered in a voice barely over a whisper.

"Change what?" he pressed.

She paused and looked back at him, answering, "My clothes."

Vinton watched as she began to remove her ball gown, curiously leaning his head.

Once again she stopped and turned her eyes to him. "Do you mind?"

"Actually, yes. It's getting dark and we need to get back."

She just stared at him for a few seconds, then insisted just above a whisper, "I need to change."

He loosed an impatient breath and conceded, "Fine, then go ahead."

They just stared at each other for half a moment.

"Do you mind?" she repeated.

"I've already told you I do, so do it if you're going to and be quick about it."

"Can you turn around?" she hissed through her teeth.

"For what?" he demanded. "If I move someone will see you in there."

"I don't want you watching me change!"

"Why?"

"Please just turn around. Make sure no one sees me."

"They aren't supposed to see me, either! Just hurry up!"

"Turn around!" she whispered with little voice.

He finally complied, turning away from her. "Fine, if it will hurry you up." The sounds of her struggling to quickly get out of her ball gown were new to Vinton and he looked back at her, asking, "Are you okay?"

No longer wearing the ball gown—or anything for that matter—she jerked the servant's dress up to her chest and hissed, "What are you doing? I'm not dressed yet!"

Vinton froze as someone walked by in the distance and he kept his eyes on her until she was gone, then he whickered back to the Princess, "If you would talk less and do whatever it is you are doing then you can get done with it!"

She hurried to gather the skirt of the dress, her eyes on the unicorn as he scanned the area again. "Just don't look back here until I say."

"You act like there's something I'm not supposed to see going on back there."

"There is! I'm trying to get dressed!" Finally mustering her courage, she raised the dress above her head and slipped it on, allowing it to drape over her. One problem: It was a little too small! "Great!" she snarled, trying to tug the dress down over her hips.

"Now what?" the unicorn growled.

"It's too tight."

"What is?"

"The dress!"

He half turned his head. "What does that mean?"

With much effort she squeezed herself into the rest of it, worrying over the way she bulged out of it around her hips and chest, and at the skirt which did not quite cover her ankles. "Oh, this won't do." She smoothed it over and straightened herself, asking, "How do I look."

Vinton turned and looked her up and down. "You look bluer."

"No, how do I look in this dress?"

"I don't know how you are *supposed* to look in that dress."

Faelon loosed a sigh and shook her head, reaching up to tie her hair back with the white ribbon. "Never mind. We need to get going. They'll be closing the gates for the night and we won't be able to get out after that."

"Ralligor destroyed the gate, remember?"

"Oh, yes. He did, didn't he? In that case they'll double or triple the guards."

Vinton half turned his head, then he turned fully and backed away, folding his essence around himself.

"You there!" a gruff woman's voice beckoned.

Faelon's eyes snapped to the heavy set woman in a similar light blue dress that approached, walking onto the lamplight from somewhere out where the hanger lines were. She wore a dirty white apron and was almost a man's height tall. Her graying black hair was worn in a tight bun on the back of her head and many seasons of hard work showed itself on her rough looking features. Faelon expected Vinton's deception to hide her as well, but discovered that it did not when the woman walked right up to her and set her hands on her hips.

With tight, angry lips, the woman demanded, "What are you doing out here like this? Those linens'll not be gettin' themselves from the line. Fetch a basket and get'em down before dark or you'll find yourself sloppin' hogs from now on!"

Feeling very intimidated by this woman, Faelon simply nodded, staring dumbly back up at her.

"Get to it!" the woman shouted, pointing at the hanging laundry.

Sheepishly creeping past, the Princess strode to the linens, turning concern filled eyes back to where the unicorn had last been seen. She could not see him either. Having seen the castle servant women collect linens before, she took a wicker basket that waited near one of the poles and reached for the first one. It came off easily and she gathered it as well as she had remembered seeing this done and got it into the basket without it touching the ground.

The woman shouted, "You'll be out here all night if ya don't hurry it up!"

"Yes, miss," she replied, reaching for the next a little faster. She was halfway down the line when she heard a footfall and expected to see the big woman when she turned, seeing to her relief the stallion behind her instead.

"What are you doing?" Vinton asked

"Why didn't you hide me?" she countered.

"She had already seen you," was his answer. "Okay, you've taken enough of those things. We need to go now."

Seeing movement toward the palace, Faelon shook her head and whimpered, "Oh, no."

Vinton also looked, seeing three more humans approach, all young women in the same light blue dresses Faelon now wore.

"Hide somewhere," she ordered. "I'll find you."

"I'll be near the gate Ralligor destroyed," he informed.

The Princess could feel the unicorn's essence again, and then he was gone. Suddenly feeling alone, Faelon continued what she had been doing as the other girls approached. Around Faelon's age, but for the tall one who appeared to be near eighteen, they talked casually amongst themselves, two of them giggling as one gossiped about one of the stable boys. They all had dark hair and one's was black. The tallest of them, the one talking, seemed to have brown hair. The third might have had red hair, but in the low light it was hard to tell. Two already carried baskets and the third, the tallest of them, reached for a waiting basket near one of the poles.

As they set about the task of reclaiming the linins, the black haired one was almost laughing as she asked, "What makes you think he'll be back for more?"

"What stable boy wouldn't want a pretty young castle maid more than once?" the tall girl countered.

"If that's so, then why would she want you?"

The other two girls giggled again as the tall one set her hands on her hips. "I'll have you know..." She turned unexpectedly, her eyes finding the Princess. "Hello. I didn't expect anyone else to be out here with this task."

Faelon swallowed hard and just kept working. "I was told to get these in before dark. She seemed rather upset that it hadn't already been done."

"When is she not upset?" the tall girl replied.

The other girls laughed and one confirmed, "Aye, I'll wager her temper is even worse than that dragon over there."

"Did you have to remind me about that?" the third complained.

"Stop whining," the tall one ordered, going back about her labor. "It's been properly lashed down and won't be coming through your window tonight."

"I'll bet that stable boy does," the third girl said right before bursting into loud giggles with the black haired girl.

"Only in your dreams," the tall girl spat. She looked over her shoulder at Faelon, informing, "You look familiar. Haven't I seen you about the castle before?"

"Um," Faelon stammered, "I just arrived today so we haven't met."

"Are you sure? I'm certain I've seen you before."

The black haired girl asked, "Whose ire did you raise to get stuck with doing this?"

"Beats slopping hogs," the Princess answered straightly.

The three girls giggled. "You sound like you know for sure."

"I've never done it," Faelon confessed. "It just doesn't sound very pleasant."

"Ever worked in the stable?" the third asked.

"I leave that to the stable boys," the Princess replied. In this simple conversing, she actually found herself starting to relax.

"Oh," the girl conceded. "I thought I recognized you *as* a stable boy."

As the girls laughed, Faelon just smiled and countered, "You might have seen me while you were living there."

"Oh!" the other two girls said in concert.

The third girl stopped what she was doing and turned narrow eyes on the Princess, setting her hands on her hips as she tried to fight back an embarrassed smile.

"Okay," the tall one cut in. "Let's get this done before Miss Ordrene comes out to remove our heads. And hurry it up, new girl. You won't last so long here working so slowly."

Faelon sighed and worked a little faster.

In short order the baskets were full and they were carrying them into a door that entered a part of the palace Faelon had never ventured into. Down a corridor and up a flight of stairs with her burden, the Princess found herself winded quickly as she was so unaccustomed to this kind of work and had not eaten anything since that morning. She was already exhausted when they reached a large room that did not look well kept, one that had linens folded and neatly stacked everywhere. Bed sheets and tablecloths were kept on separate wooden shelves while the attire worn by the castle's servants was distributed neatly on many more. Bath towels filled the shelves on an entire wall. Such things were what she had always taken for granted. How they got cleaned and folded and into the rooms where they were needed was always far fro her mind. Now, she found herself sitting on a bench with the tall girl sorting out linins to be folded, and once the folding began she did not know where to even begin and followed along as best she could.

It did not take long for the tall girl to give her an exasperated look and demand, "Have you never done this before?"

That sheepish feeling overtook Faelon again and she looked back into the girl's eyes and just shook her head.

Clearly frustrated, the tall girl sighed and grumbled, "I finally get some help and she's no idea what she's doing."

"I'm sorry," Faelon offered. For the first time in her life she was out of her element and in the place of a commoner, and she was not any good at it. But for her station, she would be just another commoner, just someone else to labor around the castle. This was a humbling realization. Before her parents' deaths she did nothing but play around the castle. After, she had done little more than wander and grieve. Now, her eyes were opening to those she had given barely a second thought to.

"Let me show you," the tall girl offered, suddenly sounding a little more patient.

As the fates would have it, the Princess was a quick study and soon found herself nearly as fast at this task as the other girls. She also found herself engaged in the gossip the other girls talked about, which mostly involved the boys who worked around the castle. Eventually, mention was made of the squires who had been assembled at the banquet for Duke Malchor and two of the girls were simply giddy as they spoke of them.

"I don't care what anyone thinks," the black haired girl admitted, "That blond boy who is squire to Sir Elwinn is the cutest of them."

"Oh, now I know you've been in the wine, Cenna," the tall girl barked. "I wouldn't have him anywhere near me."

The third girl agreed, "He's a little handsome, yet he's so creepy."

"He's not creepy at all!" Cenna defended. Looking to the tall girl, she snarled, "At least he's not a stable boy. Darree, you can't tell me you would settle for a stable boy for the rest of your life."

"No," the tall girl confirmed, looking down to what she was folding, "just for the night."

All of them laughed a hearty laugh about that.

"You wouldn't turn down a cute squire," the third girl said flatly. "Admit it."

With her eyes still on the bed sheet that she and the Princess folded, she smiled slightly and confessed, "Oh, I probably wouldn't."

"And if he talked marriage?"

Darree smiled a little more. "I can think of worse fates than being married to a knight." She turned her eyes to Faelon and asked, "What about you? Would you settle for a knight or are you holding out for a prince?"

The other two girls giggled.

Meeting her eyes only briefly, Faelon felt a choke and looked back to the bed sheet, admitting, "I'm not anymore."

The black haired girl nodded. "At least you have your vision set high. I wouldn't mind a knight or a Duke. I've seen many of the princes that have passed through here and I'd not want to wake up beside any of them."

"I've seen them, too," Cenna informed. "The lot of them was spoiled and looked down his nose and everyone around him."

"Much the way our own stuck-up princess does," the black haired girl snarled.

Darree glanced at her. "Do you mean Bellith or the one the dragon ate?"

"Well, not Princess Bellith. At least she is a little kind to us common folk. Faelon would not give you a second glance unless you were made of gold."

That stung and the Princess' lips tightened. She had no idea that the people saw her in that way and hearing it was painful.

"At least we don't have to worry about her anymore," the black haired girl went on. "She's that dragon's sour stomach now."

Cenna glanced at her. "You know, I heard she wasn't eaten. I heard she was held in an old fortress not far from here awaiting rescue."

"She can just wait," the black haired girl said flatly. "We're all the better without her." She looked to Faelon and prodded, "Wouldn't you say?"

The Princess shrugged and softly answered, "I didn't know her."

"We sure did," Cenna went on. "Couldn't even get a sharp look from her."

"Her parents both died a season ago," Darree pointed out. "We'd all be moping if that had happened to us."

"She wasn't a copious lot more pleasant before," the black haired girl complained.

"True," the tall girl agreed. "I guess it's just the place of royalty to be spoiled." She looked to Faelon and raised her chin. "So you haven't spoken of your own conquests. Did you just give up on that prince or did you see one and change your mind?"

The other two girls giggled.

Something in Faelon's chest hurt terribly and her jaw quivered as she struggled for an answer. "I... I didn't... Someone came along and stole my heart."

The three girls just looked to each other, then they turned their full attention on the Princess. When she did not elaborate, they all approached and the tall girl nudged her, ordering, "Go on. Don't leave us suspended so."

Faelon found she could not look at them. Her eyes were on the folded sheet she still held and she answered without thought or reason. "He… I was…." She shook her head, trying to find the words for them. "He whisked me away in the night and saved me from an uncertain fate."

All of the girls' eyes were wide and they leaned toward her.

"And then what?" Cenna prodded.

Taking a deep breath to collect herself, the Princess finally continued, "He took me on his horse deep into the forest. He found a place hidden in the trees so that the men who were looking for me would never find me. He made a bed and kept me safe and warm all night."

Another moment of silence passed and Darree asked, "So, how was he?"

Faelon finally smiled a little, and shook her head. "I don't know. He was the perfect gentleman and—and just… He didn't try to take advantage of me. He just held me and kept me warm. He protected me all night."

Cenna covered her mouth, shaking her head as tears filled her eyes.

"That is the sweetest thing I've ever heard," the tall girl said softly.

"What is his name?" the black haired girl asked.

As tears finally rolled from her eyes, Faelon simply answered, "Garrin."

The girls exchanged looks again and Darree informed, "I've seen him before. Wasn't he Sir Kessler's squire?"

Faelon nodded.

The tall girl went on, "Oh, I'm so sorry. I heard about what happened."

"What happened?" the black haired girl asked, almost demanded.

"He went with Sir Kessler and that dragonslayer to fight the dragon. He was killed with his knight when the other dragon attacked them."

"No," the Princess corrected, "he wasn't." She was fighting hard not to cry.

The girls looked to her again.

All of Faelon's strength drained and she dropped the sheet and raised her hands to cover her face, sinking to her knees as the pain from that morning surged forth once again. The wound stung anew as if a sword had been rammed into her chest and she could not control the avalanche of sorrow that poured from her.

The other girls knelt down beside her, trying to reassure her, but she could not be consoled.

Many moments later she finally mustered enough strength to stop crying, and as Darree put her arms around her, she leaned into the tall girl to hug her back. The other girls also embraced her. Slowly, and with the help of the other girls, the Princess stood as best she could, then turned and sat on the bench, raising a hand to her eyes as she offered, "I'm sorry."

"Don't be," Darree insisted. "You've nothing to be sorry for."

The black haired girl asked, "If he didn't die with Sir Kessler, then what happened to him?"

Faelon found her courage taxed, but managed, "He was betrayed. He fell defending me, and fought to his last breath."

"Defending you from whom?" the tall girl questioned.

Wiping tears from her cheeks, the Princess looked into Darree's eyes and shook her head. "Someone we thought we could trust. Someone who betrayed Caipiervell."

Her eyes narrowing, the tall girl breathed, "What?"

"We thought we could trust him," Faelon whimpered. "He killed Garrin. He was going to kill me."

Darree slowly stood and backed away, shaking her head, her wide eyes locked on Faelon's. "This can't be."

The other girls turned to the tall girl.

"What is it?" Cenna hesitantly asked.

"I thought I recognized you," the tall girl breathed.

Her own eyes widening, the Princess' lips parted as if to speak, yet she could not. She had been discovered in a weak moment. Now, everything was in jeopardy.

The black haired girl looked to Faelon, then to the tall girl and demanded, "You recognize her from where? What's going on?"

Darree breathed with some difficulty and finally knelt, her eyes on Faelon's as she slowly shook her head, not sure what to say.

Cenna's eyes also widened as she pointed at the Princess and almost whimpered, "You mean this is...."

"That's impossible!" the black haired girl shouted, backing away. "Princess Faelon is dead. The dragon ate her!"

Faelon looked up to her and shook her head. "It was a plot hatched by my uncle."

"Prince Tahmrof," Darree breathed. "I'd heard talk around the castle, but..." She stood and looked to the other girls. "I can't believe I'm saying this, but if it's true we need to protect her."

"Protect her?" the black haired girl demanded. "This isn't her!"

"Keep your voice down!" the tall girl hissed.

Faelon finally stood. "It's true. I am Princess Faelon. I have to let them believe that I am dead. If discovered I will be killed."

The other girls exchanged looks that told the Princess that they did not know what to believe.

"I can't prove it," Faelon went on, "not until my uncle has been dealt with. Please don't reveal me."

Suddenly very uneasy, the black haired girl stepped toward her, her eyes on the floor as she tried to say, "About what I said earlier—"

"You spoke from your heart," the Princess interrupted.

The black haired girl's eyes snapped to her.

Shaking her head, Faelon took the girl's hands and continued, "I didn't know people saw me so. It's not the kind of thing anyone will come out and tell a princess. You spoke from your heart and I'll be grateful for it." She winked and finished, "For once."

The black haired girl smiled just a little.

Faelon glanced around at them, something solemn in her young features as she informed, "I need to go. Someone is waiting for me."

The large woman, clearly the overseer of this group, entered the room and set her hands on her hips, bellowing, "So *this* is why nothing gets done!"

All of the girls spun to face her.

"And to think I was actually expecting some progress tonight," Ordrene ranted on. "I took you girls in to work for this kingdom, not stand around and gossip the night away. Get these baskets folded. No one eats until you are finished."

"Yes, miss," Darree confirmed with a nod. "I will see to them. I'm sorry it wasn't already done." She looked to Faelon and ordered, "We need those line clips from the last of the hanging line. Take a basket out and fetch them at once."

Fighting back a smile, the Princess nodded to the tall girl and acknowledged, "At once." She could not meet the large woman's eyes as she slipped by her.

"Stop," Ordrene commanded.

Faelon froze where she was, too terrified to turn around, but finally managed it and faced the large woman.

Ordrene took a small basket from a shelf near the doorway and tossed it to her. "It might be easier than trying to carry all of those in your pockets. Now hurry or I'll feed you to that dragon out there."

Nodding to her, the Princess turned and fled the room, racing down the corridor. As she got outside, her mind had shifted and she found herself concocting ways to get even, but she quickly dismissed such thoughts, for the moment, anyway.

She hurried to the hanger lines and dropped the basket there, then made her way to the main gate, pausing as she saw that the guards had doubled. With tight lips, she turned back toward the palace, stopping right at the wall near a sealed and well lit doorway. How to get past her own palace guards would be a problem. She did not notice how empty the courtyard was. No other people were outside the palace but for her and the guards at the gate.

A very old woman approached and the Princess moved aside to allow her to enter. Her mind was still very much on how to escape and not on the woman who neared.

"Still alive, I see," the old woman said in her ancient voice.

Faelon finally looked to her, her brow arching and her lips parting slightly at the appearance of this ancient person who stood less than a pace away. Bent from age and much shorter than Faelon, she had a long nose and very old grey eyes. She squinted, trying to see clearly. Wearing a heavy grey dress and a black wool cloak that seemed to be way too hot for this time of the season, her body trembled beneath and she held onto a short walking stick with twisted and crooked fingers. Little skin on her showed, and with good reason. Much of her was covered with spotty sores, many on her hands that had bled recently.

Her eyes scrutinized the Princess, looking her up and down and she continued, "Shouldn't be. Should be dead. Should be rotting."

Backing away, Faelon was stopped by the cold stone wall behind her. The horror in her eyes was clear. When the old woman raised a hand to her face, she shied away, begging, "Please, just leave me alone."

"Would be doing the land good to kill you now," the old woman went on. "Give you to that doomed dragon. Let her end you before it's too late."

Faelon slipped away and retreated. "I'm not who you think. I'm just a servant girl from the castle." She grasped her skirt as if to show the old woman and said, "See?"

Pursuing, the ancient woman scoffed, "No servant girl in there. You can't hide from me inner eye, Princess. Your death must bring order to the land, yours and that beast over there. Seen it in the water, I have. You care for more than yourself, you put the blade through you own breast."

Shaking her head, Faelon breathed, "Please, just leave me alone."

Someone grasped her from behind and she shrieked, trying to pull away until she heard the wizard say, "She'll have her end in her own time, but not for many seasons."

The old woman's eyes narrowed and she pointed a shaking, twisted finger at him. "You know as well as I the fate of the land, wizard. The dragon and the girl must die. It must be. It will be or they'll doom us all. You know it."

"I know no such thing," the wizard countered.

"It's your own doing," the woman cackled. "You've brought doom to the lot of us!"

"Of course I have," he assured with a patronizing tone. "I've brought long, hard winters, the wrath of dragons, and your own deep wrinkles."

The ancient woman snarled, showing very few teeth left in her mouth. "You're the heart. It can only be stopped with her death and the dragon."

The wizard's eyes narrowed. "If that dragon dies then this kingdom and every one of us will be doomed before sundown tomorrow. Look into your enchanted water again and see if you can see something accurate this time."

She pointed at him again, warning, "You've brought us this doom, you and yours. Interfere with what is to be and your end will come before winter."

"I'll take my chances," he chided. "Now run along and hobble back under your mushroom."

"Fah!" the old woman scoffed as she slowly turned and limped away.

Still trying to catch her breath, Faelon looked over her shoulder and up into the eyes of the wizard, feeling some comfort there.

He smiled at her. "Don't listen to that senile old witch. She stirs a cauldron of mischief wherever she goes. Come along, now. Let's get you away from this place."

As he took her under his arm, she walked with him and said aloud, "I wish I could just go up to my own bed."

"I know you do," the wizard assured. "Perhaps tomorrow night. I'll take you to some place comfortable, though, no worries."

"How did you know to find me?" she asked.

"Vinton mentioned that something had gone wrong, that you had been put to task by someone who did not know you, so I thought I would do something to help."

She grew more and more nervous as they approached the heavily guarded gate, but the wizard remained perfectly calm and strode right toward them. When one of them approached, he simply held his hand out and said, "It would seem I came an hour late. That dragon left his mark and went on."

"That he did," the guard confirmed, taking the wizard's hand. "After the other one, we think. Prince Tahmrof has ordered that no one is to be in this part of the courtyard. You have business here?"

"I once served King Elner," the wizard replied.

"Did you, now?"

"Many seasons ago," the wizard confirmed. "I heard about the incident with the dragon and thought I'd lend my talents. If you mean to do battle with the Desert Lord then you'll need every scrap of help you might muster."

"Have you spoken to Duke Malchor?" the guard asked suspiciously.

"I answer to the throne of this castle," the wizard informed, "not to a wandering dragonslayer who has brought this dragon's wrath to your door."

The guard looked to Faelon, not recognizing her as she wisely kept her head bowed. "And where would you be going with this girl?"

"She's on loan from Prince Tahmrof. My services will cost him more than gold."

Nodding, the guard agreed, "Whatever it takes to rid us of this menace, but for now you must leave this part of the castle. Go on through and enjoy her, sorcerer."

"Wizard," the wizard corrected. "There is a huge difference in the disciplines." He walked past the guards and out the gate, bidding, "Good night and good morrow to you all. You'd better rest up. Tomorrow will prove to be an eventful day."

With Faelon still under his arm, he strode into the darkness outside the castle without fear. An unknown time later they finally got to the forest and the Princess grew even more nervous, clinging to this man she barely knew for protection against the unknown and unseen horrors of the forest night.

Hoof beats from one side drew her attention and she could barely make out the form of a horse in the darkness, but when this horse spoke, she understood.

"I see you found her," Vinton observed.

"And so did someone else," the wizard confirmed. "We have preparations ahead of us, like figuring out how to get Falloah out of there."

"They don't mean to keep her in there," Faelon informed. "They said something about taking her to a battlefield of their choice and using her to draw the black dragon to them."

"As I suspected they would," the wizard said flatly. "Did they say where?"

"Just somewhere away from the castle," she answered. "They don't want people seeing someone called Ckammilon. I don't know how he's involved."

The wizard stopped.

Vinton observed, "That sounds like a dragon's name."

"It is," the wizard confirmed. "Faelon, are you certain of the name?"

"Yes," she replied. "I thought it was an unusual name."

"Where are the horses?" the wizard asked.

"They're with Shahly in the forest."

Nodding, the wizard said, "That will give us some time to collect our thoughts before morning. That is when they are most likely to make their move. We must be at the ready."

Vinton looked to him. "I should tell you that the safety of Shahly and Falloah are foremost in my mind."

"As they should be. It is in mine as well."

"We'll have to find some way to get that black dragon of yours to control himself or he could likely get someone killed."

"I have ways of calming him. His rage is not entirely out of control yet."

"He's still too reckless."

The wizard nodded, softly admitting, "I know." He turned his eyes up, faintly hearing something approaching from the night sky, and feeling a powerful presence with it.

CHAPTER 11

The pain was awful and constant. There was no relief from it, even in her thoughts.

Falloah clung to one hope and one alone, the hope that her *unisponsus,* her one chosen would come for her soon. She also knew that the humans who surrounded her would kill her before he could get her away from them. That dragonslayer might also have attained the power to kill the Desert Lord. For this reason, she hoped he would not come. It only left her with an appetite for revenge, and that taste in itself was a bitter one.

The shackles and heavy chains that held her were hard, cold and uncomfortable. Moving even slightly as she had to lay more comfortably had rubbed the steel through her skin in places, leaving raw and painful wounds beneath. She had never known such suffering and prayed it would end soon in rescue or death.

She moved her head slightly, trying to bring her jaw from something sharp. Turning her eyes to the ever constant guards, she noticed them missing. They had not been absent since she awoke in this cage. Something about that was a little comforting, but even more frightening.

Still, their absence was a relief and she drew a long breath, enjoying the smell of air with little human stench.

Glancing around, she noticed there were no humans in eyeshot. Even the windows of the palace were closed and blocked. Something was wrong.

She sensed movement overhead, powerful wings cutting the air and descending toward her, but not wings she knew. Her eyes widened and turned down.

The white dragon settled gently onto the ground nearby, taking his time as he folded his wings and stretched his muscles. Slowly, he took a couple of steps toward her, folding his arms as he stared down at her as if she was his fallen prey.

Falloah turned her eyes away, not wanting to see him.

"You were offered food and water," the white dragon observed. "Why haven't you taken it?"

She did not answer.

"It's almost over," he assured. "You don't have to be a victim in all of this."

She loosed a breath, making sure he heard it, then she weakly growled back, "Live as your mate or die, Ckammilon? What's the difference?"

"Life or death is the difference," he snarled.

"You have a short memory."

"I remember plenty, Falloah. You need to understand that the land is changing. You can be part of that change or you can be swept aside as Ralligor will be."

"Did your human keepers tell you that?" she taunted.

He growled and dropped to all fours, bringing his nose as close to hers as the timber cage would allow. "Listen, Falloah the Scarlet. You have little time left. Your life is in *my* hands now, not his."

"And whose hands hold your life?" she countered.

"My own," he growled.

"Until someone tears them from you." Falloah finally turned her eyes to him. "Even if you do manage to defeat him, are you forgetting about someone else?"

"We haven't forgotten," he assured. "He is very much a part of our plans."

"Your plans," she said almost in a laugh. "You mean you and your human keepers."

"I have no keepers, Falloah."

"I am to believe that they follow *you?*" This time she did huff a laugh. "You're a big pet, Ckammilon, nothing more."

His lips rolled back, baring his many long teeth.

"You still don't impress me," she snarled back. "You never have. Just remember that when you go into battle with Ralligor your life will be at its sunset."

"His will!" the white dragon roared, standing fully.

"Aren't you supposed to be quiet?" she asked. "We wouldn't want anyone knowing the truth about you, would we? What would your master do if he knew you were here?"

"Malchor knows I'm here," Ckammilon replied, "and he's not my master. He is nothing without me."

"Nor you without him," she pointed out. "You aren't ready for Ralligor. You and your humans will all die when you meet him."

One of his eyebrows cocked up. "Don't be so sure, Falloah the Scarlet. The magics we have now are more than a match for him. They are magics born of the blood of unicorns."

Falloah looked away from him, finally knowing fear for her powerful mate.

"Compliments of our allies," the white dragon continued. "I assume you remember them and the power they wield? Do you?"

"I remember," she confessed.

"Despite Ralligor's interference," Ckammilon continued, "they have grown in strength and with us as their allies they cannot be stopped from bringing order to the land."

"You're a pawn," she observed softly. "You're just a pawn."

"This isn't chess, Falloah."

"Isn't it?" She turned her eyes back to him. "You, Malchor, this wizard, this warlock, all of these humans... You're all pawns. You're just too involved with the rewards you've been promised to realize it."

He sighed and turned his eyes up. "Very well, Falloah. Pawns we are." His eyes slid back to her. "But we are pawns with more than enough power to rule the land as it needs to be ruled."

She raised a brow. "You speak just like your human keepers, Ckammilon. It's no wonder you can't seem to live with other dragons."

He glared back down at her for long seconds, then he reached into her cage and grabbed the chain that bound her wrist, yanking hard on it.

Falloah closed her eyes and trumpeted in pain, her claws curling inward.

"See there?" he mocked. "Who is the pawn now? I decide how much pain you feel. I decide whether or not you can go free."

She trained her narrow eyes on him. "Only because your master says you can."

"You're running out of time," he snarled. "Join us or die, Falloah. This is the last time I will offer."

"You are more human than dragon," she hissed back. "I will die, Ckammilon, and I will die horribly. I will be in such pain that you cannot even imagine. I will suffer like no other dragon has. But hear this and remember. I will die with satisfaction you will never know. I have known the life of a free dragon, one loved by one who chose me so long ago. You will never know the freedom I do."

He turned and strode away. "You don't look free right now, do you? How will you enjoy it from in there?"

"You're right, Ckammilon," she spat back. "I'm no more free than you are."

He stopped.

"You never have been," she taunted. "You've never been accepted by a Landmaster, or any dragoness who's ever seen you. The most I could ever feel for you would be pity."

Slowly, the white dragon turned, his scaly lips peeled back from his teeth as he turned deadly eyes on her. "I will be Landmaster here within the month. Perhaps you should think about that when you feel pity for me."

"Well," she sighed, "at least you still have a sense of humor."

He turned and strode back to her, reached into the cage once again and took the dead sheep meant for her out. As he turned away again and flung it out into the courtyard, he snapped back, "Who is in need of pity now? Enjoy your death, Falloah."

"Oh, I will," she assured. "I will enjoy it very much, especially knowing that yours won't be far behind mine."

Ckammilon hesitated, then he opened his wings and swept himself into the night sky.

Once again, Falloah shifted to get comfortable, wincing as the chains and shackles rubbed on raw and torn flesh. Finally getting herself somewhat settled, she closed her eyes and waited, a certain sense of satisfaction within her. She knew that there were those on the outside plotting to free her and that this dragonslayer and his men and pet dragon were to pay a horrible price for her captivity. She did not stir as she heard someone else approaching her timber cage. She just opened her eyes and stared forward. She did not have to look to know who it was who came to see her this time.

Duke Malchor leaned against a timber of her cage, staring blankly at the dragon within. His wizard stopped beside him. Neither spoke for some time.

It was the Duke who finally spoke first. "He departed in quite a huff. Doesn't look like things went well."

"You expected them to?" the wizard questioned.

"Truthfully, no. I couldn't very well deprive him of the chance, though. He's too important to our plans."

"What about this dragon?"

"I suppose we know of her position and she seems to be of status among her kind. Will you be able to restore her once this is all over?"

The wizard nodded. "I think so. Swaying her, on the other hand, will not be so easy."

"We'll deal with that when the time comes," the Duke sighed. "What of the spells to attack the Desert Lord?"

"They'll be finished by morning. He won't know how to repel them, wizard trained or not. Even dragons have their vulnerabilities."

"Let's hope the warlock can find his."

"A unicorn's essence is something no dragon can withstand." He turned his eyes to the Duke and asked, "How did you acquire that, anyway?"

The wizard got but a glance from the dragonslayer who simply answered, "I got it from someone who chooses to remain anonymous. That is all I will say."

Nodding, the wizard replied, "Then I won't press the issue." He turned to walk away, saying, "We should make sure she doesn't lose too much more strength. If she's too far gone then I won't be able to restore her, and I'm certain Ckammilon would be rather irked about that."

Malchor stared at Falloah a while longer, then he turned and followed the wizard.

A few moments later the guards returned. Their presence seemed to drive away her feeling of hope. Falloah slowly closed her eyes and retreated into her memories of her Ralligor.

CHAPTER 12

The eastern horizon was aglow with the light of the coming sun and already time was running short. There was so much to do, such unknown ahead. The coming battle was one that humans would write about for centuries, one that would be the thing of legend, and yet at the moments before dawn only one concern haunted a stallion unicorn.

He stood at the edge of the tree line, looking down at the white form that was curled up in the grass. Shahly had never been one to wake early and this day would prove to be no exception. Lying curled up beside her was the Princess of Caipiervell. She was covered with the wizard's cloak and pressed up as closely as she could be against the white unicorn's side. The cloak and unicorn were both covered with morning dew that glistened in the dim light.

The wizard approached, folding his arms as he also looked down at them, observing, "They'll sleep until high sun if we let them."

Vinton shook his head. "Is it the nature of mares of all species to sleep so late?"

Smiling, the wizard shrugged. "Well, Shahly, Faelon, Falloah... It would seem to be. Perhaps we should wake them."

With a glance at the wizard, the stallion bent to Faelon and nudged her ever so slightly with his nose.

She blinked back to consciousness, clearly from a deep, sound sleep. Drawing a deep breath and reaching her arms over her head to stretch, the Princess seemed to awaken fully and rubbed her eyes, then she looked around her, trying to get her bearings.

The wizard smiled pleasantly and greeted, "Good morning, Faelon. I trust you slept well?"

She nodded, then turned to see Shahly still asleep beside her. Slowly, hesitantly, she reached up to stroke the unicorn's mane. Shahly did not stir and just slept soundly. Faelon's hand drifted to the unicorn's spiral and she gingerly ran her fingers to the point. "Am I truly awake?" she asked almost in a whisper.

"You're awake," the wizard assured.

Vinton added, "And she should be."

Turning her eyes to the stallion, the Princess arched her brow as she saw him, admitting, "I had hoped it was all just a dream, and I hoped it was not."

The bay unicorn leaned his head. "That's a little confusing, but then I'm getting used to that in your odd race."

She smiled and slowly pulled the cloak from her, handing it to the wizard and taking his hand. As he helped her up, she looked back down to the sleeping white unicorn and bit her lower lip, smiling as she observed, "She looks so peaceful and innocent."

Vinton glanced at her, then bent his head to the white unicorn and whickered in her ear.

She stirred ever so slightly.

The stallion whickered again, and she simply took a breath and did not awaken. He snorted, then bit her ear.

With a sharp whinny, Shahly kicked and finally sprang to her hooves, stumbling sideways and shaking her head as she snorted and tried to get her wits about her. Finally looking around her, she noticed the sun was not up and actually looked a little upset as she turned her eyes to the stallion, complaining, "It isn't even dawn!"

"We have much to do," the stallion countered. "You can't sleep until high sun today."

Huffing a breath, Shahly shook her head again, her mane flailing in every direction, then falling evenly to the sides of her neck when she stopped. With half open eyes, she wandered to her stallion and nuzzled him, running her nose along the side of his neck, and he did the same.

Tears filled Faelon's eyes as she watched and she raised a hand to her mouth. "They're so beautiful."

The wizard smiled. "Yes, they are." He raised his chin and summoned, "Vinton, we should all eat something and find Ralligor."

His eyes closing as he nuzzled his young mare, the stallion nodded, finally saying, "There is a fruit tree a few paces past those trees behind you."

Shahly jerked her head up and looked at him. "What kind of fruit?"

"I don't know," the stallion confessed, "fruit. Sweet green orbs."

The white unicorn walked around her stallion and made her way to the trees behind the wizard, mumbling, "Good, I'm really hungry!"

Looking to the wizard, Vinton asked, "Where will we find the black dragon?"

"We'll go back to the river," the wizard replied. "He'll have plenty of room to land near the bank where there are no trees."

"That's going to be awfully close to the castle," the stallion warned.

"Still closer for them," the wizard countered. "I expect Malchor and his men to set up where they did before. I also expect them to be ready for him this time. They'll be expecting a stand up fight to the death. We need to deprive them of that."

Vinton raised his head. "Why?"

"As you said last night, my friend, Falloah is our first concern. If he can draw them away, we can move in and rescue her."

"She's too weak to fly," the bay unicorn pointed out.

The wizard nodded. "I realize that. It's an obstacle I'm working on."

Nodding, Vinton looked behind him where Shahly was just emerging from the trees.

The white unicorn did not look happy as she snapped, "I can't reach any of them!"

Faelon smiled and walked to her, offering, "I'll help. I was quite the tree climber in my youth." She took Shahly's side and they disappeared into the forest.

"How quickly they grow up," the wizard observed. "I still fondly remember the little girl who was so amused at the tricks I would perform for her. Now she is fighting for her kingdom and the freedom of a dragon she does not even know."

Vinton paced to him and said, "She's changing, and finally learning her purpose among her people."

Glancing at the unicorn, the wizard smiled. "I sense a certain fondness for her in you now. I don't recall it being there yesterday when you left with her to find that old fortress."

The stallion whickered a laugh. "You know how we unicorns feel about those with pure hearts. She dreamed of my kind from the time she was very young and said she dreams of us even now. She even told me that we are free to graze the land around the castle openly once she wins her status back."

With a nod, the wizard confirmed, "Yes, she's always had a giving heart. A pity more people of her station don't. Should we claim a few of those apples before they eat them all?"

Vinton walked with him toward the trees. "You know Shahly pretty well, don't you?"

Spirits among them were high, but not even a league away one heart felt such turmoil as never before. With half of his heart held prisoner, the other half slowly withered.

Ralligor lay by the riverbank where he expected to meet the wizard and unicorns. He had been there since sundown, close to the castle and the scarlet dragon that was so much a part of him. He had not slept the entire night. He stared toward the castle where he knew Falloah was held captive as if to see her through the league of forest and stone walls that separated them. Fatigue would have a firm grip on most creatures, but this dragon's rage kept him fresh. The teachings of the *wizaridi* dictate that a student of the craft must be separate from such brash emotions, that the power is best channeled and wielded with a clear mind and a pure heart. He could not clear his mind or quiet his heart. His heart burned within him. The dragon that he was had urged him to attack all night, while the wizard within him urged caution. Only Falloah's safety gave strength to the cautious wizard that he was. Still, the struggle continued.

The sun finally broke the horizon behind the trees, partly masked by the clouds that slowly rolled in from the West. A battle was to come, a fight of legendary proportions. He had done battle with humans calling themselves dragonslayers before and had killed them all, but none held the power this one did, and none before had held his mate.

Unwittingly, he had lain in clear view of the road to Caipiervell all night, only twenty paces away. While this was accidental, he simply did not care.

As the sun climbed, he was alerted to the approach of riders and turned his eyes toward the road, seeing five Caipiervell soldiers on a patrol that they had ridden without incident for many seasons. Today, that changed in an instant as they saw the gigantic form lying beside the river, and they stopped.

Ignoring them, Ralligor turned his gaze back toward the castle.

"That the one Malchor met a couple of days ago?" one of the solders asked.

"Must be," another guessed. "You think it's dead?"

"I ain't going down there to find out."

"Well, it ain't moving. Must be dead."

"Go down closer and see if it's breathing."

"Do I look like an idiot? I ain't going close to that thing! Go yourself!"

"I'm your commander. You do as I say."

"Then you can lead someone down there. I ain't going."

"You some kind of coward?"

Their bickering began to wear thin the black dragon's patience and his brow lowered slightly.

"Just go down and have a look."

"You know, I think it's breathing. Do you think the Duke wounded it and it's come here to die?"

"If that's the case then we could be heroes if we finish it off. Go down there and see if you can get a sword in its skull."

"*That* ain't gonna happen. Take your own sword down there."

"Should we go back for a pike?"

Ralligor finally lifted his head, his brow low over his eyes and lower between them as he turned his massive head toward the arguing soldiers.

They suddenly fell very silent. They did not even seem to be breathing.

For a moment, soldiers and dragon just stared at each other.

"We should go," one of the soldiers suggested in a low voice.

Very slowly, they turned their horses and rode out of sight. The hoof beats grew faster as they put some distance between themselves and the dragon.

Ralligor laid his head back down, staring toward where he had been all night.

Some time later more riders happened along. There were four sets of hooves this time, and this time they actually came looking for him. Even as they rode right up to him and the two horses became agitated at his presence, he just stared toward the castle. Two riders dismounted and a familiar voice asked, "Faelon, would you be a dear and take these horses for some water."

"Of course," she answered.

The wizard walked toward his head, patting his neck as he asked, "How are you doing?"

The dragon grunted back.

"I know," the wizard comforted. "We'll have her back today, mighty friend."

"I could have freed her yesterday," Ralligor informed sharply.

Vinton whinnied, "You also could have gotten her killed yesterday!"

"Go straight to Hell, Plow Mule," the dragon snarled.

Snorting, the stallion paced forward, his gaze on the dragon's eye as he scolded, "What were you thinking? Attacking the castle like that was the most reckless and irresponsible thing I've ever seen anyone do! Were you trying to get them to kill her?"

Shahly backed away. She had never seen her stallion so angry.

Little would have been needed to rouse this dragon's temper, and the stallion had pushed well over that line.

Raising his head, Ralligor swung his jaws over the wizard, baring his teeth as he growled back, "I sent them a message and probably kept them from harming her."

"Humans are too unpredictable to do that!" the stallion shouted back. "You above all should know that! We're lucky they didn't kill her for that stunt!"

"I knew what I was doing," the dragon snarled back, "and I stand by it! *They're* lucky I didn't kill more of them!"

"If you had they would have killed her for sure! I heard them talking about it!"

Ralligor stood and turned fully on the unicorn, blasting back, "And you did what to get her out of there? Nothing, that's what! That shows me just how much her life means to you!"

"You didn't see my pride overwhelming my judgment and endangering her."

"Nor did I see you doing anything to help free her."

"Call it inaction if you will, but their rage against her is not my doing, it's yours!"

His eyes glowing red, the Desert Lord dropped to all fours and bent his neck down to bring his nose less than a pace from the bay unicorn's, his teeth bared as he growled.

A bright red glow burst from Vinton's horn and eyes as he snorted back, not wavering as this massive predator glared down at him.

This was the moment the wizard needed to step between them, and he did. Pushing their noses apart, he ordered, "Enough of this! Both of you back away at once!"

Ralligor growled again.

Vinton pulled his nose from the wizard's hand and snorted, still glaring up at the dragon.

Faelon had approached unnoticed and was shaking her head as she cried, "Please, stop! Please!"

Dragon and unicorn turned and looked at her.

Trembling, she wept as she looked to them in turn. "She doesn't want this. She wants the same thing I do, to just go home." The Princess looked to Vinton, her own pitiful eyes looking so much like those of the dragoness. "Didn't you see her? Didn't you see how she's hurt and wants to be freed?" She looked to the dragon, pitifully asking, "Can you even imagine what *he's* enduring?"

Vinton looked away from her.

Ralligor did as well, snarling, "I don't want your pity."

Faelon approached the dragon despite her fear of him and raised her hands to grasp his jaw. "I knew Garrin for only a day and when I lost him I was devastated. You were with Falloah before my parents were even born, so I cannot even imagine the pain you feel now without her."

He pulled his jaw from her gentle grip and turned away from her, his head swinging many paces away.

She just stood where she was, watching him, and finally begged, "Please, let's free her and get her to you alive."

"You have no stake in her freedom," the dragon growled.

"My heart does," she corrected.

Ralligor turned his eyes to her.

She wiped a tear from her cheek and raised her brow. "I will do whatever I can to help you, even if it means I sacrifice my life to do so."

He looked away and growled a sigh. "Well, I *am* a little hungry."

Faelon gasped and backed away.

The dragon glanced at her and scoffed, "Nah. I'll find something bigger."

The wizard smiled. "That's the spirit. At least your sense of humor is still about you. Now, I have a plan, but it will require all of us to work as one." He raised his brow at the dragon. "Can you keep your ire at bay until it's time?"

"I'll see to it," Ralligor grumbled. "If anything happens to Falloah...."

"We will all happily join you on your rampage," the wizard assured.

Faelon raised her chin and added, "Once I am restored then all who were a part of this plot to bring that dragonslayer to my castle will be brought to justice. You have my word as the rightful heir and ruler of Caipiervell."

"Which I'll hold you to," the dragon growled. He looked to Shahly and ordered, "I need you to go to the castle and let me know as soon as they move her."

Even as the white unicorn's ears perked up, Vinton stomped forward and bayed, "I don't think so! You are *not* placing Shahly in danger too!"

"Then *you* go do it!" the dragon roared back.

"Fine!"

"Fine!"

The wizard patted Vinton's neck and calmly advised, "Just go. We will await word of your findings."

He nodded, then turned to snort at the dragon once more before galloping away.

Ralligor growled back through bared teeth.

Smiling, the wizard said, "Good to see you two are getting along better." He looked toward the river and asked, "Faelon, where are the horses?"

She also glanced that way, then turned her eyes down as she answered, "They ran off when Ralligor roared so angrily. I could not hold them."

Shahly trotted to the Princess and turned to bump her with her side. "Let's go get them. On my back."

Faelon glanced at the wizard.

He smiled at her and shrugged.

"Come on!" Shahly urged. "Let's go and get them!"

Though she seemed reluctant, the Princess awkwardly climbed on Shahly's back, riding her side-saddle as the skirt was too narrow to allow her to straddle the unicorn's back. When Shahly took off running, Faelon held on as best she could.

Turning his eyes to the dragon, the wizard observed, "They all rally around you and Falloah, even those you barely know, yet the battle itself will be yours alone to fight."

Ralligor looked back at him. "I only ask that you take care of Falloah no matter what happens."

"Take care of her I will," the wizard assured. "I need you to listen, now. The plan I have may not be to your liking, but it will get Falloah out of there alive. That's all that should be in your thoughts."

Growling another sigh, the dragon looked away and nodded.

"Don't let my teachings be wasted," the wizard urged.

"I won't, *Magister*," Ralligor assured.

A scream and a splash near the river told them that the Princess was unable to hold onto the unicorn's back, and a whinny and a laugh confirmed that.

Hours of meditation were in order. The wizard had sent Shahly and Faelon up river to look for food, grapes or fruit trees, anything they could find. This was not a task of necessity, but more one to keep them busy and away from the already agitated dragon. They did not need to know this. Still, it was a productive venture and they returned sooner than they were expected to. Faelon carried quite a burden of fruit and nuts in her skirt, one that appeared to be rather heavy as she and the unicorn made their way back up the bank.

When they arrived, they said nothing as they saw the dragon sitting catlike before the wizard with his eyes closed. The wizard stood before him, staring at him with intense eyes.

"Release the burden," the wizard commanded. "Feel your strength grow from around you. Allow your *facultas* to flow through you from the land and sky. Calmness and focus will give rise to great power and strength within and without."

A soft growl erupted from within the dragon and he slowly opened his eyes. "*Magister*, I could meditate until next spring and–"

"You don't have until next spring," the wizard snapped. "You have to regain control of that dragon rage within you now. The *wizaridi* will be the key to her survival and your victory. Put thoughts of vengeance from you until the time."

Ralligor drew a soothing breath, one that growled all the way out of him. Tension was still in his eyes, but not rage.

Faelon softly informed, "We found something to eat."

The wizard turned his eyes to her and smiled. "That you did, and it looks like quite a burden for such a small girl."

"Shahly helped to lighten the weight as we walked back," she informed. "Has Vinton returned?"

"He hasn't yet," the wizard replied. "Every moment before this starts is precious."

The white unicorn approached the dragon, looking tenderly up at him as she asked, "Are you feeling better?"

Without looking at her, he just nodded.

Snorting, Shahly flatly said, "If that dragonslayer has any wisdom in him he'll release Falloah and not want to fight you again. If he's smart that's what he'll do."

"I don't think he's that wise," Ralligor growled.

The unicorn walked to him and nuzzled his forearm. "If he knew what I do, he would be much wiser and he would be afraid. He would know he doesn't really have a chance against you. He would run back to wherever he came from and never return."

"He'll be wiser soon enough," the dragon assured.

The wizard agreed, "That he will be."

Hearing fast hoof beats approaching, they all turned their eyes to the road as Vinton galloped into view.

The stallion stopped just before reaching them. His breath was short and he first blurted out, "They've moved her."

"Where?" the wizard demanded.

Glancing up at the dragon, Vinton replied, "Not far from the castle, perhaps fifty paces from the tree line. The wall and towers are crawling with soldiers and several hundred were moving out of the wall and into the field. There was plenty of activity around her when I left, but they did not appear to be making any efforts to restrain her."

"They know she cannot fly," the wizard informed.

Faelon was the first to say, "That doesn't make any sense."

"What doesn't?" Vinton questioned. "They have hundreds of human soldiers ready to attack as soon as Ralligor lands."

"She's right," the wizard agreed. "It doesn't make any sense. He would obliterate them from the air before they had a chance to fight back. Even if he was on the ground no number of men could hope to defeat him. Did you see the dragonslayer among them?"

"I can't tell one human from another," the stallion admitted, "but among the soldiers were two older humans in coverings like yours only gray."

"Two?" the dragon questioned.

Vinton looked up at him. "One on each side of a human covered in shiny metal and armed with a long spear."

"A knight," Shahly added.

The wizard's eyes narrowed. "Archers and spearmen on the towers and battlements, catapults at the ready... Everything that would make one think that they are prepared to do battle with a dragon." He turned his eyes up to Ralligor's.

Raising a brow, the Desert Lord said, "It would be a shame to disappoint them."

Smiling slightly, the wizard agreed, "That it would, mighty friend."

Vinton's eyes shifted from wizard to dragon, dragon to wizard. "Wait a second. I thought we were counting on meeting them in that field where they first fought."

Faelon added, "They wanted the fight away from the castle."

"Plans change," Ralligor informed, "but ours does not have to. If they want death to rain on them from above, then I can accommodate them."

Stepping toward him, the Princess dropped the fold in her skirt and the fruit contained within scattered on the ground. She clasped her hands and begged, "Please don't. It is not the fault of my people that they are being misled."

Ralligor turned his eyes from her to the wizard.

"Give us enough time to get into position before you strike," the wizard ordered, "and remember what we talked about."

Nodding, the black dragon opened his wings and swept himself into the air and over the trees.

Faelon strode to the wizard, grasping his arm as she demanded, "You cannot allow him to kill all of those people! None of this is their fault!"

He turned his eyes down to her and assured, "This is not a matter of fault, Faelon, and I think you've just proven yourself more than capable of sitting on the throne of your kingdom. I'm happy to see your father's compassion in you."

She blinked, slowly shaking her head.

The wizard smiled and patted her hand. "Perhaps this was not such a horrible experience for you after all, so long as you remember the lessons learned." A crunching behind her drew his attention and he looked to see Shahly eating one of the apples the Princess had dropped. "She has the right idea. We'll need all the strength we can muster for what is to come."

CHAPTER 13

Not for four seasons had the army of Caipiervell been mobilized so. With half of its force of soldiers and mounted knights in front of the castle and on the battlements, one would think they were preparing for all out war. Catapults were loaded and ready to spray boulders all over the green field. Bolts were locked into crossbows and archers stood at the ready. Repelling human invaders usually involved boiling oil and large stones to be dropped on them as they tried to breech the defenses, but these weapons would be useless against the enemy they waited for. Sharpened wooden poles were lashed to the battlements all over the castle, pointing skyward in anticipation of an attack from above. Many eyes scanned the skies in all directions and nerves were taut. All people here who were not soldiers were safely in the center bowels and catacombs of the castle itself, awaiting the inevitable.

Out in front of the main force of over two thousand men were thirty men mounted on large, powerful steeds, all wearing armor and carrying shields but for two. They wore only the hooded robes of a wizard.

The field in front of this assembled army was abandoned, but for one lonely form lying in the early morning sunlight a little over fifty paces from the tree line. Red scales would normally glisten in the morning light, but they were dull and darkened by sickness and many wounds about her were darker yet.

Falloah did not watch the sky. While she craved rescue, she also hoped that she would not see the form of the black dragon coming for her. She knew what awaited him and prayed he would stay away—and prayed death would find her soon.

Almost an hour had passed since she had been moved from the palace and left to die in the lush grass. Her entire body hurt and ached from injury and a want of food and water. She thought about using the last of her strength to rise and attack the hidden army that awaited the Desert Lord, knowing that the humans would strike quickly and hopefully kill her just as fast. It was not to be. She barely had the strength left to raise her head.

So, she waited.

What she both feared and hoped for happened in an instant.

An alarm sounded within the castle. Trumpets blared and humans scrambled to find their places and aim their weapons. Then, a horrible roar from above shook the very air all around Caipiervell. The Desert Lord was coming to meet their challenge.

Falloah turned her eyes up, seeing a dark winged form soar into view.

Ralligor swept in fast, angling toward the castle and the couple of thousand soldiers who stood ready for battle. As he predicted, panic ensued and they fled in all directions as he neared. Without warning, he veered sharply toward the forest, toward Falloah, and loosed seven bursts of fire into the trees nearby.

With fire slamming into the forest and exploding with devastating force, chaos ran amuck with those who hid among the trees, those who he was not even supposed to know about. Plans to attack the Desert Lord by surprise were now a shambles as they tried to find cover and just survive this killing onslaught.

The Desert Lord circled and blasted them again before he landed near the scarlet dragon. The humans found they did not have time to react but for the order to loose the catapults. Boulders flew randomly and sporadically from behind the castle wall, only one of them finding its target—square on the big dragon's back.

He lurched forward as the boulder slammed into his dorsal scale ridge and glanced off, and he turned an irritated snarl to the castle. Quickly gathering the limp dragoness in his arms, the black dragon turned into the wind, running toward the palace as he swept his wings and lifted himself into the sky. A few bursts of fire into the courtyard of the palace and the catapults scattered around it sent the soldiers trying to reload them scrambling. Arrows flew from everywhere, but only a few found their mark, their steel heads glancing harmlessly off of the Desert Lord's heavy scales. With one more burst of fire at the tallest tower, he turned away from the castle, heading due south to a battlefield of *his* choosing.

Barely able to lift her head or fight the passing wind, Falloah turned her eyes to her huge mate and crooned, "*Unisponsus...*"

"Save your strength," he ordered, stroking his wings for more speed. "This is far from over. I'm getting you to safety first and foremost."

"They've prepared for you," she slurred.

He glanced at her, assuring, "And I for them."

"Leave me to them," she begged. "Go back to the desert. Please, they know how to kill you."

Even as she fought for her own life, her thoughts were of him first, and this was not lost on him.

"They know how to kill you," she repeated weakly.

He leveled out and began to descend, turning his eyes tenderly to hers as he countered, "Then that's what they'll have to do."

Behind him, Duke Malchor, his wizard and the half of his men who had survived the onslaught emerged from the smoldering trees and spotty fires at the edge of the forest, looking skyward for a glimpse of their quarry.

With clenched teeth and dressed for battle with a dragon, the Duke growled, "He's craftier than I thought he was. We'll have to face him at the red's lair."

His wizard's eyes narrowed and he corrected, "He's not taking her there. He intends to meet us a league away—right where we encountered him before."

Turning his horse, the dragonslayer shouted, "Then let's accept his invitation. Signal Ckammilon that there has been a change of plan."

Landing as gingerly as he could about a league away, Ralligor gently laid his injured mate into the tall grass of the clearing where he had found her days before, right after her first encounter with this dragonslayer. "This is where it began. This is where it will end."

She cooed to him, very weak and now unable to raise her head.

Looking skyward, the black dragon scanned the heavy, dark clouds that rolled relentlessly toward the East, then he turned his eyes back down to the dragoness. "My *magister* and some friends will be along shortly. When I finish with this dragonslayer, I'll be back for you." Not waiting for a response, he turned and swept himself into the sky, flying toward a clearing not far away, a clearing where Falloah had been baited in to be killed. No innocent maidens would be needed this time. It was time to end this, one way or another.

Falloah was right to fear for him. This dragonslayer was well prepared this time. Her mate was a powerful dragon, but she had seen what awaited him and knew how they meant to attack. She had been meant to see.

Approaching riders drew her attention and her eyes shifted to the South. As she watched them approach, she knew this ordeal would finally be over.

They dismounted and the heavy riding boots of four Caipiervell soldiers slowly approached the dying dragon. These were not humans who were in any way especially brave or cowardly. They just followed the commands of those who led them.

"That wizard said we can easily spear it through one of its wounds," one advised. "That'll kill it easier than trying to get through its hide."

"I'll be taking some teeth with me," another informed.

"Worry over your trophies once it's dead," one with a deeper, gruff voice ordered. "Let's be quick about it before that big one comes back."

Falloah watched as swords were unsheathed and two of them poised long, metal tipped spears. Fearing Ralligor's return, at least they would finish her quickly.

A spear plunged into her injured side and she closed her eyes tightly, trumpeting weakly against this new wave of pain.

More horses approached and a young woman cried, "Stop!"

They all backed away, clearly surprised.

Faelon stopped her horse between the soldiers and the dragon, her eyes boring into them as she shouted, "The next one who touches her will hang the lot of you!"

Exchanging glances, the soldiers looked back up at her and one asked, "Who are you to be talking to—"

"You don't know who I am?" she almost screamed. With tight lips and a slight scowl, she slid down from her horse and approached a few steps, setting her hands on her hips as she glared up at the largest soldier and shouted "I should have your head for that?"

His eyes narrowed and he hesitantly asked, "Princess Faelon?"

"At least one of you gets to keep his head," she spat. "Now get on your horses and get back to the palace. I'll deal with you when I return."

They all exchanged glances again.

"Do as I command," she ordered loudly, her eyes shifting back and forth between the four. When they still did not comply, she snarled, "This would be treason. Are you to tell me that you are all in league with my uncle as well?"

The largest of the soldiers raised his brow. "He *is* a stronger leader. Why, I can't even be sure you aren't even some imposter." He glanced at one of the others and suggested, "Perhaps she should be left here with that dragon."

One of the other soldiers reminded, "Prince Tahmrof does want her out of his way."

She scanned them again, taking a couple of steps back. "Prince Tahmrof is not your rightful ruler. I am!" She was trying to add authority to her girlish voice, but to no avail.

Looking down at his sword, the largest soldier informed, "After your death, Prince Tahmrof *will* be the rightful and legal ruler of Caipiervell, won't he?"

She backed away a few steps more, her feet stopped by the dragon behind her. "He will die long before I do."

Turning his eyes to her, the large soldier shook his head and countered, "Don't think so." He quickly lunged and thrust his sword toward her heart.

The blade was met by a unicorn spiral and parried away. A unicorn's horn is harder than even a dragon's scales—or a steel sword.

All four backed away as Vinton positioned himself between the Princess and the soldiers, his narrow eyes on the largest of them.

The big man slowly shook his head, breathing, "This is an omen."

The man to his left scoffed, "It's a unicorn. How dangerous can it be?"

Vinton looked right at him and bored into his mind with his essence.

His eyes widening, the man backed away, then screamed as terror burst from him.

All four men turned and ran, dropping their weapons.

As they fled, Vinton turned to Faelon and asked, "Are all of your kind that afraid of spiders?"

"I know I am," she confessed. Looking down to the dragon's face, she knelt down and gently stroked her head, gently assuring, "It's okay. You're going to be okay now."

Ever so slowly, Falloah turned her eyes up to the Princess.

Shahly and the wizard emerged from the trees behind the dragoness and the wizard bade, "Well done!" He rushed to the dragoness, looking her over, and his eyes widened. "This is going to take some time." As gently as he could, the wizard pulled the spear from her, offering, "I'm sorry," as she crooned in pain again.

Everyone's attention was drawn to the East by the Desert Lord's roar only about three hundred paces away.

Vinton informed, "We don't seem to have much time."

The pole they had sunk into the ground to bind the maiden to was still there. This time it was the dragon who waited, his brow low over piercing eyes that were locked on the trees across the meadow. Standing at his full six men's heights tall with his wings fully open, he watched as the dragonslayer emerged from the trees and stopped.

As his wizard and fifty men assembled around him, Duke Malchor met the dragon's eyes with little more than confidence and contempt.

Ralligor glared back at the dragonslayer as his men got themselves organized in a wide line that spanned most of that end of the meadow. Quickly scanning their ranks, it was clear that every man he faced this day wielded enchanted weapons, not just steel and wood. Truly, this Duke Malchor was ready for him this time. His eyes panning from one end of the line to the other, the black dragon knew the wizard's strategy. It was very simple. He was expected to charge the dragonslayer while the dragonslayer's men surrounded him in a sweeping motion. He almost laughed at how simple it was, and at how this duke actually expected him to cooperate.

Holding lanced, spears and shields at the ready, the men almost simultaneously kicked their horses forward.

Ralligor slowly lowered his head and body and half folded his wings, his eyes now locked on the dragonslayer as he prepared to charge.

The fifty horses cantered at first, slowly picking up speed as they crossed the meadow. Their riders raised their weapons, preparing to strike.

His eyes sweeping across the line of advancing men once more, the Desert Lord finally bared his teeth, then he swung his jaws open and roared as he charged into battle himself. As before, his neck, body and tail were almost parallel to the ground. He folded his wings tightly to his sides as he picked up speed. Less than forty paces away he suddenly veered to his right, kicked his long stride into a sprint and opening his wings. Sweeping himself air-born for only a few seconds, he gaped and belched nearly white hot fire into the right side of the line of men, then swung around and swept his tail across their ranks. Sharp scales on the top and sides of his tail were pulled erect and sliced through shields and armor, flesh and bone as he easily dismounted nine of them. Slamming into the ground on all fours, he loosed his fire again at the six who remained on the end of the line.

Their screams and the whinnies of the horses were brief. They were incinerated quickly despite enchanted armor. In seconds, only smoldering bones and blackened metal were all that remained of them.

Ralligor stood and turned toward the remaining bulk of his enemies as they tried desperately to regroup and reform their shattered ranks.

The men in the dragonslayer's company, now only thirty-five strong, no longer seemed to be quite as brave as they were a moment ago, and many were reluctant to take their positions with him.

Ralligor charged again, loosing another burst of flame this time directly at the dragonslayer and wizard.

Men raised their shields against the flames and the wizard threw his hands up, a quick spell repelling the fire barely in time. Their ranks scattered again as the black dragon rampaged through them once more. Many did not clear his path in time.

Ralligor batted one from his horse on the way by, slammed his jaws shut around the body of another and slung him in two pieces across the battlefield. The swing of his other arm collided with the shield of another, sending him and his horse to the ground. One horse and rider were simply crushed beneath the dragon's foot.

As the dragon turned, Malchor finally brought his sword to bear on him.

Stumbling as the blue fireball exploded on his neck, the Desert Lord realized these weapons were far stronger than they were before. His sweeping tail killed two more riders and horses before they could get out of range and he turned his attention to the dragonslayer, his neck stinging from the power of the attack. He sent another burst of fire in response, then raised his hand and caught the white, lightning-like power of the wizard on a green cushion of light in his palm, more by instinct than thought.

An enchanted spear pierced the scales on his thigh and he roared as the power exploded inside of his flesh. He wrenched it from his leg, then swept his hand quickly to ward off a second. As the wizard and dragonslayer regrouped with nine of his men for another charge from almost sixty paces away, Ralligor looked to his left, seeing another knight charging him with a lance that was engulfed in enchanted blue flames. Three riders with spears were behind him, preparing to hurl their weapons. The spears they carried had the same blue flame burning from the metal heads, flames that seemed to make the steel burn red hot.

They were twenty paces away when the black dragon turned and counter attacked with a hellish storm of fire from his gaping jaws. Their armor was more effective against his fire, but not enough. Less than ten paces away from him the charred and smoking bones of the riders and the horses crumbled to the ground.

Ralligor ran over what was left, circling around the charging dragonslayer and his men.

Duke Malchor and his wizard attacked together and the dragon answered both strikes, shielding himself from the wizard's lightning as he batted the blue fireball away. All of the men had also hurled their spears and two found their marks, one exploding through the webbing of the dragon's left wing and the other piercing his upper arm on the same side, the blue fire exploding within him as before.

Roaring in pain and anger again, the Desert Lord unexpectedly charged, pulling the spear from him and throwing it back at the riders as they tried to veer from his path. The wizard got a shot in at his side, the lightning barely tearing through his armor scales and hide and burning the flesh within. The dragonslayer sliced with his sword and found the more heavily armored tail, his weapon not making it all the way through these thicker scales.

Turning quickly as he killed his way through their ranks again, Ralligor did not wait for them to reform their lines before he blasted some of the men with his deadly fire, and three more fell to the ground as smoldering ash.

Even before the Duke and his wizard and men turned fully, something slammed into Ralligor's back, ripping through his armor scales and knocking him to the ground. Stunned, he was slower to push himself up, lifting his head as he looked upon this new menace.

White scales shimmered against the green of the forest and the grey of the sky above. Powerful wings grabbed huge amounts of air as the other dragon turned and slammed onto the ground right behind the Duke and his remaining men.

As the black dragon slowly stood, he knew immediately that the white dragon before him had opened three deep gashes in his back and right shoulder, the longest one almost a man's height in length, and rivers of blood already flowed from them.

The dragonslayer and his men quickly regrouped. Ckammilon glared back at the Desert Lord, his wings half open and his claws curling for battle.

The larger of the two, Ralligor regarded the white dragon as coldly as he did the dragonslayer, and Ckammilon could see in the Desert Lord's eyes that his appearance had not been completely unexpected. Still, he had drawn first blood and, with the humans on his side, felt he had and advantage over this old rival at last.

There would be no reunion, no words between the dragons.

Ralligor's jaws swung open and a mighty roar exploded from him.

Ckammilon responded in kind.

The humans raised their weapons.

Both sides charged, exchanging fire, lightning bolts and spears.

Ralligor, with his wings folded tightly to his back, took many direct hits to his chest, belly and throat, and a few to his head. Ckammilon bore the brunt of the Desert Lord's wrath as his chest was blasted by his enemy's fire and he was almost knocked down. Once again the black dragon sliced through his human enemies and the Duke and wizard barely escaped his wrath. Half of the remaining soldiers did not.

Spinning around, the black dragon swung his tail hard and slammed it into Ckammilon's belly, doubling him over and sending him backward to the ground.

Ralligor's massive strength was truly an advantage and his armor scales protected him well, but he was wearing down, bleeding from many wounds and burned by his enemy's assaults. While they were trying to reorganize themselves and Ckammilon was down was a good time for a tactical retreat.

Blasting the dragonslayer and wizard once more with fire, he opened his wings and ran into the wind, hoisting himself aloft on powerful wings. His enemies did not have the chance to strike at him as he withdrew and, once over the trees, he veered south and flew low and fast. Already tired and out of breath from the fight, he did not want to fly far. A clearing in the trees ahead offered a good place to land and he stroked his wings forward, descending into the clearing and landing hard in the center.

Dropping to all fours, he laid his wings against the ground to relax them for a moment and worked to catch his breath. Closing his eyes, he concentrated on suppressing the pain from his injuries.

A shadow fell over the clearing and he opened his eyes, staring at the ground before him as something big landed behind him. A few more deep breaths and he folded his wings to his sides and said, "I didn't expect you so soon."

"Just came to see how the battle is going," Agarxus informed. "Doesn't seem very promising from the look of you."

Ralligor stood and slowly turned, looking up at the massive dragon as he assured, "Everything is going according to plan."

The Landmaster nodded, looking the Desert Lord over once again. "I can see that. Is Falloah safe?"

"That's the first thing I attended to," Ralligor said straightly. "She's not far from here."

"Then not far from your enemies," Agarxus countered.

Looking aside, the black dragon growled, "Ckammilon may have seen her when he flew in on me."

"Should I deal with him?" the Landmaster asked.

Shaking his head, the Desert Lord said, "No. I will attend to him *and* these humans."

"Very well," Agarxus sighed. "When you are through *attending* to Ckammilon, send him my way. I would like to have a word or two with him."

Ralligor nodded. "I will, if he's still alive when I'm through with him."

Shahly and Faelon watched with wide eyes as the wizard held his hands over Falloah. The worst of her wounds glowed an eerie blue.

Standing a pace away from the scarlet dragon, the wizard held his palms to her, his head bowed and his eyes closed. A blue light sprayed from his hands, gently bathing the dragoness in his power.

In a moment he lowered his hands and opened his eyes. When he did, the blue light faded from her.

With a deep, soothing breath, he raised his head, looking on her with a little despair in his eyes as he informed, "That's all I can do for now."

Shahly hopefully asked, "Will she be all right?"

Looking away, the wizard answered, "She will live a little longer, but I don't have the power to heal a dragon with such injuries."

"Vinton can do it!" the white unicorn declared, looking to the big bay who stood a few paces behind the wizard.

Meeting her eyes, the stallion shook his head. "My essence would kill her, Shahly. There's nothing either of us can do."

"We have to do something!" Faelon cried. "We can't just let her die!"

"Ralligor can save her," the wizard said softly. "He just has to survive this battle he's locked in and get here in time, and then find what's inside of him."

Shahly trotted to Falloah's face, holding her nose close to the dragoness' ear as she bade, "Just hold on, Falloah. Please, don't give up."

Faelon followed her, and gently stroked the dragon's head. "You heard her. Help is coming and he will make you better, then you can get your strength back with the finest sheep my kingdom can offer you."

Slowly, Falloah opened her eyes and looked to the Princess.

Smiling, Faelon assured, "Our sheep are considered the best in the land. I'll even see to it they are sheared before I give them to you."

Vinton slowly approached, assuring, "That black lizard you're mated to will be back shortly to heal you. You just hang on."

Falloah turned her eyes to the stallion, and seemed to smile ever so slightly.

When she closed her eyes again, the wizard's lips tightened and he said, "When I have my wind back I will do more, but the most I can do is prolong her life and suffering. Ralligor needs to hurry."

Raising his head, Vinton whickered, "In that case, he's going to need some help." He looked to Shahly and ordered, "Stay here with Falloah. I'm going to stir things up there a little."

Even before he turned, the white unicorn spun to him and insisted, "I should come and help you!"

He gave her a sharp look and snapped, "Shahly! You are staying here!" With that, he galloped across the meadow and into the forest on the other side.

Shahly's eyes were narrow as she snorted. "I could be of help. You don't have to treat me like I'm a foal all the time."

A moment later the black dragon landed across the meadow, not fully folding his wings as he strode toward the dragoness and informed, "Move aside. They know where Falloah is and I'm taking her to a safer place."

Still facing the dragoness, the wizard slowly raised his head and agreed, "That would be a splendid idea—if you were Ralligor."

The dragon stopped.

Faelon and the white unicorn turned their wide eyes up to the black dragon.

Snorting, Shahly's eyes narrowed and her horn burst into a bright emerald fire as she paced toward the dragon, her gaze locked intently on him.

The wizard wheeled around and raised a hand at the dragon as he belched a burst of fire at the advancing unicorn. The fire hit an invisible wall only a few paces away from her and could not reach her.

Turning her face and tightly closed eyes away from the heat, Shahly danced backward. When it was gone, she glared back up at the dragon and whinnied, "You aren't Ralligor and you aren't taking her anywhere!"

The dragon bared his teeth, his eyes glowing red as he challenged, "What makes you think you can stop me, you pathetic little unicorn?"

Shahly trained her spiral on his chest, her eyes boring into him as she snorted again and challenged, "Come through me if you can."

The dragon snarled and strode toward her.

Ralligor slammed talons-first into the other dragon, knocking him violently across the meadow and into the waiting trees on the other side where he slammed into them hard enough to knock one over.

Sweeping his wings forward, the Desert Lord set down right in front of Shahly, his eyes locked on his fallen enemy. Looking down at the unicorn, he nodded once to her.

She nodded once back, whinnying, "We showed him, didn't we?"

"Yes we did," he agreed, looking back to see the other dragon staggering from the trees. "Go stand by Falloah and ward him off should he get past me."

She whinnied back to him, then looked at the other dragon and sneered at him, flicking her tail as she trotted back to the waiting wizard and dragoness.

His scales fading back to white, Ckammilon raised a hand to his bleeding head as he got his wits back about him, then he turned his eyes to the Desert Lord and growled through bared teeth.

Ralligor growled back and advanced on him. This fight was one on one now.

"You can't win," Ckammilon snarled.

His eyes narrowing, the Desert Lord poised himself for battle and challenged, "I've been told that many times, rodent. I hope the forest scavengers like the taste of you."

Ckammilon slowed his advance and began to circle. He was making Ralligor turn his back toward the forest across the meadow. That was the direction the dragonslayer was in. That was where the dragonslayer would emerge. With his brow held low, the white dragon seemed to smile as he heard hoof beats coming from the forest and he said, "It is time for you to die, Ralligor."

A streak of red light lanced right past the Desert Lord's arm, barely missing him, and slammed into the white dragon's shoulder, spinning him half way around in an explosion of ruby light.

As Ckammilon roared in pain, Ralligor charged, slamming his claws into the side of the white dragon's head. The Desert Lord pursued, striking again and spinning his enemy around, then he lunged and slammed his jaws shut at the base of the white dragon's neck, his teeth plunging through Ckammilon's armor with a sickening crunch. Roaring in pain, the white dragon struggled to free himself, finally ripping away and staggering toward the forest as he spun to face his enemy.

Ralligor stroked his wings and kicked hard with both legs, his talons slamming squarely into Ckammilon's chest and sending him back-first into the trees again. Ckammilon bounced off of one big tree and hit another, finally crumpling to the ground.

With his eyes on the white dragon as the dust settled around him, Vinton galloped to the black dragon. He stopped a few paces away and looked up at him, scolding, "Do you want to move over a little next time?"

The black dragon responded with a sour look and snarled back, "I see you broke loose from your plow again."

Vinton looked him up and down. "Wow. You look like hell."

Ralligor grunted back and they both turned and strode toward Falloah.

"I disrupted them," the stallion informed, "but I don't think they'll be delayed long."

"I'm not surprised," Ralligor growled back.

"You're welcome, dung-head."

When Ralligor reached Falloah, something in his eyes changed. Confidence seemed to leave him. He looked her over, looked at her wounds, then placed a hand on her back. An emerald glow enveloped it and part of her and a similar emerald glow rimmed his eyes. His jaw tightened and he backed away a step, looking down to the wizard in what appeared to be a plea for reassurance. "You can help her, can't you?"

"I can do no more," the wizard answered bluntly. "It is entirely up to you now."

The dragon looked behind him, right where he expected the dragonslayer and his men to emerge from the forest any second. "*Magister,* my studies in the *medici facultas* are incomplete. I could kill her if I—"

"Ralligor," the wizard interrupted, "she will die if you do nothing. You are the last hope she has to defend her as you are her last hope to live."

The black dragon looked away. "I—I've taken a toll on them, but they are still very much a threat. Perhaps I should attend to them first."

"She won't be alive when your battle ends," the wizard informed straightly. "If you want her to survive, then you must act now. Heal her, mighty friend. Find the power and the courage within you to do more than fight today. Find the wizard inside of you who will save her life."

His confidence clearly shaken, Ralligor shook his head and replied, "I'm not sure I can, *Magister*. What if I... If I do something wrong? I could kill her."

"Then she will die," the wizard said flatly. "We should leave her here so that they can finish her quickly and end her suffering and her pain."

The Desert Lord's eyes found the wizard master, then turned back to his mate. Hesitantly, he placed his hands on her, ever so gently, and a green light sprayed from between his fingers.

Falloah tensed and flinched, crooning in pain.

Ralligor withdrew his hands and backed away, shaking his head. "I—I can't, *Magister*. I don't have the power. I don't know how to call upon what... I don't know what to do!"

"Clear your mind and emotions," the wizard ordered. "Find the power and the confidence within yourself."

"But what if I kill her?"

"You won't, mighty friend, but you must act quickly. Her life force is weakening by the second."

"Ralligor," the stallion prodded, "you can do this. Just heal her."

Even encouraging words from an enemy did not seem to stoke the fires of his confidence. Once again, and reluctantly, he laid his hands on her, the emerald spray from between his fingers returning as he tried to call upon his power once again. He could feel that her strength was almost gone, that her life force held on only by one hope, and that he could not give her what she needed. When she crooned in pain, he retreated from her once again and looked away. Such despair he had never experienced. With all of this power at his disposal, he simply could not use it.

Shahly stepped forward, looking tenderly up at the black dragon as she said, "Ralligor, just love her. Don't you see? Your love for her is all the power you will ever need."

The black dragon turned his eyes on the trusting little white unicorn and he just stared at her for long seconds. What she had said went entirely against his teachings, and yet it seemed to make sense. In this moment, it was all that made sense.

Approaching Falloah a third time, he opened his heart and laid his hands gently upon her once again, and as his feelings for her poured forth, the emerald light from between his fingers shined brighter and did not just spray from between his fingers, it raged like an emerald fire. His eyes burned red, then green as he channeled all of the power he could muster for the first time. Radiating outward, the glow from his hands began to envelope her and soon she was cocooned in an emerald light. The light sprayed from her many wounds, glowing a hot red as it emerged and fading through the spectrum to green. Slowly, the wounds closed up until only the emerald glow about her body remained.

Watching his student wield the *wizaridi* like this for the first time, the wizard smiled.

Power poured forth from Ralligor like never before. As he should have been quickly drained by such use of his *facultas,* his love for Falloah fed him such power that he had never experienced. The full discipline that he had struggled to master for forty seasons now raged like some uncontrollable fire. Wizard and dragon were finally one within him.

Faelon's eyes streamed tears as she watched, then, out of the corner of her eye near the fallen white dragon, she saw movement. Turning fully, she gasped as she saw the white dragon struggle to his feet, holding onto a tree for balance as he got his wits about him again. Looking across the meadow, she shook her head and breathed, "Oh, no," as Duke Malchor and his wizard with sixteen survivors behind them charged from the trees.

The emerald glow in Ralligor's eyes faded, as did the glow that enveloped Falloah.

She opened her eyes, not looking half dead, but looking alive and alert. She raised her head and looked up at her huge, wounded mate, her jaws parting slightly as she saw him clearly for the first time in many days.

He smiled back and offered her his hand, easily helping her to her feet.

Still staring up at him, Falloah shook her head in disbelief. A moment ago she was on the brink of crossing over. Now, she felt as strong as she ever had—and felt for the first time everything in her huge mate's heart.

Seeing movement behind him, she gasped and did not have time to warn him as a blue fireball from the dragonslayer's sword streaked toward Ralligor's back.

She did not have to.

Ralligor spun half around and raised his hand, catching the fireball in his palm. It exploded with killing force, sending a shock of wind and heat across the meadow and into the forest, but the black dragon did not even flinch.

The Duke's wizard raised his hands and struck with everything he had and Ralligor caught this attack as well. The green cushion of light he characteristically used was not in his palm, rather he seemed to just consume their powers.

Seeing this, the dragonslayer and his men stopped about thirty paces away.

Turning fully, Ralligor took a few steps toward them, watching as Ckammilon strode to them and stood right beside the dragonslayer. He was within range of the enchanted spears and crossbows used by the soldiers, and yet he made no effort to poise himself to dodge as they all took aim at him. He just stood there, looking back down at them, and he spread his wings and arms and raised his head, making his chest and belly an inviting target.

"On my word," the Duke ordered, allowing his sword to fully regain its strength.

The wizard held his hands above his head, conjuring a bright white orb of energy that discharged small and random bursts of lightning, mostly between his hands. The soldiers aimed their weapons carefully, weapons that burned with that same blue fire that had wounded him before.

Ralligor watched them prepare. That familiar red glow overtook his eyes, glowing brightly in the overcast light. It was overtaken by an even brighter emerald glow, one that looked more like flames from his eyes. He snarled, showing them his teeth as he said, "Whenever you primates are ready."

"Now!" the dragonslayer shouted.

All of the men loosed their weapons at once and Ckammilon belched a hellish burst of bright white and yellow fire.

All of the weapons found their mark on the black dragon's chest and belly and all of them exploded against a flash of emerald light as they struck him.

The barrage was only a few seconds old when it ended. The Duke's sword, firing a long burst slowly died out until all of the flame from it was gone. The wizard's attack was the longest, but even it lost strength, thinned and finally faded from sight.

In the aftermath, Ralligor stood where he had been, unmarked and unharmed.

The Duke and his men slowly backed away. Ckammilon shook his head as he retreated, his wide eyes locked on this powerful old rival.

Ralligor's eyes narrowed as he growled, "My turn." Falloah had felt his love for her as he healed her, now his enemies would feel his rage in battle. He raised a hand, sending a blinding green blast toward the dragonslayer, who raised his enchanted shield to ward it off. On impact, the shield exploded and he was thrown from his horse, landing almost thirty paces away and rolling to a stop.

The wizard struck again with the same results, then crossed his arms before him as Ralligor struck back. The explosion of green and white light hurled the wizard backward in the air in burning pieces, all the way to the far side of the meadow and into the forest.

All of the soldiers dropped their weapons and fled, many of them screaming.

Ckammilon took another step back as the Desert Lord's eyes found him again.

Slowly, Ralligor raised his other hand and struck with a burst of emerald fire that was so powerful it didn't just blow the white dragon into the trees fifty paces behind him, the explosion sent a shockwave all the way to the unicorns, wizard and waiting Princess.

Once again, the white dragon was slow to rise, but this time did not stand fully. As Ralligor strode to him, he submissively raised his snout and cooed pitifully.

Reaching his vanquished rival, Ralligor folded his arms and leaned his head, looking down at the defeated smaller dragon without even pity in his eyes that still burned green. "Well, now," he started. "I can't win, huh?"

The white dragon turned his eyes away, not daring to move from his submissive position as he pitifully cooed again.

Raising his head, the Desert Lord advised, "The next time you are foolish enough to cross paths with me will be the last time you take a breath in this world. Do you think you can remember that?"

"I'll remember," the white dragon assured.

"Good to know," the black dragon drawled. He stared down at the white dragon for long seconds, then simply ordered, "Go."

Slowly crawling past the Desert Lord on all fours, the beaten dragon did not dare relinquish his submissive posture. As he got to about forty paces away, he opened his wings and finally stood, leaping into the air and retreating as fast as his battered wings would go.

Duke Malchor stirred, sitting up and cradling a burnt and broken left arm. Nothing was left of the shield that was supposed to protect him from any dragon fire or magic but a piece of leather, one of two, that had been meant to hold it onto his arm. Gripped by the pain of his broken, burnt arm, he did not realize right away where he still was—until a shadow fell over him. Ever so slowly, he turned his head and looked up, his eyes widening more as he saw the Desert Lord staring down at him.

"A word of advice," Ralligor said, baring his murderous teeth. "You might want to find a new occupation."

Struggling to his feet, the dragonslayer backed away from the Desert Lord many steps, his eyes on the dragon's as he pitifully said, "I stand before you a beaten man. My life is yours. Spare me, I beg you and I'll never venture into your land again." He was actually weeping as he cried, "Spare me! I beg you!"

"Such a brave and noble man you are," the dragon almost laughed. "If I kill you I would be doing you a huge favor, but I'm not in such a charitable mood today. I will be tomorrow. You've been a hunter for some time, but from now on you'd better get used to being hunted." Ralligor turned and strode back toward his mate with long, heavy steps, finishing, "Be sure that when I look this way again you aren't still here or that charitable mood may just return." As the Duke fled, Ralligor strode right up to Falloah and took her shoulders, the emerald fire in his eyes fading to the natural pale blue there. He stared down into her eyes for long seconds and finally said, "Now you know the truth, Falloah. You know I hesitated when you were in your greatest need."

Tears rolled from her eyes and she nodded. "I also know why, *Unisponsus*. I know you risked everything to save me from that horrible human. I know you did not want to hurt me. You need to know that I shall always be yours."

He simply nodded to her.

Faelon dared to approach and observed, "You're badly injured. We should get you to the castle to get bandaged up."

"Appreciated," the black dragon offered, his gaze still on his smaller mate's eyes, "but not necessary. I will heal up in short order." He finally turned his eyes down to the wizard, who smiled proudly back up at him, and offered, "Thank you, *Magister*. Your wisdom is finally a part of me."

"It has been for forty seasons," the wizard informed. "Today you found your own, with the aid of a little unicorn. Today we both learned that your power is not in a clear mind. It is in your heart. We still have much work to do, but I think it will wait. You and Falloah should spend some time together."

He nodded. "I should hunt. We'll both need a good meal after all of this."

"Don't," Faelon bade. "Please come to Caipiervell. We have an abundance of sheep and I've read somewhere that dragons really like sheep."

He looked down at her and confirmed, "What you read was true. I do believe I'll take you up on that." He raised a brow.

"First things first, though. I understand you are having problems with an uncle who wants your throne and to see you dead."

"I do," she assured. "I think I can muster enough support to depose him. This kind wizard has offered his services to me and—"

"You'll need an army," the dragon interrupted. "No one knows who you can trust and who you can't there. You'll also need someone to make sure you get there safely. Assassins could be waiting behind every tree. A good show of force will likely frighten them away."

She smiled slightly. "With the help of my unicorn friends here we won't even be noticed."

Ralligor shook his head. "You don't want to sneak back into the castle, you want them to see you coming." He looked down to the wizard *and* unicorns. "In flamboyant style, of course."

The wizard laughed. "Mighty friend, you and I think a lot alike."

"And that, *Magister,* is what I call a compliment." He glanced around at them and offered, "You all have my thanks for your help today." He looked down to Vinton and finished, "You too, I suppose, plow mule."

Vinton rolled his eyes and snorted.

Looking almost tenderly down to the white unicorn, the black dragon added, "Shahly, I would have lost Falloah but for you."

"It's what best friends do for each other," she said to him straightly.

His jaw tightened and he just nodded to her.

The wizard strode to Faelon and took her hands, smiling at her as he said, "Let's go get you your throne back."

"I should probably not get directly involved, *Magister,*" the black dragon advised. "Under the circumstances my presence may not be well taken."

Nodding, the wizard agreed, "I see your wisdom, mighty friend. Still, I would not want you very far away."

Faelon turned her eyes up to the dragon's. "I would not, either." She looked to Falloah and added, "You and I both have scores to settle with my uncle."

With a glance up at her mate, the scarlet dragon agreed, "Yes, we sure do."

"And yet," the wizard interjected, "the thoughts of the people of Caipiervell are not favorable toward dragons. I would agree with Ralligor. Let this affair of men be settled by men." He looked up to the black dragon and added, "I still would not want you very far away, though. You'll have a debt of sheep to collect from Princess Faelon once she reclaims her throne."

"And her army?" Ralligor asked.

The wizard smiled and assured, "It's been taken care of."

Battered and bleeding, Ckammilon found himself too exhausted to fly more than about a league. Ahead of him was a large clearing in the ten height tall trees of the forest, one just large enough for a weary and beaten dragon to land.

Settling down gently and favoring an injured leg, he hobbled forward, carried by the momentum of his own weight, then he swept his wings forward to stabilize himself. Finally, he folded his wings to him and reached for an aching shoulder. Even with a dragonslayer, a wizard and all of those other humans with their enchanted weapons, he was no match for the Desert Lord. This burned inside of him. His brow lowered as anger brewed and he growled aloud, his eyes on the trees fifty paces in front of him.

He took deep breaths, not to calm himself, but to fuel his anger and he bared his teeth. In his eyes was nothing but hate. In the tongue of our kind, of dragon kind, he vowed, "I'll have my revenge. Not today, perhaps not tomorrow, perhaps not for a hundred seasons, but I'll have my revenge on him! His mate will be mine, his hoard will be mine, his territory will be mine!" The white dragon growled again, turning his eyes to the sky. "With my last breath I vow to kill Ralligor and his entire line! He is in the eye of my vengeance and has evoked my wrath! He has stoked the fires of my rage!"

"Ralligor tends to do that," a deep, distantly familiar voice boomed from behind him.

Slowly turning his gaze forward, Ckammilon's eyes widened, his jaw dropped open. Without moving, he looked as far to one side as he could.

Something moved behind him, something massive. Wood and ground crunched as it was brought under tremendous weight.

Both reluctantly and slowly, the white dragon turned, raising his eyes to meet the eyes of the Landmaster—a dragon more than twice his size—as he stood.

Agarxus folded his massive arms, his gaze locked on the puny dragon who stood before him.

Ckammilon wanted to flee more than he had ever wanted anything in his life, but his body, stiff and battered from combat and paralyzed by fear, would not move.

Agarxus lifted an eyebrow ever so slightly as he thundered, "Perhaps you and I should talk about what happens to a dragon who violates my borders. Then, right after we talk, I'll show you."

CHAPTER 14

Despite the offer of help from two dragons, two unicorns and a wizard, Faelon decided to try to reclaim her throne by herself. Besides, if anything went horribly wrong then she would have those two dragons, two unicorns and that wizard to call in. It seemed easy enough. Her strongest allies waited less than half a league away and could be there in moments should her uncle decide not to step down and return her kingdom to her.

She rode right up to the main gate, sidesaddle on her horse as the skirt on the servant girl's dress she still wore, now dirty and horribly stained, was too narrow to allow her to straddle her mount. As workers labored to repair the front gate Ralligor had destroyed, they all paused as she rode right past them, her eyes on the elaborately dressed man under the tent about twenty paces inside. Stopping right outside of the open tent, she slid from her saddle and approached a few paces more, folding her arms as she shouted, "Prince Tahmrof. I would see you before me now!"

He and his three advisors looked up from the simple wooden table and the papers on it, locking their eyes on the young woman who glared back.

She pointed to the ground right in front of her, a gesture that demanded his immediate presence.

Setting his jaw, the Prince, who now only wore comfortable riding trousers and a loosely fitting swordsman's shirt, strode around the table and right up to the girl, snapping his fingers at two nearby guards as he approached her. Once in front of her, he also folded his arms, little more than contempt in his eyes as he glared down at her.

Faelon raised her chin, informing, "You've failed, uncle. I still live, and I want you out of my castle within the hour."

He raised a brow and held his ground.

She continued, "That means get moving. If you aren't gone within the hour you will find yourself in the dungeon and will be tried for treason against the crown."

"I *am* the crown, little girl," he countered. "I don't know what you are trying to pull, but my niece is dead and this kingdom is mine now. You should run along before you find my temper and end up in trouble you can't really cope with."

As he turned to go back to the tent, she shouted, "Don't turn your back on me, you treacherous snake. I said I want you out of my castle and my kingdom—now!"

He stopped and raised his head. Slowly, he turned back and approached her, eyeing her with contempt as he said to those around him, "We seem to have a little girl here who either has a fever or is touched in her little mind." His eyes narrowed, his brow low between them as he ordered with clenched teeth, "This will be your last warning, little girl. Walk out that gate and never return or feel my wrath."

Her lips tightened and she snarled, "Your wrath doesn't frighten me. Now get out of my kingdom you conniving imposter!" She never saw his hand move and didn't realize it was until the back of it slammed into her cheek, spinning her around. Her next realization was lying face down on the hard dirt road. Slowly pushing herself back up, she went to stand and was seized by the arms and yanked violently from the ground. The two guards held her arms tightly and turned her back toward her uncle. As blood trickled from her nose and mouth, she looked up at him and felt fear for the first time.

"Now," he started slowly. "What shall we do with you?"

"You will release her," a woman answered as she rode up to him.

Tahmrof and his advisors took a step back and the guards holding Faelon looked over their shoulders, then they let her go and turned fully.

The woman who approached was taller than all of the men present and had a heavy and muscular build for a woman. Her long blond hair was restrained behind her face and her light, Zondaen armor was polished and clean. On her left side of her belt was a sword at the ready. On the right side were two daggers.

The fifty women behind her were dressed similarly. Many of them had bows in their hands that were ready to respond to any threat. The rest of the riders already had their swords in their hands and ready for battle.

The tall woman dismounted and walked right up to Faelon, looking down at her with her thumbs hooked into her black swordsman's belt. Looking the Princess up and down, she finally asked, "Would you be Princess Faelon?"

Faelon hesitantly nodded.

"I am Captain Pa'lesh," the blond woman continued. "I am a field captain from Zondae. A friend of yours asked that we send some troops this way to ensure that you reclaim your throne." Her eyes turned to Tahmrof, her brow low over them. "And, we are to make certain there are no problems when you do so."

One of the guards grasped the hilt of his sword and defiantly observed, "There are only forty or fifty of you."

Pa'lesh turned her eyes to him and informed, "The other five hundred are waiting outside. There are also a thousand more on the way from Zondae and another thousand from Enulam so I suggest you think hard about where your loyalties lie." She looked around and shouted, "Soldiers of Caipiervell. I've come from Zondae to support the restoration of Princess Faelon to her rightful place. Those loyal to the legitimate heir to the throne should come forward and join us. Those not loyal will probably not live through the day." She turned her eyes to Tahmrof and finished, "Starting with you."

He raised his chin and snarled back, "You have no claims here. I shall have you all arrested if you don't leave immediately."

A rare smile curled the Field Captain's lips. "Try it. You'll find most of your loyalists lying dead before they even get their weapons drawn." In two steps she closed the couple of paces between them and said, "Oh, and one other thing." She swung hard, slamming the back of her hand into his jaw and spinning him around. As he crumbled to the ground, Pa'lesh's eyes narrowed and she snarled, "It isn't wise to strike your princess. Very bad things can happen to you when you do."

Many loyal soldiers as well as a group of commoners began to gather around.

Setting her hands on her hips, Captain Pa'lesh looked down to Princess Faelon and straightly said, "I have orders to keep you safe until the other garrisons are here, so I won't be leaving your side for a while. What are your first commands, Princess Faelon of Caipiervell?"

The Princess turned her eyes to the moaning man on the ground and nodded toward him.

Pa'lesh looked to two Caipiervell guards and motioned to the stirring Prince with her head.

As the guards took his arms and hoisted him from the ground, they were not gentle or in any way courteous. They treated him like a common criminal, and turned him to the Princess for judgment.

Staring back up at him, Faelon rubbed her sore cheek, then looked down at her hand where some blood from her mouth had smeared onto her fingers. Rubbing the blood off on her dress, she turned her eyes back to her uncle and said, "You are still family, so I will not have you executed. However, you are a treacherous bastard who is now banished from the kingdom of Caipiervell and all of her surrounding territories for the rest of your life." She looked to another guard and ordered, "Find all of those loyal to him and enough horses to carry them. I want them gone."

The guard glanced at Pa'lesh, then bowed and hurried on his way, collecting more men as he headed toward the palace.

Faelon's eyes narrowed as she looked at a home she had not been in for three days. "You know, there's something else that requires my immediate attention."

Pa'lesh followed as the Princess strode toward the palace. Only a few paces away, she turned and signaled three of the Zondaen women still on horseback to follow her.

With an entourage of four tall and powerful Zondaen warriors behind her, Faelon fearlessly stormed into the palace, past the banquet hall, through the elaborate dignitaries hall and up the stairs. Ahead was the Hall of the Legion of Knights and it was time to find out who was loyal and who was not.

She turned the door handle and pushed it open, striding in to find only about half of the knights present. With them were their squires who froze from their tasks as they saw her.

Faelon stopped about four paces inside and folded her arms, her narrow eyes scanning the knights within with the look of an angry predator.

No one spoke for long seconds.

"Well, now," she finally said. "It seems that some of you would support my uncle. Some of you were actually involved in a plot to kill me so that he could have the throne. I will offer one chance for you to live and only one chance. If you support my uncle, then get on your horses and get the hell out of my palace—and do it now!"

Four of the fifteen or so knights strode to her, one folding his arms as he informed, "You no longer rule Caipiervell. Prince Tahmrof does."

Her eyes narrowed. "Well we know where your loyalties lie."

"Princess Faelon," he said, sounding as if he was trying to be patient with an undisciplined child, "it was decided that we need a strong leader for this kingdom. That clearly is not you. Please, make the transition of power as smooth as possible."

Raising her chin, she demanded, "And why should I do that?"

"Civil war will tear the kingdom apart," he explained, as if he was speaking to a child again. "Your first concern should be your people. How many should die so that you can get what you want?"

She just stared coldly up at him for long seconds, then she turned her eyes down.

He smiled. "I think you understand now."

Nodding, Faelon confirmed, "Yes, I understand. You are right to support my uncle, especially feeling as you do." Her lips tightened and she stared at his polished boots for a moment, then she asked, "Captain Pa'lesh, when will your other garrisons be here?"

Staring coldly at the defiant knight, the Zondaen Captain folded her arms and reported, "Within the hour."

Knights glanced at each other and mumbles of uncertainty rippled through the room.

Faelon nodded, then she turned her eyes back to the knight before her and offered, "Thank you for your honesty." She glanced around at the other knights present and asked, "Does everyone here feel the same?"

"No," one at the rear of the room said loudly. He was a younger man with a short beard and sharp eyes. Wearing a grey arming shirt and his lower armor, he strode toward the front of the room, his eyes on the four knights standing before the Princess. "They do not speak for us all. There are still some of us loyal to your father."

"King Elner is dead," another of the four knights pointed out.

"And his heir lives," the younger knight countered. "You would follow a man who would have a girl barely of marrying age murdered to get the throne?"

Again, uneasy looks were exchanged.

This younger knight, one knighted shortly before King Elner's death, looked to Princess Faelon, to Pa'lesh, then he turned to the room and shouted, "What is wrong with you men? Does honor no longer have its place in the Knight's Hall of Caipiervell?" Scanning their ranks once more, he shook his head and declared, "You are all spineless sheep of Tahmrof. Very well. Boy, bring my armor. I'll not have it rusting in the stench of this foul place another moment." He turned to leave, pausing beside Pa'lesh to whisper, "I'll rally what troops and support I can and meet your garrisons at the grain fields half a league from here. Send them word to pause there."

Without looking at him, she nodded. As he left, she turned and whispered something to one of the other Zondaen soldiers, who turned and hurried out herself.

Shaking his head, the knight regarded Faelon with condescending eyes and a half smile. "So. We're a spoiled little girl after all."

She turned her eyes up to his.

"Very well," he went on. "In the name of honor I will allow you and your girlfriends here to leave the castle unharmed. Take with you whoever would follow you and leave Caipiervell Castle. After that, King Tahmrof will decide what to do with you." His eyes shifted to Pa'lesh and he finished, "I shall look forward to meeting you on the battlefield, Zondaen."

She half smiled back at him. "You'll change your mind once we're there, dog."

Faelon had heard enough and she turned to leave.

Following, Pa'lesh and the other Zondaen warriors quickly took positions in front of her, behind her, and the Captain beside her.

"What now?" Pa'lesh asked. She glanced down to see Faelon wiping a tear from her cheek. "Oh, what's that about?"

"I didn't want this," the Princess answered softly.

Nudging her with an elbow, the Field Captain countered, "What kind of leader would you be if you did?"

Faelon glanced up at the tall woman beside her. "Do you think it would be wiser to just surrender Caipiervell to him and leave? No one would be killed in battle that way."

"What would you be surrendering your people to?" Pa'lesh countered. "It seems to me that a man who would strike a little girl like that would have no feeling for the misery of those around him." She glanced down at the Princess. "I would much rather have a queen who actually cares about her people on the throne of my kingdom than a man like that, even if some do consider him a strong leader."

"You hit him too," Faelon reminded.

Pa'lesh smirked and looked down to her, meeting her eyes. "I'm a soldier. I'm supposed to."

Smiling back, Faelon offered, "Thank you for helping me."

"We aren't out of the fire yet," the Field Captain assured. She raised her chin, seeing five more Zondaens coming toward them and she ordered, "Report."

The two groups stopped about a pace apart.

One of the five Zondaens reported, "Loyalists to Tahmrof got to him. He's been freed."

Pa'lesh nodded. "I expected he would be. What about support for Princess Faelon? How many can we count on?"

The Zondaen soldier shook her head. "The army around here is in chaos."

Faelon stepped forward and ordered, "Find any who are still loyal to King Elner and have them meet us outside of the castle walls within the hour. Tell them to bring whatever they can with them. Make it look like we are fleeing."

The soldier looked to Pa'lesh.

Raising her brow, the Field Captain asked, "Should she repeat all of that?"

Shaking her head, the solder assured, "No, Captain," as she turned and hurried on her way.

Looking down at Faelon again, Pa'lesh observed, "You are a devious and crafty little bitch, aren't you?" She smiled slightly. "I like that."

"Thank you," the Princess offered softly. Considering for a moment, she bade, "Come on," as she hurried down the corridor. "There is someone we need to talk to."

The Zondaen soldiers strode after her, Pa'lesh protesting, "Bear in mind my orders are to keep you safe until the garrisons arrive."

"I realize that," Faelon assured. "I would only ask that you trust me."

"We're going the wrong way," Pa'lesh tried to explain once again.

"I know where I'm going," the Princess assured.

A voice from the forest agreed, "As you should."

Faelon stopped her horse and looked, seeing the wizard leaning against a tree by the road, his arms folded and his eyes on her. A slight smile was on his mouth. Sliding from her horse, the Princess ran to him and threw her arms around his chest, burying her face in his robes. She wept as he hugged her back and held him even more tightly. "I didn't want this!" she cried. "That's why I kept you away. I thought he would back away. I thought my people would support me. I just didn't want anyone to get hurt!"

Ever so gently, he stroked her long black hair, offering, "Shh. There now, child. No one said this would be easy. It is one of the many trials you will face as Queen."

"I don't want to go to war with my own people," she sobbed. "I don't want to go to war with anybody!"

"Those of conscience never do." He looked up from her as the Field Captain approached, and he nodded to her, greeting, "Pa'lesh."

She nodded back. "Nessar of Enulam sends her regards."

He smiled. "She is a dear friend."

Looking with wide eyes up to the wizard, Faelon breathed, "You know each other?"

Pa'lesh answered, "This old wizard gets around, it seems. He's one of the few men who were ever allowed to wander in and out of Zondae at will over the seasons. It's good to see you again. I'm guessing you are why she came this way?"

He nodded. "Faelon and I have been getting reacquainted over the last few days."

"What do you know about her uncle?" the Field Captain asked.

"Nothing I like," the wizard replied.

Pa'lesh nodded. "That's good enough for me. You asked for a garrison from Zondae, but Prince Chail sent for one from Enulam as well. If this Tahmrof bastard wants a fight then he'll get one."

His bushy eyebrows dropping, the wizard asked, "He is *still* at Zondae?"

Pa'lesh rolled her eyes and confirmed, "He's still at Zondae. It would seem that he and Le'ell are doing some reacquainting of their own. One would think that they're conjoined most of the time."

The wizard offered only a slight shrug in response, then he looked back down to Faelon and assured, "We'll get through this, and we'll get you home soon."

She laid her head on his chest again, nuzzling into his shoulder as she softly said, "I'm not sure I even belong there anymore."

"Nonsense," he scoffed. "There are those at Caipiervell awaiting your return so that they can be liberated from that uncle of yours."

"Liberated to what?" was her response. An impatient sigh from Pa'lesh drew her attention but she did not look that way. She tried hard to compose herself and finally asked, "Am I really worth all of this?"

The wizard met the Zondaen's eyes and he did not answer himself.

"That is for history to decide," Pa'lesh finally answered. "Right now it is important that you pull yourself together and lead your people. We have a war to win and our leader will need her wits about her."

Hearing that stirred something in Faelon and she finally looked to her Zondaen protectors. Nodding, she assured, "You're right. I suppose I have people counting on me."

"That you do." Pa'lesh confirmed. "Now we'd best be on our way to the rendezvous with my people at this grain field. I don't like being in the open like this."

"You're in no danger," the wizard assured, "and we can't leave yet."

"We have to go," the Field Captain insisted.

Turning such a calm yet steely gaze on her, the wizard assured, "No, we don't. You'll see why shortly." He turned his eyes up the road as hoof beats approached.

All of the Zondaens turned, their hands on their weapons, then they froze as Vinton galloped around a bend in the road and straight toward the wizard. He seemed to completely ignore the warriors as he stopped and informed, "As you thought. That dragonslayer went right back to Caipiervell."

The wizard nodded and looked back to Pa'lesh. "*Now* we can go."

"Dragonslayer?" one of the Zondaen soldiers asked. "What exactly are we up against?"

"He's nothing for you to be concerned with," the wizard assured. "My apprentice will handle him. In the meantime, we have—"

"Another unicorn," Pa'lesh cried. "A dragonslayer… What's next? A dragon?"

Faelon looked to her and suggested, "You know, we should talk about that."

The Field Captain's wide eyes turned to the wizard.

The grain field on one side of the road was soon an encampment and the nearby village gratefully took in the Princess and officers. Within the village hall, one that had been ordered built by Faelon's grandfather, two Zondaen and three Caipiervell officers and eleven knights of Caipiervell sat at the same table, one that filled most of the front room which was fifteen paces long and five wide. This was supposed to be a place of safety for the villagers, a place to gather and a place where the King of Caipiervell could have an audience with his subjects. That had not been for over a season.

Now, Princess Faelon sat in that place of honor, still dressed as a servant girl of her castle. With her forehead in her hands, she really did not pay attention to the battle plans the military people talked about. She wanted more than anything to avoid it. The wizard was wandering the Zondaen and Caipiervell camp and was not present, and she felt a little lost without him. The task of getting everyone to agree on what to do about reclaiming the kingdom seemed impossible.

The door at the far end of the large room finally opened and Faelon slowly raised her head, looking to the squire who entered. He stiffly strode around the table and right to Princess Faelon, faced her and snapped to attention. He did not even look as old as she was and had terror on his features. He would not even look directly at her.

"Report," one of the knights ordered. When the boy hesitated, the knight barked, "Out with it, boy!"

The squire flinched.

Faelon looked to him and snapped, "Sir Daldwan!" She looked back to the boy and ordered in a calmer voice, "What did they say?"

He took a deep breath and reported, "About one quarter of your forces, my Lady."

That was not good news and sparked mumbling around the table.

The Princess turned her eyes down and nodded, offering, "Thank you."

"I'm sorry, my Lady," he said, then he threw his chest out and assured, "We will win the day, anyway."

She turned her eyes back to him and smiled. "With such bravery as yours in our ranks we cannot fail."

He nodded, then bowed to her and hurried out.

As the door closed, a Caipiervell officer slouched in his chair and mumbled, "That isn't good. Even with the promised garrisons helping us we're hopelessly outnumbered."

Pa'lesh turned an impatient glare on him and snarled, "It's a wonder your castle didn't fall seasons ago with that attitude."

He glared back and barked, "Mind your place, woman!"

When the Field Captain stood, Faelon raised a hand to her and shouted, "That's enough!" She waited for the tension to ease and Pa'lesh to take her seat before she spoke again. "Don't you think we should be fighting my uncle instead of each other?" Glancing around, she noticed no one looking at her and somehow felt even more out of place. Finally, a little anger began to well up inside of her. "Listen to me carefully. I did not want this war. I don't want anyone dying for me. Things are as they are, so make a choice now who you would rather have under the crown." She scanned the room again. Still, no one would even look at her. Nodding, she continued, "I see. Very well." Standing, she went on, "Disband the camp in the morning and be on your way."

Pa'lesh also stood, looking down at Faelon with steely eyes as she informed, "My soldiers and I came here to fight, and fight we will, with or without your own troops."

A red haired knight with a well groomed beard streaked with white looked to Pa'lesh and assured, "You'll be fighting along side me and my men. I served under the banner of King Elner for many seasons. He was a good man and king, a man of the people, a man of honor and integrity." He turned his eyes to Faelon and continued, "His daughter has those qualities. Even if she will not fight to reclaim the kingdom herself, I'll be at her side until the end of my days."

Faelon offered him a slight smile.

The other Zondaen officer also stood. She was not quite as tall as Pa'lesh, but her build was unmistakably Zondaen, as was the light armor and fur she wore. "I didn't lead my garrison here to tuck my tail and return home."

"Nor did I," another knight of Caipiervell said straightly.

"So we just march our men to slaughter?" an older knight asked.

Silence gripped the room again.

The door burst open again and was filled with a man of massive proportions.

Faelon's eyes were nearly as wide open as her mouth as she saw him duck inside and close the door. She had never seen a man so big in her life! The white swordsman's shirt he wore was open half way down and was almost completely filled with his massive chest and arms. The lace that was meant to hold it together was not even there anymore. His riding trousers fit him very tightly and his black boots made the room echo as he walked, his steps telling everyone he was a very heavy man. Brown hair was restrained behind his head. His eyes darted around the table and he asked, "Did I miss anything?"

Everyone at the table stood.

The massive man walked right toward Pa'lesh and nodded to her.

"Where is Le'ell?" the Field Captain asked.

"Got thrown from her horse again," was his answer.

She sat down and propped her elbow on the table, covering her eyes as she said in an impatient voice, "Oh, for Goddess' sake."

Grabbing one of the crude, wooden chairs, he carried it down the table as he countered, "Nasty sprain on her sword arm's wrist. Her mother and I ganged up on her and made her remain at Zondae. But, she only has herself to blame. She's the one who wanted that big Northern mare." He placed the chair between Pa'lesh and the Princess Faelon, looking down at Princess Faelon as he asked, "And you are?"

Staring dumbly back up at him, she just stood there and blinked. Her neck was craned back and her eyes were locked wide on him.

Pa'lesh answered, "That would be Princess Faelon. Princess Faelon, this is Prince Chail of Enulam."

He gently reached to her and took her hand, bending way over to kiss her fingers. "It is a pleasure, your Highness."

She managed to nod to him.

Pa'lesh looked around the big prince and suggested to Faelon, "Why don't we sit down and continue?"

She nodded again and took her seat, everyone else following suit as she did.

Prince Chail's chair creaked under his weight as he settled into it. He folded his hands on the table and looked around at those who were present, finally asking, "We still don't have a battle plan, do we?"

That awkward feeling gripped the room again.

He nodded and looked to Pa'lesh. "You are all for a full frontal assault, of course."

She raised her brow and did not answer.

The Prince nodded then looked to the men across the table. "And you are advocating caution over there, aren't you?"

They all looked away from him.

He nodded again, then looked to Faelon. "What would you recommend?"

Still wide eyed, she shrugged and replied, "Whatever you think."

Pa'lesh rested her head in her hand, grumbling, "Why does every woman act that way around him?"

"It's my charm," the Prince assured. "Okay, how about we compromise?"

A brown bearded knight sitting across the table answered, "We're outnumbered three to one. We have no catapults, no siege engines, and nowhere but here to fall back to once the fighting begins."

Chail nodded, agreeing, "It does sound rather dismal, doesn't it? Is the other side expecting Zondae and Enulam to help?"

The knight nodded.

Looking to Pa'lesh, the Prince seemed astonished as he asked, "And they still haven't surrendered? I simply can't believe that!"

"Believe it," she grumbled back, still rubbing her head.

He nodded again. "Okay, so our enemy knows we're outnumbered, he knows we have no siege engines and no hope of taking the castle." He raised his brow and looked to Faelon. "Do you think he'll give us time to strengthen our forces, acquire what we need and sign on more allies?"

The Princess blinked, then her eyes widened.

Pa'lesh raised her head and looked up at him.

Many in the room exchanged looks.

"No," Faelon confirmed. "If he knows where we are... He's going to attack us as soon as possible!"

Chail nodded. "Probably at first light when he thinks our guard is down, and he'll most likely wipe out the village and all in it for aiding us."

Pa'lesh finished, "And the forces he sends will be vulnerable as hell on the march here."

The Prince nodded. "They certainly will."

"They're still my people," Faelon insisted. "I don't want them slaughtered."

Pa'lesh barked back, "Right now they are your enemy."

"For the moment," the Prince agreed. "We need to remember that Caipiervell will someday have to defend herself again so we don't want her forces too badly depleted."

Raising her brow, the Field Captain asked, "So we are to fight nicely?"

Chail turned and smiled at her, assuring, "I didn't bring my special axe to fight nicely."

"Oh, good," she chided. "You brought your special axe. I feel better already."

"Well what can we do?" Faelon asked desperately.

Pa'lesh answered, "We can quit throwing obstacles in the way, for starters."

The door opened once again and this time the wizard entered, his eyes on the Prince of Enulam and a huge smile on his face as he greeted, "Chail, you midget ogre!"

"Well," the Prince countered. "Look what the wind blew in." He stood as the wizard approached and the two men of drastically different size exchanged a hearty embrace.

The Zondaen Field Captain looked back at the wizard and barked, "Is there anyone you don't know?"

"I have many friends," the wizard assured, backing away as Chail sat back down.

"Sorry I missed you during your visit to Enulam," the Prince offered.

"I'm sure you had other business," the wizard said. "Right now I sense a bit of tension. Am I to assume no plan of attack has been finalized?" When no one volunteered an answer, the wizard glanced around and informed, "Good. I would hate to have to change all your minds."

A blond haired Caipiervell knight leaned forward, folding his hands on the table as he asked, "What do you mean? Are you saying you have a plan, yourself?"

"Of course," the wizard answered. "I've been outside preparing the troops, the villagers."

"For what?" a Caipiervell knight asked dryly.

The wizard smiled at him and informed, "For the nasty surprise awaiting Prince Tahmrof and his men."

Once again the door burst open and an armored soldier of Caipiervell stormed in.

Expecting a threat of some kind, Pa'lesh stood, her eyes boring into him.

Instead, the young soldier strode to within three paces of the Princess and bowed to her. "I bring news from the castle, my Lady. Prince Tahmrof means to execute a hundred people he claims are loyal to you."

Faelon's lips slowly parted, her wide eyes filled with tears and locked on the soldier as she slowly shook her head.

"He's trying to force our hand," Chail informed straightly.

Looking away, Pa'lesh snarled, "And he'll be waiting to ambush us on our way back to the castle."

"How can he do that?" the Princess breathed. "How can anyone do something so horrible?"

The wizard countered, "You mean like murder a sixteen season old girl to capture the throne?"

She looked away.

Clearing his throat, the soldier informed, "There is a messenger outside awaiting your word, my Lady."

The room fell silent.

Faelon raised a hand to her mouth, trying hard to compose herself, and slowly turned her eyes to the Prince of Enulam. She did not know what to do.

Prince Chail sensed this as he looked back at her, then he folded his arms and turned steely eyes on the soldier as he ordered, "Tell this messenger—"

The wizard interrupted, "That the Princess will be there in the morning to discuss terms."

Everyone's eyes snapped to him.

Sir Daldwan snapped, "Are you insane? After—"

"Do it!" the Prince barked harshly, his eyes on the wizard, who met his gaze and smiled ever so slightly.

The soldier looked to Princess Faelon.

She finally nodded to him.

As he hurried out, a somber moment followed. No one spoke. Pa'lesh sat back down, turning her displeased eyes to the Prince.

He looked back to her and asked, "Okay, so now how do we convince him to surrender?"

All eyes snapped to him.

And cheers erupted from the meeting hall.

CHAPTER 15

King Elner's study had changed little since his death. A large room, it was not as elaborately decorated as one would have thought. In fact, there were few decorations in it at all. Shelves full of books, scrolls and maps lined the walls on two sides. A simple wooden desk sat under a window that overlooked the Southern gate of the castle's perimeter wall and right across the room from the only door in. Ten paces square, half of the space left in the room was occupied by a large wooden table, two paces wide by four long. A chair sat at each end, three on the edges, and papers and maps littered most of the surface. Three wine flasks, a pitcher of ale and a few tankards sat neglected near one of the room's two occupants.

Sitting in the chair that faced the door, Prince Tahmrof, already dressed in his arming shirt and pants, held his head up by his palms as he studied a parchment before him. The dark figure behind him, who stood near the desk and stared out the window, gave him a feeling of uneasiness, but he knew he dare not speak up. He would not even give a glance back at the man who stood there, dressed in the dark, hooded robes of a warlock. His eyes were fixed on the parchment, and there they would stay.

A knock on the door finally broke his concentration and he looked up from the parchment, bidding "Come in." He stood as Duke Malchor limped in.

His arm in a sling, splinted and bandaged, the dragonslayer was a pitiable sight. His white swordsman's shirt had the left sleeve split and it dangled from his shoulder. This was a beaten man, one who felt horribly dethroned from the larger than life figure he felt he might have once been. His eyes finally met the Prince's and he asked in a soft voice, "You wanted to see me?"

"Under different circumstances," Tahmrof replied. "Do we stand a chance should that dragon return?"

"He won't," the dragonslayer assured. "He has what he wanted."

"You sound awfully certain about that," the Prince observed, "much like that man who was sure that he would return victorious today."

Nodding, the Duke admitted, "I know. The riders I sent to find Ckammilon have returned. I told the guards to send the commander here."

"He won't rejoin us," Prince Tahmrof insisted. "After what you told me happened to him he's sure to be long gone."

"We'll see." He turned as someone else knocked on the door.

"Come in," the Prince bade.

A soldier entered the room, one who had clearly been riding for some hours. He would not meet the eyes of his prince or the Duke, instead keeping his gaze trained on the ground before him. He carried something wrapped in a cloth under his arm, something bloody.

Raising his chin, Malchor demanded, "Did you find him?"

Hesitantly, the soldier nodded, then he walked past the Duke and laid the bundle on the table.

The Prince's eyes narrowed and he asked, "Will he be coming back?"

The soldier shook his head, staring at the bundle before him.

"Damn," Malchor growled. "What excuse did he come up with this time?"

Glancing at him, the soldier took one edge of the cloth and pulled it up, allowing the object within, one the length of a man's forearm, to roll free.

The Duke's eyes widened slightly as the dragon's tooth rolled onto the table, then he set his jaw as he said, "You'd better have pried that from the coward's head."

"We didn't find all of his head," the soldier reported.

Ever so slowly, Tahmrof stood, his eyes on the tooth. "You said the black dragon spared him!"

"He did," the Duke assured. "He spared us both."

Still looking out the window, the warlock laughed, an ancient, evil laugh.

The three other men just glanced at him.

"We found what is left of him in a clearing about a league south of where you fought him," the soldier continued. "He had been torn apart."

"So, he's dead?" the Prince questioned.

Looking right at the Prince, the soldier corrected, "He's been torn apart. The clearing we found him in is as large as the western courtyard of this castle, and he was all over it. We didn't find but a few pieces bigger than a sheep."

Raising his chin, Duke Malchor accused, "You're lying. Ckammilon was not such a weak and defenseless dragon. Not even that black dragon could have done something like that to him."

The warlock laughed again, saying, "You simple minded fool." He finally turned from the window. Ancient, hairless skin was pulled taut over his half fleshless skull and teeth that seemed too big for his head gleamed in the lamplight of the room. Slowly, he approached, eyeing the other men one at a time and finally turning his eyes to the tooth when he reached that end of the table. "What indeed would do something like this to a dragon of Ckammilon's size and power? What indeed?"

His brow low over his eyes, Malchor demanded, "Tell me what you know, Zelkton. What does this mean?"

The old warlock picked up the tooth and looked it over, and finally answered, "It means the time has come for me to depart."

"Enough of your foolishness and your riddles," the dragonslayer shouted. "Tell me what it means!"

"The meaning is clear," Zelkton replied. "You have crossed the wrong dragon. I warned you to stay north of the Dark Mountains, and now you have the attention of a dragon you should have let sleep."

"You know as well as I that staying there was impossible," Duke Malchor snapped. "Had Mettegrawr discovered us there again before we…" A hearty laugh from the warlock stopped him.

"At least you've made this journey here an enjoyable one," Zelkton laughed. "That old drake is the least of your problems now."

"What do you mean?" the Prince demanded fearfully.

"You fear one Landmaster," the warlock answered, "and flee into the territory of another. Ckammilon wasn't killed by magic or a dragon his own size. He was killed by the Tyrant. Pray that he felt all of the Tyrant's ire and left none for you." Clearly enjoying himself, Zelkton shook his head and observed, "You two are an amusing pair. Perhaps you should take this pathetic little act of yours from castle to castle and try to make a little gold off of it."

Drawing his dagger, the Duke held it a finger length away from the warlock's chest and snarled, "Perhaps I should arrange the untimely death of a warlock instead?"

The smile never left Zelkton's skeleton-like face as he looked down at the blade, then back to Malchor's eyes. "I am one hundred and forty-three seasons old. Nothing about my death would be untimely at this point." He raised a hand to the Duke's chest and pushed him out of the way as he walked past. "Think about your own future, Malchor. The lands you claim to have are no doubt withering to dust without you." He laughed again as he slowly left the room, and laughed more as he made his way down the corridor outside.

A long, silent moment passed.

The soldier looked to Prince Tahmrof and bowed to him. "By your leave, your Highness." He then turned and left the room.

The Prince sighed, shaking his head. "Now what do we do?"

"We hope that old warlock is right," the Duke answered, "and we prepare for that other problem."

"Other problem?"

"Your niece."

"Oh, yes."

"She still has a quarter of the army with her and whatever forces that Zondaen brought with her."

"I didn't see that many Zondaens out there, and she said she only had five hundred with her."

"And another thousand on the way, assuming she wasn't lying about that. Of course, we should not assume that she was lying." The Duke walked to the other end of the table, absently picking up a tankard. As he poured it full of ale, he asked, "Why would Zondae send forces here, anyway? What interest is Caipiervell to them?"

"I can't answer that. She also said Enulam is sending a thousand men." The Prince raised his chin, his narrow eyes on Duke Malchor as he asked, "Aren't they arch enemies?"

Nodding, the Duke confirmed, "Yes, of course they are. She must have been lying about the extra troops she says they are sending."

"Should we assume she is?"

"No, it's best to be prepared, that is unless we get word of their surrender."

A knock on the open door drew their attention and a palace guard entered, saying, "Excuse me, my Lord, the courier has returned with word from the rebels."

"Go on," the Prince demanded.

Another soldier, the courier himself, entered the room, clearly weary from a long and swift ride and reported, "Princess Faelon has sent word that she will be here sometime after sunup to discuss terms."

Silence gripped the room again and the Duke and Prince shot surprised and satisfied looks to each other.

"Well now," the Prince said in a lighthearted tone. "It would seem that this ugly situation has resolved itself."

His eyes narrowing, the Duke turned to the courier and asked, "How many did you see in their camp?"

"I was stopped at the edge of the village," the soldier replied. "I saw no encampment, but I did see smoke from many fires."

Nodding, Malchor looked back to Prince Tahmrof, eyeing him for a moment before he spoke again. "What of the Zondaens?"

"I didn't see any," the messenger answered, "just the sentries posted on the road into the village."

"How many sentries?"

"Four, my Lord."

The Duke nodded again, then ordered, "That will be all."

The two soldiers bowed and left the room.

Nodding, the dragonslayer absently said, "Wants to discuss terms, does she? It all seems a little too easy."

"She's just a little girl," the Prince pointed out. "She clearly does not know how to wage war any more than her father did and she has had time to think about it."

"And what do you intend to do when she comes to discuss these terms?"

Tahmrof shrugged. "I suppose I'll hear her out. At this point, if she is willing to surrender her troops and swear her loyalty to me then wasting our time and soldiers in battle would seem pointless."

"Until she decides to return the favor you tried to do her," the Duke pointed out.

"What do you mean?"

"I mean this little girl will grow up someday and may just seek revenge against the uncle who took the throne from her and had her parents killed."

The Prince raised his chin, his eyes widening slightly. "Well. I suppose I could offer her a comfortable and carefree life, or marry her off. She's an attractive young lady. What man would turn her down?"

"Marry her off to another kingdom where she will have a whole army and that kingdom's allies to strike at you with. Brilliant."

"Are... Are you saying I should kill her?"

"And all loyal to her," the Duke replied.

"Killing her outright could be dangerous."

"She's leading a rebellion against the crown. I believe that is called treason."

Prince Tahmrof turned and looked out the window.

"We made this deal to get her out of your way," Malchor reminded. "Don't tell me you've grown a soft belly for her now."

"I suppose I did not expect to actually see her killed."

"That's why you hired others to get their hands bloody." Taking a gulp from his tankard, the Duke continued, "Now is a prime opportunity to show your metal to the people you mean to lead."

Tahmrof sighed and turned his eyes down. He finally nodded and agreed, "She is quite a threat as long as she lives, isn't she?"

"How surprising would an answer of yes be?"

The Prince nodded again. "What should we do?"

"Once she publicly recognizes you as the rightful ruler of Caipiervell, she should be arrested, tried, and then executed. It's as simple as that."

His lips tightening, Prince Tahmrof drew a breath and looked toward the desk where his brother, King Elner had ruled the kingdom for so long.

Duke Malchor gulped down the rest of the ale, then he slammed the tankard down on the table, glaring at the Prince as he snarled, "You're going soft, Tahmrof. This girl is the one obstacle you have left."

"That's why you were invited here," the Prince reminded. "But for your incompetence she would not be an obstacle."

Grabbing the Prince's arm, Duke Malchor turned him and growled back, "Just remember that *I* put you where you are and I can remove you just as easily!"

Tahmrof jerked his arm free and glared back. "You did no such thing, and should my ally to the north hear you speaking so you will be removed with a thought."

"Where is your ally now?" the dragonslayer questioned.

The Prince raised an eyebrow. "Two garrisons are a league north of here, awaiting my word."

"Are they, now?" The Duke almost smiled. "I have three hundred men to the South."

They stared at each other for a moment, then both men smiled.

The Prince patted Malchor's shoulder. "Perhaps she will never arrive to discuss these terms of hers."

The dragonslayer looked to the table and picked up the pitcher of ale, pouring his own goblet full and another, then he picked his up and held it to the Prince.

Tahmrof picked up the other and bumped the Duke's saying, "May my lovely niece die well in battle with her Zondaen allies."

Another knock and the guard outside entered again. "My Lord, there is someone here to see you."

Malchor and Tahmrof turned to see an old man with a long white beard and long white hair enter. He was dressed in the green robes of a wizard and wore a pleasant smile. "Gentlemen," he greeted. "I've come to propose an end to this war before it begins. Do you have a moment?"

They glanced at each other, then the Prince nodded and assured, "A moment, perhaps. State your business."

Folding his hands before him, the old man suggested, "What if I can deliver this girl to you without having to go to the messy step of war with her?"

Tahmrof raised his chin and bade, "Go on."

"I'll escort her to the gate," the old man continued. "We will have words and you will simply let us in."

"That sounds too easy," the Duke observed. "What is in this for you?"

"Restored peace in the land," was the wizard's answer. "The black dragon has his mate back so there should be no more reason for further bloodshed.

The Duke and Prince exchanged looks again.

Raising his bushy eyebrows, the old wizard leaned his head slightly.

Nodding, the Prince offered, "Have a seat. We shall discuss your terms."

As they all took their places at the table the dragon's tooth still lay on, the old wizard's eyes narrowed and he sniffed twice, then asked, "Was there an old warlock in here?"

CHAPTER 16

The morning sun had not fully broken the horizon and the land was bathed in that glow from the East. Long shadows from the forest and the buildings of the village were cast. Horses and cattle mingled in the grain field. Not much was heard, no discussion and no preparations of battle. Tents were as they had been the night before and not disturbed. Campfires still smoldered everywhere. The village itself was very quiet. Even the farmers who rose at this hour were absent.

Still in the castle servant's dress, Faelon stood just outside of the meeting hall, her eyes on the ground as she leaned against the cold stone wall.

Vinton butted her with his nose. "Come on, now. It's almost time."

She turned her eyes to him, feeling a little ashamed as she asked, "Are you sure about this?"

"Your soldiers need every horse here," the unicorn explained, "and Ralligor was right when he said you should return in flamboyant fashion."

A slight smile touched her lips. "Are all unicorns so giving?"

Vinton shrugged. "I don't know all unicorns. I do know that you are worth the sacrifice. Come on, now. Let's get that thing in place."

Faelon vented a deep breath, then hesitantly reached up and slipped the halter over his nose. He lowered his head, allowing her to buckle it behind his ears, and when he did, her eyes filled with tears. "Thank you for this, Vinton. I have no truer friend in all the world than you."

He raised his head, smiling at her as he said, "I feel honored."

"A girl in the village lent me some undergarments," she informed, "so I can ride properly now. I don't know what I'm going to do about this skirt, but I can at least ride properly. Should I put a blanket on your back? It might make you more comfortable."

"I didn't need one yesterday," the unicorn reminded. "Besides. You aren't heavy at all. I barely even notice you."

She smiled again, much broader this time, and she wrapped her arms around his neck, hugging him as tightly as she dared.

He whickered and nuzzled her.

Pa'lesh emerged, dressed for battle as always. "Princess Faelon, it's nearly time."

Still holding onto the unicorn, she nodded, then finally tore herself away and looked up to the Field Captain. "Is everyone ready?"

Half smiling the way she always did, Pa'lesh nodded and confirmed, "Oh, yes. I'm always ready." She looked the Princess up and down and asked, "How do you intend to ride wearing that?"

Faelon shrugged.

The Field Captain pursed her lips, then she drew her dagger and ordered, "Spread your legs."

Her eyes widening, the Princess stepped back, watching almost in horror as the big Zondaen reached down with the dagger and stabbed it into the skirt, running it downward and splitting it all the way to the ground.

"Turn around," Pa'lesh ordered.

Hesitantly, Faelon complied.

Vinton watched the Zondaen split the back of the skirt and nodded. "That seems to fix things."

"If you intend to wear it," the Field Captain said, "it will have to work in battle."

"Thank you," Faelon offered.

Prince Chail emerged, now wearing battle armor over his upper arms, shoulders and torso. He also wore light armor over his thighs and greaves over his boots. As usual, he wore no helmet. No sword hung from his belt, but a sword breaker and dagger hung from the right side. His eyes quickly found the women and he asked, "Are we ready?"

Pa'lesh turned to him and folded her arms, looking up at him with absolute confidence as she replied, "You know I am, Chail of Enulam. Are you?"

"Can't wait," he answered with a smile. Looking to Faelon, the Prince turned his eyes down to her split skirt and observed, "Well, you seem ready to go."

She blushed and looked away from him.

Rolling her eyes, the Field Captain turned to walk away. "I should take up my position."

Chail grabbed her arm and stopped her. "You *are* in position, Captain."

Once again a mix of shock and rage was in her eyes as she turned them up to him.

"I mean it," the Prince informed harshly. "We have things covered in the field. Princess Faelon's safety is more important than one more sword out there."

"More important than having the best sword we have out there?" she snarled back.

He nodded. "The best sword should be protecting the Princess."

Pa'lesh folded her arms. "Any reason *you* can't baby sit her?"

"I didn't bring my special axe for that," he answered with a smile.

"So you're going to use your status to get your way with me again, aren't you?"

"Of course I am," he confirmed.

Faelon glanced back and forth between them. "Can you both stay with me?" When they both turned their eyes to her, she cringed a little and admitted, "I'm scared to death. I don't know what to expect out there."

"You aren't going out there," Pa'lesh informed. "You will leave the fighting to the warriors."

Faelon looked to Prince Chail.

He raised his brow.

She turned and looked to the stallion, who simply stared back, giving her his absolute confidence. Looking back to the Prince and Field Captain, the Princess folded her arms and informed, "My soldiers are going to need to see what they are fighting for. I shall not cringe in the shadows while people die for me."

Chail exchanged glances with Pa'lesh, then looked back to the Princess and explained, "Highness, the last thing we—"

"The matter is settled," she insisted. "When they march on this village they will see me here waiting to meet them."

"Really bad idea," the Field Captain said straightly.

"And fighting a war like this is a good one?" she snapped back. "We're outnumbered, Captain Pa'lesh. The spirits of the soldiers who fight for me must be kept high. I can at least do that for them."

Vinton finally stepped forward and assured, "She will be kept safe, especially with the three of us guarding her."

Pa'lesh turned her eyes down, shaking her head. "I really don't like this."

Prince Chail snapped, "Your opinion is noted, Captain."

"As is yours," Princess Faelon informed.

A young Enulam soldier wheeled around the corner of the meeting hall and stopped abruptly, reporting, "They're coming, about four hundred paces from the bend. Garrison strength from the look of them."

Chail nodded to him and watched as he ran back toward his post, then he turned his eyes down to Faelon and said, "The moment's at hand, Princess."

Staring back up at him with wide eyes, she swallowed hard and nodded to him. When Vinton butted her in the back with his nose, she turned and looked to his eyes for reassurance, finding it there. She felt his essence envelope her, felt that warm, safe place around her and finally drew a calming breath. Once again with some difficulty, she got onto his back, this time astride him and took the reins. From here, she looked to Chail and said, "Let's get this done."

He smiled slightly, then slapped Pa'lesh on the back, making her stumble forward a step. "Let's get to our mounts, Captain."

Vinton paced around the meeting hall, the first structure the soldiers would encounter in the village, and into the middle of the road beside it. Ahead was that bend in the road that the enemy forces would charge around. The road was wide enough at this point for four or five horsemen to ride abreast, and most likely they would be the first to attack.

Faelon stared blankly down the road, feeling fear for the village that had taken her in for the night. Her future would take a serious turn in the next few moments. Victory would mean her restoration, defeat her death. Never had she felt such burden.

The first horses rounded the bend. It was time.

Faelon was the first and only one they saw as they closed the distance. They seemed fearless of battle and did not even bother drawing their weapons as they neared to within a hundred paces.

Her heart thundering, the Princess simply stared back, never taking her eyes from the approaching riders. When they were only fifty paces away, she made a startling discovery, and her eyes widened.

These soldiers were not from Caipiervell!

The over-armor tunics that the officers wore were red and trimmed in black and purple. The horses were also armored about their necks and flanks. That was something the mounted soldiers of Caipiervell never did. Their helmets, even those worn by the mounted soldiers and foot soldiers behind had three steel all the way over the top, one high one in the center and two slightly lower ones just above eye and temple height. Only one wore no helmet. He was a big man—a very big man!—who only wore light armor, the tunic of an officer and little armor over his legs. His head was shaved bald and a thin black beard surrounded his mouth. Alone, he was an intimidating sight, but he was being followed by at least a thousand soldiers, none of which seemed to be from Caipiervell.

Vinton raised his head, glancing back at the Princess as he whickered, "Steady."

She nodded, her wide eyes locked on the approaching soldiers.

The four officers in front turned their attention to the camp behind the Princess and the big man with them raised his chin toward it.

"Stop!" Faelon ordered before she realized.

The approaching soldiers seemed stunned at hearing her voice and actually stopped.

Swallowing hard, she scanned their ranks once again and informed, "You are not welcome in this village. Either surrender or go back where you came from."

The four officers exchanged glances and many of the men behind them laughed.

The big man regarded her with apathetic eyes as he asked, "Would you be the tribute meant to pay us to turn us around or is this someone's idea of humor?"

Another of the officers leaned toward him and suggested, "We should attack before she alarms the sleeping army. Our orders are to finish them quickly."

Chail and Pa'lesh rounded the meeting hall on their large war horses and took up positions flanking Princess Faelon.

The bald man's eyes found Chail immediately, locking on him in a deadly glare. The Prince of Enulam returned this look but with the hint of a smile.

The officer directly facing Pa'lesh raised his chin and demanded, "Who would dare challenge us?"

"Permit me to introduce us," the Field Captain offered in an uncharacteristically sweet voice. "I would be Captain Pa'lesh of Zondae. The big fellow over there is Prince Chail of Enulam and this girl between us is Princess Faelon of Caipiervell. And you are?"

"In no mood for such foolishness," he growled, drawing his sword. "You will surrender the girl and disband this army or you will all die today."

Chail smiled slightly, slowly pulling his axe from its place behind him. His eyes never left the big bald man as he challenged, "Perhaps you'd like to try and come through us."

His eyes narrowing, the bald soldier pulled his sword and kicked his horse forward.

"Now!" Pa'lesh shouted as she also drew her weapon.

A hail of arrows, some three hundred or more, was shot from the right side of the road, almost all of them finding their mark. Chaos ensued as the soldiers who had not been struck turned and armed themselves, raising their shields against a second volley. Most of this volley found shields, but many got through and struck down many more of the enemy soldiers. As they tried to advance into the forest to engage the archers, the Enulam garrison attacked from the forest on the other side, blindsiding them and felling a quarter of them before they realized what was happening. Turning again, they found themselves under attack by the Zondaen garrison from the right side.

The four officers charged the Prince and Field Captain. With a snort from Vinton, two of the horses panicked and reared up, throwing their riders. Chail and the big bald man swung their weapons with true aim and steel met steel over and over. Pa'lesh engaged the other with her inherent ferocity. The four of them battled from horseback for several moments as Vinton quietly folded his essence around himself and the Princess and backed away.

As the battle started to go badly for them, many of the surviving enemy soldiers tried to retreat, but no quarter was granted.

The two officers who had been thrown from their horses recognized that the battle was lost and one attempted to flee, finally throwing his weapon to the ground as he found himself confronted by three Zondaen warriors. The other simply disarmed himself and did not rise from his knees.

The man Pa'lesh fought vastly underestimated her speed and ferocity with the sword and found himself impaled before he realized.

Prince Chail seemed to have his hands full with an opponent that seemed to match his size and strength. They backed away from each other, then, together, they dismounted and their fight raged on. Axe met sword, sword met axe. This fight came down to skill against skill, but the heavier weapon was taking its toll on the bald man as well as Chail's arm. Both men tired, but neither would yield. Even as the rest of the battle ended, these two men continued to fight. Everyone around them seemed to realize that they should not intervene, and no one did. Zondaen, Enulam and even a few enemy soldiers who had surrendered gathered around them for a closer look.

Eventually, blades would find flesh on both men and scar armor, but even slightly wounded they continued to strike and parry with the same savage cries that they started with. These were two evenly matched opponents fighting to the death, evenly matched but for two small details. Youth favored Chail. Experience favored the bald man. Strength and speed favored them both.

One thrust of the bald man's sword got past the Prince's defenses and a hand's length of the blade rammed into Chail's shoulder. Yelling in pain and rage, the Prince brought his axe up into the bald man's side, finding both flesh and armor. The bald man yelled back and stumbled away. Chail pursued, barely acknowledging his wound as he swung the heavy axe again. The bald man met the axe with his sword but the parry was weak and almost collapsed. Half turning, the Prince kicked the bald man hard in the chest but only stunned him. As he staggered backward further, Chail shouted a mighty cry and swung his weapon with all the strength he had left, sinking it deep into the bald man's chest armor and his ribs.

Spitting blood, the bald man staggered backward as the Prince wrenched the axe from him, and before he fell, the axe found its mark again, this time sinking into his skull.

Stained with his enemy's blood, his chest heaving with each breath, Chail backed away from his vanquished enemy and watched him fall, just staring down at him for a moment after.

Also eyeing the bald man's cleaved head, Pa'lesh approached the Prince and asked, "What took you so long? I thought I was going to have to deal with him myself."

Chail still struggled to catch his breath, but he met the Field Captain's eyes with a smile and managed. "Just enjoying the moment."

She smiled back and nodded. "Next time, I get the big one."

He laughed, nodding back in agreement.

A small group of prisoners was escorted to them, numbering less than twenty. When they reached the location of the two surviving officers, they were forced to their knees. No more fight was in them. They were surrounded by some of the best warriors of the Abtont forest and knew it. The whole battle had lasted only a few moments.

Sheathing her weapon, Pa'lesh walked to within a pace of the enemy officers and folded her arms, looking down at him with little more than contempt as she snarled, "You call these warriors? I expected a greater challenge than these squirrels you put in armor and gave swords."

None of the enemy soldiers had an answer for her. None would even look at her face.

Chail approached, settling his axe over his healthy shoulder as he asked, "When can we expect the next attack?"

The two officers exchanged looks.

Pa'lesh kicked one of them, knocking him to his back as she shouted, "Answer him!"

The Prince nudged her with his elbow and scolded, "Now, Captain. That's no way to treat our guests, even if they are completely incompetent on the battlefield."

The other officer glared up at him. "You will not survive the day."

Motioning to the bald man's body with his head, the Prince informed, "He didn't think so, either. Now tell me how far behind you the next attack is."

"Perhaps you should just kill me," the officer growled back.

Pa'lesh met the Prince's eyes, then shrugged and drew her dagger. Before it arrived at her enemy's throat, her wrist was grabbed by Prince Chail, who pulled it back to her and removed the dagger from her hand.

"You won't get answers from him if you kill him," Chail reminded.

"Perhaps not," she conceded, "but the others surely will if I open this one's throat and pull his entrails through the hole."

Turning his eyes to the horrified soldier, the Prince admitted, "You know, you may just have a point there. However, the powers over us may just be a little irked if we should have to kill them all like that."

"I'm sure the common soldiers back there don't have any knowledge," the Field Captain guessed, "so we're clearly going to have to get it from these two."

Chail nodded in agreement, then suggested, "Okay, how about you go and interrogate this one in private and I'll stay here with the other."

"Agreed," the Zondaen accepted. Reaching down, she grabbed his tunic and hoisted the enemy officer from his knees, demonstrating strength legendary to her people. "I'll be done with him within the hour," she informed as she led him into the village by the tunic she still held.

The Prince watched her depart, then he looked down to the remaining officer and shook his head. "Well, I suppose you're the lucky one who gets to talk to me." He looked up to an approaching Zondaen and ordered, "Have the rest of the prisoners taken to the village hall and put them under heavy guard. Make certain none of them are hiding arms."

She nodded to the Prince and motioned to some of the Enulam and Zondaen soldiers.

Chail watched as the prisoners were collected and marched away, then he looked to the officer who was still on his knees. He took the axe from his shoulder and looked over the blood stained blades. Nodding, he admitted, "I'd hoped this thing would cleave more sculls than it did." He turned his eyes back down to the officer.

The enemy officer seemed to maintain his composure, but the color began to leave his face, his eyes widening as he stared at the big battle axe the huge man before him held.

"What are you called?" the Prince asked in a casual voice.

The officer raised his head, replying, "Barrek."

Chail nodded. "You may call me Prince Chail."

Barrek raised his chin, and his eyes actually widened more.

"Perhaps you and I can talk like gentlemen," the Prince suggested hopefully.

A man screamed from somewhere in the village. Everyone grew silent and looked that way.

Shaking his head, the Prince looked back to his axe and said, "Aren't you glad you're not your colleague right now? Captain Pa'lesh is one of the most ruthless women at Zondae. You know, she once gutted a man who wouldn't cooperate with her. That didn't kill him. She ended up strangling him to death with his own entrails."

Barrek's eyes narrowed. "Do you expect me to believe that? I know that your kingdom and hers are mortal enemies."

"Things change," Chail sighed. "As you can see, we tend to work very well together on the battlefield." He turned his eyes to the enemy officer. "You came from Ravenhold, didn't you?"

"What if I did?" Barrek countered in a challenging tone.

Slowly shaking his head, the Prince informed, "I know quite a bit about your kingdom. It isn't very large, not very rich, and now I see you've been coerced into being the sacrificial lambs for this Tahmrof who does not seem to want to commit his own troops for his own needs. He would rather see yours led to slaughter than leave his comfortable palace himself."

"I do as Lord Nemlivv commands," the Ravenhold officer informed straightly. "And I don't know a Tamrof."

"Weren't your orders to destroy Princess Faelon's forces before they could march on the castle?" Prince Chail asked. "Looks like you've failed. You're entire garrison was wiped out today, and for what? I have a feeling you aren't the only troops from Ravenhold we will encounter today, and further clashes between your people and mine, especially so close to Zondae, now our ally, could very well lead your kingdom and mine to war, and you can be sure Zondae would jump right into that."

Barrek said nothing.

"If I release you," the Prince continued, "We are sure to meet in battle again, that is unless this Lord Nemlivv has you hung for failing him. I'm sure that would also strain relations between your kingdom and Caipiervell, especially if you find yourselves at war with us."

"That is none of my concern," the Ravenhold officer growled back.

Chail shrugged. "I don't really care what you are concerned with. What you are going to do is tell me is how many more of your people's troops we can expect to encounter today."

"What makes you think I even know anything?" Barrek sneered.

"Well," the Prince sighed, "if you don't then you're Captain Pa'lesh's problem, not mine. Good luck with her." He settled the axe back onto his shoulder and turned to leave.

"We weren't told any more than we had to know," the Ravenhold officer shouted. When the Prince did not stop, he added, "We were commanded to take the village and hold it."

Chail stopped, half turning his head. "Hold it for whom?"

"That's all I know," Barrek assured. "That is what we were commanded to do."

"And the villagers?" the Prince prodded.

The officer was a long time in answering, but finally said, "We were to fight and kill those who resisted. That's all."

"Your people don't exactly have such a reputation," the Prince informed. "History tells a story of your armies taking villages and killing everyone, men, women *and* children. Perhaps you would like to clear that up for me."

"That is rumor and innuendo," Barrek scoffed. "I've heard similar stories about your people."

"Of course you have," Chail said flatly. "However, I didn't just lose a costly battle to you. I owe you no answers and I really have no more time to waste on you. Good day."

The Ravenhold officer stood. "Think hard about it, Prince of Enulam. If we are forming an alliance with this Tahmrof of Caipiervell then why would we slaughter his people? Perhaps he wanted to make sure the village remains loyal."

"Peasants don't care who is in charge," the Prince informed. "They are simply struggling to survive most of the time." His eyes finally found Princess Faelon, who slowly strode to him. "Am I right, Princess?"

She looked up at him and nodded, then turned her eyes back to the Ravenhold officer.

Chail turned and took her shoulder. "Oh, and by the way, this is Princess Faelon, the rightful heir to the throne of Caipiervell. She's the girl you and your men were sent here to murder today."

Barrek took a step back, his gaze shifting back up to the Prince.

Motioning with his head to the fallen bald man, Chail continued, "That little fellow right there was sent specifically for that purpose. Or didn't you know that?"

Glancing at the fallen bald man, the Ravenhold officer shrugged. "I—I didn't even know him until a couple of seasons ago."

"Let me enlighten you," the Prince continued. "He was a fugitive from Enulam who fled three seasons ago. I'm not sure what his crime was, but I know he was not man enough to face punishment. I see he's been hiring himself out as a mercenary to any kingdom that needs a good sword." His eyes narrowed. "He also seems to be for hire for those who would need an honor-less bastard who could see to it an innocent girl gets murdered. Or were you sent to do that?"

Barrek frantically shook his head. "Only to take the village. I knew nothing of this girl, I swear! None of us did!"

Chail pursed his lips and nodded. "So, you weren't sent to murder her. I see. You were just sent to slaughter an army that was returning to the castle to discuss terms of surrender."

"I—I wasn't informed. We would not engage an army that..." He looked away. "Apparently word did not reach us that you meant to surrender."

"How far behind you is the next garrison?" the Prince asked straightly.

Turning his eyes down, Barrek replied, "I don't know of another garrison."

"You didn't leave your castle alone," Chail informed. "Your men were split up by number and clearly inexperience. That tells me you were meant to fail and that there are more of you waiting for us somewhere. That also means you'll be taking the lead when we ride back to the castle."

Hesitantly, Faelon approached Barrek, absently tugging on her thumb as she stared up at him.

Vinton strode up with her, standing beside her and eying this human himself, then he looked to the Prince and reported in a whicker, "That is truly all he knows. It would seem that they were not all trusted with all of the information."

"But they were sent here to kill me," the Princess breathed, her eyes still on the enemy soldier. When he would not even look at her, she turned and hurried away, toward the forest.

Chail's eyes were still locked on the Ravenhold officer's as he ordered, "Bring this incompetent coward his horse and send him on his way. He has a report to give to his superiors."

Prince and unicorn watched as Barrek mounted his horse and fled, then Vinton looked to Chail's injured shoulder and asked, "Would you like for me to attend to that?"

There was much activity in the village, but Faelon's mind was far from it. So many people lay dead and she knew she was at the center of it. She had wept before, but now sat at the base of a tree, her legs drawn to her and her arms wrapped around them. Just staring into the forest, she put her thoughts as far away from this ordeal as she could, but she kept running into a squire, one who cared for her, loved her, and really should not have.

When she heard someone approaching, she did not even look up. She just stared into the forest.

Pa'lesh sat down beside her and turned her eyes into the forest as well, munching on an apple.

Long moments passed before the Princess spoke. "How many died out there?"

The Field Captain shrugged. "I didn't get a report on enemy casualties. We had twenty-seven wounded, no dead. Not surprisingly. They never knew what hit them."

Faelon nodded. "Any reason you kept my solders out of the battle?"

Pa'lesh took another bite of her apple. "Your soldiers need to be leading the way when we go back to retake the castle. It's best that they're fresh and ready. We'll bring up the rear and reinforce them."

"I can't do this," the Princess said softly. She felt herself beginning to cry again. Try as she may she could not hold back the flood of tears that resumed. "I just can't do it. I'm not the great queen everyone wants me to be." She held onto her legs tighter, burying her face between her knees. "Why did this have to happen?"

Glancing down at the huddled, sobbing Princess, Pa'lesh sighed impatiently and asked, "Do you want to lead your people?"

Hesitantly, Faelon shrugged, still crying as she answered, "I don't know. They would probably be better off if I had been killed by that dragon."

Pa'lesh glanced at her again. "You know, many seasons ago I found myself promoted to Field Captain shortly after my queen *and* my commander were both killed in an ambush. My new queen found herself thrust into a position of power she didn't seem ready for and she was no more prepared for it than you are now."

Faelon turned her eyes up to the Zondaen.

Pa'lesh continued, "I knew she wasn't ready, but she put her trust in me, enough to promote me young and believe that I would be able to perform my duties to Zondae despite my inexperience, and she had my absolute trust in return."

"You both knew about the art of war," the Princess pointed out. "I know nothing of it."

"But you do know about the art of compassion. You also make decisions and stand by them. That's when those who follow you see your strength." She turned her eyes down to the Princess and half smiled. "You don't have to lead your army with a sword in your hand, just let them be soldiers. Be their rallying point. Let them know they have your trust and that you're as dedicated to them as they are to you. That's how Queen Le'errin won my absolute trust and the trust of those all around her."

"What if I make a mistake?"

"What if you do? Are you going to let that keep you from doing anything? Don't worry about making mistakes and just be the leader they need you to be."

Faelon nodded and turned her eyes back into the forest. "Do you trust Prince Chail?"

Pa'lesh huffed a laugh and admitted, "I suppose I do. We're sworn enemies, but he's an honest man and a strong leader. He's a hell of a good soldier and tactician as well."

"You trust him even though your people were enemies for so long?"

"That trust was earned. Princess Le'ell was always a flighty, spoiled little brat with little discipline despite my best efforts, but around him I saw her mother's traits emerge from her. I saw confidence glow from her. She actually started making decisions for the good of Zondae." Pa'lesh looked down to Faelon and nodded. "You can do this. I keep hearing about what a great leader your father was and how people see him in you. Just let them see him there, and show them your confidence."

"Even if I don't feel any confidence?"

"Especially when you don't feel it." The Field captain stood and tossed the half eaten apple from her, then she offered Faelon her hand and said, "Your people are waiting to see you, and your allies are looking for a good fight."

Taking Pa'lesh's hand, the Princess was pulled easily to her feet, then she ordered, "Just don't get yourself killed because of me. I wouldn't want to live with that."

Pa'lesh half smiled and corrected, "If I die on the battlefield then I will die a fulfilled woman and Zondaen warrior. Just know that I would be proud to die in your service as I would my own queen's."

Smiling slightly, Faelon offered, "Thank you."

They emerged from the forest side by side and Faelon felt compelled to ask, "What did you do to that soldier you were questioning."

The Field Captain half smiled again and replied, "I used some techniques to get what I wanted from him."

"You didn't hurt him badly, did you?"

With a glance at the Princess, Pa'lesh huffed a laugh and informed, "He'll pull through. I'm sure he enjoyed my interrogation as much as I did."

Faelon's brow lowered. "Huh?"

"I'll explain when you're older." Pa'lesh raised her chin and greeted, "Chail. Is everything ready?"

He strode to them and answered, "Just waiting on you two."

Seeing the blood stain on his torn shirt, the Princess gasped and raised her hand to his formally wounded shoulder, running her hand over the rock hard muscle as she asked, "Are you hurt?"

"Our unicorn friend saw to my injury," the Prince assured. "I feel good as new. In fact, he treated all of our wounded. Tired him out a bit but he sure seemed eager to help. He even healed our enemies."

"Why?" Pa'lesh snarled.

"He has a compassionate heart," was the Princess' answer. "I would expect no less from him."

Chail went on, "The villagers will watch the prisoners as we march on the castle."

"That's good," Pa'lesh said straightly. "According to the man I questioned we have at least two more garrisons waiting to meet us half a league from the castle. We'll have our hands full long before we have to try and breech the castle itself. Assuming we get through them, do you have a plan to deal with Tahmrof and the castle defenses?"

The wizard appeared behind her and assured, "I'm sure they'll have their hands full when we arrive. Faelon, how do you feel, lass?"

Glancing up at the Field Captain, the Princess nodded and assured, "I feel like it's time to free my people. I also feel like my belly is full of very nervous worms."

"Our mounts await," the wizard said, "and you've got a unicorn who's been asking about you."

She could not help but smile a little. "By the way. Has anyone seen Shahly?"

"Put to task," the wizard assured. "You'll be seeing her by the end of the day. Right now you need to get on your mount and address your soldiers. They are eagerly waiting to hear from you."

This news did not sit easily and she turned her eyes down. Now, she was far more nervous than before.

Pa'lesh patted her shoulder and assured, "We'll be right there beside you."

"What if I say something foolish?" the Princess asked grimly. "What if—"

"What if you get up there before them and inspire them to win the day?" The Field Captain interrupted. "What if you are such a princess to rally around as they've never seen?"

Turning her eyes down, Faelon admitted, "I don't know what to say to them."

Chail took her other shoulder and straightly said, "I'm sure your father didn't either. I'm sure he spoke from his heart. That's where you will find the words you need."

Slowly, she turned her eyes up to his, then she turned and slipped her arms around his waist, hugging him as tightly as she could. "I'll try not to disappoint you."

"You won't disappoint anyone," he assured.

"Well, now," the wizard announced. "It seems that the troops are awaiting their princess." He turned and led the way to their mounts.

Faelon held on to the mammoth Prince Chail the whole way. Her head barely came up to his broad shoulders and she felt very safe with his very thick arm around her. That and he was such a man as she had never seen!

Vinton waited for them by the horses and raised his head as he saw her.

She finally let go of the Prince and approached the unicorn, slowly raising her hands to him. She scratched him behind the ears and offered, "Thank you for this. I need to inspire the soldiers and having you nearby is of great comfort to me."

He whickered a laugh. "What can be more inspiring than seeing their princess on the back of a unicorn?"

She smiled at him and patted his neck, confirming, "Nothing."

With Prince Chail's help she got mounted and took the reins, though she would not guide him with them. They were more for show than anything. With the Prince of Enulam, Field Captain Pa'lesh and that trusted wizard behind her, she felt much more confident, yet was still more nervous than she had ever been, even more so than she had been the last few days.

One of the grain fields was now a staging area and all of the troops were neatly assembled, lined up and facing the road, all on horseback. Caipiervell troops made up the front two rows and a mix of troops from Enulam and Zondae behind them. They grew silent as they saw Princess Faelon and her entourage approach them. All of their eyes were on her, and the moment became ever so tense.

She stopped before the formation, her eyes panning from one side to the other. This was the moment of truth. They awaited word from their princess. She managed to swallow back her fear and somehow found a voice they could all hear.

"Um, you probably all know by now that I won't be marching into battle with you." She shrugged. "As you can see I'm really not dressed for it and to be honest I think I would just be in your way." The soft laughter that rippled through the troops broke the tension and she actually felt herself relax a little. Still, she was much more somber as she continued. "I will understand if some of you do not want to fight this battle. There will be no dishonor for any who choose to leave. But if you do stay, I implore you, do not fight this battle for me. Do not fight for the crown. Fight for your people. Fight for your families. Fight for those still at the castle who would live horrible lives under my uncle's boots. I'm not important enough to risk your lives for. You see me as I would be without title and privilege, dressed as a servant of the kingdom, and that's what I am with my crown, your servant.

"I haven't been the perfect princess. Since the deaths of my parents I've barely noticed the real presence about the castle. I barely noticed all of those who have made life for me bearable. I did not deserve to be given the throne of Caipiervell. I had no purpose. I was just one more unworthy noble to be served and protected. For that I am sorry. The people of Caipiervell deserve better. I want to give them better. I want to give you better.

"Today we go to face the bulk of the Caipiervell army. My uncle kept the loyalty of the larger part of the army, but not the best part.

The best of the Caipiervell army stands before me now, and the best of the Caipiervell army and those who have come to aid us will take the day!"

Weapons were drawn and cheers went up and Faelon felt the unicorn beneath her flinch. The cheers and shouting died down as the Princess raised her hand, and she continued, "Please fight bravely, but I would implore you not to sacrifice yourselves." Her eyes darted around the ranks again. "As I said before, any who choose not to fight today may leave with no disgrace. I would only ask that you approach me before you do so that I might thank you for standing with me as long as you have."

Silently, looks among the waiting troops were exchanged. No one moved otherwise.

Finally, a horse was kicked forward, one with a fully armored knight on his back.

Faelon raised her chin as the knight approached, and her heart broke a little as she saw the face of a man she had trusted since childhood. "Sir Daldwan."

He just stared back at her for a moment, then he nodded and observed, "You have your mother's eyes, and your father's heart." He turned his horse and looked to the waiting men, shouting, "King Elner lives within the heart of his daughter. I will see her restored to the throne she belongs on or I shall die in the attempt! Her Highness has granted pardon to those who would not fight today. I would ask you to come forward and be recognized."

Again, looks were exchanged among the men. Many shook their heads. One finally shouted back, "Sir Daldwan, can we quit wasting time and get to our enemy while we're all still young enough to enjoy the fight?"

Shouts and cheers were raised again, louder this time.

The knight turned back to his princess and informed, "We await your command to march, your Highness." He leaned toward her. "Don't make us wait too long. This fight has been a long time coming." He finished with a wink.

She smiled back and offered, "Thank you, Sir Daldwan. Thank you."

CHAPTER 17

Insurmountable obstacles were all they had to look forward to. At a slow pace, the castle was not quite an hour away and a ragtag army of three kingdoms was quiet for the most part. There was little to talk about, really. With no siege engines and barely enough soldiers to even begin an assault on a castle that size, they had almost no hope of succeeding, but for the reassurances of their leadership.

Leading the procession were three people who rode abreast, two of them warriors.

Princess Faelon rode between Prince Chail and Field Captain Pa'lesh. Still on Vinton's back, she could not settle her thoughts. She knew there was little hope of success or even survival. Somehow, the people around her felt differently. They seemed convinced that the day would be won. However, no matter how she tried to convince herself of that, the truth of their situation loomed like a storm on the horizon. She needed a distraction.

Looking to the Field Captain, she timidly asked, "Pa'lesh, did you ever think of starting a family?"

Glancing at her, the big Zondaen countered, "What do you mean?"

"Did you ever want any children?"

Pa'lesh glanced at her again. "What makes you think I haven't any?"

Turning her eyes down, the Princess offered, "I'm sorry. I didn't mean to pry."

"I have no such secrets from you," Pa'lesh assured. "I have three children."

Faelon and Chail both snapped their eyes to her.

She regarded them casually. "You look surprised."

"Uh," the Prince stammered, "I must admit that I am."

"I had them young," the Field Captain said wistfully. "I was still in training and continued to train almost until the moment I delivered my first. Well, my second, too. They were sired by yobs at Zondae and were born yobs themselves. You can imagine my disappointment when that happened."

"Yobs?" Faelon asked.

Chail answered, "Zondaen men."

Pa'lesh continued, "It seemed that if I wanted a warrior girl to raise then she would not be sired from the yobs at Zondae, so I took the matter elsewhere." She glanced at them, seeing that she had their full attention and now had the attention of the unicorn. "It seemed that if I wanted that warrior girl then she would have to be sired by a warrior."

The Prince shook his head. "Oh, don't tell me."

She nodded. "I figured after two tries it was time to find someone strong enough to sire me a girl."

Glancing at Chail, Faelon hesitantly asked, "What did you do?"

"I found a soldier from Enulam," the Field Captain answered straightly. "All I had to do was get across the border and find a soldier I liked without getting myself captured or killed. It seemed easy enough until I was actually over there. The funny thing about Enulam patrols is they are always at least five strong. I didn't want to take my chances against five of them so I had to wait for one to get separated from the others."

"Wait a minute," the Prince insisted. "You, a woman and warrior from Zondae, crossed into Enulam territory with rape on your mind?"

"Is that so hard to believe?" she countered. "Of course, it really wasn't like that."

"Sure it wasn't."

"No, it wasn't. When I found one that I wanted I just waited for them to stop, and yes the Goddess smiled on me that day when he separated from his patrol. He was young and very easy on the eyes with a very well made body not so unlike yours."

Chail nodded. "I see. And you ambushed him and hoped to overpower him to get what you wanted. You women are all alike. Only one thing on your minds. Did it occur to you that we might want to be respected?"

"No, it didn't," she answered with a slight laugh, "and that's not how it happened. It was a hot day and he looked like he was going to the river for a swim or something. He took off his armor and arming shirt and it wasn't until I got a good look at him that I finally approached."

Faelon blushed and covered her mouth. "Oh, my!"

Pa'lesh smiled. "That's what I was thinking, too. I did what any good warrior would do. I announced my approach and made my intentions clear."

The Prince nodded again. "And he was more than willing to oblige."

"Of course he was," she confirmed. "In fact, he obliged almost every day that month. It seems that the King of Enulam at the time was pretty loose about soldiers on detached duties, and that played into my hands quite nicely. We met at the same place about the same time of day, one or both of us would bring wine and something to eat and he would oblige me."

"This sounds disturbingly familiar," the Prince informed in a low voice.

Pa'lesh shook her head. "Oh, you two weren't the first and you're sure not to be the last."

"Yes. I've seen that you still have a taste for Enulam men."

She shot him a sidelong glance. "And you a taste for Zondaen women."

"Only one," he defended.

Pa'lesh shook her head and admitted, "Well, I'll trust your word on that, but I sure don't know how you do it. I would get bored with the same one over and over."

Faelon informed, "Marriage is about spending your life with someone and being faithful only to them, in bed and out." She looked to Vinton and urged, "Right?"

The stallion nodded. "I intend to be only with Shahly for the rest of my life."

Smiling, the Field Captain said, "Well, joy to you both." She raised her chin, turning her eyes forward as she asked, "Who is that coming? Is he one of ours?"

Chail turned his eyes to the approaching rider, and as the rider turned his horse to ride abreast of him he ordered, "Report."

The Enulam soldier, fully armored and ready for battle, kept his eyes forward and said in a monotone voice, "They're assembled in a field that is perhaps two hundred paces square less than a quarter league ahead."

"How many?" the Prince asked.

"Seems nearly a thousand in four columns. A quarter are heavy horse, about five hundred infantry and archers behind."

"What banners did you see?"

"No banners, but their colors are those of Ravenhold Castle."

Nodding, Chail said, "As I thought. That will be all."

The soldier nodded back and kicked his horse back into a full run.

Pa'lesh glanced at the Prince. "I didn't know you sent scouts."

He smiled slightly. "I like to know what I'm walking into."

"I see," the Field Captain said with narrow eyes. "It doesn't sound like they outnumber us."

"Nor us them," Chail pointed out. "It is another mission that was sent to fail."

Faelon looked up at him and asked, "Why would they do that?"

Pa'lesh answered, "To get us to commit our forces early. They don't necessarily want to win out here. What they want is to inflict casualties and slow our approach to the castle, that way they have an easy victory once we finally arrive." She looked to the Prince. "So, I suppose you have a plan to deal with them?"

"I sure do," he confirmed. "We're going to hit them head-on."

The Field Captain just stared at him for many paces. "You mean you're going to give them exactly what they want."

"That I am," he said straightly. "We'll take up our formations just as we planned, but we'll stay as far on the other side of the field as we can."

"I hope you know what you're doing," Pa'lesh growled.

"Of course I do. We'll move the Caipiervell forces out first and I'll back them up with my garrison and half of yours. You will hold back with the other half and charge into the clearing and into one side of them once the fighting starts."

"You intend to go into the fight outnumbered?"

"Exactly. They'll plan their attack and set their confidence based on what we show them. Your little surprise should take some of the fight out of them. Be warned, though. I'm sending Princess Faelon your way once the battle begins."

The Princess raised her chin and snapped, "Shouldn't I stay on the battlefield to—"

Chail and Pa'lesh answered together, "No."

She fell silent and looked down to the unicorn.

Vinton glanced back at her and admitted, "I agree with them."

Her lips tightened and she looked away. "I still think I could help inspire the soldiers."

"I'm sure you would inspire them," the Prince agreed, "but bear in mind that our enemy's main goal is to kill you. If your soldiers see you slain on the battlefield then they won't be inspired at all, now will they?"

She sighed and admitted, "I suppose not."

"Well," Pa'lesh announced. "I'm glad we can all agree. I'll go back and see to your little surprise." She turned her horse and guided it toward the rear of the formation, selectively picking solders out of the lines as she went.

"You can ride out at my side," the Prince told Faelon, "but as the fighting starts you are going to follow your escorts back this way."

"If you say so," she conceded.

Slowly, Caipiervell soldiers filed into the clearing, hanging a hard left to form up directly across the field from their waiting enemies. Their Princess led them and her ally Prince Chail was at her side. As the Caipiervell soldiers took their positions in a single line abreast of each other and about two paces apart, the soldiers from Enulam and Zondae filed into the field and formed a second line right behind them. They were quickly in formation and facing an enemy with a numerical superiority.

Once the troops were in position and Chail and Faelon were sitting before them, two squires rode up beside them and stopped.

Chail leaned his head to the Princess and said in a low voice, "We'll wait and see what they do. If they charge, you will follow these boys back the way we came."

"What if they send a delegation to talk?" she asked.

"We'll talk," the Prince assured, his eyes tense and locked on the enemy that was less than two hundred paces away, "then you will follow these boys back the way we came."

"But what if they don't want to fight?"

"They've come to kill you and as many of us as they can, especially any soldiers from Caipiervell. I don't think they will just give up."

She nodded, then raised her chin as a group of four enemy soldiers rode out toward the middle of the field.

"Here we go," the Prince murmured, then he half turned his head and ordered, "Sir Daldwan, I need you and two volunteers with capable arms."

The knight rode forward with about a dozen men following him.

Chail glanced back at them. "I appreciate your enthusiasm, but I should only have two of you."

Sir Daldwan pointed at two of them and they rode abreast of the Prince, Princess and the squires.

The group rode toward the middle of the field to meet their opponents, all of them on edge and expecting treachery at any moment. Instead, they reached the center and stopped three paces away from them.

This small group was made up of one Ravenhold officer who was dressed as the last had been and three large soldiers, one of whom carried a loaded crossbow.

The officer quickly scanned Princess Faelon's entourage, his eyes locking on Prince Chail, and he raised his chin before he spoke. "We are here to escort you to Caipiervell Castle. Princess Faelon shall be in my custody during the journey. Your knights and officers may keep their swords, but your soldiers will surrender their weapons and march on foot between our ranks. Are Prince Tahmrof's terms clear?"

Chail glanced at Faelon, then he looked back to the officer and asked, "What is your kingdom's stake in this?"

"That is none of your concern," the officer snapped. "Are the terms clear?"

Looking to Sir Daldwan, the Prince asked, "Should I have him repeat the terms?"

The knight shrugged. "Only if you want to hear them again. Frankly, I find them insulting."

Chail nodded, then looked to the officer and smiled ever so slightly. "I have some terms of my own. How about we each ride back to our respective armies, put our weapons in our hands and fight like you really came here to do?"

His eyes narrowing, the officer snarled, "You are outnumbered and I don't see any archers set. What makes you think you have so much as a chance, you insolent boy?"

"I really hate when people address me so. I think I shall kill you personally."

The officer set his jaw, grinding his teeth as he growled, "You will surrender the girl and your forces immediately."

"I know you think that," the Prince countered, "but it isn't going to happen. Now go back to your lines so that my forces and I can slaughter you with honor."

Glaring at Chail for long seconds, the officer abruptly turned his horse and led his men back to their waiting formations.

Chail raised his hand as his own men started to turn and he ordered, "Hold." His eyes narrowed as he watched the enemy riders return. His gaze was locked on the man with the crossbow. He held the reins tightly with one hand and the other drew up toward his chest. As the soldier with the crossbow turned, the Prince reached to Faelon and grabbed the back of her dress, tearing the fabric as he pulled her quickly her from Vinton's back and laid her across his lap on the saddle.

The crossbow bolt passed right over the unicorn's head.

As the Princess turned over and sat up, pressing her back to the Prince as his arm wrapped around her and held her tightly to him, then he turned his horse and led the retreat back toward his own lines.

"How did you know he was going to do that?" Sir Daldwan shouted.

Chail answered, "If you're going to talk terms of surrender, you don't send one man with a crossbow."

Her dress had been torn halfway down the back and slid from her shoulder. She raised a hand to her chest to keep it from coming all the way off and turned her eyes to the Prince, offering, "Thank you."

He just glanced at her and smiled.

She added, "I just hope I have some dress left by the time we reach the castle."

Chail laughed as they neared the lines. "I don't think anyone around you would object if you didn't."

Her mouth fell open. A second later an arrow whizzed by, then another, then much of the volley rained down and stabbed into the ground. One slammed into the Prince's left shoulder, right outside of his armor. When he lurched forward, she reached up to him and held on, then she noticed a sharp bulge beneath his shirt to one side of his breast plate. As they reached their lines and got out of range of the arrows, Faelon shouted, "I need help! He's hurt!"

Vinton darted to the front of the horse and stopped it.

Twisting her body to turn toward him, the Princess reached up and strained to tear his shirt away from the bulge, wincing as she saw the steel point of an arrow protruding through his skin high on his shoulder.

"Get down," the Prince strained to say.

Hesitantly, she complied and slid from his horse.

As a few soldiers from all three kingdoms began to gather around, he harshly ordered, "Stay in position!" He took a few deep breaths, then he reached over his shoulder and grabbed the arrow, snapping the shaft with his thumb. With another strained breath, he seized the arrow head in his fist and clenched his teeth, then tore the arrow from his shoulder with one quick jerk.

As he groaned in pain, Faelon reached up to him and ordered, "Come on down. We need to attend to that."

Turning his eyes to her, he actually smiled and corrected, "I'm fine. Get to your mount and get out of here. All Hell is about to erupt from this battlefield."

"You're hurt," she insisted.

"I agree," Sir Daldwan said flatly. "You aren't much use to us if you're injured."

Chail looked to him and assured, "Believe me when I say wounding me was the last thing they should have done." He turned his horse and guided it back to the line.

When Faelon looked up to the knight, he just shrugged and turned his horse as well. She shook her head as Vinton approached her. "I don't know if he's more brave or foolish, but he sure looks brave." She took the reins that dangled from the unicorn's nose and this time got on his back with one try. Looking back toward the enemy forces, she winced as she saw more enemy solders rapidly emerging from a road across the clearing. "That isn't good."

"I wonder if he anticipated that," Vinton said. "Come on. We need to get you to safety before the fighting really starts."

"I'm not leaving," she insisted.

He looked back at her. "Faelon, we talked about this."

"And I never quite agreed with you, did I?" she countered.

Only thirty or forty of the enemy charged from the road and Faelon's eyes narrowed as she said aloud as if to herself, "That doesn't look like very many soldiers." They were yelling, and as they charged in front of the enemy formation, many of them turned toward the road and drew their weapons.

One of the Caipiervell officers looked to Chail and asked, "Do we charge?"

Shaking his head, the Prince answered, "Not yet."

Enulam solders on horseback poured from the road, yelling and swinging their ready weapons at the closest of the Ravenhold troops. As they emerged, more darted from the trees and began hacking the archers to pieces.

Prince Chail pulled the axe from behind him and shouted "Now!"

All of the Caipiervell, Enulam and Zondaen solders drew their weapons and charged, forming one solid wall that quickly advanced on the chaotic scene before them. They veered toward the left, and in a moment were across the field and attacking only that part of the enemy lines. As the other part of the Ravenhold formation reorganized and tried to flank around Chail and his garrisons, Captain Pa'lesh charged from the road to Faelon's right and sent their horses galloping toward the circling Ravenhold men.

As before, the fight was bloody and brief.

When it seemed over, one Ravenhold rider kicked his horse as fast as it would go, charging right at Princess Faelon. He had been wounded and blood stained his face and his blade.

Her eyes widening, Faelon raised her chin and said, "Okay. You win. We should leave."

"He's already seen you," the unicorn informed, his eyes on the approaching rider.

The Princess had forgotten about the two squires who were supposed to escort her from the battlefield. Seeing the threat, they drew their weapons and charged out to meet him. Fighting together, they quickly overwhelmed him and he found himself unable to fight them both, and one's sword plunged into his ribs. When he turned and raised his sword, the other swung his blade and caught him in the body.

As blood sprayed from the mortally wounded Ravenhold soldier, Faelon turned her eyes away and covered her mouth.

Vinton observed, "Yours is truly a species of barbarians."

She turned her eyes down and nodded, lowering her hand as she agreed, "Yes, the last few days have convinced me of that."

The squires returned, the older of the two raising his chin as he announced, "We have taken down the enemy, your Highness. You are safe now."

She smiled at them and said, "I am thanks to your bravery. Thank you."

They nodded back, then turned their horses toward the fray that had raged across the field. That side was relatively quiet now as the fight had ended.

As the troops and officers took stock, Chail and Pa'lesh rode back to the Princess they were to defend. When they arrived, the Prince finally dismounted and looked over his shoulder at the fallen Ravenhold soldier who meant to kill Faelon. "Well now. It looks like one slipped through."

The older squire snapped to attention and reported, "He came through your lines, my Lord, but we stopped him."

Chail roughed the boy's hair as he walked passed him, offering, "Good work, lad. Good work." He walked right up to the Princess and folded his thick arms, raising an eyebrow as he scolded, "Weren't you supposed to leave the battlefield?"

She glanced at Vinton, then looked him square in the eye and countered, "I never actually agreed to that. Besides, you are in Caipiervell territory and since I am the Princess here I am in charge."

The Prince also looked to the unicorn, then he shook his head and strode back to his horse.

Pa'lesh walked by him and ordered, "Get that shoulder tended to," then she approached Faelon and shook her head. "I didn't know keeping you safe was going to be so complicated. What happened to leaving the battlefield?"

Setting her hands on her hips, the Princess informed, "I won't leave my soldiers in their darkest hour. I belong—"

"You belong right where we told you to be," the Field Captain snapped, "and until I'm confident that you can defend yourself you will do as we tell you, is that clear?"

The older squire approached and informed, "Captain, we successfully defended our Princess, so all of this really isn't necessary."

He got but a glance from the big Zondaen before her scolding eyes found the Princess again. "You're reminding me of another pain in my backside right now. Don't make me do to you what I have had to do to her many times." With that she turned and strode to the Prince, barking, "Unicorn, can you give us a hand?"

Vinton looked to Faelon and commented, "She's a demanding one, isn't she?"

As he walked past, she just nodded, then she pulled her dress back up and looked away, toward the road across the field. Half a league away was her home, and the most important fight of her life.

❧

There would be no homecoming celebration. The field surrounding the castle had no livestock or tenders in it. Much of the grasses had been trampled down. Smoke rose from behind the castle wall and the battlements were thick with Caipiervell soldiers who expected to repel a siege.

This time, Faelon led the precession of soldiers and was the first to emerge into the field and approach the castle. Lookouts in the towers and on the battlements saw her coming and those within were alerted with horns and other alarms. It seemed chaotic in there. It also seemed impregnable.

Behind her, Chail and Pa'lesh were still discussing the battle, and the Field Captain did not seem happy with him.

"All I'm saying," Pa'lesh argued, "is it would be a good idea to keep me apprised of your plans. What if something had gone wrong?"

"Pa'lesh," he sighed, "nobody knew about Dahkam's garrison. I didn't know who in the camp could be trusted."

"Oh, so now you don't trust me. I thought we were beyond that."

"Now you're sounding like Le'ell."

"Another comment like that and I'm knocking you right off that horse!"

"Sure you are,"

Faelon shot them an irritated look and snapped, "Do you two mind?"

They looked to each other, then to the castle.

Pa'lesh nodded. "A pretty little palace you have. Whitewashed stonework and that wall must be four heights tall. River running under the wall on the north side…"

"What we have to worry about is what's behind the wall," Faelon informed. "My father commissioned a dozen catapults to be built to defend the castle when we were at war with Red Stone. They'll be striking at us before we are halfway across this field."

"Not good," the Prince said grimly.

"Oh, it gets worse," the Princess informed. "Most of the men you see on the wall are archers. We aren't getting anywhere close to the palace."

Pa'lesh looked to Chail and asked, "So, Prince of Enulam, do you have a plan to lay siege to this place?"

"How long can they hold out under siege?" he asked.

Faelon answered, "A whole season or more."

The wizard rode to them from within the forest, his eyes also on the castle as he asked, "How was your journey to the castle?"

"They tried to ambush us," the Field Captain reported, "but Chail of Enulam here seemed to have another garrison up his sleeves that he didn't tell anyone about."

Nodding the wizard observed, "I see. Well, don't get comfortable. Just have the soldiers form up and spread the word that they are not to retreat no matter what they see." He looked to the Princess and said, "Faelon, let's go see if we can talk any sense into them."

Pulling her dress back up onto her shoulder, she turned her eyes to Chail, her brow arched as uncertainty took her features.

The Prince looked to the Wizard and raised his chin.

He smiled back and assured, "No need for concern today. She will be safe with me."

Chail nodded to him.

"Come along," the wizard urged. "We haven't much time."

She took his side, holding her dress up with one hand as she loosely held Vinton's reins with the other.

As they neared, the unicorn looked to the wizard and asked, "This seems awfully dangerous. Are you sure you know what you're doing?"

With a glance and a smile, he simply replied, "You'll just have to trust me, my friend. No matter what you see or hear, you'll just have to trust me."

Faelon looked ahead of them to the hastily rebuilt southern gate.

Turning his eyes to her, the wizard assured, "Everything will be all right, child. You'll be home before you realize."

She nodded, fearing what was to come.

They stopped about fifteen paces from the wall and the wizard looked to the men standing directly over the gate, shouting, "I believe I have an audience with Prince Tahmrof. Would you be kind enough to tell him I'm here?"

One of them nodded and hurried to one of the staircases that would take him down.

Moments passed and Faelon grew more and more uneasy.

"Relax," the unicorn advised. "They aren't shooting at us and no one's charged. I'm sure the wizard knows what he's doing."

Faelon nodded again, saying, "I'm just afraid to see him again."

The wizard reached to her and patted her shoulder. "You needn't be afraid, child. Everything will be all right."

Prince Tahmrof appeared, dressed for battle in highly polished armor as he looked over the battlement and shouted down, "You brought her, wizard?"

"She's right here beside me," the wizard confirmed. "And the dragonslayer?"

"On his way," the Prince replied. "I shall have the gate opened."

"As soon as I see the dragonslayer," the wizard corrected. "We wouldn't want any misunderstandings when we are so close to resolving this matter."

Nodding in agreement, Tahmrof turned to speak to a soldier beside him.

"What are you doing?" the stallion whickered.

"I would think that it is obvious," the wizard answered. "I am trading the girl for the dragonslayer."

Faelon turned her eyes to him, her mouth falling open as she slowly shook her head.

He looked to her and smiled. "You wanted to avoid bloodshed. This is the best way. In a way, everyone wins."

"But," she protested, "he'll kill me. That's all he wants to do is kill me!"

Shaking his head, the wizard corrected, "That simply will not happen. As I said, just trust me. I worked hard to negotiate this."

He turned his eyes back up to the palace wall as Duke Malchor appeared beside the Prince. The Duke was dressed for battle but his arm was still splinted and in a sling.

"He's here," the Prince shouted down. "Say to him what you want to and surrender the girl as you promised."

"I have nothing to say to him," the wizard informed. "However, my apprentice would like to have words with him."

The Prince and Duke exchanged glances.

Panic erupted among the men on the battlements and many of them ran for cover.

Ralligor swept in low and landed gently about ten paces from the wizard, looking down at him for a moment before he folded his wings. Finally, he said, "You thought it would be a good idea to have Shahly watch over Falloah and me all night?"

Falloah landed behind him, folded her wings and also looked down to the wizard.

The wizard master simply smiled. "I'm certain you enjoyed every moment of her company last night, mighty friend."

Cocking an eyebrow up slightly, the black dragon turned and approached the castle, his scarlet mate following.

The Prince and Duke backed away, as did the men around them. It was clearly too late to flee and they seemed to know it. Instead, their wide eyes were locked on the dragon as he approached.

Leaning against the wall with one arm laid over the battlements, the black dragon looked down at the puny humans with a certain calmness in his eyes and just stared at them for a long moment. The claw of one finger tapped rhythmically on the stone wall.

A hush fell over the land all around the castle.

"You were good to your word," the dragon finally said. "You brought this parasite right to me, so I'll probably not chew you in half today." He raised his other hand and looked down at his long claws. "On the other hand, the dragonslayer has my full attention, as does the fact that you harbored him. What shall we do about that?"

Prince Tahmrof swallowed hard and assured, "I have no quarrel with you, dragon."

Ralligor gave him a casual glance. "Your lamed up little friend there made a quarrel with me. He nearly killed my mate. Can you understand why that might upset me?"

"What would you have of me?" the Prince demanded.

"I want the dragonslayer," Ralligor answered straightly. He finally looked to them and added, "But not like this. I don't want him just given over to me. I want him running for his life. I want him to know what it is to be hunted." His eyes locked on the Duke. "Perhaps, right before I make the kill, he will feel the despair and terror he's brought to so many others. I don't care about his crimes elsewhere, but he's been sentenced to death for his crimes here." His gaze shifted to the Prince. "See to it I have my hunt."

Tahmrof hesitantly nodded.

The Dragonslayer slowly backed away from the Prince, shaking his head as he shouted, "Traitor!"

The Prince nodded to his soldiers and two of them took the Duke's arms. "Get him to his horse and get him out of here." He watched with hollow eyes as his men took the dragonslayer away.

Looking back with fury in his eyes, Malchor shouted, "You will pay for this, you traitorous bastard! I'll be back and I'll have your head on the end of my lance!"

Hesitantly, Prince Tahmrof looked back to the dragon.

Ralligor nodded. "That's a good first step to getting off of my bad side, but it still does not erase your role in this matter." He looked over the castle, his eyes sweeping it from one side to the other.

As his gaze swept across the palace, the wall and the courtyards below, catapults suddenly fell apart, bowstrings broke, handles broke off of swords, wagon wheels fell off, horses panicked and retreated toward the north side of the palace, many throwing their riders. As the dragon looked back to Prince Tahmrof, the recently rebuilt southern gate simply fell over, free from its hinges by unseen forces. A fiery green glow overtook the dragon's eyes. The ground trembled and a similar green fire erupted from the base of the wall, running its entire span but for the section the dragon leaned on, a section about ten paces wide. Slowly, the rest of the wall sank into the earth below and in a moment the battlements and the men who stood at the ready on them were at ground level. The wall itself was otherwise gone, but for that ten pace wide part the dragon leaned on.

The emerald glow in the dragon's eyes faded away and he just stared down at the Prince, simply saying, "Oops."

Frantically glancing around him, Prince Tahmrof realized that his army had been disarmed and his castle was now almost defenseless, and facing several thousand soldiers from Enulam and Zondae as well as those from Caipiervell who wanted their princess back on her throne.

"Too bad," the dragon drawled. "Looks like your defenses don't work anymore. You might reconsider the battle you were about to wage, and make sure that dragonslayer is far away from your castle when I return tomorrow." He looked out over the half panicked men in the courtyard and those who retreated from the grounded battlements. "Keep one thing in mind, people of Caipiervell. I won't attack a castle and the people within so long as the one who leads them is in my favor." He looked down at Tahmrof and added, "He is not in my favor." He pushed off of the wall and walked toward one of the roads that led away from the castle, calling back, "Just something to think about before I return tomorrow."

The wizard laughed to himself and shook his head.

As the black dragon strode into the forest and out of sight with the scarlet behind him, soldiers all over Caipiervell exchanged looks and a mumbling stirred among them.

It started with one man. This one man walked over the sunken wall and approached Princess Faelon. He stared up at her for a moment, then bowed deeply to her and said, "I am yours to command, your Highness."

She nodded to him, then watched him walk around behind her and turn back toward the castle.

Others began to trickle out, each stopping to bow to their Princess before they joined the first behind her. This trickle became an exodus.

Prince Tahmrof watched in disbelieve as his entire army began to abandon him. Out of sheer desperation, he shouted to the men below, "Arrest and execute anyone who tries to leave!" That did not even slow them. Even many of the soldiers who stood on the wall with him gave him one final look before they descended the stairs to go join their comrades.

Sir Daldwan led the rest of the Caipiervell forces and their allies to the Princess, stopping right behind those who had just abandoned Prince Tahmrof.

His eyes ablaze with rage, the Prince yelled, "This is treason! I will have you all hung if you don't return to your posts at once!"

None complied.

Faelon looked up at her uncle, who now stared back down at her, and she offered, "Would you like to join us down here or should I call my dragon friend back to fetch you down?"

He raised his chin, then looked to the few men he had left and turned toward the stairway, storming down to meet her. Those with him, those few who were still loyal followed. He stomped over the fallen gate and strode right up to her with about a score of men following and he stopped four paces away, glaring at her as he folded his arms. "I was willing to give you an easy life. I was willing to let you live and be happy. You could have enjoyed all of the comforts of the castle until marriage, but you just had to behave like a spoiled brat and bring all of this upon me. Well, I've indulged you too much, young lady."

Faelon pulled her dress back onto her shoulder, then folded her arms as she listened without expression.

"Now," he continued, "you've cost me my patience. There will be no easy, comfortable life for you. You are a traitor to the crown and you will be punished so." He raised his head and ordered, "Take her. It's time she learned about the consequences of her actions."

All of the soldiers behind the Princess drew their weapons in one motion.

The men behind him glanced at each other. Many of them looked into the field where almost all of the Caipiervell army now stood. Behind them were three garrisons of Enulam and Zondaen warriors, people who in their own right most would not want to meet in battle.

When no one complied, the Prince looked around him and growled, "Must I do everything myself?" He strode forward and reached for her, but stopped when Vinton snorted at him.

Chail and Pa'lesh guided their hoses through the crowd of soldiers and stopped behind the Princess and wizard. Together, they dismounted and strode around the horse and unicorn to stand right in front of the Prince, and they both folded their arms as they stared defiantly down at him.

Prince Tahmrof backed away. Just the sight of Chail was enough to make him doubt his very manhood, but he had already tasted the wrath of the big Zondaen and knew fear of her. He swallowed hard and looked back to Faelon. "This isn't over, little girl."

"It's over enough," the wizard informed.

Chail nodded and added, "And so is your reign here. You lose, and as you can see, you are no longer welcome at this castle."

Pa'lesh's eyes narrowed. "It's time for you to leave, little man."

He stared defiantly back, informing, "This will mean war!"

Nodding again, Prince Chail countered, "Okay, war it is. But, you might need more than twenty men if you mean to fight Enulam *and* Zondae."

Princess Faelon finally raised her chin, adding, "And Caipiervell. You had my parents killed. You tried to have me killed. You are responsible for the deaths of many brave men and nearly the death of at least one innocent dragon. As I said before, Uncle, you are family so I will not have you executed, but you are banished from Caipiervell and all of her surrounding lands for the rest of your life." Her brow lowered over her eyes and she harshly ordered, "Go!"

He pointed at her one last time as he retreated and snarled, "This isn't over, you treasonous little brat. I'll have my kingdom back and I'll see you die slowly!"

She nodded and looked away from him. "Blah blah blah… Someone get him out of my sight."

He and those loyal to him were escorted to the palace by more than a hundred soldiers of Caipiervell, Enulam and Zondae. He would not leave with much, only what could be carried in their horse's saddlebags.

Faelon slid down from Vinton's back, then reached to his head and unbuckled the halter. "I owe you for this. I shall be in your debt the rest of my life."

"I told you," he said flatly, "I hold no such debts over anyone."

She smiled at him, then hugged him tightly around the neck. "Thank you, Vinton. You are truly my dearest friend and I love you with all my heart."

He whickered back to her.

Stepping away from him, she patted his neck and said, "I would be honored if you would stay and graze for a while."

"I would be honored to stay for a while," he replied, then he turned and paced toward the waiting grains.

The Princess watched after him for a long moment, a slight smile curling her lips.

Pa'lesh nudged her and ordered, "Okay, snap out of it. We have work to do."

Faelon glanced at the Field Captain, then she turned her eyes to Prince Chail and asked, "Can you attend to matters here?"

He nodded. "I think I can get things organized." He unfastened and removed his light armor, handing it off to an attentive squire, then he removed his shirt and used it to blot perspiration from his face.

Looking over his massive, unclothed build, Faelon's eyes widened and her lips parted ever so slightly. She watched intently as he turned and strode to a group of approaching Enulam and Caipiervell soldiers, then realized she was not breathing.

Pa'lesh loudly cleared her throat, then leaned down to the Princess and whispered, "He's spoken for."

Faelon blinked and glanced at her, then looked back to the Prince and nodded, admitting, "Oh. That's a shame."

The wizard dismounted and assured, "I'll do what I can to help as well."

She tore her eyes from Chail and gave the wizard a nod, offering, "Thank you," then she looked to Pa'lesh and informed, "I have some things that need my attention." She raised her brow.

Half smiling the way she did, the Field Captain assured, "Your bodyguard will be right there with you."

As they strode toward the palace, Faelon felt compelled to ask, "So, how many other Enulam warriors look like that?"

"You saw many of them," Pa'lesh reminded. "Prince Chail, I think, is one of the best looking of them and is the second largest man from Enulam that I've seen."

Faelon stopped and raised a hand to stop the Field Captain, slowly asking, "*Second* largest?"

Patting her shoulder, Pa'lesh assured, "I don't think the other would quite be your taste." She pushed the girl along and said, "You should just put men from your mind until you have your life back in order."

They entered the palace amid much confusion. People were unsure how to accept her or how she would react to them, so they gave her a wide berth for the most part.

Faelon led the way up the stairs to the second and then the third level of the palace and went right to her room. Once there, she changed into a light spring dress, nothing fancy, just something that was comfortable and not torn. It was white trimmed in red and pink with flowers embroidered around the low neckline. It had no sleeves, rather it had wide straps that held it up to her shoulders.

She looked up to Pa'lesh and twirled around, asking, "What do you think?"

"It looks good on you," the Field Captain answered. "I wouldn't be caught dead wearing it, but it works on you."

The Princess rolled her eyes and bade, "Come on," as she left the room again.

They did not make it far when Princess Bellith emerged from her room, saw Faelon and froze. She was dressed in something light and comfortable as well, a blue dress that resembled her cousin's but was trimmed in lace.

Faelon strode right up to her and folded her arms, her lips tight and her eyes narrow.

Raising her hands before her, Bellith backed away and insisted, "Faelon, I didn't know what he was doing. I swear! I really didn't! I've always been loyal to you."

"Sure you have," Princess Faelon snarled.

Glancing at the big Zondaen, Bellith shook her head and assured, "I just did as he said. I stayed out of the way and out of his business. That's all he wanted from me. I enjoyed living here and—"

"You enjoyed an easy and comfortable life," Faelon interrupted, "at the cost of the kingdom of Caipiervell. Have you given anything back or were you just going to wait for your father to die so that you could get your greedy little hands on my throne?"

Shaking her head, Bellith cried, "I don't want your throne! I—I just... Faelon, we've been friends and playmates since we were little. You were always my best friend!"

"I still think you're loyal to your snake of a father," Faelon accused.

"I'm not!" Bellith insisted. "Faelon, he just wanted me to stay out of his way until he wanted me for something. He showed me off and then pushed me aside. I swear I have no loyalties to him. Please, you have to believe me!"

Looking over her shoulder to Pa'lesh, Princess Faelon asked, "What do you think?"

The Field Captain raised her chin and replied, "Not sure, but I know who would know for sure if she's telling the truth." She winked.

Faelon nodded, then turned her attention back on her cousin and ordered, "Follow me."

Bellith glanced fearfully up at the big Zondaen warrior as she strode nervously by.

Leading the way back out of the palace, Faelon paused as she looked around and saw that the castle wall was standing to its full four heights again. She strode to the main gate, which was back on its hinges and standing open and found Sir Daldwan ordering people about to reorganize the castle.

When he saw her, he turned and bowed his head to her, greeting, "Your Highness."

She scanned the wall again and pointed at it.

Before she could speak, the knight raised his hand and assured, "You don't want to know. Believe me, you don't want to know."

She looked to Bellith, then to Pa'lesh and shrugged, then led the way outside of the wall.

Wringing her hands together, Bellith timidly asked, "You aren't going to banish me, are you? Please say you aren't going to have me arrested and imprisoned. Do you know what could happen to a princess in the dungeon?"

Faelon glanced back at her, then approached two forms that were only fifteen or so paces away.

Vinton looked up from the grasses he was munching on. Grazing behind him, Shahly also looked up. She had rejoined him only moments ago.

Princess Bellith gasped and grasped her chest as she saw the unicorns, her eyes locked wide on the stallion. She watched in clear disbelief as her cousin walked right up to him.

Smiling at her dear friend, Faelon scratched the bay unicorn under the jaw and said, "There is someone who needs to talk to you."

Slow to approach, Bellith had her mouth covered as her gaze was fixed on the big unicorn before her. Tears began to escape from her eyes and she slowly shook her head. She stopped a pace away, still barely believing that she was in the presence of an actual unicorn.

Vinton, still chewing on some grass, turned and walked right up to the blond haired girl who wept at the sight of him. As she reached out to gently touch him, he looked back at Shahly, who stood only three paces behind him watching, and he smiled, teasing, "Jealous?"

The white unicorn's eyes narrowed and she snorted.

Bellith slowly stroked the stallion's mane, tears streaming from her eyes. She looked back to her cousin, her mouth quivering, then she turned fully and threw her arms around Faelon's neck, hugging her tightly.

Unsure what to do at first, Faelon hesitantly slid her arms around her cousin and returned her embrace.

"Thank you," Bellith sobbed.

Looking to Vinton, Faelon raised her brow.

He whickered back to her.

Faelon pushed her cousin away and held onto her shoulders. "Okay, Bellith. You have a long journey to win my trust, but I'll allow you to stay. But, you must go to the food stores and get these unicorns some apples. Do you understand?"

Shahly's ears perked and she whinnied sharply and cantered to the stallion's side, her wide eyes on the Princesses.

Bellith glanced back at the unicorns, then she looked to her cousin and nodded. "Can I stay with them for a while?"

Faelon combed some of Bellith's hair back with her fingers, assuring, "You can stay as long as they'll let you, and I'm sure that white unicorn will stay longer if you bring her some apples."

Nodding, Bellith smiled, then she turned to the unicorns and assured, "I'll be right back." Even before they could respond, she turned and ran toward the palace.

Faelon looked to the unicorns and said, "You are safe and welcome here for as long as you care to stay."

Vinton nodded and informed, "I don't think we'll be leaving for a while."

"Thank you," the Princess offered. She hesitantly turned and walked back toward the palace, lost in her thoughts.

Pa'lesh strode up behind her and asked, "So, what's next on your itinerary?"

Her eyes narrowing, Faelon replied, "One important thing stands out in my mind. Come on." She led the way to the side of the palace, past the hanging lines and into an open door. Not too deep inside the castle was a little room she had visited for the first time only a couple of days before. There was some unfinished business within. This was her palace, yet she found herself nervous about entering.

Three girls were inside the room with several baskets of linens and bath towels. As they had days before, they sat on the two benches, folding and gossiping. The black haired girl sat on the far bench, facing the other two as she talked away.

Faelon stood just inside the doorway, watching and feeling like an outsider among them. She found herself hesitant to approach, but when the black haired girl looked up at her and froze she found herself a little more afraid to be there.

The other two girls looked over their shoulders. Dropping what they were doing, they stood and faced the Princess.

A tense, silent moment followed.

Hesitantly, Faelon entered the room, not meeting any of their eyes. She walked slowly to the black haired girl, then turned and sat down on the bench.

The three girls also sat down.

Her eyes on the basket of towels before her, Faelon slowly pulled one out and ran it over her hand, finding two corners of it. As she made the first fold, she raised her eyes to the tall girl and asked, "Has that stable boy visited you of late?"

The tall girl just shook her head.

The girl sitting beside her glanced around and informed, "He didn't, but she was talking to one of those squires yesterday."

Gasping, the tall girl nudged her with an elbow and barked, "Narra!"

Narra giggled and pushed herself back up, insisting, "You know it's true, Darree."

"We were just talking!" the tall girl spat back.

The black haired girl smiled and said, "Sure you were." She looked to Faelon and continued, "I saw them *talking* with their mouths pressed together." The bed sheet Darree had been folding hit Cenna in the head.

Faelon raised a hand to her mouth and giggled.

Pa'lesh finally entered the room and stood beside the doorway, leaning against the wall with her arms folded as she watched the activity within.

Turning her eyes to the big Zondaen, Faelon asked, "Would you like to join us?"

Slowly shaking her head, the Field Captain replied, "No, you girls just go ahead. I'm fine."

The other girls turned and looked at her and suddenly grew very silent.

Pa'lesh stared back without expression.

Faelon broke the silence with, "I would like you to meet Pa'lesh. Pa'lesh, this is Cenna, Narra and Darree."

The Field Captain nodded once to them.

They nodded back to her, still looking back at Pa'lesh with wide eyes.

Faelon continued, "Captain Pa'lesh is from Zondae. She will help look after things for a while until we can get the kingdom organized again."

"And," the Field Captain added, "I'll be keeping all of the drooling little boys away from your Princess."

Cenna giggled and asked, "So she's not to have fun while you're around?"

The tall girl looked to her and scolded, "Cenna!"

Pa'lesh just smiled and assured, "That's the plan. No fun on my watch."

"You're really from Zondae?" a wide eyed Narra asked.

The Field Captain nodded.

Darree was clearly hesitant to speak, but finally asked, "Do you really keep men as property there like I've heard?"

That half smile returned to Pa'lesh's face as she informed, "I have three."

The girls just exchanged wide eyed looks, even Faelon.

"I want to live at Zondae!" Cenna announced.

Giggles burst from the girls there.

Before they could get control of themselves, the doorway was filled by a large woman who strode in a pace and stopped, setting her hands on her hips as she announced, "Once again I come to check and find you all idle and nothing accomplished!"

Darree stood and spun to face her, reporting, "Miss, we've already finished six baskets."

"You should have finished them all!" the overseer countered. She looked down at Faelon and sneered, "What are you so dressed up for?"

The Princess raised her chin, staring defiantly back with narrow eyes.

Ordrene continued, "Did you think I forgot about you? Where did you go the other night? You skipped away and left all of this work undone with this kingdom on the brink of war! Do you think I'll be letting you have an easy task like laundry after that? Get off of your duff and come with me. You and that pretty little dress will be slopping hogs from now on."

Faelon's brow lowered slightly and she spat back, "Go slop them yourself. Perhaps if you would do something other than yell around here more work would get done, that and I'm sure those hogs would love the company of one of their own."

The three servant girls gasped, watching with wide eyes as they expected the worst.

Her eyes flaring, the overseer strode toward the Princess, reaching for her as she shouted, "That was the last word from you, missy!"

Pa'lesh grabbed the large woman's shoulder from behind and informed, "You really don't want to do that."

Spinning around, the look on Ordrene's face went from rage to fear as she looked up to the Zondaen's eyes.

Folding her arms, Pa'lesh asked, "Princess Faelon, what should we do with this insolent and very loud cow we have here?"

Her eyes widening further, Ordrene slowly turned back to the Princess and gasped, "Princess Faelon?"

Faelon half smiled like she had seen Pa'lesh do and she nodded. "That would be me, and the woman behind you would be my bodyguard from Zondae." The Princess stood and slowly strode up to the overseer, glaring up at her without fear in her eyes this time. "I've taken power fully from my uncle. He's gone now. If you would like to join him then go ahead. Otherwise, your abusive posture toward the people of this kingdom ends now. Do we understand each other?"

Ordrene nodded, replying, "Yes, Highness. I understand."

Smiling back, the Princess patted the overseer's arm and said, "That's good." Her brow lowered over her eyes and she ordered, "Go!"

Turning quickly, the overseer almost ran into Pa'lesh. She raised her hands before her and hesitated, then sidestepped and fled the room.

The servant girls within stood and applauded their princess, cheering her.

Faelon, a satisfied little smile on her face, turned and curtsied to them.

They all sat back down and the Princess looked to Pa'lesh, who stood by watching her and she asked, "So, what's it like to live at Zondae and have three men?"

The other girls looked up at her and Cenna demanded, "How did you get three?"

Fighting back a smile, the Field Captain raised her eyes, then she strode to the bench and waved her hand, sitting down as Cenna and Faelon moved over. She rested her elbows on her knees and looked to the girls across from her. "You girls have a lot to learn about men. Bottom line is they tend to be very needy, it's sometimes difficult to get them to do what you want and they are often nearly impossible to train."

"Train?" Darree asked with wide eyes.

Pa'lesh looked to her and nodded. "Do you think they'll do what you want them to if you don't train them? If a man doesn't satisfy you every time he's with you then what good is he?"

She hesitantly shrugged.

Shaking her head, the Field Captain looked down at Faelon and nudged her with her shoulder. "I can see I have a lot to teach your people while I'm here."

Faelon smiled and nodded to her.

"How long have you been a warrior?" Narra asked.

Raising her brow, Pa'lesh replied, "Since I was about your age. Bear in mind that life as a Zondaen is quite a bit more demanding than it is here." She looked to the Princess again. "I guess you're work is just starting, isn't it?"

Faelon nodded, then turned her eyes to the basket of towels in front of her and picked one up. "It sure is. Even after this laundry is folded we have much to prepare for." She looked to the tall girl and winked. "Life isn't all banquets and parties, nor is it all linens and stable boys."

Darree smiled at her.

Pa'lesh met the Princess' eyes and nodded to her. "You're getting the right idea, Princess Faelon. You're going to do okay. But I'm still not folding."

They all laughed.

The Field Captain nudged the Princess with her elbow. "So what about you? Did the princess of this castle have any conquests?"

Faelon was silent for a moment, then she turned her eyes up to the Zondaen's and replied, "I had but one. You would like him. He fell in battle defending me."

Pa'lesh nodded. "Sounds like a brave lad. Why don't you tell us about him?"

Turning her eyes down, Faelon replied, "He fought as a squire, and died a knight."

CHAPTER 18

The end is near...

Darkness had fallen some time ago and torchlight lit the way. Ahead was a mountainous castle. Ahead was a place Prince Tahmrof did not really want to go.

The sentries opened the gates and allowed the twenty plus riders to enter. They were escorted by palace guards who wore red and black arming tunics over their chain mail shirts. Black arming pants made them difficult to see in the insufficient torchlight. The procession circled around the castle, heading for the stables. Once there, the riders dismounted and the horses were led away. Men with open torches were kept away from the stables. Only closed lamps were burning within.

Tahmrof strode to one of the palace guards, one who looked like he might have a bit of rank to him, and ordered, "Take us into the castle. I must get myself cleaned up after that long ride before I see her Majesty."

The guard corrected, "*He* wants to see you first."

Even the dragon's visit to the castle did not cause Tahmrof such uneasiness. He swallowed hard, then beckoned to his men to follow.

The guard raised his hand and ordered, "They will remain here. Follow us."

With his last bastion of comfort and security left behind, the Prince nervously followed the four red and black clad palace guards who surrounded him deeper into the darkness. The stables behind the main stable were dark. No torchlight and no lamplight, only light from the one lamp carried by one of the guards who led the way. They abruptly stopped beside the second building.

"Well?" a deep, raspy voice demanded from the shadows.

Tahmrof stiffened and slowly turned to face the voice. A slight violet glow came from that way. "I, uh… I—I bring news from Caipiervell."

"You failed," the voice growled.

"There's been a small setback," the Prince informed nervously. "That dragonslayer failed us both."

"And Princess Faelon still lives." Something sighed in the darkness. "And to think I trusted you with such an easy task."

"I was close," Tahmrof assured. "I—I can get the kingdom back. I just need more men and some time to—"

"Drop it!" the voice ordered. "You've failed. The plan is in ruins now!"

"It wasn't my fault!" the Prince insisted. "I did everything as you said. Faelon was the last obstacle. Duke Malchor assured me that his dragon would kill her but even that failed to work. He attacked a dragon that had a very powerful mate to come to her defense that he simply was not ready for."

"So this is all Malchor's fault, is it?"

"Of course it is. But for his failure and incompetence Caipiervell would be in our hands right now."

"My informants told me that your army surrendered without a fight," the voice informed. "It doesn't sound like you were able to properly motivate them."

Hesitant to respond, Tahmrof finally said, "It was that dragon that caused them to surrender. But for him arriving when he did—"

"What dragon?" the voice demanded.

The Prince glanced around, grasping for an answer. "I don't know, some large black beast that came from nowhere. I think it is mated to the red dragon that Duke Malchor attacked."

The voice growled in the darkness. "Black dragon. You involved the Desert Lord himself and you wonder why you failed."

"I didn't," Tahmrof insisted, "it was that dragonslayer. *He* involved the black dragon. I told him not to go out and challenge the beast but he simply would not listen. He concocted weapons and potions and went out anyway."

"So once again it is someone else's fault. I see." A deep breath was loosed in the darkness. "I have tired of this dragon interfering in my business. Send word out to find dragonslayers and have them brought here, and collect gold enough to show a bounty that they cannot refuse."

Tahmrof nodded, assuring, "I'll take care of it at once."

The voice growled, "I'm not talking to you. I need someone competent for this task, not the village idiot. I've heard of a knight who travels the land and has claimed to have killed four dragons already. One of them is rumored to have been the Desert Lord's size or close to it. I believe those who speak of him called him Sir Rayce. Send messengers and get word to him and any other dragonslayers who can be found that their presence is requested for such a task and a generous bounty will be paid to whoever rids me of this damn dragon. I want the Desert Lord dead!"

One of the palace guards bowed, then turned and hurried away.

Huffing another breath, the voice grumbled, "I am surrounded by weak minded fools."

"I've done my best for you," the Prince assured.

"I'm sure you have," the voice growled. "Are soldiers from Zondae and Enulam still at Caipiervell?"

"They were when I left. I don't know how or why they're involved—"

"The unfortunate truth is they are involved now. How or why is no longer important. They should be at war with each other right now, but someone else's incompetence shined brightly there as well."

"I can assure you that I—"

"You assured me three seasons ago that Caipiervell would be in my possession by now! Would you care to explain why you are here and not sitting on its throne?"

Prince Tahmrof turned his eyes down. "I understand that this has upset you, but please believe I did my best. It was the dragonslayer who failed."

"Where is Duke Malchor now?"

"He is running for his life, fleeing the wrath of that black dragon."

"As he should. It's a wonder the Desert Lord has allowed him to live this long. Very well. I've much to think about and many plans to rework."

The voice in the darkness turned to leave, heavy footfalls sounding from the shadows somewhere.

"What shall I do now?" Prince Tahmrof asked abruptly. "I served you as best I could and I can still be of service to you. I just need more men and time to formulate a plan to reclaim Caipiervell from that little girl. Surely she can't stand against us both."

The form in the shadows stopped and those violet glowing eyes turned back to the Prince. "You always need something, don't you? I assume you are tired and would like to rest first?"

The Prince nodded, admitting, "It has been a long and trying day. I could use some rest I suppose."

"Very well," the voice in the darkness conceded. "Guards, the would-be King of Caipiervell is weary from his long travel and lost battle. He is in dire need of a good, long rest. Kill him."